New York Times bestselling author **Christine Feehan** has over 30 novels published and has thrilled legions of fans with her seductive and sensual 'Dark' Carpathian tales. She has received numerous honours throughout her career including being a nominee for the Romance Writers of America RITA, and receiving a Career Achievement Award from *Romantic Times*, and has been published in multiple languages and in many formats, including audio book, e-book, and large print.

For more information about Christine Feehan visit her website: www.christinefeehan.com

Praise for Christine Feehan:

'After Bram Stoker, Anne Rice and Joss Whedon
(who created the venerated *Buffy the Vampire* series),
Feehan is the person most credited with
popularizing the neck gripper'
Time Magazine

'The queen of paranormal romance'
USA Today

'Feehan has a knack for bringing vampiric Carpathians
to vivid, virile life in her Dark Carpathian novels'
Publishers Weekly

DARK SLAYER

A CARPATHIAN NOVEL

CHRISTINE FEEHAN

piatkus

PIATKUS

First published in the US in 2009 by The Berkley Publishing Group,
A division of Penguin Group (USA) Inc., New York
First published in Great Britain as a paperback original in 2009 by Piatkus
This paperback edition published in 2010 by Piatkus
Reprinted 2010

Typeset in Caslon by M Rules
Printed in the UK by CPI Mackays, Chatham ME5 8TD

Papers used by Piatkus are natural, renewable and
recyclable products sourced from well-managed forests and certified
in accordance with the rules of the Forest Stewardship Council.

Mixed Sources
Product group from well-managed
forests and other controlled sources
www.fsc.org   Cert no. SGS-COC-004081
© 1996 Forest Stewardship Council

FSC

Piatkus
An imprint of
Little, Brown Book Group
100 Victoria Embankment
London EC4Y 0DY

An Hachette UK Company
www.hachette.co.uk

www.piatkus.co.uk

To Christopher Walker,
who, according to Domini,
is not as Zen as Razvan, but I disagree.

ACKNOWLEDGMENTS

I have so many people to thank for their invaluable help with this book:

Anita Toste, my sister, who writes poetry and always answers the call when I run out of rhymes and ideas for spells!

Dr. Christopher Tong, who is incredibly intelligent and can do just about *anything*. Did I say "just about"? I meant, Thank you so much for always, *always* being there no matter how busy you are. You are truly a gifted man and an amazing friend.

Cheryl Wilson, my dear friend, who came through just when I was in my darkest hour.

Domini Stottsberry, Kathie Frizlaff and Brian Feehan, who worked so hard to make this book the best it could be in every respect.

For Lisset and Jack, who gave me something precious beyond measure for this book. In loving, beautiful memory . . .

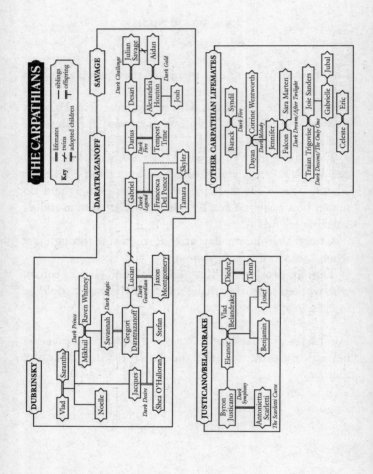

THE CARPATHIANS

Key === lifemates   — siblings   ⊥ offspring   ⋏ adopted children

THE CARPATHIANS

Key ══ lifemates ⫞ siblings ⋏ cousins ⋎ twins ⋏ triplets V parents not lifemates

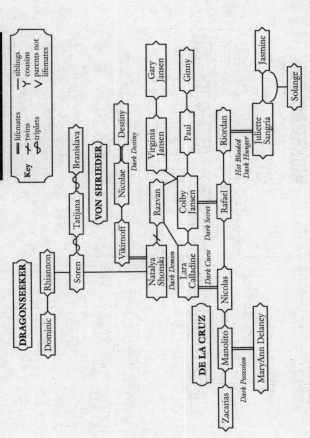

THE MAGE

The mage walks forth as the Hell Gate closes
Lightning strikes with his first order
Energy spirals from his fingertips
A spell does form upon his lips
Tall and dark, handsomely slender
His silver eyes burn like lighted embers
A power, a presence one cannot explain
A drawing feeling that will not leave the brain
A longing, a yearning that burns like fire
To be wanted and taken with heated desire
The mage walks forth, unfolding his arms
His victim comes quietly, succumbed by his charms
The embers of passion burst forth in flame
As the mage draws heart's blood from deep within
Consuming all, leaving no remains
The victim languishes in untold pain
The mage, having taken body and soul,
Now turns from the broken to seek one who is whole
The pattern is set, the ending the same
The mage needs heart's blood to be whole and remain

—ANITA TOSTE

1

Swirling mist veiled the mountains and crept into the deep forest, stringing layers of white through the snow-laden trees. Pockets of deep snow hid life beneath the cap of ice crystals and along the banks of the stream. Shrubs and fields of grass rose like statues, frozen in time. The snow gave the world a bluish cast. The forest, where icicles hung, and the stream, with its water frozen in bizarre shapes, seemed an eerie, alien world.

Clear, crisp and cold, the night sky shone bright with stars, and a full, glowing moon spilled a silvery light over the frozen ground. Silent shadows slipped through the trees and ice-coated bushes, moving with absolute stealth. Large paws made tracks in the snow, a good six inches in diameter, single file, the trail winding in and out through the trees and thick shrubbery.

Although they looked in good health, strong with steel muscles rippling beneath thick fur, the wolves were hungry and needed food to keep the pack alive through the long, brutal winter. The alpha suddenly stopped, going very still, sniffing the trail around him, lifting his nose to scent the wind. The others halted, wraiths only, silent shadows that immediately fanned out. The alpha moved forward, staying downwind while the others sank low, waiting.

A yard away, a large piece of raw meat lay on the trail, fresh, the scent wafting temptingly back toward the wolf. Wary, he circled, using his nose to detect potential danger. Scenting nothing but the meat, with his saliva running and his belly empty, he approached again, going downwind, angling toward the large piece of lifesaving food. He went in three times and backed away, but no hint of danger presented itself. He nosed in a fourth time and something slipped over his neck.

The alpha leapt back and the wire tightened. The more he struggled, the more the wire cut into him, strangling the air from his lungs and sawing through flesh. The pack circled, pacing, his female rushing to aid him. She began to struggle as another wire snared her neck, nearly knocking her off her feet.

For a moment there was a hush, broken only by the gasping breaths of the two trapped wolves. A twig snapped. The pack whirled and dissolved in a rush of fleeing shadows, back into the thicker cover of the trees. The bushes parted and a woman stepped into the open. She was dressed in black winter boots, black pants that rode low on her hips and a sleeveless vest of black that left her midriff bare and had three sets of steel buckles running down the middle of it. The six buckles were shiny, almost ornamental, with tiny crosses running up and around, embedded in the squared silver pieces.

A wealth of blue-black hair spilled beyond her waist, pulled back in a thick woven braid. The long hooded coat she wore, made of what appeared to be a single silver-tipped wolf pelt, fell all the way to her ankles. She carried a crossbow in one hand, a sword at one hip and a knife at the other. Arrows were slung in a quiver on her shoulder and all down the inside of the long wolf skin were small loops containing various sharp-bladed weapons. A low-slung holster adorned with rows of very small, flat, razor-sharp arrowheads housed a pistol on her hip.

She paused for a moment, surveying the scene. "Be still," she hissed, both annoyance and authority in her soft voice.

At her command, both wolves ceased struggling instantly, waiting, bodies trembling, sides heaving and heads held low to ease the terrible pressure closing around their throats. The woman moved with fluid grace, flowing over the surface rather than sinking into the ice-crusted snow. She studied the snares, a multitude of them, disgust in her dark eyes.

"They have done this before," she scolded. "I showed them to you, but you were too greedy, looking for an easy meal. I should let you die here in agony." Even as she rebuked the wolves, she withdrew a pair of utility cutters from inside the wolf pelt and snipped the wires, freeing the wolves. She pushed her fingers into their fur and over the cuts deep in their throats, then clamped her palm over the slashes, chanting softly. White light burst under her hand, glowing around and through the wolves' fur.

"That should make you feel better," she said, affection creeping into her tone as she scratched the ears of both wolves.

The alpha growled a warning and his mate bared her teeth; both were facing away from the woman. She smiled. "I smell him. It is impossible not to smell the foul stench of vampire."

She turned her head and looked over her shoulder at the tall, powerful male emerging from the twisted, gnarled trunk of a large evergreen fir. The trunk gaped open, split nearly in two, blackened and peeled back, the needles on

3

the outstretched limbs withering as the tree expelled the venomous creature from its depths. Icicles rained down like small spears as the branches shivered and shook, trembling from contact with such a foul creature.

The woman rose gracefully, turning to face her enemy, signaling to the wolves to melt back into the forest. "I see you have resorted to setting traps to get sustenance these days, Cristofor. Are you so slow and foul that you can no longer lure a human to use as food?"

"Slayer!" The vampire's voice seemed rusty, as if his vocal cords were rarely used. "I knew, if I brought your pack to me, you would come."

Her eyebrow shot up. "A pretty invitation then, Cristofor. I remember you from the old days when you were a young man, still handsome to look upon. I left you alone for old times' sake, but I see you crave the sweet release of death. Well, old friend, so be it."

"They say you cannot be killed," Cristofor said. "The legend that haunts all vampires. Our leaders say to leave you alone."

"Your leaders? You have joined them then, banded together against the prince and his people? Why seek death when you have a plan to rule every country? The world?" She laughed softly. "It seems to me that this is a silly wish, and a lot of work. In the old days, we lived simply. Those were happy days. Do you not recall them?"

Cristofor studied her flawless face. "I was told you were pieced together, one strip of flesh at a time, yet your face and body are as you were in the old days."

She shrugged her shoulders, refusing to allow the images of those dark years, the suffering and pain—agony really—when her body refused to die and lay deep in the earth, stripped of flesh and open to the crawling insects

4

abounding in the dirt. She kept her face serene, smiling, but inside she was still, coiled, ready to explode into action.

"Why not join us? You have more reason than any other to hate the prince."

"And join the very ones who betrayed and mutilated me? I do not think so. I wage war where it is due." She flexed her fingers inside the skintight, thin gloves. "You really should not have touched my wolves, Cristofor. You have left me little choice."

"I want your secret. Give it to me and I will let you live."

She smiled then, a beautiful smile, her teeth small and pearl white. Her lips were red and full, a teasing, sexy curve inviting him to share the humor. She tilted her head to one side, her gaze moving over his face, assessing him carefully. "I had no idea you had become such a fool, Cristo." She called him the name she had used when they were children playing together. *Before.* When the world was right. "I am the slayer of vampires. You summoned me with your traps"—she waved a contemptuous hand—"and you think I should be intimidated by you?"

He grinned at her, an evil, malicious smile. "You have become arrogant, Slayer. And careless. You had no idea the trap was for you and not your precious wolves. You have no choice but to give me what I want, or you die this night."

Ivory shrugged her slender shoulders and the silvery full-length coat rippled, moved as if alive. One moment it loosely flowed around her ankles and the next it was gone, settling over her skin until six ferocious wolf tattoos adorned her body from the small of her back to her neck, wrapping around each arm like sleeves.

"So be it," she said softly, her eyes on his.

Spinning, she drew her sword with one hand, rushing toward him, going up and over a snowcapped boulder to launch her body into the air. She felt the bite of a hidden snare, and inwardly cursed as the noose closed around her neck. Already she was dissolving, but blood spattered across the snow in bright-crimson drops.

Cristofor laughed and leaned down to scoop up a handful of snow to lick at the droplets, savoring the taste of pure Carpathian blood. Not just pure—the slayer was Ivory Malinov, from one of the strongest Carpathian lineages possible. He followed the arc of blood, saw her forming a few feet from him, closer to the tree line, and satisfaction made him cackle.

Ivory saluted him with two fingers, touched the thin line running across her neck and put her finger in her mouth, sucking off the blood. "Nice score. I did not see that coming and I shall have to apologize to my wolves for scolding them. But, Cristo, if you believe your partner back there in the woods is going to help you after slaying my wolf pack, you are doing some serious underestimating of your own."

She ran forward again, her hand low, drawing and throwing the small arrowheads, snapping them with tremendous strength so each buried itself deep into his body, in a straight line from belly to neck. The vampire roared and tried to shift. His legs disappeared, melting into vapor. His head swirled and disappeared. Fog drifted in from the trees in an attempt to help conceal him, congealing around his body, forming a thick veil. The torso remained, that straight, damaging line from belly to neck exposing his heart.

Her sword sank deep, her body weight, strength and momentum from her run driving the blade through the body right beneath the heart. The vampire screamed horribly. Acidlike blood poured from the wound, sizzling over the sword and splattering across the snow. The metal should have been eaten through, but the coating the slayer used protected it, as well as prevented that portion of his body from shifting. She turned her body in a dancer's spin, sword over her head, still stuck inside his chest so that she cut a circular hole around his heart.

Ivory withdrew the sword and plunged her hand deep. "I showed you my secret," she whispered. "Take it to your grave." She withdrew the heart and flung it away from her, lifting her arms to call down a sword of lightning.

The jagged bolt incinerated the heart and then jumped to the body, burning it clean. "Find peace, Cristofor," she whispered and hung her head, leaning on her sword, tears shimmering briefly for her lost boyhood friend.

So many were gone now. Nothing remained of the life she'd once known. She took a deep breath, drawing in the crisp night before cleaning her sword and all trace of the vampire's blood from the snow. She retrieved the eight small arrowheads and slid them into the loops on her holster before holding out her arms for the silver-tipped pelt. The tattoos moved, emerging, sliding once more over her body in the form of a coat. She allowed the silvery full-length garment to settle over her body slowly before picking up her weapons and drawing up the hood. At once she seemed to disappear, blending seamlessly with the layers of white fog.

Ivory moved in silence, feeling the hostile energy radiating from her pack. They were under attack and her wall of protection was weakening. She'd thrown the shield up around them hastily when she scented the second predator. Had he not been quite so eager for the kill, and stayed downwind, he might have managed to kill her wild wolf pack. She couldn't reuse the arrowheads on him; the vampire's acidic blood would have eaten through most of the coating. She had very little time to kill her enemy once she buried the small, lethal wedges in the vampire's body before that acidic blood ate through the coating and allowed her enemy to shift.

Weaving through the trees, the slayer stayed low to the ground, taking on the shape of a wolf. With her silver-tipped pelt it would be difficult to distinguish her from the other wolves in the area as she slipped through the trees toward the second vampire. She sank behind a fallen tree, studying the man hurling fireballs at the wolves. He had cornered them just at the water's edge, where the ice was thin and dangerous. She could see cracks spreading along the thin shield she'd thrown up where the vampire continually battered at it.

She took a breath, released it, and let herself find that place deep inside where there was stillness. Where there was resolve. In human form now, she stood and ran at the vampire, firing the crossbow as she went. Again, her aim was for his torso. She caught him as he turned, one arrow slicing into his lower back, the second missing altogether. He flung the fireball at her and Ivory somersaulted on the ground, letting it fly over her head. Then she was up on her feet, still running, always advancing, shooting at him with the crossbow.

The vampire howled in rage, the sound cut off abruptly as an arrow slammed deep into his throat. Her wolves threw themselves at the wall, frantic to come to her aid, but she knew the vampire would simply destroy them all. On the other hand . . .

The slayer shrugged, this time sending her thick, silver-tipped wolf pelt away from her. The heavy coat landed in the snow, widespread, the fur rippling as if alive. The hood stretched and elongated, and each sleeve did the same, moving with life as the body of the coat formed three separate shapes to match the ones emerging from the hood and sleeves. Ivory didn't wait for her companions to shift to their normal forms; she rolled across the snow, coming up on one knee, firing two more coated arrows into the vampire's chest while he was distracted by the six newly formed wolves.

The vampire hissed, his eyes glowing hot with hatred. He tried to shift, but only his legs, belly and head took the shape of a multi-armed beast, leaving his heart exposed. He realized he was trapped, but was fully aware of the small arrow weakening in his back as the metal was destroyed by his acidic blood. He whirled, sending up a spout of snow, gathering the wind to him and hurling it outward, creating an instant blizzard as the snow was drawn into his circle and flung out around him.

It was impossible to see the vampire in the center of that storm, but the wolves leapt through the swirl of icy snow, guided by scent to attack, tearing at his legs and arms, the alpha going for the throat in an effort to bring him down. The slayer followed them into the circle, knife in hand, hurling herself into the frenzied fray. One of the wolves yelped, and then screamed as the vampire ripped open its sides with curled, slashing talons and flung its body at her.

Ivory dropped her crossbow and caught the wolf as it slammed into her chest, driving her backward. The blizzard slashed across her face without mercy, tearing at her exposed skin as she went down, the wolf on top of her. She put the alpha's injured body aside as gently as possible and crawled forward fast, covering the snowcapped ground like a snake, picking up the crossbow and loading it as she slithered forward. Firing rapidly, she struck him three more times, exploding to her feet right in front of him, driving the knife deep, her hand wrapped around the hilt, following as the blade sliced through bone and sinew in an effort to get to the heart.

The vampire reared back, spittle and blood foaming around his mouth. He slammed his fist at her chest, trying to get at her heart, striking the double row of buckles. Howling, he withdrew his hand, the burn marks evident in the flesh of his knuckles. The tiny imprints of crosses woven into the silver and blessed with holy water had burned through his flesh almost to the bone.

The vampire roared, clubbing at her throat in spite of the wolves hanging on his arms. His nails scraped across her neck and shoulder, gouging flesh away as he struggled wildly. The alpha male hit him full force in the torso, driving him back and away from Ivory before those poison-tipped talons could pierce her jugular.

Ivory leapt on him, punching down with her fist, reaching for the heart, ignoring the acid as it poured over her coated gloves and began burning through them quickly. The vampire thrashed and ripped at her, but the wolves pinned him down as she extracted the pulsing black heart, before flinging it from her and raising her hand toward the sky.

Lightning zigzagged, streaked down and slammed into the heart, jolting the ground. The wolves leapt out of the way and the bolt of cleansing energy jumped to the body, incinerating the vampire and cleaning her arrows. Wearily, Ivory bathed her gloves in the light and then sank down into the snow, sitting for a moment, hanging her head, struggling to draw in air when her lungs were burning with need.

One of the wolves licked at her wounds in an effort to heal her. She managed a small smile and laid her fingers in the fur of the alpha female, rubbing her face in the soft pelt for comfort. These wolves, saved from death so many years earlier, more even than she remembered, were her only companions—her family. They were her true pack and she owed no loyalty to any other but them.

"Come here, Raja," she crooned to the big male. "Let me take a look at the damage."

Still trapped behind the shield she'd created to protect the natural wolf pack from the vampire, the alpha roared a challenge. Raja ignored him as he'd done so many others over the years. The natural pack lived and died, the cycle of nature intervening, and he'd learned such petty rivalries didn't touch him. He sent the natural alpha a look of pure disdain and crawled to Ivory, then lay on his side so she could inspect his wounds. She'd healed him countless times over the years, just as his sisters and brothers healed the slayer's wounds, their saliva containing the healing agents.

She scraped snow from the frozen ground and dug deep until she had good soil. After mixing her saliva with the soil, she packed the wounds and then hugged him. "Thank you, my brother. As so many times before, you've saved my life."

He nuzzled her and waited patiently while she inspected each of the pack. The strongest female, Ayame, named after the demon princess wolf, cuddled close to him, inspecting his wounds and passing her tongue over the other scratches he'd received. Their littermates formed the rest of the pack: Blaez, his second in command; Farkas, the last male; and Rikki and Gynger, the two smaller females. They crowded around Ivory, pressing close to her battered and bruised body in an effort to aid her.

The littermates, born of different parents, were very distinctive with their thick, silver-tipped coats, a shimmering fall of luxurious fur, all larger than normal, even the two smaller females. All had the blue eyes from their puppy days when Ivory had tracked blood and death back to the den, finding the mangled bodies of her natural wolf pack all those years ago. Even then, she'd become a scourge to the vampires, a whisper, the beginnings of legend and they'd sought to destroy her. Instead, they'd killed and mutilated the bodies of the wolf pack she'd befriended.

She had found the puppies dying, their torn bodies wriggling across the blood-soaked ground, trying to find their mothers. She couldn't bear to lose them, her only family, her only contact with warmth and affection, and she'd fed them her blood out of sheer desperation to keep them alive. Carpathian blood. Hot and healing. She'd stayed in the den with them, back away from the light of day, nearly starving herself. Forced, again out of desperation, to take small amounts of blood from them to stay alive. She hadn't realized she was giving blood exchanges, until the largest and most dominant of the pups underwent the change.

The pups had retained their blue eyes as they'd grown, the Carpathian blood giving them the ability to shift. Their ability to communicate with Ivory had saved them, giving them the necessary psychic brain function to live through the conversion. Like Ivory, they had been wounded a thousand times in battle, but over the past century they'd learned how to successfully bring down a vampire, the seven of them working as a team.

She lay back in the snow, catching her breath, letting her body absorb the pain of her wounds. The one in her neck throbbed and burned and she knew she had to cleanse it immediately. She was impervious to the cold, as were all Carpathians. Her race was as old as time, nearly immortal, as she had discovered, to her horror, when the prince's son had betrayed her to the vampires for his own gain. She'd never known such agony, an endless battle deep in the earth as years went by and her body refused to die.

She must have made a sound, although she didn't hear herself. She thought her cry was silent, but the wolves pressed closer, trying to comfort her, and the natural pack behind the shield took up the cry. Looking up at the night sky, she let her wolves soothe her, their love and devotion a balm whenever she thought too much about her former life. Time was creeping forward. This time of day was as much an enemy as the vampire. She had to hurry to get to her lair, and there was still much to be done before dawn.

Ivory pressed her fingers to her burning eyes and forced her body to move. First, she removed the poison from the lesions in her flesh, where the vampire's poison-tipped claws had torn her open. The vampires who'd banned together used tiny wormlike parasites to identify one another, and those parasites infected any open wound. She had to push them through her pores fast, before they could take hold and require a much more in-depth healing. Again she brought down the lightning to kill them before mixing soil and saliva to pack her own wounds.

"Ready?" she asked her family, picking up her weapons and shoving the used arrows back into her pack. She never left a weapon or an arrow behind, careful that her formula didn't fall into the hands of the vampires, or worse: Xavier, her mortal enemy.

Ivory stretched out her arms and the pack leapt together, forming the full-length coat in the air as they shifted, covering her body, the hood over her head and flowing pelt surrounding her with warmth and affection.

She was never alone when she traveled with her pack. No matter where she went, how many days or weeks she traveled, they traveled with her, keeping her from going insane. She'd learned to be alone and had the wolf's natural wariness of strangers. She had no friends, only enemies, and she was comfortable that way.

Striding through the snow, she waved her hand and allowed the shield to disintegrate. The natural wolf pack milled around her, weaving in and out between her legs and sniffing at her coat and boots, greeting her as a member of the pack. The alpha marked every bush and tree in the vicinity to cover Raja's scent marks. Ivory rolled her eyes at the display of dominance.

"Males are the same the world over, no matter what the species," she said aloud and checked the wolves one by one, assuring herself the vampire hadn't harmed any of them.

"All right. Let's get you fed before dawn. I have a ways to travel and the night's fading," she told the pack. Catching the alpha's muzzle, she looked into his eyes. *Find and drive prey to me and I'll bring it down for you. Hurry though, I don't have much time.*

Although she talked to her own pack all the time and they understood her, it was easier with a wild pack to convey the order in images, rather than in words. She added a sense of urgency at the same time. She needed to begin the trek back to her lair. Ordinarily she would fly, and each of her weapons was made of something natural that could shift with her, to transport her arsenal over long distances. But first she had to help the pack find food. She didn't want to lose them over the winter, and another storm was coming in soon.

The wolf pack melted away, once again fading into the forest to look for prey. She shouldered her crossbow and

14

began walking through the wilderness in the direction of her home. She'd only make a few miles before the pack would flush something her way, but she would be that much closer to home—and safety.

She understood little about the modern way of life. She'd been buried beneath the ground for so long, the world was unrecognizable when she'd risen. She'd learned, over time, that the prince's son Mikhail had replaced him as the ruler of the Carpathians, and his second in command, as always, was a Daratrazanoff. She knew little else of them, but even the Carpathian world had changed drastically.

There were so few of her species, the race nearing extinction, and who knew? Maybe it was for the best. Maybe their time was long past. So few women and children had been born over the last few centuries that the race was nearly wiped out. She wasn't part of that world any longer, any more than she was part of the human modern-day world. She knew little of technology, other than from books she read, and she had no concept of what it would be like to live in a house or village, town or—God forbid—a city.

She quickened her steps, and again glanced at the sky. She would give the wolf pack another twenty minutes to flush game before she took flight. As it was, she was pushing her luck. She didn't want to be caught out in the light of dawn. She'd spent so much of her life underground that she hadn't developed the resistance to the sun as many of her kind had done, able to stay out in the early-morning hours. The moment the sun began to rise she could feel the burn.

Of course, it might have something to do with her skin taking so long to renew itself, scraped from her body as it

15

had been until she'd been nothing but bones and a mass of raw tissue. Sometimes, when she first woke, she still felt the blades going through bone and organs as they chopped her into little pieces and scattered her across the meadow, left to be eaten by the wolves. She remembered the sound of their rasping laughter as they carried out the orders given to them by her worst enemy—Xavier.

The wind began to increase in strength and dark clouds drifted overhead, heralding the coming storm. She sought the haven of the trees and took refuge, closing her eyes to seek the wolf pack. They had discovered a doe, thin and drawn from the winter, hobbling a bit from an injury to her old body. Giving chase, the pack had taken turns, running her toward Ivory.

She whispered softly, asking for the doe's forgiveness, explaining the need to feed the pack as she lifted her weapon and waited. Minutes passed. Ice cracked with a loud snap, disturbing the silence. Hard breath burst from lungs in a rapid puff of steam as the deer broke through the trees and ran full-out over the icy ground.

Behind the doe, a wolf ran, silent, deadly, hungry, moving across the expanse of ice on large paws. Surrounding them, the pack came in from various angles, keeping the doe running straight toward Ivory. They'd hunted this way more than once, bringing the prey to her in desperate times.

Ivory waited until she had a killing shot, not wanting the doe to suffer before releasing her arrow and taking the animal down. Before the alpha could approach the carcass, snarling at the others to wait until he had his fill, she hurried to it and retrieved her arrow, striding away fast, not wanting to use energy to control a starving pack when there was a banquet in front of them.

Increasing her speed until she was running, Ivory sprang into the sky, shifting, the wolves sliding over her skin to become ferocious tattoos as they streaked through the clouds with her. She always felt the joy of traveling this way, as if a burden was lifted from her shoulders each time she took to the air. Spinning dark clouds helped to ease the light on her skin as she moved quickly toward her home. Maybe that was what made her feel less weighted down— that she was heading home, where she felt safe and secure.

She'd never learned to be relaxed and at ease above-ground where her enemies could come at her from any direction. She kept her lair secret, leaving no traces near her entrance, so no one had the opportunity to track her. Her unique warning/protection system would never be detected; of that she was certain. The entrance wasn't protected with the usual spell, so, if a Carpathian or vampire found her lair, they wouldn't know it was occupied or even existed. She'd learned many years earlier what levels underground her enemies were most comfortable at, and she avoided them.

Ten miles from her lair, she went to earth, landing, still running, skimming across the surface, arms outstretched so her wolves could hunt. They all needed blood, and, with all seven of them spreading out, they'd run across a hunter or a cabin. If not, she would go into the closest village and bring back enough to sustain the pack. She was very careful not to hunt near home, not unless she absolutely had to.

As she slipped through the trees, the mountain rising high in the distance, she came across tracks. An early-morning wanderer out to get wood perhaps, or doing some hunting himself. She crouched low and touched the tracks in the snow. A big man. That was always good. And he was alone. That was even better. Hunger gnawed at her now that she'd allowed herself to become aware of it. Ivory ran in the footsteps, following the male as he made his way through the trees.

The forest gave way to a clearing where a small cabin and outhouse sat, a stream bisecting the meadow surrounding it. Ordinarily the cabin was empty, but the tracks led through the snow and inside. A thin trail of smoke began to float from the chimney, telling her he'd just come to the hunting cabin and lit a fire.

Ivory threw her head back and howled, calling to her pack. She waited on the edge of the clearing and the man stepped outside, rifle in his hands, looking at the surrounding forest. That lonely call had spooked him and he waited, quartering the area around his house.

Ivory took to the sky again, moving with the wind, part of the drifting mist surrounding the house. She stood above her prey on the roof while he studied the forest and then, with a small curse, went inside. She saw the shadows flitting among the trees and gestured to them. The pack sank down, waiting.

The crack beneath the cabin door was wide enough for the mist to flow through, and Ivory entered the room, warm now from the crackling fire. Only one room, with a small fireplace and cooking stove, the cabin had the barest of amenities. In modern times, even the poorest of the villagers had such few trappings. She watched the man from a dark corner of the room as he poured water into a pot and set it on the fire to boil.

Crossing the room, she materialized almost in front of him, slipping between him and the fire, her will already reaching for his to calm him and make him more accepting. His eyes widened and then glazed over. Ivory led him to a chair where she could seat him. She was tall, much

18

taller than many women in the villages, a gift from her Carpathian heritage, but this mountain of a man was still taller. She found the pulse beating on the side of his neck and sank her teeth deep.

The taste was exquisite, hot blood flowing, cells filling and bursting with life. Sometimes she forgot just how good it was to feast on the real thing. Animal blood could sustain life, but true strength and energy came from humans. She savored every drop, appreciating the life-giving blood, grateful to the man, although he wouldn't remember he had donated. She planted a dream, slightly erotic, wholly pleasing, not wanting the experience to be unpleasant for him.

She flicked her tongue across the puncture wounds to close the two holes and erase all evidence that she'd been there. She got him a drink of water and pressed it to his mouth, commanding him to drink, and then she set another one beside him and tucked a blanket close to keep his body heat up before leaving.

The pack met her in the deeper woods, surrounding her the moment she called to them. The alpha male came first, leaning against her knee as she knelt and offered her wrist, the blood welling up. He licked the wound from her left wrist while the female fed from her right one. She fed all six wolves and then sat for a moment in the snow, recovering. She'd taken quite a lot from the woodsman, although she'd been careful that he could still function, not wanting to risk him freezing to death before he recovered, and she was a little drained after the fight with the vampires and then feeding the pack.

She rose slowly and held out her arms, waiting for the wolves to shift back into tattoos covering her skin. As they merged with her, she felt a little more revived, the wolves

19

giving her their energy. Again she ran and leapt into the sky, shifting as she did so, giving her body wings as she flew over the forest, heading home.

The clouds were heavy and full, and small gusts of wind blew in the mist, blotting out the rising sun. The mountains rose in front of her—snowcapped and high—hiding warmth and home beneath the layers of rock. She found herself smiling. *We're home*, she sent to the pack. *Almost.* She had to scout before she dropped down, check for strangers in her area.

She felt the wolves reach out with each of their senses just as she did, never taking safety for granted. It was how she'd managed to stay alive for so many years. Trusting no one. Speaking to no one unless she was far from her dwelling. Leaving no tracks. No trace. The slayer appeared and then vanished.

She worked her way in an ever-tightening circle, closer and closer to her lair, all the while scanning for blank spaces that might indicate a vampire, or for the disruption of energy that meant a mage could be in the area. Smoke and noise might be humans. Carpathians were more difficult, but she had a sixth sense about them and could hide herself if she felt one near.

As she began her spiral downward, unease rippled through her body and then through the wolves. Below her, through the layers of mist, she caught glimpses of something dark lying motionless in the snow. The snow began to fall, adding to her loss of vision, and she knew by the prickly sensation crawling over her skin that the sun had begun to rise. Every instinct told her to increase her speed and make it to her lair before the sun broke over the mountain, but something far older, far deeper, deterred her.

She couldn't turn away from the sprawled body lying in

the snow, already being covered with the new falling powder. *O köd belső—darkness take it*. Cursing ancient Carpathian oaths that would have shocked her five brothers in the old days, when she remained their protected, adored baby sister, she set her feet down in the snow and threw her arms out to allow her pack to leap down.

The wolves approached the carcass wearily, circling in silence. The man didn't move. His clothes were torn, exposing part of his emaciated torso and belly to the gleaming, hungry eyes. Raja moved in, two steps only, while the pack continued to circle the body. The alpha female, Ayame, stepped in behind the male and Raja turned and snarled at her. Ayame leapt back and whirled around, baring her teeth at her mate.

Ivory took a wary step closer as Raja resumed sniffing the motionless man. He'd once been a powerful male, no doubt about it. He was taller than the average human by several inches. His hair was long and thick, a black-gray pelt that was loose and unkempt. Blood and dirt were caught in the thick strands, matting his hair in places. She leaned over Raja to get a closer look and something inside her shifted.

Gasping, she pulled back abruptly, her body actually turning, ready to flee. He had the strong bones of a Carpathian male, a straight aristocratic nose, and deep lines of suffering cut into his once-handsome face. But what really caught her attention and terrified her was the birthmark showing through his torn, thin shirt. She could see the dragon on his hip. It was no tattoo; he'd been born with that mark.

Dragonseeker. Her breath rushed from her lungs in a long gasp. Around her the snow continued to fall and the world became white, all sound muted. She could hear her

21

heartbeat, too fast, adrenaline pumping through her body, her blood roaring in her ears.

Raja nudged her leg, indicating they should leave the body where it lay. She took a breath, even though her lungs could barely drag in air. Her body actually shivered. She turned away, signaling to the wolves to leave him, but her feet refused to work. She couldn't take a single step. The man with that ravaged face, too-thin body and barely a pulse, held her to him.

She raised her face to the heavens, letting the snow cover it like a white mask. "Why now?" she asked softly. A plea. A prayer. "Why are you asking this of me now? Don't you think you've taken enough from me?" She stood waiting for an answer. Lightning to strike, maybe. Something. Anything. Her whispered entreaty was met with implacable silence.

Raja gave a series of whines. *Come away, little sister. Leave him. He obviously disturbs you. Come away before the sun is high.*

For the first time in hundreds of years, she'd forgotten the sun. She'd forgotten safety. Everything she knew, everything she'd learned—it was all gone because of this man. She wanted to go away. She *needed* to go away, but everything in her was drawn to this one man. *Päläfertiilam*—lifemate—*her* lifemate—the curse of all Carpathian women.

2

Ivory crouched down beside the fallen man, her fingers gliding over his face, around to his neck to feel his pulse. It was unnecessary. Her heart had slowed to match the impossibly slow beat of his. She brushed the snow from his face and began a minute examination of his wounds. His body was crisscrossed in scars—nearly as bad as her own, should she allow anyone to see her as she was. His skin was ice-cold. Every Carpathian learned from childhood how to control the temperature in their bodies, yet he was freezing.

Little sister! Raja's whine ended in a growl of warning. *The sun is climbing.*

If she didn't take him, he would die here in the open. Her heart stuttered as she looked back at his tracks. That had been his intention. From the old and fresh scars on his ankles and wrists, she could tell he had been chained, the links coated with vampire blood, burning into his flesh each time he moved. She knew one man who used that method of imprisonment: Xavier, the high mage. The Dragonseeker had escaped captivity and, instead of heading toward one of the villages to seek aid, he had gone into the forest interior, making his way to the most remote side of the mountain where the sun could claim him.

The pack milled around, uneasy now, casting glances up at the sky. The snow began to come down harder, coating the silvery pelts. Cursing, Ivory reached for him, pulling him into a sitting position so she could lift him.

His eyes snapped open—dark swirling pits of suffering, of determination, of resolve. This was a man honed in the fires of hell, a man who'd suffered unbearable agony and set his mind in stone. There would be no manipulating him; she could see and feel that as his energy surrounded her.

"Leave me." His voice gave a hoarse command.

She felt the mental push behind the brusque order and hastily shut out the compulsion. The telepathic coercion affected her wolves; she could see them back away, and she waved her hand to hold them. Only her long and very tight bond with the pack held them to her under the strength of that compulsion—and that told her a lot about this man. In spite of being so weak, half-starved and emaciated, he was incredibly strong—and dangerous.

She wasn't about to open her mouth. She shook her head mutely and went to lift him. The Dragonseeker pulled back and laid his hand on her arm with surprising gentleness. She felt the jolt of electricity and her body tingled, sudden awareness forcing the air from her lungs in a hissing rush.

"You do not understand," he said. "You are in terrible danger just being close to me. I have powerful enemies and they can reach you through me."

Again she felt the warning compulsion in his voice. He radiated purity—truth. He wanted her to leave him knowing it was a death sentence—not just a death sentence, but that he would die in absolute agony, one slow inch at a time. She cursed again. She had no choice but to speak and he would know the truth. Her species had one mate. One.

24

They could look the world over, through centuries of living and unless they connected to that one person, the one who shared the other half of their soul, they were not true lifemates.

If she spoke, he would know. He would see in color, he would feel emotion—not just remember it. He would know—and maybe he already did—that she was his other half. She knew she had no choice. He would fight her, try to force her to leave him and he had to know she couldn't, that it was virtually impossible to do such a thing no matter how much she might want to. Ivory gave a slow shake of her head.

The Dragonseeker put his hand up and she knew he was about to speak. She spoke first. "I cannot and I think you know why. If you do not want my pack—and me—to suffer the sun burning us, you must cooperate."

She saw the shock register on his face. His body actually flinched as if from a body blow and he squeezed his eyes shut tight for what seemed an interminable amount of time as if his returning colors and emotions were too overwhelming, too dazzling for him to process. In truth, he didn't seem to welcome the news any more than she had, but she was fully aware that he felt that same pull toward her as she did toward him. When he opened his eyes, the color was swirling, dark, almost black, and then mixing into a deep emerald green before going back to a midnight blue. He blinked and the effect was gone. He took a breath. Let it out.

"My mortal enemy is Xavier, the high mage. He can possess my body at will and often does, slipping in and out of me and committing hideous, vile crimes against all peoples: mage, human and Carpathian alike. You cannot stay near me. He is weak at the moment, which is why he has not overtaken my body and forced it back. This is my only chance to escape him."

Ivory sank back on her heels and stared into the dark, ravaged eyes. He was telling the truth. Xavier. He had set in motion things that could never be undone. He had commanded the vampires to chop her body into pieces. He was an incomparable monster like the world had never known, and he couldn't be allowed to regain power.

"Your enemy is my greatest enemy," she said. She had so many.

"Leave me. Hide yourself. If I die here, he cannot use me to harm any other."

Little sister! Come away from this place. Take us home. This time Raja bared his teeth, his voice demanding.

Sister-kin. The rest of the pack took up the desperate cry.

Ivory felt the burning itch begin along her bare neck and arms. In spite of the thick snow falling around her, she was that sensitive, or maybe it was a fear she'd developed over the years. It mattered little.

"How does he possess you?"

"I gave him an opening." His gaze held hers captive as he made his confession. "There was a young mage woman who was kind to me. At that time, without my knowledge, Xavier was experimenting with ways to possess a body. He used mine to impregnate women. He wanted a blood supply and thought having children would do it for him. I am his grandson."

Ivory raised her arms to allow the pack to merge with her skin. Grateful that she was at long last preparing to go, the pack took their places one by one, covering her back and arms as if they were only ink on her skin and not immortal creatures. She never took her eyes from her lifemate, never changed expression even though inside she could hear herself screaming.

"The young woman had my child, a little girl, quite beautiful. She was amazing and talented. We were all held prisoner. My aunts, me, my child's mother and beautiful little Lara. I didn't want him to kill Lara as he'd ultimately killed her mother, and I told him I would do anything."

She gasped in disbelief. "To the high mage? You traded your soul? To the high mage?" She felt a little idiotic repeating herself, but who did that? Who would be that . . .

"At the time, I had been tortured severely. He had left Lara's mother's dead body to rot in front of us, and I could not bear for Lara to be tortured. In truth, I was not thinking clearly." He shook his head. "I cannot remember facts accurately anymore. Time has blurred together for me. But you cannot trust me. He can take this body at any time and force me to do unspeakable things to those I love. I have betrayed everyone who ever meant anything to me."

"And yet you fought him. You still fight him."

"I am my father's son. Xavier killed him as well and tried to possess my sister. I would not let him have her. I traded my life for hers and then my soul for my daughter. I have nothing left for you."

Those piercing eyes never once left her face, and, if there was regret or remorse in his confession, she didn't hear it. He had traded his life and was willing to die this day, as the sun came up, to protect everyone else, Ivory included.

"He cannot have you," she said. "I am sorry, but if what you say is true, then I have no choice but to render you unconscious so you do not know the way to my lair."

For the first time his expression changed. "You cannot take me there, woman. I forbid it." Both hands came up, and she felt the beginnings of the spell he was casting, one to force her compliance.

She was faster. Palms out, she shattered his spell so that small sparks clashed between them. She whispered softly and he blinked and fought for a moment, but, starved and weak, his head slipped to one side as his eyes closed.

Ivory didn't hesitate once she'd made up her mind. She slung the Dragonseeker over her shoulder and took to the sky, racing the sun as it climbed toward the higher peaks. She streaked up through the driving snow, scanning the trails leading into the mountains for tracks of human vampire hunters, rare now, but still a menace to her kind. She let her senses flair out, seeking signs of the undead who may have taken refuge near her lair, or a stray hunter, one of the Carpathian males she was careful to hide her existence from.

In midflight, she found herself rolling her eyes. A fat lot of good that had done her when she'd stumbled across her lifemate, just lying out in the snow, so thin and drawn, so emaciated from starvation and suffering that she couldn't be heartless enough to leave him there.

"*O jelä peje teräd*—sun scorch you, *päläfertiilam*—lifemate," she hissed aloud.

It had never occurred to her that she would find herself in such a predicament. A male. She was bringing a sodden male to her home. Her haven. She should have told him *teräd keje*—get scorched—and been done with him, but no, she had to be a simpering female and take the blasted man home with her.

She made for the gap between the two tall, towering columns of rock rising like horns above the mountain. The rock seemed solid and no one, in all the years she'd been residing there, had ever found that thin crack in the left

28

rock that ran from the inside around to the base, where the tower met the mountain peak itself. It took a moment to disable her intricate mineralogical alarm/protection system so she could pass through with the male. She blew gently into the wind, stirring the snow into a mini-blizzard, covering her drop as she entered vaporized, pouring like fog into the crack and making her way down through the inside of the mountain.

Passing layers of rock, crystal caves and ice, all the while using the small crack that ran from the highest point to deep beneath the ground, she moved steadily lower until heat began to warm her and the pressure on her body increased. It always took a few moments to adjust to the depth beneath the earth, but over the years her body had adapted. If the Dragonseeker had been held prisoner by Xavier, then he'd been underground in the ice caves where Xavier ruled and his body would be somewhat acclimatized to the depths.

She continued down, past the caves where bats dwelled and even lower beyond the depths of the ice caves, where no Carpathian she knew ever slept. She'd found rich soil and a hollowed-out cavern. Over the centuries she'd enlarged her living quarters to include several rooms. She'd brought in books, storing them on the floor-to-ceiling shelves she'd created. She'd painstakingly re-created each spell book she'd studied when she'd attended school under Xavier, back in the old days when Xavier had been thought to be a friend of the Carpathian people.

Her furniture suited her and her candles were made with the best healing fragrances and minerals she could find. In enlarging her lair, she'd come across a small flow of water, and, although it had taken nearly seventy-five years, she'd hollowed out a natural basin in the solid rock and formed a pool for herself. She loved her pool, the cool, clean water that always flowed and cascaded down through the floor into the next bed of rock beneath them.

Once down in her lair, she reprogrammed her unique alarm system with its gems that not only weighed the mass dropping through the crack but provided light for her far beneath the surface. She shrugged off the wolves the moment she was inside her home, allowing them to take their natural forms, while she strode through the outer rooms, her sitting room where the wolves liked to curl up while she read or painted or played her instrument, and then the rooms where she did her metal work, constructing her weapons, before going down the stairs leading to the last room where they all slept.

A violin lay in a case against one wall of her bedchamber; nearby sat a deep rock basin that she'd filled with the richest soil. She set the Dragonseeker down on the rejuvenating earth and studied him a moment. He was struggling, fighting off the slumber spell. She had the feeling he hadn't been as deep as she'd intended, but all that really mattered was that he hadn't seen the location of her lair.

Taking a deep breath, she laid aside her weapons and reversed the spell. The Dragonseeker, in spite of his starved and weakened condition, came up out of the soil, his eyes mercilessly angry. She fell back away from him, landing on her rear so that she had to tilt her head up to see him.

"What have you done, woman?" he roared.

Before she could answer, Raja burst into the room and hurled himself at the intruder's throat. He launched himself high, teeth bared.

"No!" Ivory commanded.

The Dragonseeker caught the huge wolf by the neck,

the force of the attack driving him back into the bed of soil. She saw his hands clamp down like a vise. The wolf fought instinctively for air.

Little brother, he is not an enemy. He is my mate. She bared her teeth at the wolf and he went still and submissive in the Dragonseeker's hands.

"Let him go," Ivory ordered. "Do it now, or I will retaliate."

The Dragonseeker raised his eyebrow, his hands remaining firm around the wolf's neck. "You seek to threaten me with bodily harm? I doubt there is much you can do that has not already been done. And if you desire to kill me, that is my wish, so I do not believe that it will serve your purpose to intimidate me."

She spat out another curse. *"Veridet peje*—may your blood burn!"

He released the wolf a little warily, keeping his gaze fixed on the large alpha and not on Ivory, which only served to irritate her more, as if he thought the animal was more of a threat to him than she was.

"My blood has burned on many occasions, *avio päläfer-tiilam*—my lifemate."

Her breath hissed out of her lungs. "Do not *ever* say 'my lifemate' to me. I am not yours. I belong to no one. I trust no one, least of all the grandson of Xavier and a Dragonseeker on top of that." She put every ounce of contempt and disgust that she could summon into her voice.

Before he could respond, Ivory switched her attention to Raja who, picking up on her mood, was baring his teeth again, low warning growls rumbling in his throat. *Little brother, I have no patience now to deal with two males and their egos. Go to your mate who will soothe your nerves and leave me to deal with this . . . this . . .* There was no word bad enough to describe him.

The wolf sent the Dragonseeker one last look of warning and then loped out of the room, leaving them alone in the bedchamber.

Ivory moved back across the floor until there was space between herself and the Dragonseeker. She pressed her back to the wall, fighting to maintain her composure. "It has been centuries since I have been alone in a room with another person," she confessed. "I am no longer certain what one does."

"You could start by telling me your name."

He didn't smile. He didn't look at her as if the moon rose and set with her, as lifemates were reputed to do. He didn't even argue that she did belong to him as every cell in her body screamed at her was true.

Ivory moistened her lips. "I am Ivory Malinov, sister to the five raising an army and a rebellion of vampires. Sister to the ones in league with Xavier." She took a deep breath. "And this is not my true form."

"I am Razvan, grandson of Rhiannon and Xavier. I am a dealer of death and torture to any who dare come near me, especially those I care most for. I will never lay claim to you, so have no worries, Ivory. I will leave you as soon as I am able to do so." He tilted his head to one side and studied her flawless body. "Do you fear showing me your true form?"

Her chin went up. "I do not fear much of anything, Dragonseeker, least of all you."

"I can see that," he said, faint sarcasm sliding into his tone. "Though, in truth, you should fear me. Not me: Xavier. He can find me wherever I am. You must believe me in this."

"I believe you. I studied under Xavier, many years ago.

Far longer than I care to remember. I know him well—too well."

"You displeased him in some way." Razvan made it a statement.

She found she could barely breathe in the close confines of the room with the Dragonseeker's hunger beating at her. Maybe it wasn't just his hunger. Maybe it was the way his eyes moved over her with a hint of possession, a male's intense look of interest. No one had looked at her that way since the prince's eldest son—and that hadn't turned out so well.

Her skin ached. Her bones. She'd forgotten that pain, or at least pushed it so far back in her memories that it was dull and faded. Now, looking at him looking at her, asking her questions, her body remembered the feel of sharp objects slicing through bone and tissue.

"Ivory," he prompted, his voice gentle. "What did you do to displease him?"

She sank down along the wall, drew up her knees and clasped her arms around her legs, making herself much smaller. "I wanted to go to Xavier's school and learn from him. My brothers and five of their friends raised me. Ten strong warriors indulging my every whim. I learned how to fight, but was never allowed to use my knowledge. I could do things no other woman could do, yet was expected to sit home and wait for a lifemate to provide safety for me." She shook her head, remembering the frustration of having an active brain desperate for knowledge, any kind, and running into a stone wall as her brothers refused to allow her any freedoms.

She rubbed her chin on her knees. "At that time, Vlad Dubrinsky was the prince." She was giving him a very convoluted explanation, rambling on instead of making it short and succinct. She pressed her fingers to her eyes. "I think it has been so long since I have carried on a conversation with anyone but my pack that I have forgotten how." She rubbed her palm up and down her thigh.

Razvan's gaze jumped to her hand and lingered there, recognizing the sign of nerves. She was wild, like her pack, uneasy with his presence, not because he represented danger, or because he was her lifemate, but simply because she was inherently wary of everyone.

"Be calm, Ivory," he said softly, crooning as he would to tame a cornered wild animal. "I seek nothing from you. I do not believe that Xavier will hunt for my body this soon. He has grown weak and old without Carpathian blood to feed on. He will need to find his strength before he can strike at me. Lara escaped his prison first and then my aunts. So for the moment you are safe, but never turn your back on me. Consider killing me."

She ignored his last statement. "How did you escape?"

"Xavier took my body out of the ice caves when his fortress was destroyed. He needs blood now to survive and be strong." He looked down at his worn, torn body with a brief, humorless smile. "He had used my blood until little enough remained. I believe he had it in his mind to kill me, but, when the aunts escaped, he needed my blood to keep him alive. He is determined to gain immortality. As you can see, there is little left of me, and he grew weak trying to build his new fortress."

Ivory took a deep breath and let it out. He could see she struggled with herself before she made the offer.

"You need to feed."

Her voice was low, trembling, and his heart turned over in his chest. It had been long since another had offered a kindness to him.

"I thank you for your offer, but I must regretfully decline. I have taken enough blood from those I should have protected and I will not take yours."

She frowned at him. "I can feel your hunger."

"I know. I cannot control the needs spilling into the close confines of this room. I am truly sorry for causing you distress."

He didn't want her dwelling on the hunger crawling through his body, every cell crying out for sustenance. He could smell her blood, rich and hot and flowing in her veins, calling to him. He could barely think with his teeth already lengthened and his saliva in his mouth. Her heartbeat matched the irregular beat of his own, and that worried him.

He knew little of lifemates, and the last thing he had ever wanted to do was feel real emotion. It was bad enough to remember what it was like to love and feel remorse for the vile things he had done, even under another's compulsion, but she had brought it all into his mind and heart and made it real again. Where before he had been numb for hundreds of years, now every terrible, brutal act—the violation of women, feeding from his own children, stabbing his aunt, betrayal of every single person he loved and cared about—all of it was in front of him, filling him with self-loathing and disgust.

His soul was so black. The emotions poured into him with his memories. His beloved sister—he'd fought to save her, but in the end he'd betrayed her. His aunts—he'd tried so hard to save them, yet Xavier had controlled his body and he'd been the one to plunge a knife into his aunt's chest. He couldn't breathe, couldn't find air to drag into his lungs.

His throat felt raw and he choked, closing his eyes,

trying to shut out the guilt and horror of his actions. It mattered little that he had not been in control—that in itself was a terrible guilt—or that he hadn't been strong enough to stop Xavier. Fighting him every inch of the way hadn't been enough, and now this stranger, this woman, brought every horrifying, vivid and disgusting detail into his mind and branded his soul unredeemable.

"Razvan." Her voice was soft. Gentle. "Look at me."

He couldn't move. Couldn't face her. No, not her—*himself*. He cursed his body's resistance to death. How could he ever face anyone after the terrible crimes he'd committed? Bile rose and he choked on it, a bitter, metallic taste. He wiped at his face and his palm came away smeared in blood.

He scented her, although she made no sound as she drew closer to him, as silent as her deadly wolves. He shook his head. "Stay back. Don't come too close." Because hunger turned him savage, while guilt made him a little insane. Now it wasn't Xavier he feared; it was himself. He knew what even the best of his kind could do when starved, and he was so far from the best. He was damned—cursed, even—cunning and . . . so hungry. Ravenous.

Ivory crawled toward him. "You need to feed. I feed my pack often, it is truly of little importance. Just take the blood from my wrist."

Between his fingers he could see her now, in front of him, concern on her face, although she was smart enough to be wary. She didn't trust him—it was there in her eyes. One fingernail lengthened, razor sharp, and she reached down toward her wrist.

Razvan caught her hand, the rush of fear and adrenaline combining to give him strength when he really had little left. "No! I will not." The thought sickened him. Her

36

offered wrist conjured up a vision of a greedy mouth tearing at a small wrist. He choked again and turned away from her.

How do you tell someone you are damned? He shook his head. "You have to take me to the surface and let me go."

"Why won't you feed? Perhaps if you tell me . . ."

He didn't tell her. He *showed* her. She had to see—*know*—the monster she'd brought into her lair. He seized her mind, flowing into her, shoving the memories into her head, forcing her to watch him tear at a frightened child's little wrist while she pleaded with him, letting her see the mother of his child rotting while he screamed and fought and wept blood, raging at the monster who imprisoned him. He made her watch as he betrayed his twin sister, Natalya, and as he plunged the knife into the breast of a dragon desperately trying to help his daughter escape.

She paled, but she didn't pull away from his mind. He felt her move inside of him, alert, the way she was naturally, but soaking up his memories, reading his life. And he fed it to her, hundreds of years with Xavier, watching him torture and kill. Xavier had used his body over and over to commit horrendous acts, to breed with chosen psychic women, slowly taking him over, and then later, using him as a puppet to do his evil bidding. She should have recoiled, should have plunged her fist into his chest and extracted his heart there on the spot, but she stayed, looking at everything, unafraid, quiet, giving nothing of her own thoughts away.

After a while he became aware that he was weeping, deep inside, for those years of torment and regret, for the arrogance of a young man who thought he could single-handedly defeat an enemy who'd eluded warriors and minds far older and wiser than his. He realized he was lying with his head in her lap, her hand stroking his hair, the blood of his tears smearing her thighs.

"Do you see what I am?" he asked. It was a plea. He had spent the last twenty years planning to escape, planning to let the sun cleanse his soul, to take his chances in the after-life. But here she was, the one woman who could stop him—and she refused to let him go. If he'd had the strength, he would have fought his way out, but he couldn't risk hurting her and, with his mind so shredded and his body so weak, he doubted he could reach the surface without a major battle between them.

"I see more than you think I see. You have forgotten, Razvan, that I had my own experiences with Xavier." Her fingers stroked his hair and began to make small circles over his temples. "And you have revealed far more of Xavier and his spells than you know."

He didn't like the speculation in her voice, but her hands worked magic, holding anguish at bay along with physical pain.

"You cannot best him. Believe me, I have tried over the centuries and I've always failed." He should have pushed away from her, but found he could not. Her hands were inducing a magic all their own. How long had it been since someone had touched him with such gentleness?

"As did I," she replied. "I knew Rhiannon and her life-mate. And when Xavier cast a holding spell over me and dragged me into the deep woods, he told me of his plan to kill her lifemate and force her to breed with him. He already had everything in place. Of course I knew the Carpathians would defeat him; we were too strong."

She paused. Her voice had gone singsong, lower pitched, almost velvet. He felt the soft notes sliding inside of him, stroking at the painful memories, pushing them back ever so gently. Everything about Ivory seemed soft and smooth and so peaceful.

"No one defeats Xavier."

She leaned close to him and whispered in his ear. "Because he has help. He *always* has help. Every memory you have shown me, a lesser mage first found the platform for the spell he cast. When he took me, and then later took Rhiannon's lifemate and murdered him, it was not Xavier who committed the actual murder—although I have heard he took the credit. It was Draven, Prince Vlad's eldest son. He betrayed our people to Xavier. He delivered Rhiannon's lifemate, dead, into Xavier's hands."

Razvan tried to stir, but his limbs were heavy. He felt his mind drifting a little as she built up doors, then slowly and gently pushed them shut to trap the pain and guilt where it couldn't reach him. One by one, the memories of his defeat and his crimes were slowly blocked until his mind could accept, from a distance, the centuries of failure, of torture and of self-revulsion. Her voice was the most beautiful thing he'd ever heard and he concentrated on it, on that soft, sweet melody that seemed to take him somewhere far away from the stark brutality of his existence.

"I remember Draven. He is a distant memory. A murderous, treacherous man who demanded young mage women from Xavier in return for his information. He disappeared one day and Xavier was furious, spewing vile curses on Gregori Daratrazanoff for weeks after. I assumed Gregori had finally found out his betrayal and administered justice." He tried to open his eyes to look at her, but his eyelids were too heavy and he didn't want to disturb her soothing fingers. "Why would Draven kill Rhiannon's lifemate?" He choked a little over his grandmother's name. He had his father's memories of her, the soft-spoken woman

Xavier had fed off of until his children were old enough to take her place.

"Draven was obsessed with me. I was not his true lifemate, but he wanted me. He had the sickness in him that some of our males get, and he believed, because he was in line to be prince, that he should have any woman he wanted. My brothers refused him when I told them I knew I was not his lifemate. When they were gone in battle, Prince Vlad sent me to Xavier's school, I think to keep me away from Draven."

"So Draven bought you from Xavier with the body of Rhiannon's lifemate." Razvan made it a statement.

His mind seemed at peace, drifting with the stroke of her fingers and the soft melody of her voice. It mattered little that the subject they discussed was abhorrent, his mind could process without fear or guilt or the overwhelming emotions that had poured into him at the sound of her voice. Now, his mind simply accepted and for the moment he was at peace. He didn't want that ever to end. He imagined this moment must be close to heaven, a haven where nothing bad could happen, even for just a brief interim.

"Yes, but Draven didn't count on the fact that I had ten strong warriors who had spent my lifetime teaching me to fight in battle. My five brothers and the De La Cruz brothers." Ivory rubbed the strands of his hair between her fingers and then shifted him, just the slightest of movements, turning him so that his head was facing upward toward hers.

Razvan's eyelids fluttered. He opened his eyes to narrow slits and looked up at her. His breath caught in his throat and he stared at the woman above him. Her face was still that of an angel, skin so flawless and pure, but now he could see the scars—terrible scars that started on her throat and ran down her body as if she'd been pieced together by barbed wire.

"He did this to you?" He breathed out the words in shock, knowing Carpathians didn't scar—not as a rule—yet her body was covered with lines, the disfigurement a patchwork of skin sewn back together almost haphazardly.

"Draven did not like a woman defeating him, the mighty, soon-to-be prince, if his plans with Xavier succeeded. He could not resist bragging, telling me how he was going to kill his own father, because it never occurred to him that I could fight and defeat him in battle. He was so furious."

Her voice sounded far away, a distant song of peace and warmth in spite of the chilling tale she told. He found, try as he might, that he couldn't experience the horror of her words, the extent of Draven Dubrinsky's betrayal of not only his people but his own father. Xavier was the devil himself, a monster unrivaled, and yet Draven had deliberately sought an alliance with him.

"I was caught by four vampires on my way back to my people," Ivory continued, shifting him again, cradling his head to her.

Her body felt warm and soft and so giving against his. She smelled of the forest, of the wilds, deep and green and secret. There was a touch of snow, distant and compelling, an ice princess yielding to no one, yet giving of herself to him. It was fanciful. He'd long forgotten fanciful and his wayward thoughts didn't belong in the midst of her retelling such a traumatic event in her life. Everything seemed so dreamlike, yet he'd ceased to dream, knowing Xavier extracted information from his sister when he dreamt. He hadn't even been able to stop that and save

Natalya such grief. He knew she'd been attacked by Xavier, but four vampires? *Four?*

He struggled to get up, to try to go to his sister's aid.

The singsong voice soothed him. "Not Natalya, Dragonseeker, the vampires attacked me. Xavier wanted the most horrendous death he could envision for one like me. He had them chop off my head and then cut me to pieces, scattering me across a field so the wolves could consume me. They should have incinerated my heart. I did not have the will to die, not when I needed to see Draven and Xavier gone from this earth."

For a moment the horror and agony of what she had endured was in her mind—and his—and then, before he could possibly assimilate and process what she had given to him, it was gone, replaced once more by the soothing touch of her fingers stroking over his temples and her whispered, seductive voice.

You are so hungry, Dragonseeker. You have been starved for so long and kept without true strength. I am offering you life. Strength. A chance to join me in defeating the devil himself. You have only to take what is freely given. If, when you are at full strength, you choose to walk away, I will take you from here and you are free to go your own way.

The thought of separation from her gave him pain somewhere in his tattered soul. She was his lifemate; once found, he could not simply abandon her, yet he knew—frowning—that there was a reason he must not utter the words that would bind them together.

She rubbed gently at the frown lines between his eyes. *Be at peace. You are safe here.*

He shook his head, although it was difficult to do so. More than anything he wanted the touch of her magic fingers and the warmth of her body after he'd been cold for so many centuries. He'd existed in the ice caves with so little blood to live on, Xavier determined to keep him from strength, that he had all but forgotten warmth—or kindness. He didn't want to destroy the illusion that someone cared enough for him to render him aid without strings.

It wasn't true, of course; he'd learned that painful lesson over the centuries. No one could be trusted, least of all himself, but the illusion could sustain him when his starving body and his shredded mind could no longer function properly.

She leaned closer. Her breast grazed his face and his body tightened strangely in reaction. *Hear the beat of my heart. Match your rhythm to mine.*

He could hear her heart, steady, like an unfaltering beacon, a signal for him to find his way home.

Ivory looked over his ravaged face and her heart contracted painfully. She hadn't felt compassion for another in centuries. She'd been careful to avoid the traps and pitfalls of emotion. Her beloved brothers had betrayed her. *Her own family.* She would never forget how she sought them out, crawling out of the ground, her flesh barely intact, fighting every inch of the way back home, only to discover that centuries had passed and her brothers had joined the very ones who had chopped her into little pieces and left her for the starving wolves.

Hearing Razvan confess to the betrayal of his own sister and aunts, of his child, she had thought to aid him to find the dawn, even though it would mean condemning herself. But once inside his mind, she realized more than he did the centuries of struggle, of fighting to protect everyone around him from a monster. And he had held out in spite of torture and starvation and anything else she could ever conceive of.

In some ways it scared her to think what his will and determination would be when he was at full strength. Never once during the time Xavier held him captive had he been at full strength. He'd been a youth when Xavier had taken him, and even then, as a mere boy, he'd protected his sister. He didn't consider himself good with spells—his sister was a far better mage—but he was Carpathian male through and through, strong and protective and unflinching in his fight, no matter how weak he had grown.

Hear the blood rushing in my veins. It flows like the tide itself, like sap in the trees, nectar of life, flowing for you. Can you smell it? Do you feel your body crying out for life?

She drew a line across her breast, one of many lines, but this one welled bright-red blood. Shifting him again, she pressed his mouth to her. There was a heartbeat. Two. Everything in her stilled. *Veri olen elid—blood is life. Saasz hän ku andam szabadon—take what I freely offer.* She put every ounce of compulsion she had into her soft entreaty.

She felt him stir. His tongue licked over the raw wound and her womb clenched. Teeth sank deep, a biting, burning pain that gave way to a rush of heated pleasure.

She stroked back his hair and began to chant the Carpathian Lesser Healing Chant. Her voice rose, soft and melodious, filling the chamber with the rich gift of song.

Kuñasz, nélkül sivdobbanás, nélkül fesztelen löyly—
    You lie as if asleep, without beat of heart, without
    airy breath.
Ot élidamet andam szabadon élidadér—I offer freely
    my life for your life.
O jelä sielam jörem ot ainamet és soñe ot élidadet—My
    spirit of light forgets my body and enters your body.

O jelä sielam pukta kinn minden szelemeket belső—
   My spirit of light sends all the dark spirits within
   fleeing without.
Pajňak o susu hanyet és o nyelv nyálamet
   sielametsívadabat—I press the earth of our
   homeland and the spit of my tongue into your
   soulheart.
Vii, o verim soɳe o verid andam—At last, I give you
   my blood for your blood.

Weary, Ivory closed her eyes. She dared not give him
more blood than she was able. One healing session and one
feeding was not going to be nearly enough. A week, a
month . . . time mattered little, but she would heal him.
For now, she'd done all that she could do.

Find peace, Dragonseeker.

Pressing her hand to his mouth, she whispered for him
to stop before placing him in the deep, rich loam of her
bed. Calling to her pack, she signaled them to take their
places around her lifemate—claimed or not—and she
pressed close to him before allowing the dark soil to engulf
them, her protections around their bedchamber the
strongest she knew.

3

The search for Razvan had been intense over the past three weeks. Ivory crouched below the snow-covered slope, raising herself just enough to study the forest beneath her. She couldn't see anything, but the wind had shifted enough on its own to bring her the scent of blood and death. Along with that scent came the soft sobbing of a child.

She had been careful to feed far from her lair, but then her travels had taken her closer to the Carpathian world where Mikhail Dubrinsky, the prince of the Carpathian people, and his legendary guard, Gregori, made their homes. There seemed to be far more Carpathians than the last time she'd been this close. That meant, when she hunted for food enough to feed her pack, she had to avoid not only vampires, Xavier and his servants, but the hunters as well.

She knew the vampires and Xavier searched for Razvan. They had visited the cabin where she'd fed from the human in the forest, but, thankfully, the human had been long gone. The stench of vampire remained in the cabin, and fortunately the vampires were unable to track her. They found the spot where Razvan had fallen. Footprints circled the area and the foul stench of vampire radiated from that central spot for days before they'd moved on.

She'd made certain neither she nor her pack set foot on the ground close to her lair after that. She'd even resorted to visiting the village to bring rich blood back to feed Razvan, barely rousing him, healing him each night and keeping his mind free of the damaging images and memories that haunted and tormented him. If, after he was at full strength and fully healed, he chose to meet the dawn, she vowed to herself that she wouldn't stop him a second time. But night after night, holding him in her arms and singing the healing chant, her blood flowing into him, she knew it would be difficult to let him go. She would though. She would set him free, with no guilt, because saving him had been *her* choice. Staying to help her defeat Xavier had to be his.

The child's cry drew her attention back to the forest below her. Why hadn't an adult answered that distress call? What kind of parents would leave a young one to the dangers of a snow-covered wood at night? Even the villagers crossed themselves, hung garlic and crosses in the windows and over doors, believing in the persistent rumors of the undead walking the night.

She sank back on her heels. She didn't do children. She hadn't even held a baby, not once in her entire life cycle. She couldn't remember interacting with children when she was younger—*before*—in the before. If a child saw her in her true form, especially a Carpathian child used to the perfection of form, the child might run from her.

She touched her neck. In this form, she never gave a vampire the satisfaction of seeing her scars. The vampires and Xavier had done their worst to her, but she remained flawless, untouched, unmarred by their barbarity. If nothing else, it gave her a psychological boost to know they were so shocked by her beautiful appearance.

The child's voice crescendoed and Ivory winced. She was going to have to at least check that the little thing wasn't injured, but that meant exposing herself when she was certain there were both vampires and hunters in the vicinity. She took a deep breath and shrugged, allowing her pack to merge with her skin in the form of tattoos. They would watch her back, and could draw more information from the wind than even she could. With six pairs of intelligent eyes and six noses gathering every detail around them, she felt more secure.

Let us get this done. And when we find the child, no scaring it. We will take it back to its mother and be done with this.

The pack didn't seem anymore enthusiastic than she was. She hadn't let them run free for some time, knowing the vampires often searched out the wolf packs, hoping to find evidence to track them back to her lair. *Soon*, she assured.

She dissolved into vapor and streaked over the snow, staying low to the ground, giving the wolves every opportunity to take in every scent.

Foul ones. Humans. Carpathians. Blood. The walking dead.

Ivory processed the information and directions as fast as the wolves fed it to her. *Foul ones* was the wolf name for vampires. But the walking dead were puppets—nonpsychic humans given vampire blood and promised immortality. The vampires often used them to attack during the day. They were nearly as foul as the vampires themselves.

She moved even faster, suddenly afraid for the child. For one moment, below her, she caught a glimpse of a man running through the snow, and then he disappeared in the trees. The child's father? If so, he was arriving a little late.

She spotted a little boy, thin, with a mop of dark hair reaching his shoulders, struggling against the type of snares that had trapped the wild wolves. Her heart dropped. Another trap. She wasn't fool enough to believe that the boy had walked into the mass of snares himself. He'd been forcibly taken from somewhere—she knew by the smell of death and blood—and staked out like a sacrificial goat, the thin wires cutting into his hands and ankles. There was one around his neck. He was crying, but he stood stoically, refusing to fight and worsen the already deep cuts.

She didn't believe this boy had been set out as bait for her—more likely for Razvan. He had a child and he had given his soul, or at least a piece of it, to save her. Xavier would know he would risk everything to save a child. She was in for a fight, but she couldn't leave that child. The vampires were expecting a starving, sick, tortured Razvan, not the slayer, scourge of all undead.

She formed close to the boy, noting that he didn't wince or scream out in fright, which meant he'd seen a Carpathian before and they had allowed him to retain his memories. "It's a trap," he mouthed. He stared at the wolf tattoos with their bared teeth and lifelike eyes covering her shoulders and arms as she bent to gently set her crossbow in the snow and withdraw a pair of cutters.

She nodded her understanding. "Keep crying," she hissed as she snipped his left wrist free. It was brave of him to try to warn her when he must have been terrified.

The boy didn't miss a beat, keeping up a lively rendition of wailing while she cut loose the wire on his neck and carefully removed it. Her fingertips brushed the thin necklace of blood circling his neck. Her fingers crept up to her own neck, fluttered there for one moment as she remembered the bite of the sharp blade.

The boy couldn't be more than eight or nine, with his thin face and large, intelligent eyes. He was watching her carefully, studying her closely as she reached across him to snip at his other hand.

Behind you.

The alpha gave her the warning and she felt the large wolf shift in preparation for the attack. Raja's head lay across her neck, his eyes looking straight back. Ever so slightly he turned his head and the movement made the boy gasp. Ivory thrust the cutters into his hands and held out her arms away from her body, bending her knees until she was in a crouch, her right arm slowly dropping to reach for her crossbow.

The child's eyes widened in alarm and fear as he looked over her shoulder and saw the large man coming up behind her with an axe gripped in his hands. The woodsman's face had a blank look and he shuffled, his eyes a strange red. He lifted the axe above Ivory's head, still several feet out. The boy opened his mouth to call a warning, but no sound emerged.

Ivory felt the slight wrench of pain that always accompanied her pack separating themselves from her as the savage wolves leapt, completely silent as they made their concentrated attack, the communication in their minds only. Her fingers closed over the crossbow and she grasped it, winking at the boy to reassure him as she dove away from him, somersaulted and came up on one knee, her crossbow aimed at the attacker. The boy stared open-mouthed at the six silver-tipped wolves, more shocked at the sight of them than the soulless attacker.

The wolves drove the ghoul backward, teeth clamped around each arm, the alpha going for the throat while the other wolves grasped legs and held him. Vampire puppets were extremely strong, programmed by their masters for one task; very few things could stop them once they were set on a path. The wolves tearing at him did little other than keep him on the ground beneath the writhing mass of silver fur.

Ivory felt the surge of power crackling in the air and rolled closer to the boy. "Hurry up. We are about to have some very unpleasant company." She kept her body between the child and the snarling, writhing ghoul and whatever else was coming at them.

A man broke from the trees, sprinting fast. "Travis! Trav! Are you all right?" He skidded to a halt, taking in the ghoul, the wolves and the woman aiming the very lethal-looking crossbow right at his heart.

"Gary! That's Gary," the boy yelled, his voice bursting with relief.

"Stay away from the wolves," Ivory cautioned. Her gut tightened. Now she had two humans to protect. Neither seemed shocked at the ghoul, nor at her appearance, as if a female hunter, a pack of wolves and a mindless assassin were everyday occurrences. She knew little about Carpathian politics, and didn't want to know more. She was a slayer. And a vampire was close.

One of the wolves yelped, and out of the corner of her eye she caught movement as the ghoul flung one of the smaller females. The body dropped almost at the feet of the man called Gary. He leapt back, eyeing her warily.

"You have a vampire coming down on top of you," Ivory pointed out. "Move or die."

Above his head, in the whirling mist of snowflakes and fog, she could see the outline of the grisly form of a vampire. Power radiated from him, and her heartbeat ratcheted up a notch. This was no lesser vampire; she'd fought enough of them to know.

Gary dove toward the boy, landing belly down, crawling

51

the rest of the way. Travis sank down in the snow in an attempt to cut the wires from his ankles.

The vampire struck at her wolves, raising his hand to call down the lightning, thrusting the white-hot bolt at her pack, uncaring that the monster he'd created might be in the path of destruction. She slammed the bolt with a second one, driving the sizzling, crackling energy away from the writhing bodies. A tree exploded just beyond the wolves, the splinters and debris raining down on the ghoul and the pack. Her pack leapt back, circling the puppet, paying no attention to the vampire, leaving him to Ivory.

Gary rolled to finish extracting the boy, shielding the small body with his own as Ivory fired one of her small arrows into the vampire's chest. It hit him just below his heart, and he turned his head, deigning to acknowledge her for the first time.

Ivory's breath caught in her throat. A small sound escaped. Stunned, she could barely stammer, nothing coherent emerging from her.

Gary looked at her sharply, and then up at the vampire as the creature slowly lowered himself to the ground. The caricature of a man had probably been handsome at one time. He was well built, with wide shoulders and long hair that once had been thick and full, but now the vampire obviously didn't bother to hide his evil appearance. His skin was pulled tight on his skull and his teeth were sharp and pointed. He not only looked strong, but the power radiating from him hung in the air. The glowing eyes were locked on the female hunter, but he looked nearly as shocked as she did.

"Sergey," Ivory whispered.

The vampire winced visibly at the sound of her sweet,

pure voice. He stood a long moment in silence, his looks subtly changing. In the blink of an eye his teeth were not long, pointed and stained, but white and straight. The face was fuller and the eyes had gone dark. The ghoul moved and the vampire merely flicked a hand toward him to freeze him where he was. Even the wolves didn't move; they were statues, staring at the woman and the vampire as they faced one another.

"Ivory?" The voice grated. He cleared his throat. "Ivory?" he repeated and this time the tone was beautiful. Gentle. Affectionate. His hands came up to cup the shaft of the arrow where black blood dripped down his chest. "You are alive."

Her hands trembled and she took a breath. One. Just held it and then released the air in a long gasp as if she was fighting to breathe. Her gaze dropped to the arrow in his body, the blood slowly dripping down his shirt and welling around the entry wound.

"Yes," she whispered. "I am alive and my soul is intact. How is it that you, my beloved brother, would join the ranks of the evil ones who would destroy your sister? Answer this for me." Each word was squeezed painfully from her heart, constricting her throat, threatening to strangle her with raw grief and the terrible sense of betrayal.

Ivory's throat was clogged with tears. She doubted she could say another word without bursting into sobs. She refused to look away from the vampire, not even for a moment, although it was much more difficult to think of him as an enemy when his form was so dear and familiar. She longed to fling herself into the comfort of his arms and rest her head against his shoulder, crying for her lost past.

She sought the path she might best use to warn the human. *Take the boy and slip away. Get far from this place. I am not certain I can defeat this one in battle.*

Sergey. He'd been a genius fighter. Few compared. Now he had centuries of battles with some of the best Carpathian hunters, not to mention the vampires that he'd defeated to add to his experience. She tried not to see the sly, cunning intelligence slipping into the depths of his eyes. She didn't want to believe her first vision of him. She had avoided her brothers once she'd confirmed the whispered rumors.

Gary caught Travis by his upper arm and began to slowly ease him back into the woods. The vampire's head turned slowly toward them, and for a moment that soft, dark color was ringed in red and glowed at them like a feral animal.

"Do not look at them, Sergey," Ivory snapped. "Or should I call you *hän ku vie elidet*—vampire, thief of life."

His gaze flicked back to her and he looked sad. "You are my beloved sister . . ."

"Do *not* call me beloved when you betrayed me. You are in league with those who would have stolen my life."

"They have been brought to justice."

"Have they?" She stood, tall and straight, the moon gleaming off her blue-black hair. "You cannot lie to me, Sergey. Others perhaps might believe you, but I have hunted the vampire for many centuries now and I know the ones who took me to the meadow of our father and chopped my body into pieces and left them for the wolves. I know they live, so do not tell your pretty lies to me."

"Did they really do that to her, Gary?" The boy sounded fearful with his loud whisper.

She caught a glimpse of the man holding the boy closer,

trying to soothe him. Each time they moved, the ghoul stepped with them in a macabre dance of death. Every time the ghoul shifted, the wolves circled and darted toward him, teeth bared.

"Leave us, Sergey," Ivory said, "and take your *kuly* with you."

"What is *kuly*?" Travis asked.

She turned her head toward the boy, but she kept her gaze on the vampire. "It is a worm that lives in the intestines, a demon who possesses and devours souls. So really, that is what Sergey is, as he possesses that worm's soul." With her chin she indicated the ghoul.

"I need a weapon," Gary hissed at her.

Ivory sighed. What man would run into the forest chasing a ghoul who had taken a child without a weapon? At least neither was hysterical, and that was a plus when she needed every ounce of concentration she could have. In any case, there was no use whispering; any vampire, let alone a master vampire, had excellent hearing.

"You have forgotten your manners, Ivory," Sergey reprimanded, looking more sorrowful than ever. He dragged the arrow from his body, watched it disintegrate in his palm and dropped the metal scraps in the snow. "Your arrow nearly pierced my heart."

Ivory marked where the pieces fell. "If you still had a heart, those who desecrated my body would have been brought to justice. Instead, you torture a child with your pathetic puppet. Take your servant and go, Sergey. You do not want to fight me."

He laughed, a soaring wicked sound that seemed to fill the skies around them. The trees shivered, shaking the snow from their branches so that ice crystals were flung into the air. The vampire lifted his head and coughed hard.

As the icy flakes hardened and changed form, raining down, Ivory threw out her hand and the snow turned to vapor, a great gust of wind blowing it back into Sergey's face.

He coughed again and gagged, choking, holding one hand to his mouth. Behind his palm she could make out a small trickle of blood, then crimson drops stained the snow below him. He coughed and more blood spilled. Above his hand, his eyes glowed bright red and she heard the child give a strangled, frightened cry.

Keep his face against your chest, she ordered Gary. *He put his parasites in the snow and they can be lethal. You cannot allow the boy to breathe them in.*

Sergey spit into the snow, staining the pristine white powder with tiny wiggling wormlike creatures. "I am losing patience, Ivory. You must join with me now."

She felt her body respond to the sweet compulsion in his voice. Her fingers closed tighter on the crossbow. "Do you believe I am still that young girl you last saw? I do not respond to compulsion."

He opened his arms. "Come to me, sister. You belong here, with us. We fight against the prince—for *you.* We fight against the prince—for *you.* But for the cowardice of his father, but for the sickness in his lineage, none of what happened to you would have. He sent you away, knowing there was danger to you, against the wishes of your brothers. Would you fight for his son? Would you join with the brother of the man who set in motion a war?"

Was he maneuvering closer? She couldn't tell. His body swayed when he talked and she couldn't tell if he was using that to inch forward, not with the snow swirling around her head. Each time the ghoul moved, the wolves reacted, but their attention was centered on the puppet, leaving the master to her. Her vision seemed a little hazy. Or maybe it was her mind. When he talked, his voice conjured up images she kept buried deep in order to keep her sanity. She could distance herself and remember that moment when all was lost and Draven had handed her over to the vampires with a smirk on his face. He'd caught her face in his hands and kissed her. She'd had the satisfaction of biting him hard, nearly tearing off his lip. He'd punched her hard enough to make her lose focus, just as she seemed to be doing now.

Sister! Raja snapped at her.

Sister! Sister! The rest of the pack took up the cry.

Ayame lifted her face to the sky and howled, the sound piercing through Ivory's brain. She blinked. The blood spots in the snow were no longer there or, if they were, she couldn't see them because the undead had glided forward just those scant few inches. She could feel the crossbow in her hand, still loosely pointed at her brother. Her hands trembled. She'd battled a master vampire once or twice in the intervening years, and she'd barely escaped with her life.

She knew Sergey had been considered one of the Carpathian's greatest hunters long before he'd ever turned.

"Back off," she ordered. "You do not want to do this."

"My patience grows thin." Sergey snapped his fingers. "This child is the beginning. We will have the others soon and they will either join us or die. Once hope is gone, we will have little trouble picking off the Carpathians. You belong with us in this. Come here to your brother and feed. I offer you *everything*."

She noticed he could barely sustain his pleasant tone, one more indication of how far gone he was. Too many years as a vampire had left his memories of better days tattered. The slow rot had claimed even the recollection of what love had been, what family meant. She had run out of time, hoping that by stalling him the Carpathian hunters would feel the dark power so close to their realm. And if the boy was really part of the Carpathian world, where were his keepers?

"My heart and body died a long time ago, Sergey, and now you so graciously offer me the death of my soul. I choose to remain true to the teachings of my brothers."

"We were wrong to follow the prince. He was unworthy. He allowed his son to destroy all that we held dear." He stretched his hand to her again, beckoning with his fingers. "Maxim dwells in the land of the shadows. As does Kirja, both slain by villainous Carpathian hunters, betrayers of their own people. Ruslan and Vadim need to see their beloved *sisar*—sister."

Her heart contracted. The pull of the past was strong. She fought the memories, the compulsion, shaking her head to ward off the lure. She didn't change position as she looked guilelessly up at her beloved brother. Her finger squeezed the trigger on her crossbow, releasing the arrow. She tossed the bow to the human male and rushed Sergey, snapping the coated arrowheads hard in a straight line up his chest.

It was an act of desperation to attack a master vampire, but she couldn't wait for his strike. *Go! Take the boy and run. My pack will hold off the ghoul to give you a chance.* She hoped Gary understood that his chance was slim and he shouldn't waste it. His first priority had to be the life of the child—especially when Sergey admitted they planned to turn or kill the boy.

She didn't look to see if Gary obeyed; her entire being concentrated on Sergey. The arrowheads would keep him

58

from shifting, but then, it didn't look as if he had any intention of shifting. He waited for her with that small half-smirk on his face.

The ghoul jerked up and lumbered forward. The wolves sprang and he tried to smash their bodies together as they tore at his dead flesh.

Gary picked up Travis like a football, tucking the boy under one arm while he grasped the crossbow in the other and raced back into the shelter of the trees, weaving his way through the brush to present a more difficult target.

Lightning slammed from sky to earth, strike after strike as the vampire sought to stop him, slowing the man, forcing him to fall several times in the snow. All the while, Sergey stood his ground, his glowing eyes burning, pitiless holes, glaring at Ivory as she rushed him, sword drawn.

At the last moment, before that tip of a sword could sink into his flesh, he moved so fast he blurred, raking across her face with poison-tipped claws, creating gouges in her skin. She traveled beyond him, somersaulting into the soothing icy powder, before coming up on one knee behind him and hurling a much more lethal star toward the back of his neck. It caught him as he spun to face her, a lucky break, the spinning points slicing through the side of his neck, cutting through the jugular.

Black blood sprayed across the snow and all pretense of civility and sibling affection was gone in an instant. Sergey threw back his head and howled, the sound excruciating, an energy wave that blasted everything in its path, knocking her back and setting the wolves whimpering.

Ivory landed flat on her back, the air rushing from her lungs, leaving her gasping. Automatically she rolled several times, saving her life. Jagged bolts of lightning hit the ground where she'd been and followed her across the snow, leaving great gaping holes where each white-hot strike landed.

She came to her feet a short distance away, blurring her body and sending replicas of her form at him from every direction, rushing in, slamming the sword deep into his chest. Before she could twist the hilt or withdraw, he sank his teeth into her shoulder, clamping his mouth down around the thin bone and grinding. She screamed as pain burst through her, radiating outward, her flesh burning away from the acid blood pouring over her.

"Mmm, *sisar*—sister, you taste delicious," he whispered, a contemptuous smirk in his voice. "I have not tasted Carpathian blood in a long while. Perhaps I will keep you to myself instead of sharing your delightful taste with my brothers."

Ivory clawed at his face, trying to gain enough leverage to get him off her. She dared not take the wolves off the ghoul, afraid the child wouldn't get away. Her knee came up into Sergey's crotch, the heel of her boot raking down his leg to smash into the side of his knee. His bite deepened, tore at her flesh as if he were trying to consume her.

She fought to stay conscious through the pain, drawing both hands back and smashing her fists to either side of his jaw, driving through bone. His mouth blew open in a screaming gasp and he lifted his head.

Gary fired the crossbow, hitting the vampire in his right eye.

The boy? Ivory gasped as she dropped to the ground, blood pumping from her mangled shoulder. She dissolved as Sergey reached for her, his claws going through vapor. Droplets of blood followed her across the snow as she streaked away from Sergey.

Gary backpedaled when the vampire snarled and turned to look at him with one glowing eye. "I sent him back to the village. I couldn't leave you behind."

"You will wish you were never born," Sergey promised him and reached up to yank the arrow from his eye. Black blood poured down his face. The vampire didn't bother to wipe it away; instead he bared his savage teeth at the human.

Ivory materialized over the ghoul, slicing through his neck with one hard stroke, sending the head bouncing obscenely across the slope. The wolves pinned the thrashing body to the ground, holding him there while she gathered energy from the sky.

Move! Already she hurled the bolt toward the soulless creature, striking just as the wolves leapt back, in a move they'd perfected countless times.

Orange-red flames erupted, turned black, a foul stench filling the air as the carcass burned. Ivory kicked the head into the flames and faced the vampire over the rising fetid smoke. Her sides heaved for air; her body was covered in her blood—and his. Trails of blackened flesh streaked her shoulder and went down her arm, but she faced him stoically, with one eyebrow raised.

"You look a little worse for wear there, brother," she commented. "You must be getting old and feeble to allow a human to creep up on you like that."

As she spoke she circled around to try to put her body between Sergey and the human male. The man had risked his life for her and he was still standing there, waiting for another shot, when he had to know that her crossbow wasn't going to take down a master vampire. She'd rarely had dealings with humans, but she had to admire his courageous stand, even though she feared for his life.

"One of mine for one of yours, little sister," Sergey hissed, his body suddenly moving with blurred speed.

Even with her specially coated metal in him, she could barely follow his path, the master vampire moved so quickly. She saw him grasp little Farkas and slam the wolf's body over his knee. There was an audible crack and the animal screamed. Cackling, Sergey threw the wolf away from him so that the body hit a snowcapped boulder where the animal lay broken and panting in pain.

The metal arrowheads fell to the ground in pieces, and already the vampire's body was regenerating, while her own grew weaker from blood loss. She dared not close off the wound and trap parasites in her where they could take hold. For a moment she just faced her brother, trying to decide the best way to get luck on her side—it was the only possible chance she had of defeating the vampire.

The air around them charged with electricity, making the hair on the back of her neck stand up. She felt the compression in her lungs and thought it was the undead attacking, but he stepped back, giving a wary glance right and left and then upward toward the sky.

"Another time, Ivory." Sergey raised his hands and the ground erupted into violent upheavals, sending both Gary and Ivory pitching forward. Gary went down headfirst and Ivory leapt to try to cover him against whatever form Sergey's latest aggression would take. Snow burst into the air in a spinning cyclone so that everything went white. She felt the impact of his blow on her left side, slamming her down and over the male. The blow might have killed a human; as it was she felt bones crack under the force.

Ivory rolled and rocked forward, allowing the momentum to take her to her feet in a half-crouch, ignoring the waves of pain coursing through her body. She turned in a circle. Sergey was gone. There was silence, broken only by heavy, ragged breathing. Ivory sagged, the strength leaving her body in a rush.

On hands and knees she crawled to Farkas as the other wolves circled around them. Ivory gathered the wolf into her arms, judging how much time she had to heal him. She was definitely weak and needed blood.

Gary pushed himself to his feet. "Are you all right?"

"Yes. Thank you." It came out stiffer than she intended. "How did the ghoul get that child? Why was he not kept safe?" She cast him a swift look of reprimand, her hand stroking gently along the back of her wolf, finding the breaks along the spine.

"He is the adopted child of Sara and Falcon and, although psychic, is human. During the day the children attend school and participate in the regular activities other children in the village have. Falcon and Sara have guardians in place. I was with several of them in the schoolhouse, but Travis had gone to attend a function with a woman who helps us out. We had no idea there was a threat in the area."

Ivory sighed. "Master vampires have learned to hide their presence from hunters. Some of the lesser vampires have slowly been acquiring the skill as well. Your hunters should know that and take better precautions."

Above them, thunder boomed and an answering crash blasted across the sky as if two powerful forces met and clashed in the heavens above them.

Sergey had sent another blast toward them, hoping to score a hit from a distance, but an unseen hand had sheltered them. The energy was much closer, and she knew she didn't have much time. She had to leave before the Carpathian hunters arrived.

Another burst of energy swept through the area, rocking the earth and making the trees tremble. Several rocks dislodged and rolled, drawing Ivory's attention to the pieces of metal strewn through the snow. She raised her palm, calling them back to her, careful that each piece was found and placed in a small pouch on her belt.

Gary frowned. "What are those?"

"Weapons." She shrugged her shoulders, not wanting to draw attention to her secret. "I have to take care of my wolf. You can leave the crossbow here and go with my thanks."

"I think I'll wait until I'm certain you're all right."

Ivory gave a dismissing grunt, closed her eyes and laid her hands over the wolf's broken bones, drawing as much energy as she dared to heal Farkas enough so that he could at least travel. Light burst from beneath her palms and radiated heat along the animal's spine.

"Would you give him blood?" Ivory looked up at the man standing above her.

"What?"

"I am not asking for myself. He needs blood to heal. He will not harm you, I guarantee you." She kept her gaze locked with his. "I would not force you. It is solely your choice."

Gary crouched down beside the woman, aware of the five large wolves pressing close to him. None of them acted threatening, but they were big brutes and fierce looking. Some had burns in their fur and around their muzzles from the acid blood where they'd taken the ghoul down. Up close he could see numerous old scars from other battles. He laid the crossbow next to her hand and nodded, rolling up his sleeve.

Ivory handed him a knife. Gary took it and without

hesitation cut across his skin and pressed his wrist to the wolf's muzzle. The wolf licked at the blood while Ivory murmured a soft healing chant. "Enough," she said, only minutes later. "That will get us traveling. I am in your debt."

"Let me give you blood," Gary offered. "If you wait, the others will be here soon and they can heal your wounds."

"We are here," said a voice behind them.

Ivory gasped and spun around, taking up her crossbow and aiming the arrow at the heart of the newcomer. She hadn't heard him approach, nor had the wolves. One moment there was no one and the next he stood there, tall and powerful with slashing silver eyes. He kept his gaze on her, and she had the feeling he took in everything—her wolves, Gary, the battle scene and every wound.

"Are you all right, Gary?"

"She saved our lives, Gregori," Gary explained.

Ivory had known exactly who this man was the moment she'd laid eyes on him. She'd known his elder brothers, Lucian and Gabriel, but Gregori was a legend in his own right—and she wanted no part of him. She stood slowly, careful not to make any sudden moves, keeping the arrow trained on him. She signaled to the wolves and they all moved behind her.

"We are in your debt, lady," Gregori said, inclining his head. "I am a healer. Perhaps I could aid you in return for the great service you rendered."

She knew he was deliberately formal in his speech, recognizing her as an ancient, but she refused to allow him to lull her into a false sense of security. She didn't trust him any more than she had Sergey. Behind him another man materialized and she heard herself gasp. For one horrible instant she was certain Draven was alive and had come for her again. It took her a moment to realize this had to be Mikhail Dubrinsky, Draven's younger brother, the reigning prince of the Carpathian people.

She took a step back, the arrow switching immediately to cover the intruder's heart. Gregori stepped deliberately in front of the prince, holding his hand palm outward toward her. "No one wants to hurt you. We are in your debt."

Behind him, the prince gently guided Gregori to one side. "I am Mikhail Dubrinsky and we are in your debt."

"I know who you are." She couldn't keep the bitterness from her voice. "I gave my aid freely to the child, and this man has more than repaid any debt owed to me." *Farkas, on your feet now.*

The wolf rose obediently and stumbled, nearly falling again. She cursed, knowing he was too weak to cross the distance on his own. She couldn't go back to her lair, not wounded and bleeding. She'd leave a blood trail in the sky. It wouldn't be visible, but the droplets could be scented and anyone who wished to could find her.

Gregori took a step closer and her other hand went to her holster. Ivory shook her head. "I do not wish to do battle with you, but, if you insist, I will do so."

"I wish only to aid you."

"Do so by giving me free passage through your land. I will take my pack and go."

"You are a Carpathian woman without a lifemate and in need of our protection," Gregori said, his voice soft and compelling.

"I am an ancient warrior with a lifemate and I fight my own battles. I have no allegiance to your people and none to your prince. Know this, dark one—I will fight to the death to retain my freedom. I wish only to be left alone." She took another step back.

"If you leave without aid, you will be vulnerable to any attack," Gregori answered, his voice more gentle than ever. "As a Carpathian warrior, a male, the healer of our people, I cannot allow you to go without first seeing to your care."

Her sword swung up, her dark eyes catching fire even as despair swept through her. "Then know it will be a fight to the death. I want no help from you or from any of your people."

Her wolves spread out, even Farkas, facing the Carpathian males—enemies now—circling the men with teeth bared.

4

Razvan came aware slowly. At first he thought he was dreaming, but dreams such as lying in soil had long ago disappeared from his imagination. He was certain though, absolutely certain, he could feel loam, rich in minerals, surrounding him like a warm comforting blanket, the earth cradling him, his body warm, hunger a distant memory. And that made no sense.

His eyes snapped open, power consuming him, shaking him, more than he'd ever imagined, more than he'd ever conceived of or dreamt. It ran through his body like a rising tidal wave, rushing through veins, pumping through his heart, exploding through organs and sinew until he was filled with power. Light radiated from his body as he burst through the layers of soil to the surface. Dirt geysered up, hitting the high rock ceiling above his head and spraying across the room.

He landed in a crouch, senses flaring out, scanning, his mind racing, trying to fit all the pieces of the puzzle together. He had escaped at last. His mind almost couldn't grasp the truth of it. He remembered running through the snow, shivering, his strength so far gone he couldn't control his body temperature, but he forced himself to keep going until he didn't have a single ounce of strength left. He had to get far enough away that Xavier and his servants wouldn't find him before the sun rose. The sun. Every Carpathian's last resort was to cleanse their soul with the bright white light. Even that had been denied him.

Xavier had been careless. Fear had been his downfall. Fear that, if he fed Razvan too much, he would lose control of him, so the mage had forced his grandson to go for weeks without blood. Yet Xavier took from him daily—until finally Razvan was too weak and sick to stand, or to supply the greedy mage with the life-giving Carpathian fluid.

He remembered that empty, weak feeling, the near insanity of hunger, his body crying out, his teeth sharp and needy every moment that he was awake. Chained, he couldn't hunt for his own food. There were not even animals near to call to him. Every cell, every organ cried out, until his brain was nothing but a red haze of need. Now he felt only mildly hungry, not the constant gnawing hunger that had ruled his life for so many centuries.

He looked around him, realizing he was still deep beneath the earth, but it was warm. Somehow, glittering moonlight streamed in from above, yet he was deep beneath the earth in a rock cavern. He heard the sound of water but little else. He waved his hands, and candles sprang to life all over the room, instantly transforming it into a feminine sanctuary. The layers of rock above them were intricately carved with beautiful pictures, sweeping landscapes and trees and shrubbery, as if the outside world had been brought inside one small piece at a time, until the walls were a thing of beauty.

Feminine—the woman—the reason he was seeing in blazing color. The light and the color dazzled his eyes, burned after so long of seeing in gray and black and white.

He remembered the soothing touch of her hands; her voice, soft and compelling; the way her blood tasted, addictive and hot as though made specifically for him. She had saved him when he'd told her not to do so. She'd worked a compulsion on him in spite of all his warnings, and now . . .

He *felt*. Everything. All of it. The guilt and the rage and the sense of absolute loneliness. He had no idea how to behave in civilized society. He had no knowledge of much other than deceit and torture, and now here he was, completely unprepared to be alive and well for the first time that he could remember in his centuries of existence.

Razvan stretched, feeling the play of muscle beneath his skin. His body felt so different, warm, alive, steel running beneath skin, so much power he trembled with it, uncertain how anyone could wield such strength without harming everything around him. He drew in a shaky breath and looked around again.

The woman—his lifemate—must have taken hundreds of years to carve out her home. It was unusual, but it appealed to him. There was something safe and comforting about it. He was upset with her for saving him. He couldn't stay to reprimand her or be tempted by her, of course, but at least he now had a fighting chance when he went after Xavier, and he knew he would. He couldn't allow the mage to continue spreading his evil through the world. He had to stop him, and now he might have the ability.

Razvan knelt to examine the large basin of soil. The depression was made of sheer rock. Impenetrable rock. The circular hollow that was her bed had been carved out, deep and wide, and then filled with the richest, purest, most heavily mineraled soil he'd ever seen. Unable to resist, he sank his hands into the black loam, feeling the soothing, rejuvenating properties.

Where had it come from? He sank back on his heels and studied the wide, deep hole. This soil had been brought here, one small bit at a time, yet now it was so many feet deep, he almost hadn't realized there was a bed of rock beneath it.

Who had the kind of patience it would take to first carve out a large chamber in a rock bed and then fill the basin with soil? It must have taken hundreds of years, yet she had conceived the idea and then painstakingly done it. He stood in one fluid motion, shocked at the way his body responded to the strength running through it, but he was more interested in the woman and what she had wrought than in how his body worked.

There was something extraordinary about the room, and not just the sheer work it had taken. The *feel* of it intrigued him. He placed his hands palm out toward the walls. Power crackled. Warmth and peace filled him. He frowned and dropped his hands, turning his head to study the rich carvings. Each wall, about thirty feet high in the shape of an oval, was carved with intricate drawings. A forest took up one wall, each needle and limb and gnarled trunk in rich detail. He moved closer. A second wall held a waterfall spilling into a pool of water, a pack of silver-tipped wolves, six of them, was etched in various positions in and around the forest and pool. He noted the shrubbery and flowers and the round moon and stars. Along the bottom of the wall, near the chamber basin where she rested, she had carved a single phrase.

Kućak és kuɲe jeläam és andsz éntölam sielerauhoet, andsz éntölam pesädet és andsz éntölam kontsíverauhoet: May the stars and moon be my guiding light and grant serenity of the soul, protection from all harm and a warrior's heart—peace.

It was more than a work of art. Embedded into each letter, every loop and whorl, the vines running in and out of each word, was the feeling of tranquility. When he ran his hands over the sentence, an inch away from the wall, he could feel vibrations and knew that woven into those words, into the very rock itself, were powerful safeguards.

Razvan laid his hands on the rock wall. Again the wall hummed with life. The walls were solid rock, impenetrable like her basin of soil. But more than that, each wall held safeguards, potent ones. He recognized the beginnings as mage, but they were so different it would be nearly impossible to unravel them. Nothing was going to get through those walls. No one would ever find her, and she was perfectly safe.

He groaned aloud. *She had brought him to her sanctuary.* He was probably the first person to ever see her home, and, with him, he brought an enemy beyond all others. Xavier could possess his body and, now that it was strong and fit and filled with power, the evil mage would want Razvan's body for his own more than ever.

Razvan touched her violin, and felt the joy and artistry of her music. Her emotions were everywhere, buried in the art she created in the warmth and sanctuary of her home. He went up smooth, polished rock steps and through the narrow opening into the largest room. This was obviously her living quarters, where she spent the most time. The cavern walls had been etched out one inch at a time until she had created a round tower, rising up a good forty feet. Although relatively small, the chamber appeared spacious in its simplicity.

There were a couple of chairs and a thick rug of wool

with a bit of wolf hair clinging to it here and there, giving evidence that her pack often lay in this room. He found a book of poetry and another on samurai battles and strategy and code of honor. Both were old and lay on the small carved table by a chair. He picked up the samurai book, told in an ancient language, and thumbed through it, noting the small writing in the margin and the underlining of phrases on every page. The book was worn, and obviously read often.

As in the bedchamber, the walls were covered in drawings, each stroke carved into the wall, which must have taken years to complete. The craftsmanship told him something about her. She was patient. She was meticulous. And a perfectionist. She was an artisan whether she knew it or not. The faces of ten young men stared out at him. Each face held an expression of love. When he lifted his hand and ran his fingertips over the smooth etchings, he *felt* the love. Her love. Their love for her. Anguish and sorrow at her loss of them. This, then, was her monument to her lost family.

Razvan had known love. His father and mother. His sister, Natalya. He carried those memories long after his emotions had faded—and it had taken a long time, even when he embraced that darkness in him, reached for it, desperate to be numb so he couldn't feel loss and guilt and an overwhelming sense of failure and despair. The blood in him ran strong whether he wanted it or not. When he touched those faces, the love there, the sorrow, nearly drove him to his knees. Every single stroke of the implement used to forge those beloved lines from memory was done with tears running down her face and absolute love in her heart.

As the pads of his fingers traced over the hair and

foreheads, down to the eyes, noses and mouths, he felt the difference in her. At first those hands had been innocent of knowledge of the fate of her brothers. Little by little, the knowledge had been gained over centuries, until she knew of the betrayal of her five older brothers. His hands stilled and he drew in his breath sharply. *Vampires*. Betrayers. Master vampires banding together and plotting the downfall of the Carpathian people with . . . His heart sank. Her enemy. Her worst enemy. *Xavier*.

It was all there in the stone. Every detail, every emotion, the blood and the tears and every ounce of love and forgiveness she had in her. She resolved never to see them as they were now, only to remember them with love in her heart where she could touch their faces here on this memorial and remember nothing but love from them.

He wanted to weep for her, for her lost family. He couldn't imagine what strength it must have taken for her to go on, so alone, so lost, the pain of her loss nearly intolerable, the strength of her love enduring. The other five faces were family—yet not blood. He felt her deep love for them, the caring, but fear was woven in there. She dreaded knowing their fate, and so he had stopped looking, afraid that they had taken the path of her brothers. The love shone through along with her dread of the truth.

Below the faces of the ten men were six wolves, carved in exquisite detail, so real looking he touched the rock to see if the fur was really of stone. Each face was different, as if she'd studied a wolf and transformed the living creature into part of the earth for all time. The room was beautiful yet very simple and felt like home and love.

He studied each face carefully, both man and wolf, knowing these were the important beings in her life. He wondered, if things had been different, whether his face would have been on the wall, immortalized with her family.

Along the bottom of the wall she had carved sentences in the Carpathian language, the letters intricate with vines and leaves weaving in and out of them along with finely etched flowers woven into the sentences.

Sív pide köd. Pitäam mustaakad sielpesäambam. Love transcends evil. I hold your memories safe in my soul.

Once again, as he passed his hand over the words, he *felt* the emotion pouring from the wall, so much so that he felt burning behind his eyes. Her love for her brothers, for her family and her pack, was tremendous and unwavering. Even with the knowledge that her brothers were dead to her, that they had betrayed her memory in the worst possible way, she not only was determined, but she succeeded in remembering them only as the family she had loved and adored.

There was courage in those words, he decided. Courage and strength and determination. If there was a way to recover the lost souls of her brothers through sheer love and forgiveness, she would find a way. He traced the small crosses cut deep beneath each of her brothers' faces and those of the De La Cruz brothers. Protection sparked back at him, as if that wall held the safeguards to protect her loving memories should she encounter the evil that her family had chosen to become.

A short tunnel veered off to the right and an open arch led through to a third room. He glanced inside the third room, which was nearly an extension of her family room to find a soothing pool, with a small real waterfall spilling out of the rock. This room had carvings, but just the faint beginnings of them. He could make out a huge tree trunk, with many long, sweeping branches reaching across the rock as if to shade the pool. It was a work in progress and he wished he'd be there to watch her work.

He ducked his head and entered the tunnel. His shoulders scraped against either side. Above the archway leading down into another room there was a cross cut deep. Already, before he even entered, he sensed a difference. Where the other rooms were feminine and homey, filled with soothing peace, love and comfort, this room was all about business and purpose. This was a workroom—a war room—and just as she had been meticulous in detailing her art, she was the same way with her weapons.

She forged her own swords and knives. Even the bullets in her gun were made by her. She appeared to be a master craftsman, her weapons as carefully and patiently forged as her carvings on the rock walls. He was amazed at the variety of weapons; some he'd seen before, others he was uncertain how to use. Books were scattered among the shelves of tools, again, well worn and often read.

One wall held shelves of books carefully penned in a feminine hand, and, opening them, Razvan recognized mage spells Xavier often used. Beside each one was penned a second spell, countering or corrupting the first. Book after book appeared to be dedicated to finding a way to defeat Xavier's spells. Razvan found it very interesting and became lost for a while, reading her notes, and her conclusions and the twists she put on the words to counter everything Xavier had ever taught. She'd obviously spent hundreds of years detailing Xavier's deeds, poring over the spell books she had used when she'd attended his school so many centuries earlier and working to find ways to defeat the mage at every turn. And it all made sense.

Excitement coursed through him. He had come to

believe, after centuries of captivity, that Xavier was invincible. The Carpathians had failed to defeat him. The Lycans had failed. The jaguars. Humans had been trapped and tortured and made into ruthless puppets. And the worst scourge of all—the undead—had made an unholy alliance with him. Razvan had seen it all. Yet, right here in this room, one person, one woman, had dedicated her life to stopping Xavier.

Razvan looked at the walls, knowing he would find an inscription. Each wall contained a single word and one held three lines. *Feldolgaztak. Kumalatak. Kutnitak.* Prepare. Sacrifice. Endure. There were no fancy letters this time, no vines and flowers interwoven in those stark words. Her mantra.

He walked across the room and crouched down beside the wall where she had carved her code, using the Carpathian language, deep into the rock wall. Four lines this time.

Köd elävä és köd nime kutni nimet. Sieljelä isäntä. Evil lives and has a name. Purity of soul triumphs.

Türelam agba kontsalamaval—Tuhanos löylyak türelamak saye diutalet. Patience is the warrior's true weapon—a thousand patient breaths bring victory.

Tõdhän lö kuraset agbapäämoroam. Knowledge flies the sword true to its aim.

Pitäsz baszú, piwtäsz igazáget. No vengeance, only justice.

All of this—everything she did—was in preparation for her ultimate battle with Xavier. This place was a safe haven, protected by extraordinary safeguards with no way to penetrate the miles of rock. The mage books, the weapons. She was assembling every possible weapon against the high mage and waiting patiently to strike while she gathered

77

information against him. The war room was a tribute to her vast knowledge of the enemy, her patience, determination and discipline. A picture of his lifemate was emerging, and he felt a sense of pride and respect for her.

Razvan lifted his head and looked around the room. A long, narrow table and workbench covered in tubes and handblown glass of all shapes and sizes caught his attention. He recognized herbs and plants, roots, dried and hung around the room. Sage was prevalent, and various plants to ward off evil. What was she making?

He peered at the book lying beside a twisted tube containing a dark, thick liquid. He sniffed cautiously toward the glass tube as he glanced over the neat, feminine scrawl. The formula had been crossed out and rewritten over and over until she seemed satisfied and had underlined the resulting mixture in thick, dark lines. He couldn't detect any odor at all. When he lifted a carved, smooth ladle, the mixture was clear, not dark. He frowned and looked at the glass tube, certain it was dark.

Along with everything else, she appeared to be a chemist. He examined several of the trays and baskets holding a variety of dried herbs. The workmanship on each of them was incredible, the patterns unique. When he touched them, he knew she had crafted each of them.

He left the room and went back to her family room, trying to think, to form an idea of what he should do. This woman—his lifemate—was patiently assembling the tools to defeat the world's greatest enemy. His memories of her rescuing him were very hazy, but he remembered her eyes, and the feel of her hands, the silk of her hair, the softness of her skin. Most of all he remembered her kindness.

He wanted more than anything to stay to help her achieve her goal, but he knew he was more dangerous to her than any other being on the face of the earth. Through him, Xavier could find and destroy her. Death was far from the worst that the high mage could do to a person; Razvan had learned that through bitter experience. He had been helpless to protect his sister and daughter—even his aunts—but he could protect his lifemate by staying away from her.

He looked around the comfortable lair—a masterpiece of beauty and courage, grateful that, before his death, he'd had a chance to meet her, to see what true light in one's soul was. He'd known only darkness and cruelty, but here he was surrounded by something altogether different—the complete opposite—and he wanted to just stay and bathe in her soul for as long as he dared before he had to leave.

He had never understood what being a lifemate truly was. Two halves of the same soul uniting. Light to darkness—darkness to light. They each needed the other. Just standing in her living quarters with the memory walls rising above him, he felt comfort and warmth, not of the body—he had that now; for the first time in centuries he wasn't shivering—but he felt warmth inside, deep where it counted. She'd given him something he hadn't known and he hadn't yet claimed her, hadn't actually bound their souls together. How much more powerful would these feelings be then?

The temptation shook him and he quickly pushed it away. He'd had no control of his life for centuries. This one moment, when he had choices, he would make the one necessary to protect this woman. Xavier would never get to her through him. She complicated things though. His first thought had been to try to kill Xavier, but he dared not risk falling into the mage's hands again, not when he would know the location of Ivory's lair.

Something stirred in him. A questing. A seeking. Something alien brushing at his mind with sharp talons, scraping at the walls. He stiffened and, without thinking, slammed a barrier so hard, so fast, it shocked him. He hadn't realized he could do such a thing. He recognized that perverted, vile touch. Xavier. The high mage was seeking him, reaching out to find him and possess him.

His heart beat so hard in his chest he thought it might explode. Fear for his lifemate lived and breathed in him, strengthening his resolve to fight Xavier's possession. He raced through the rooms, looking for a way out, fearing that Xavier might be able to see through his eyes. He kept his mind as blank as possible, knowing the mage, when merged, could read his thoughts. He couldn't remember how she'd gotten in. Everything about the journey was so hazy.

He couldn't get through miles of rock, not without knowing where he could safely emerge. He felt trapped and panicked, cursing his fate, that he would once again be the downfall of someone who needed and deserved his protection.

Finding himself in the bedchamber, he rested his hand on the wall, head down, eyes closed, trying to orient himself. To have another possess his body was a wrenching, sickening experience; the details of Xavier and his vile greed and extreme depravity were uppermost in his mind. He *would* keep him out.

Without warning, pain hit him—excruciating pain. Razvan's eyes snapped open and he looked around, trying to determine what was happening to him. The soil was there, in the deep depression, a rich, beckoning treasure he couldn't resist. He went to his knees in it, but the pain didn't subside.

His body was often taken on journeys through soil, but he had never rested in the rich, rejuvenating loam. Xavier had never dared to allow him that luxury. The soil might have healed his body and restored his strength, which Xavier could ill afford. He was left to languish in a kind of half-life in the ice caves. Razvan wasn't even certain he could survive beneath the earth, or even above it after so many centuries of cold, yet the soil filled him with strength—it just didn't stop the pain.

Xavier, unable to enter his mind, had to be attacking him from a distance. Teeth tore into his shoulder, the serrated edges slicing through bone, sinew and flesh, sawing deeper and deeper, injecting the burning parasites into the wound. He was being eaten alive—fitting justice for one such as him. His own teeth had sunk into his daughter's tiny wrist, and he had watched in horror, unable to protect her, while Xavier had done this very thing, gnawed on her as if she were a bone, a piece of meat to be consumed, his teeth tearing her delicate skin open to get at blood and bone.

He felt the spray of acid burning through his skin, deep—deeper still, vampire blood running in rivers over his flesh, long streams of it branching out over his hands and forearms and down his shoulder, and running down his arm and chest. He recognized the feeling—his wrists and ankles and even his back had often burned from the vampire blood-coated manacles. He had earned that for his failure to keep his family members safe from Xavier. Time after time, he had fought the demon mage, but he'd never been strong enough or wise enough to defeat him.

A burst of pain through his ribs shook him, radiating through his entire body. Pain was a way of life to him. He could push it away now, absorb it into his body and let it consume him. He had long ago learned how to live with agony.

The pain was not *his* pain. It was too far away. Too distant, the reaction stoic but definitely feminine. *Ivory was in trouble.* Everything else ceased to matter. He had one reason for his existence—to protect her from any enemy at all costs.

He cleared his mind and fought back the all-consuming emotions he still found difficult to deal with. He built the image of her in his mind, the image of her as he saw her. Soft and feminine, the loving woman who belonged here, in this home of raw beauty.

Ivory. You have need. Tell me how to come to you.

There was the smallest of hesitations. *They are hunting you.*

He didn't argue with her. She was hurt and she was surrounded by enemies. He could feel the burn of the vampire blood, the pain gnawing at her shoulder and ribs, and the trepidation that she was weak and might not be able to fight her way clear, although she was absolutely determined to try.

Razvan filled her mind with his strength and power, feeding her while he searched her memories and found the information he needed.

Stall them. I will be there soon. Do not fight. They will not attack you as long as you talk with them.

I do not have much time. The admission was humbling to her. *My strength is waning.*

I will come. I will be there, Ivory. Do not lose hope. He poured his determination and resolve into her mind, knowing she distrusted everyone, and with good cause. And she had every reason to fear and hate him. Xavier's genetic code was in his body.

There was another small hesitation, and then he clearly saw the crack cleverly hidden in her bedchamber where she could slip in and out of the narrow, inches-wide chimney. There was caution in her mind.

Razvan hastened to reassure her. *I will scan carefully before I emerge so there will be no trail leading back to your lair.*

Now he had the information in his head and he had to be doubly careful that Xavier could not enter his mind. Before he moved, he took that moment to build every possible defense, thickening barriers, making himself stronger than he'd ever been. Stronger than before he entered the thin crack that most would never notice. He streamed to the surface, a threadlike trail of vapor moving upward, weaving back and forth through the layers of rock bed for what seemed an interminable amount of time before he saw a sliver of sky overhead.

I will come. I will be there, Ivory. Do not lose hope.

In hundreds of years she had never relied on anyone but herself and her pack. She was Ivory Malinov, slayer of the dark ones, and she trusted no one, believed in no one. That way, no one could tear her heart out, physically or figuratively. She took a breath and pain nearly blinded her, made her stagger so that the dark one leapt toward her.

Ivory pulled a knife from her belt and stood facing him. She knew his reputation, but, thankfully, he didn't know hers. It was an advantage, no matter how small. He wasn't aware the wolves were Carpathian and all the more lethal. He would try to control them—it was standard defense—but it wouldn't work, and that would also give her a small advantage. Ordinarily she would have rushed to attack already, not wait for him to make the first move, but a part of her didn't want to start a war with the Carpathians.

Mikhail held up his hand. "Gregori. There is no need for this." It was a warning, delivered in a soft, almost gentle voice.

She remembered that same tone—his father's, so gentle and benevolent, the kind eyes, the compassionate, caring wisdom. The voice of reason. He wanted only to help her. An unselfish, gentle man who lived to serve his people. Whatever was best for them. She remembered that voice all too well. The eyes looking at her, looking through her, piercing her soul, seeing her need of knowledge, her need to learn when her brothers couldn't—or wouldn't. That voice soothing her, telling her he would make it right, that he would talk to her brothers when they returned and explain why it was necessary for her to go to the school and learn.

The prince understood. How could he not, when he knew so much more than everyone else? How could he not, when his reasons for doing everything were to serve his people. He had known that she hungered to do more than sit in her home and wait for her lifemate. She wanted to *be* something, to *do* something. The prince understood and helped her as she had known he would.

Something twisted inside her stomach. For a brief moment she couldn't feel the throbbing pain in her ribs or the terrible agony of her shoulder, not even the burn from the acid blood or sharp stabbing of the parasites as they bored into her cells. It had never occurred to her in her naivete that the prince had another agenda altogether— that he wanted to get rid of her, send her away because he knew his sick and twisted son would never leave her alone, and that her brothers or the De La Cruz brothers would kill Draven. Instead, she had happily gone off, believing the prince, in all his wisdom, knew so much more than her own family. She'd felt so grown up, so validated. She'd been hopelessly young and trusting in those days.

You have to hurry. I cannot hold out much longer.

She didn't know if her weakness was as much physical as mental. Seeing her brother had shaken her more than she'd realized. She'd vowed to avoid them and hadn't prepared herself mentally for seeing Sergey in his state of evil. He had changed his appearance when he recognized her, giving her a glimpse of her past, of a beloved man who'd held her and rocked her and spent hours teaching her to fight.

It had made her physically ill to shoot him with an arrow. She thought she had successfully separated the past from the present in her mind, but seeing him in person wasn't the same as thinking about him abstractly.

I am coming to you. Stall for time. Use the wolves if you must.

"Allow our healer to help you," Mikhail said, his voice dropping another octave, becoming almost hypnotic.

She couldn't help but feel the pull of that pure voice, even though over centuries she'd trained herself not to fall prey to sound. Farkas pressed closer to her legs, his body trembling. He was in the same shape as she was.

"I have no need of your help, Dubrinsky," she said, her voice haughty. "I neither ask nor want anything from you or anyone connected to you."

Gregori's breath came out in a long, slow hiss.

Her gaze jumped to his face, to the storm gathering in his eyes. If an attack came, it would come from him. She was weak from blood loss and pain, and was running out of time. "You evidently have never learned, in all your years of existence, how a voice can be sweet and pure to the ears, yet hide the truth behind the mask. My brothers chose the path of evil, but they were not wrong in their judgment of the Dubrinsky line. The prince you follow is not at all what you believe him to be."

Her gaze flicked to Mikhail, holding absolute, utter contempt. "You cannot deceive me, *karpatii ku köd*—liar, I am only fooled once, and your father was a champion. I wish to leave. Are you holding me prisoner?"

There was a small silence and Gregori slowly shook his head. "Do you believe you can fight all of us and emerge the victor? You are a woman, a Carpathian woman without anyone to protect her. I am sworn to carry out my duty whether you wish it or no."

Ivory took a breath, and let it out. *Be ready, Raja.*

The pack bared teeth and faced the threat of the Carpathian males without flinching.

Gary moved then, deliberately placing his body in front of hers, standing between her and the guardian of the prince, ignoring the threat of her pack.

"Please," he said. "No one wants to take you prisoner. I'm offering my blood freely to you. My life for yours. I'm not certain of the formal words, but, if you take what I offer, we'll know you'll at least have a fighting chance should you run into another vampire. No one wants to imprison you."

"She is infected with the vampire's blood," Gregori explained. "The parasites have to be removed."

"I am well aware of the infestation," Ivory retorted. "I am perfectly capable of healing myself."

Another male and female materialized just beyond the prince, and Ivory heaved a sigh, wishing she could just sink down into the snow and rest. She recognized the male, with his strong, handsome features, and a smile nearly broke out. Falcon. A friend of her family, of the De La Cruz brothers. He was a loner but a good man. She was grateful to see him, to know that at least a few of the older males still survived with their souls intact.

"Ivory!" Shock registered, shock and happiness. "*You* are the mysterious woman who saved our son?" Falcon glided forward but stopped abruptly when she stepped back and waved him off with her hand.

"*Pesäsz jeläbam ainaak*—long may you stay in the light, Falcon," she greeted. "It has been many years."

"You're injured," the woman exclaimed, hurrying forward.

Falcon stopped her by putting a restraining hand on her arm. "What is going on here?"

Ivory noted that he didn't sound judgmental, just cautious. "I wish to leave and your prince and his servant have dictated otherwise."

"Only to see to your health, lady," Gregori said with a slight bow, ignoring her taunt.

The woman frowned. "I'm Sara, Falcon's lifemate. You saved our son and we're indebted to you. No one here wants to harm you." She sent a small glare toward Gregori. "I can't imagine that anyone here would want to do anything but reward you for your help. I offer freely my blood to help heal you. Both Falcon and I will do our best to heal your wounds, although Gregori is a healer without comparison. He may look intimidating, but he is really a gentle, caring man."

"I am not intimidated by the dark one," Ivory denied. "I wish only to go my own way." The woman tempted her with her offer. A healing would certainly go a long way toward strengthening her, but, if she took the dark one's blood, he could track her all the more easily. Blood called to blood. And she would be so vulnerable. He could easily take her blood and then she would always have to worry that he could find her lair. As it was, Sergey knew she lived. He might get it in his head to try to find her.

She sighed and shook her head. "I regret that I cannot take you up on your generous offer, but thank you," she said to Sara.

Raja growled a warning and she realized that Gregori had moved closer. The dark one halted when she swung toward him, angling the knife up toward the softer parts of his body.

"You would be very foolish indeed, dark one, to try it."

"You are swaying with weariness," Gregori said. "If I said anything to make you think I wish you harm, I apologize. Surely you can see my only concern is your health. While we stand here, the parasites have had more of a chance to spread their poison through your body."

"I am well aware what parasites can and cannot do."

She reached for Razvan, desperate now. The healer was closer than she was comfortable with, perhaps within striking distance. Ivory wasn't foolish enough to disregard the man's reputation. He was known far and wide throughout the community as a dangerous, ruthless defender of the prince and of the Carpathian people.

Unless I allow him to give me blood, I have no choice but to fight my way out.

You will not have to fight. I give my life for yours. Follow my lead. Talk to the woman, distract them for another couple of minutes.

There was something reassuring in his tone. She had left him a broken, fallen warrior, but he had risen something altogether different. There was confidence in his voice. Razvan was Dragonseeker, one of the oldest and most powerful of all Carpathian lineages, and he had endured torment and suffering for hundreds of years without succumbing to darkness. She had been in his mind, and his memory was long. He had absorbed fighting skills, techniques and strategies. He knew more about Xavier than any other living being and he had more cause to destroy him than any other. She wanted to believe in him. Shaken and weak, she *needed* to believe in him.

The healer is trying to outwait me. He knows I cannot last.

You will last.

Strength poured into her. "Sara," she said softly. "I appeal to you. Ask the dark one to step aside. I have done harm to no one here and I want only to leave in peace. You indicated the need to repay me for saving the life of your child. This is what I ask. Simply have your healer step aside."

Sara looked up at Falcon and then to Mikhail. "I think she sounds reasonable. Please, Gregori, just step aside."

All of them looked at Sara, who angled closer, more protectively, toward Ivory.

Dirt geysered beneath the heels of the prince and a body materialized behind him, one arm locked tight around Mikhail's neck, the blade of a knife pressed against the heart of the prince. Stormy, merciless eyes locked on the face of the dark one with absolute resolve.

5

N o one moved. No one breathed, remaining statues frozen in time, as if one small mistake would start a bloodbath, and judging by the death in Razvan eyes—and Gregori's—there was little doubt there would be.

Gregori released his breath in a long, slow hiss. "It is a death sentence to threaten the life of the prince."

Razvan shrugged his shoulders, a casual ripple of power. "I have been under a death sentence since my fourteenth summer. It is nothing new to me. There is nothing you can conceive of to do to me that has not been done already. I accept that I will die this night." He inclined his head to Gregori, his expression unchanging, as if giving the Carpathian leave to kill him.

A man with nothing to lose, Gregori, often emerges the victor, Mikhail pointed out, a trace of humor in his voice.

Gregori's silver eyes flashed, and there was no answering amusement in them. *No one lays his knife at your heart and walks away unscathed.*

"Step away from my lifemate. Once she is away, you can do as you will," Razvan instructed.

"No," Ivory protested. "I remain with you. We will fight our way free."

Sara tried to step closer to Ivory. "This is crazy. Mikhail," she appealed to the prince. "Stop this. Let them go."

"Do you know who this man is?" Falcon asked softly. "Ivory, do you have any idea of the crimes Razvan has committed against our people?"

Again Razvan didn't flinch—and neither did the knife.

"You know nothing about him," Ivory said. "You have no right to pass judgment when you do not know the facts."

There is no need to defend me.

Razvan was shocked that she would. She stood there swaying, looking far too deceptively fragile for the warrior he knew her to be. Her body was tall and straight, her flawless skin marred now by the tracks of vampire blood and the teeth tears in her shoulder. There was something very intimate in knowing that, beneath that flawless exterior, he knew the true woman, the scars of death and defiance. The reserve of courage that it must have taken to pull her body back together and lay so broken in the ground for hundreds of years while nature tried to repair her.

He alone knew the depths and strengths of her when no other on the face of the earth did. Pride in her shook him. Her courage and ferocity humbled him.

"That is true," Falcon said, remaining calm in the midst of the tension. "You do not know *this* prince. I have given my allegiance to Mikhail. He is worthy of my respect and protection. You know me. More important, you know the De La Cruz brothers. They also have given their sworn allegiance to Mikhail. Manolito gave his life for Mikhail and Gregori restored him to this world." His gaze flicked to Razvan. "I believe your lifemate injected the poison into Manolito."

Razvan didn't flinch and the hand holding the knife was rock steady. "Ivory, I want you to come to my side and take my blood. Take enough that you can be at full strength."

She looked stricken and shook her head silently.

It is the only way. Your purpose and your preparations will be lost if you do not get away. We cannot stop them all. I knew when I came that I would be exchanging my life for yours. It is an honor.

"Her blood is infected with parasites," Mikhail said. "Keep the knife to my heart and allow my healer to rid her of Xavier's vile worms."

Ivory flinched when she heard the high mage's name.

Gregori's gaze flicked toward the prince, flashing him with a glitter of silver. *This is not amusing, Mikhail. We know too little about this man. He may very well shove that knife into your heart under Xavier's orders. You would not be wearing that smirk then.*

I have no doubt that you would find a way to save me.

"Razvan," Mikhail said. "We are not looking to harm your lifemate, only to make certain she can survive an attack on the way back to her home. We offer both of you friendship. Your sister, Natalya, is here with her lifemate, Vikirnoff. Lara, your daughter, and her lifemate, Nicolas De La Cruz, are residing among us, working to save our unborn children. She has been a tremendous asset to our people. Your aunts, Tatijana and Branislava, are safe and alive, at present under the ground healing. I offer safe passage to both of you."

Razvan flicked Ivory a quick glance. *It is up to you.*

Ivory drew in her breath. Life or death for her lifemate. He was putting his life into her hands so easily. Little did he know how abhorrent it was to her to allow favors from the Dubrinsky family. She could scarce make herself accept, yet she forced her body forward stiffly until she stood beside the healer, her fingers closed tightly around the hilt of a knife. She nodded her head toward the healer.

She'll probably stab me when I'm done. Again those silver eyes flicked toward the prince. *You won't be laughing so much when our wives give me hell for allowing someone to stab you.*

I don't know. It might be amusing. Neither will be angry with me.

Gregori's breath hissed through his teeth as he sent the prince another smoldering look before laying gentle hands on Ivory's shoulder. She trembled, much like a wild animal under the hands of a rescuer removing it from a trap. Without being consciously aware of it, the healer murmured soothing words in the ancient language, trying to reassure her by his voice and the touch of his hands that he meant her no harm.

Gregori closed his eyes and ceased to be a fierce warrior, ferocious guardian of the prince and the Carpathian people. All ego, everything he was, he surrendered, sending himself outside his body and into that of the wounded female. He became energy, a healing entity, moving through her bloodstream to find and repair all damage from the inside out.

He nearly forgot himself, one of the rare times in his centuries of healing, when he discovered the way her bones and sinew were so crudely knitted together. Ridges and evidence of inside and outside scar tissue were everywhere throughout her body, even on her organs, unheard of in Carpathian society. He pulled out of her for just one moment, shaken, unable to look at her while he tried to puzzle out how anyone could have survived what had made those scars.

Mikhail. There was shock when it was difficult to shock

Gregori. There was awe when it was nearly impossible to astonish him. Mostly there was respect. *It is as if she was chopped into small pieces. No part of her is untouched other than her face, and even her neck has these patchwork ridges. I believe she was cut into pieces, but how could she survive?*

He sent the impressions to Mikhail. *Her true skin is a patchwork. I feel blades sawing through her skin and bones, around her neck, hacking off her head. This woman has suffered greatly.* There was a breath taken. A crashing heartbeat. Abruptly Gregori pulled his mind from Mikhail's.

Tell me. The two words were a command, nothing less.

Your eldest brother assaulted her. I feel his taint, a stamp of suffering I have not felt before. He did this to her. Or he was part of it.

Mikhail closed his eyes for a moment. *She has reason to hate my family.*

Undoubtedly.

Do you feel animosity toward the Carpathian people? Would she try to destroy us?

There is great resolve, but not to end your life or to destroy us. Her determination is bred into her bones. I would like to know more of this woman.

Gregori shed his physical body once more and reentered Ivory, paying attention to the bones and organs, bathing them in healing light as he passed through, examining her blood and cells for the infestation of parasites. He forced more of the intruders from her body through her pores, incinerating them as they wiggled in the snow, trying to find a target. It was a messy, exhausting business, and she sank into the snow, her strength finally giving out.

Her wolves pushed close, forming a circle of protection, with Ivory and the healer's body inside. Gregori was dependent on Falcon to keep his physical form safe while he worked, and the ancient Carpathian remained very still, watching the wolves very carefully.

While Gregori worked, the knife never wavered, nor did Razvan ask anything about his family. His entire concentration was on Ivory's safety. He watched the others, leaving it to her wolf pack to warn him should Gregori try anything to harm her. That took discipline and restraint. At no time did the blade of the knife penetrate the prince's skin.

Mikhail allowed his body to breathe naturally. "Gregori is a tremendous healer. He will make certain no parasites remain."

"I appreciate his service."

"You have no need to continue to hold me hostage," Mikhail said. "Gregori snarls and snaps, but he has no wish to harm your lifemate, only to heal her. He is driven by his code. He will not be so understanding over your continued threats. I have given my word for safe passage for both of you. It would be foolish to escalate the situation when your woman will need care."

Razvan held the knife for a few more moments, as if weighing the truth of Mikhail's words and then the knife disappeared and he stepped back into the shadows where he had a clear path to all three male Carpathians.

Mikhail didn't move out of striking distance, maintaining his show of faith. Falcon glided a little closer so that he was in a better position to insert his body between the prince and potential harm should there be need.

"Tell me, Razvan," Mikhail said, "does Xavier still truly live?" He studied the gray-streaked hair. Few Carpathians went gray; only the gravest of all injuries could produce that kind of damage to a Carpathian. When looking closely the prince could see signs of suffering etched into the worn face. Razvan was a handsome man, but he looked older, weathered.

"He does," Razvan confirmed.

"Does he possess your body at will?"

"He does," Razvan answered, without flinching. "Although, for the first time, I was able to keep him out. I have never been at this strength before, so it is possible, with time, I can learn to keep him at bay."

Falcon stirred, his dark eyes looking deep into the shadows as if he might see their oldest, most dangerous enemy. "Do you endanger your lifemate?"

"I am a danger to anyone near."

Mikhail flicked Falcon a quick, quelling glance. "How is it you came to escape?"

"The last attack on the ice cave forced him to move me from the chamber where I was normally held. He had little time to prepare, and it wasn't as secure. I had not been fed in days. I believe he thought me too weak to make the attempt." Razvan shrugged.

Mikhail studied the face ravaged by hardship. That small shrug told him a lot about the man. He wasn't asking for sympathy, nor was he apologizing for the life he'd been forced to lead. Those simple sentences spoke volumes.

Mikhail bowed. "You are a true Dragonseeker." No Dragonseeker had ever succumbed to the darkness preying on the males of their species. If anyone had reason to embrace bitterness, hatred and anger, it was Razvan, if all that was suspected was correct. "We are in a battle for our very existence. Perhaps there are things you can tell us that might aid in our fight to save our children. Lara has been invaluable to us."

Razvan kept his gaze on Ivory, not answering. Just hearing his daughter's name was hard, and emotions swamped him, but he refused to let it show. He had centuries of practice at learning to keep his face a mask, and he didn't allow the prince to see how the mere thought of Lara twisted him up inside. Ivory lifted her lashes and looked up at him. His gaze locked with hers and his heart jumped.

She knew. She had to be in tremendous pain—she had to be fearful of the outcome of his threatening the prince of the Carpathian people—but a small half-smile curved her mouth. He knew that smile was for him. That secret smile locked them together, fit them like two pieces of a puzzle, private and intensely intimate. Her eyes were soft as she sent warmth into his mind.

Something deep inside of him twisted into hard knots. Something else melted. His heart gave a curious flutter and his throat closed. Ivory. Why had he found her now? She was the most unexpected treasure. No one, least of all him, deserved her, with her tenacious courage and generosity.

Feminine amusement slid into his mind. *Do not deceive yourself. No one but you would call me generous. I am the slayer. That is all.*

She was so much more—she was *everything*. He kept his eyes locked with hers while she shuddered again as more parasites fell from her pores to the blood-spattered ground. He filled her mind with strength and the scents he had discovered in her lair, the ones he knew soothed her, to sustain her through the rest of the healing.

The extraction of parasites was a difficult process. The healer had to be especially careful not to miss even one and, as Gregori rejoined his body, he swayed with weariness.

"She needs blood," Gregori announced, and sank into the snow beside her.

"So do you," Mikhail said, gliding over the snow to the

healer's side. He held out his wrist in a casual, easy gesture that spoke of longtime familiarity with donating blood.

Razvan hesitated. He had no idea of the extent of Xavier's hold on him. If it was cellular or molecular, if he gave his blood to Ivory, would Xavier be able to somehow possess her as well? He didn't know and he didn't want to chance it.

The healer slashed him with peculiar silver eyes, eyes that reminded him eerily of Xavier. They glittered with menace, a threat, a reprimand, and, for the first time in his encounter with these men, he felt shame.

"You protect me," Ivory said, "and I am grateful. No one here has an understanding of what you—we—deal with."

"I offer my blood freely," Sara reiterated and stepped close to Ivory, holding out her wrist in offering.

Ivory inclined her head. "I am grateful."

The blood was rich, a Carpathian's blood, hitting her system like a fireball of energy, soaking into her cells and aiding the healer's careful repair of her shoulder and ribs.

Gregori studied Razvan's face. "You fear to give your blood to your lifemate." It was more of a statement than a question, and this time a hint of respect crept in. Every male Carpathian was driven to provide for their lifemate. "You have not claimed her."

Razvan shrugged. "I cannot. I will not."

Ivory lifted her head, her tongue sliding over the pin-pricks in Sara's wrist, dark eyes gleaming, going almost amber, much like a wolf's eyes. "There is no need to explain to any of these men."

"Ivory," Mikhail said, his voice gentle, "no one is accusing Razvan of failing you. Quite the contrary. And the man who gave his services to heal you is the man who brought my eldest brother to the justice he so deserved. Gregori spent three months in the ground from the injuries he sustained."

Her chin rose. "I spent three hundred years in the ground." As soon as the words slipped out, the first sign of bitterness, she looked ashamed. "Forgive me, healer. I have long been away from the company of others and have forgotten my manners."

"There is no need to apologize," Gregori said, but he was still studying Razvan's worn face. "I would like to examine you for signs Xavier might have left behind."

There was a stunned silence. Mikhail frowned. Falcon stepped partially in front of Gregori and Razvan actually took a step farther back into the shadows.

"You have no conception of how dangerous that might be," Razvan said.

"If no one tries," Gregori pointed out, "you are lost to us."

"I have been lost these hundreds of years."

"And all the information you possess that might aid in our fight against our greatest enemy is lost as well," Gregori continued. "And your lifemate is lost as well."

"I do not factor into the equation," Ivory protested. "Do not put pressure on him to do anything he thinks is wrong by using me as your leverage."

Gregori flicked her a quelling glance. "You have much to contribute to the world at large, Dragonseeker. I wish only to take a look."

Perhaps he is right. Deliberately Ivory didn't look at Razvan. *It is solely your decision and I will back you all the way, but perhaps we can find a way to break Xavier's hold on you. I suspect there is a way.*

Razvan turned the idea over in his mind. He hadn't

thought about living, only dying. Dying represented freedom from Xavier's possession, from mental and physical torment, and now even from his memories and the emotions they elicited. Ivory had used the term *we*. He had never thought in those terms either. He looked around at the small group.

He had never thought he would be standing among Carpathians and not have to fight his way out. A part of him didn't trust their acceptance of him.

As if reading his mind, Gregori shook his head. "I do not altogether trust that you pose no threat to Carpathians, but I am willing to find out."

Razvan felt the challenge of those words. Gregori was willing to put himself in jeopardy in order to protect the Carpathian people and perhaps to aid Razvan. Did Razvan have the courage to allow him to enter his body to see for himself what Xavier had done? Guilt lay heavy in his mind.

His memories of earlier had faded behind the barriers he'd erected for sanity's sake, and he was no longer certain what he had or hadn't done. There were weeks, months, perhaps even years he no longer remembered, and he was afraid to examine what had happened. Xavier had slowly, successfully beat him down until he could no longer fight the mage.

If he allowed Gregori to enter his body and examine him, Gregori would know every humiliating and degrading moment of his life.

I will enter with the healer. I can protect your memories if anything were to be incriminating. Otherwise, whatever he finds is on Xavier, not you.

His heart turned over. She so clearly aligned herself with him, but why? They were meant to be lifemates, it was true, but they didn't know each other, and he was the most notorious criminal the Carpathians had.

I have been inside your head many times these past three weeks. I am an outsider as well. And I believe absolutely that you are the key to destroying Xavier.

That was a reason he could understand. He wasn't certain it was true, that he was the key to destroying Xavier, but he knew her purpose was absolutely unswerving. What did he have to lose? Their respect? He could care less. That had gone centuries ago. He was more than willing to face the dawn. But he didn't want her to see, to know, to live through the things he had seen and done, whether he was a party to them or not.

He knew the faces of every woman Xavier had violated with his body. The alluring lies, the sweet, deceptive promises, impregnating an innocent woman in order to take the child she conceived with him for the blood. Always the blood. He didn't remember their names, but he remembered the tears when they knew the truth. He remembered the sense of betrayal and the taunting laughter of the mage.

There had been so many killed over the centuries: mages, humans, one or two Carpathians who had been deceived and murdered by his hand. He remembered every face, every expression. They haunted him every moment he was awake. He had been dishonored so many times he couldn't remember any other way of life.

This was his moment—he could take up the burden of helping his lifemate hunt and destroy the world's greatest enemy, or he could give up and walk into the sun, telling himself he was protecting everyone. By helping, he would be exposing the sins of his past to both Ivory and the healer. There would be nowhere to hide from himself and the crimes his body had been used to commit. He would have to face them every day of his existence. And he risked falling back into Xavier's hands. He looked around him at the circle of faces. There was no impatience, no restless movements. They simply waited for a decision.

If I am tainted beyond the ability to be saved from Xavier, give me your word that you will slay me, lifemate. I want only you to see that damning evidence.

Ivory caught her breath at the enormity of what he asked of her, drawing the attention of the dark one. She kept her gaze locked with Razvan. To kill her own lifemate . . .

I ask that you carve me on your wall, that I can remain safe in your soul. Do me that service, although I may be unworthy. If you keep me safe, I will have a chance in the next life.

Ivory's fingers crept into Raja's thick fur and clutched there. Her throat closed and for a moment her eyes burned. She held his gaze, refusing to look away from his courage. *It will be my honor.*

Razvan continued to look at her, soaking her into his mind, drawing her into his lungs, feeling her courage and strength, pride in her welling up until he nearly burst with it. He took her courage for his own and, still looking at Ivory, nodded his head to the healer.

"I ask that you follow my lifemate's lead," Razvan said. "If she wants you to leave, give us your word that you will do so and all of you will leave us immediately."

Gregori exchanged a long look with the prince. *He means to commit suicide or have his lifemate slay him.*

You cannot save the world, Gregori, Mikhail sent back, his voice weary. *You can only do your best. If you can help him, do so; otherwise we leave them to their fate. It is their wish and any Carpathian, male or female, has the right to choose death over dishonor.*

"So be it," Gregori said aloud to Razvan. "Mikhail and Falcon will guard our bodies while we try this." He looked at Ivory. "Are you strong enough? If Xavier attacks him while you are in his mind, can you fend the mage off?"

Her lashes raised and she met the dark one's gaze with eyes of steel. Warrior's eyes. Calm. Cool. Remote. "Worry about yourself, healer."

Gregori inclined his head, a brief smile somewhere between amusement and respect touching his mouth. He gestured for Razvan to sit in the snow between them. As Razvan settled down, a little tense from being in such a vulnerable position, five of the six wolves made a circle around them, with Farkas lying beside Ivory, his head in her lap. Ivory laid one hand in his fur and the other on the hilt of her knife.

Mikhail, Falcon, Sara and Gary took up positions around them to better protect the circle.

Ivory closed her eyes to send herself seeking outside her body. Razvan stopped her with a gentle hand to her arm. Her lashes lifted and she met his gaze.

I just need to see you looking at me one more time. Just like this. No condemnation. No disgust. No fear. You look at me as if I am a person to you.

She lifted her chin. *You are much more than a person to me, Razvan.* She deliberately used his name. *You are my lifemate. In this world, the next, or both.*

The caressing note in her voice flooded him with warmth. A slow smile curved his mouth. It felt rusty, like his lips might crack and his jaw might break, but inside, where no one could see, he held that first smile close.

"Ready?" she asked.

"Just be careful. Both of you," Razvan cautioned.

Ivory shed her body and entered her lifemate. Gregori's light burned hot and bright, almost luminescent, the mark, she knew, of a strong healer. He allowed her to take the lead, although she sensed his reluctance. There were scars inside the body, a multitude of them, and signs of torture beyond endurance, yet Razvan had endured.

She moved to his brain. Before she allowed Gregori to delve too deep, she intended to keep her promise to Razvan. She alone would know if he had cause for the guilt that weighed so heavily on his shoulders. She alone would know whether he was truly the criminal he had been branded as for so long.

It had been difficult to maintain her objectivity when she'd encountered the scars that reminded her of her own, but his memories were a virtual minefield. Xavier's experiments and tortures were unthinkable, the things he'd forced Razvan to endure, to watch, to participate in. It was a wonder that he was sane. She moved through his brain, soaking in his memories until she felt saturated and ill. Yes, his body had been used time and again to commit crimes, but his spirit, the essence of who Razvan was, had not been present.

She moved aside and allowed the healer entrance. They moved through his brain, searching carefully for evidence of Xavier. While they worked, they had to share Razvan's burden of memories, of a life of pain and suffering, of mental anguish. Yet he had fought back, holding on to sanity, sometimes by a thin thread, by the toughness and honor that was inherently Dragonseeker. Her heart wept for that lonely warrior, and she felt Gregori, strong and disciplined, weep with her as he moved through Razvan's memories, seeking to find anything that might be Xavier's fingerprints—a way for Xavier to enter at will.

There was no way to go through centuries of torment without it taking a toll. Ivory had to pull out and take a breath. Gregori followed her closely.

"He gave up his body when he was less than twenty to save his sister. And he inadvertently traded a piece of his soul for his daughter's life." Ivory lifted wet lashes to look at Gregori and then turned her head to her lifemate. "That is your greatest crime."

"One of duty and love," Gregori added. "You are no criminal, Razvan. You are a true Dragonseeker." He sent a quick glance toward the prince. "No doubt I shall hear often how others recognized your true worth first."

"No doubt," Mikhail murmured.

"Can you remove Xavier's hold on my soul?" Razvan asked. "If he was to possess my body right now, he could see all of you, he could use me to strike at the prince, or at my own lifemate. I cannot take that kind of chance."

"If Xavier found a way to mark an entrance to your body, then we can find a way to remove it," Ivory said. "I have studied him carefully, and each time I run across a new work he has done, I have found the way to unravel it. I know this can be done."

Gregori drew in his breath. *Did you hear what she said, Mikhail?*

I am not so old that I'm deaf.

Gregori kept his grin to himself. *These two have far more information on our enemy than we have managed to gain in the time we have been trying.*

We didn't exactly know Xavier was alive until recently.

"Ivory," Sara said. "Do you know a way to stop the endless cycle of his microbes? He's mutated them in some way and grown them to penetrate the soil and find us. They cause miscarriages. Lara has been invaluable in trying to keep the women free, but she is only one person and cannot be turned fully until we find a permanent solution."

"If Xavier has used his gifts for evil, I am certain I can undo whatever he has wrought. I have long studied his methods and successfully countered each of his spells." Ivory spoke with confidence, not from bragging or ego, but obviously from experience. "I would have to study the microbes. Do you have samples?"

"We can get them," Sara said.

"I can take them to my laboratory." Ivory glanced up at the night sky. "We have a few hours left, but not enough, so I will return here tomorrow and you can bring them to me. I have spent most of my time beneath the earth and I am extremely light sensitive."

We have a few things in common. Razvan's flick of his dark eyes showed camaraderie. He had spent most of the last few centuries beneath the earth as well, in the ice caves, and he was equally as sensitive.

Again there was that flood of warmth he associated with her. Comforting. Easing the aching loneliness that was such a part of him.

"You are welcome to come to my home. My lifemate is with child and staying close. She would very much like to meet you," Mikhail offered. "And my brother's lifemate, Shea, and Gary have been working nonstop on trying to find a solution. Perhaps if you spoke with them it might eliminate several steps for your work."

Ivory shrugged. "I thank you for the invitation, but until we know whether we can prevent Xavier from knowing our moves, it would be best to stay as far from you as possible."

"I agree," Gregori said before Mikhail could answer. He sent the prince a smoldering glare. "You and Raven must be protected at all times."

Mikhail flashed Razvan a small grin. "Do you see what

it is like to live with him? Nag, nag, nag. And he is my daughter's lifemate as well."

"In this instance, I have to agree with him," Razvan said. "If Xavier had an entrance through me to strike at you, he would be unable to resist. The thought of torturing me mentally amuses him. He is particularly fond of using me to harm my sister. If he could use me to harm the prince of the Carpathian people, and make certain I knew it, he would be elated."

Ivory felt the wrenching pain in Razvan, although his voice was steady and his expression gave nothing away. Sorrow weighed heavily on him. With his emotions so new and raw, difficult to control, his love for Natalya, his determination to keep her safe at all costs, had infuriated Xavier, and now Razvan could remember and feel every betrayal as if it were the cut of a knife.

"If we can find his portal, Dragonseeker," Gregori said, "we might be able to close it." Once more he looked to Ivory. "Let's get it done."

Ivory stroked her fingertips over his jaw, her touch lingering on his skin for just a moment. Abruptly, she shed her body and followed Gregori, pure light and energy, seeking darkness that had to be hiding somewhere inside her lifemate. While she didn't want to admire anything about Gregori, she couldn't help herself. He sorted through memories fast, processing each horrible event quickly and discarding it, looking for that moment Razvan had traded his body for his sister's life.

They reached that memory, so long ago, centuries, a young boy offering himself to a madman, to a killer, to keep his sister from harm. Ivory had to fight to stay in the form of energy. It was so difficult exploring those old memories, that boy beaten down but valiant, trying to shield those he loved, seeing too much evil every day. She examined everything from all angles of that memory, looking for something that had allowed Xavier to take possession.

Not here. Gregori moved forward in time quickly, sorting through data fast, looking for something that Xavier had done, some trigger word, something that might indicate he had possessed Razvan's body at will.

Wait! Ivory had been paying more attention to Razvan's memories of himself. The way he looked at what was happening around him. He was Dragonseeker, turned fully by his aunts in their effort to give him the necessary strength to escape. He had the mind of a true Dragonseeker. He had resolved to travel the world in spirit, rather than allow Xavier to continue to "use" him. He wasn't aware, but the use of his body at that time was an illusion Xavier created to make Razvan believe the mage was all-powerful.

Realizing he had little hope of escape, kept starving and weak, Razvan used his waning strength to shed his body, leaving it vulnerable to Xavier's attack. Ivory saw the exact instant Xavier entered into that shell and left pieces of himself behind. Now they knew the time and the how, but they still had to find the small pieces of Xavier and find a way to extract them.

Ivory began to chant softly in the Carpathian language, sending the words vibrating through both Razvan and Gregori.

I call to me all that is good to aid me in my
    desperate plight.
Sky send to me the purest light.
I plead for the song that I may sing to reveal that
    which is evil buried within.

Light of sky, burning bright, find that which is
   dark and make it light.
Evil one, I call forth the blight you left behind.

Light burst through Ivory and she directed it into
Razvan's body, allowing it to seek out the darkness left
behind. The light swam into his bloodstream, rushed
through his mind and heart, and sought to go deeper into
the very essence of his soul until Razvan's being was
entirely illuminated. In his mind there was a dark scar, a
very small ridge that Ivory recognized. There was one in
his heart, one pumping through his bloodstream and the
last in his soul. *Four*. Heart, mind, body and soul. No
wonder Xavier managed to possess Razvan's body at will.
Even with that, Razvan had fought back for centuries.

Razvan appeared splintered, as if he'd been broken apart
and put back together wrong. Ivory's breath rushed out in a
long, slow hiss. She had been in pieces, her body filtering
through the soil, struggling to pull itself together, so fractured she couldn't even knit her skin and bones back
together evenly. This was worse than mere flesh. This was
the very essence of who Razvan was. As each point of darkness was revealed, Ivory attached a thread of white light,
anchoring it so that all of the pieces could be kept connected.

Ivory knew without Gregori having to tell her that she
had to provide the light to repair the fractures to Razvan's
soul and drive out that small splinter of evil. Words were
powerful, the truth and rightness of them to bring his
fractured mind together. They could tune sound to the
true rhythm of Razvan's body to restore balance and push
the fragment of evil from his bloodstream. But the
heart . . .

I do not know how to love, healer. There was despair in her voice. I lost that emotion a long time ago. He will be lost because of me.

There are all kinds of love, Ivory, and you are capable of all of them. He is a warrior first. Love him for that. He is a man alone who fought for all those around him and did not succumb to darkness when others embraced the darkness with far less to drive them. Love him for that. Find what you have to give and it will be enough when he's never had anything.

Ivory took a breath and steadied herself. The healer's faith was convincing. She felt herself settle. This was a battle for a man's sanity, for his very soul, and they would win because they had to.

When we chase out the pieces of Xavier, the splinters will need to find a host. Gregori spoke to both Razvan and Ivory.

Something in Gregori's voice made everything in her go still.

Long ago, I experimented with the forbidden and broke our laws. I have a need to understand how things work and I violated our sacred laws to find out.

The confession was given freely, but Ivory knew it was more than that. Gregori not only wanted to warn them what to expect, but he was also giving Razvan and Ivory a piece of himself because he knew so many terrible things in Razvan's life. It was a great risk for Gregori to admit such a thing and she respected the healer a lot more.

What was put inside of you, Razvan, can be removed. I have done this myself.

Razvan was silent a long moment while Gregori waited for his condemnation. Razvan sighed before he spoke. *Sometimes, what started as wrong can be turned to good. I pray that is the case. I am ready, but take no chances that you may open yourself to him.*

Ivory began to sing, synching her tones to Razvan's

body's natural rhythm. Gregori and Ivory matched the beat of his heart, the breath in his lungs, so that the notes flowed through all of them together, vibrating in every cell and organ. Blood rushed in and out of his heart, ebbing and flowing in his veins.

I call to blood flowing, hot like the tide,
Seek that which is dark, holding it still inside.
Pulsing heat, spread and sear,
Cleansing and cleaning that which is unclear.

Like the sound of waves rolling, the chant spread through Razvan's veins so that heat spread like molten lava, hot and thick and cleansing. Every cell embraced the steaming inferno, muscles and organs reaching for it. The heat gathered steam, rising, picking up speed as the song changed tempo. The notes provided the cleansing, each of them tuned to the exact same rhythm so that only that small dark splinter hiding in his veins, running before the purifying heat, was discordant.

Gregori moved quickly now that the splinter was running, murmuring the words to exorcise Xavier from Razvan's body. He trapped the tiny fragment so that it couldn't burrow or hide, his words holding it prisoner.

Ivory began to sing again, the notes changing to those of immense power, her words resonating throughout Razvan's mind. Gregori's voice joined hers, in perfect harmony, and then counterpointing, calling, commanding.

We seek that which is dark, that which has lain fallow.
We command you forth from the darkness and shadow.

We command you, Xavier, come forth into the
  light.
We abolish every part of you, Xavier, from Razvan's
  mind.

Razvan could hear, as if from a great distance away, the
sound of Gregori and Ivory's voices rising, the notes tuned
exactly to his body's rhythm, the words powerful and commanding. He knew words were powerful. Names. He
heard them call to the high mage, the name reverberating
through his mind, demanding he leave, demanding their
bitter enemy leave and not return. He heard the ancient
Carpathian language, the beat of his heart, his pulse, and
knew he wasn't alone.

Gregori and Ivory walked with him, striding toward the
parasitic fragment with absolute confidence and mastery.
He actually felt the moment the splinter rolled into a ball,
desperate to escape the trueness and purity of the cleansing words. Once again it was Gregori who drove the
fragment into the holding prison with the first one.

Ivory's song changed. Her voice grew soft and loving as
she called on memories of her lost childhood and strong
brothers holding her close. She remembered the love she
had for her family, intense and consuming. She poured that
love into her song. Her voice was powerful and persuasive,
bringing tears to the eyes of all who heard.

Heart that is pure with body worn,
I find you beautiful standing tired and alone.
I give you my heart, I will shed your tears,
Take my hand, I will hold all of your fears.
I give you my word, no bindings attached,
I give my love freely so no harm may attack.

Having fought a long war, withstanding many
    sorrows,
Know that, though you are weary, I am your
    tomorrow.
Cling to my words, hear the song that I sing,
Let it sink deep that you may find peace once
    again.

She changed her words, singing tribute to a warrior, strong and pure and all alone in a world of madness. Honor drove him, love of his sister, of his people, a code that he refused to break no matter what was done to him. She sang the song of tribute to a warrior, love pouring into every note. The more she moved through Razvan's memories and saw his life, the way he struggled to maintain honor in the madness surrounding him, the way he barely clung to sanity when he faced what Xavier had forced his body to do, the killings, impregnating women, feeding from his own children, stabbing his aunt. Tears choked her, and love flowed from her heart to his, filling his until there was no other emotion but love. The splinter fled, unable to stand the genuine, untainted emotion that Xavier could never feel. Gregori surrounded the fragment with his strength and herded it to join the others in darkness.

Ivory knew saving Razvan's soul was her task alone. She was his other half. His soul was hers as well. An intruder had invaded and dared to dwell, to take what was rightfully hers. Razvan had not claimed her, had not joined their souls together, but each time they were near, she felt the pull between them, strong and intense. She changed her song again, this time singing from her soul to his, calling to her true lifemate to accept her, to join with her, to accept her merging. Her light would be too much for someone as evil as Xavier.

Light to dark, dark to light.
My soul to yours together we fight.
Half of a whole, together one.
Mend and heal for two now are one.
Blood, body, bone mended, together our light it
   shone.

Light burst through Razvan's body, bright and pure, the light of an innocent soul—that of his lifemate. Though he had not claimed her, their souls, two halves of the same whole, shimmered with dazzling brilliance, side by side, only a thin gap between them. Her half seemed to illuminate his as she moved her soul over his, and then merged, letting her light go into his darkness. The fragment ran before the light, smoldering with smoke around the edges as if burned, the cells shrinking away so that Gregori could herd it to join the others.

Razvan felt complete. Whole. The sensation of their merged souls shook him. He felt tiny threads weaving them back together as the two halves recognized one another and reached for what had been lost. He knew her intimately, every struggle, every part of her determination and her courage, all that she was, what she was. He held her safe and she held him safe. For the first time since he was a young boy he felt he could breathe freely.

Gregori began to chant. The words were in the ancient language, a healer's greatest command, greatest gift, to force out the darkness of evil from Razvan. His voice was powerful, vibrating through both Razvan and Ivory, a tool of immense strength.

Kuuluam hän ku köd és hän ku Karpatiiak altenak—I
  take that which is dark and banned.
Saam te Szavéar—I name you Xavier.
It éntölam kuulua ainadet—Your body I now claim
  and command.
Ottiam sa éset veriet és luwet—I see the sinew, blood
  and bone.
Muonìam ainadet belső és kinn—From its core I hold
  and hone.
Muonìam ködaltepoårak, it poårak juttam—I
  command these abominations, these fragments left I
  now bind.
Totellosz sarnaakam, kaδasz kontalik, kaik kaδasz—
  Do my bidding, go from this warrior, leave nothing
  behind.

The splinters did their best to struggle against his
commands, but they were too fearful of the light. Each
time his energy touched on them, they smoked and withered more.

Get back to your body, Ivory. They were both at risk as the
slivers of Xavier's blackened and malevolent soul fled
Razvan's body to seek another host.

Ivory and Gregori merged their spirits back in their
bodies as Razvan rose over them, protecting them in that
first disorienting moment. The ground rumbled ominously.
Dirt spewed up like a geyser. The sky darkened overhead.
For one moment they could hear the rustling of the leaves
on the trees, and then a swelling noise like a wall of rushing water.

Within moments the clouds and a sliver of the moon
were wiped out under the heavy migration of huge bats.
The bats neared, showing dripping fangs, some landing on

the ground in a circle around the group, using their wings to walk. Others flew at their faces, teeth gnashing together.

The earth opened up right beneath Razvan and a giant worm burst from beneath, jaws open, serrated teeth clamping around Razvan's ankle. For a heartbeat, the thirty-foot worm hovered, with Razvan locked in its teeth, and then it slid back beneath the ground, the dirt pouring in after it.

6

Ivory drew a wicked-looking, circular, crystal-centered weapon and held out her arms. "Now," she called to her pack.

The wolves leapt into the air, diving for her back. Ivory was already plunging, straight down, hands in front of her face like a modern-day Olympic diver, changing form as she went, pushing through the dirt to follow the path of the large worm dragging Razvan deep.

Look to me. At me. I am with you.

No! Go back. He cannot have you.

Nor can he have you. Ivory blocked out everything happening on the surface. Gregori would fight his way clear of Xavier's mutations and get the prince free; he had to. She had one duty, and that was to her lifemate—keeping him out of the hands of the high mage.

I cannot shift and get away.

You have seen the worm, bred to travel through the earth. Once his teeth meet in the middle, he holds your form. She knew. She'd extracted that very venom to use with her own combination of chemicals to make the coating on her weapons to prevent vampires from shifting. *He cannot have you. Do not struggle. Stay very still so it injects less poison. Keep your mind in mine. You have to trust me.*

She felt him holding himself utterly still. It had to take a great deal of courage not to fight the worm dragging him deeper beneath the earth. It was easier for the worm to go through its tunnel, already carved through the layers of soil as it headed back to its master to deliver its prize. Razvan had to know where and to whom the worm was taking him, yet he ceased fighting.

Razvan had never been able to trust anyone once his father had died and his sister was lost to him. To give her that—to put his life, no, his soul in her hands—had to be nothing short of a rebirthing by fire because never before had he put his very soul into someone else's keeping.

I trust you.

It would take trust. Fighting a worm was extremely dangerous. Practically everything about the worm was venomous. The spikes that ran along his body to dig and propel himself forward and back through the tunnel, and the barb on the end of his lashing tail, all contained the same poison as the fangs and double rows of serrated teeth. The tail itself could break every bone in a warrior's body. The hide was tough and could slice through a hand or arm if brushed against.

Close your ears, Razvan. You cannot listen. The sound will be bothersome to you. It was the only way she could think to describe it, but she had to slow the worm down, disorient it. With the tunnel already dug, it could warp time with alarming speed. *When it releases you, you will have only seconds to push the poison from your body so you can shift. You have to be ready. Seconds only.* She had to trust that he would feel the urgency in her and obey.

Knife in one hand, arms outstretched toward Razvan, eyes locked with his, she began to chant.

I call to the element of air used for sound.
Drum to the heartbeat of evil that digs through the
   ground.
Pitch, harmonics, combine and align,
Fight by attaching to warp evil's mind.

The notes she used were pitched to vibrate and disorient, triggering vertigo and time loss in the worm. The earth responded to the discordant notes of her command. The cadence of her song continued, but Ivory's tones altered, changing the vibrations of the earth so that they became in tune with the surrounding soil, drawing it inward so that it began to collapse and fill the tube. The wave of sound moved through the earth. The ground shuddered, trembled. Dirt rained in all around them.

Keep looking at me. Ivory kept moving toward Razvan, propelling herself down the long, wide hole. *Remember, push the poison out fast when the worm releases you.*

She had shifted form and was nothing but molecules traveling at a high speed but still not fast enough to catch up.

Keep your arms outstretched above your head, toward me, toward the surface.

More soil tumbled into the tube. A clap like thunder roared down the tube behind the worm and the creature hesitated. It was enough for Ivory to close the gap between them, her hands materializing. She shoved the weapon into Razvan's right hand and caught his left wrist. At once she began to sing again, this time the notes resounding through the earth. The sound was painful, crashing through their bodies and minds, turning their insides to jelly.

The worm completely stopped moving, opening its

mouth wide in a scream that reverberated through the ground, releasing Razvan at the same time.

Now! Now! Shift when you can, holding the weapon. Follow me in. Fearlessly, Ivory became vapor only, streaming inside the giant opening of the worm's mouth.

Razvan pushed the poison from his body, ignoring the wrenching pain, closing off his mind to anything but following her. He felt the disc in his hand vibrating as he shifted and knew he still held it, which meant it was no mere illusion, but was constructed of natural earth and gems. He followed her without hesitation, past the double rows of serrated teeth, past the dripping fangs and pockets of thick amber venom, down the very throat of the beast.

Touch nothing inside; not the walls, nothing. These worms have two vulnerable spots, and both of them are deep inside Even going for their eyes does nothing. Look for scar tissue inside the throat—you will know it when you see it. Everything else is coated. The spot is where Xavier attaches himself to give instructions. The second place is much deeper and much more perilous to find.

Razvan didn't want to know how she'd discovered this information, but there was no doubt in his mind it had been hard won through firsthand experience. She was too confident in her assessment, and her voice was tight with tension.

He scanned the walls of the worm's throat. Bumps and ridges in dark purple and black covered the membranes above and all around them. The worm pitched and bucked, fighting to get out of the collapsing tunnel, making it doubly difficult to avoid accidentally skimming along the wall. Venom dripped from the ceiling, raining down around them. As vapor, it was easier to avoid the drops.

There! Above and to your right, on the roof of his throat.

Razvan spotted the small circle and recognized the stamp of Xavier. Welts and splotches made tiny rings and whorls, damaged for all time after contact with the mage.

We will only have seconds to get out again. The disc is iolite, a violet stone that enhances vision on the astral realm. Follow what I do and then move fast out of here.

Razvan realized there was a thin thread of blue-violet light emanating from the disc. Ivory took her normal form, hovering in the center of the worm's throat, dodging the strings of poisonous saliva. Hairy fibers sprang into action, reaching like tentacles toward the heat source. Ivory grimly eluded them and, using deadly aim, struck hard and fast with the light, using it like a spear or a laser, penetrating into the worm's tough wall, anchoring deep. She let go of the disc and it followed, slamming hard into the ring of scars.

Razvan mimicked Ivory's actions, releasing first the light and then the disc within a heartbeat of hers. Light burst from the two discs and lit up the walls of the throat, bathing them in a violet wash. Sound came next, high-pitched, the notes threatening to shred all reason, so that Razvan hastily muted the sound.

Ivory was already streaming back toward the mouth of the worm. The huge, cavernous body thrashed back and forth, rolling and bucking harder than ever. *Hurry.* The urgency in her mind convinced him to double his speed as nothing else could. Behind them, the violet light spread like a cancer, staining the venomous throat bluish-purple. Steam rose.

Ivory hovered just behind the double rows of teeth. *Be ready.*

Razvan had no idea what he was ready for, but the worm seemed more unstable than ever as all around them smoky blue-violet vapor curled, pouring from the two discs. He heard Ivory mentally counting, concentrating hard. Deep in her mind, he felt the exact moment she began to burst forward.

The worm opened its mouth to cough. The throat contracted, muscles squeezing down behind them, closing the gap as they shot from inside the worm.

Move. Move. Ivory didn't slow down, but kept driving through the soil, back up toward the surface.

Razvan followed, amazed at her skills, at her knowledge of the enemy and at the fast, efficient and utterly calm way in which she went about destroying it.

When we surface, the bats will be attacking. Come up near the prince to add to his protection. All of Xavier's twisted abominations will be fighting to get to him.

Around him he could feel the unstable ground quivering, rolling, as the worm thrashed and fought, sending shock waves undulating deep beneath the earth. The ground sank all around them, falling in on itself.

Faster. Ivory hissed the command in his mind. *Take the lead.*

She might be one of the best warriors he'd ever encountered, and by far the most knowledgeable dealing with Xavier's army, but he was still a Carpathian male and her lifemate. She wasn't going to be protecting his back, not when he could be protecting hers.

Keep moving. We are close to the surface, he informed her. *Whatever is up there is not as bad as the evil Xavier had inside of me. Watch yourself.*

He will go for the prince, Ivory reiterated. *The one sure way to destroy the Carpathian people is to destroy the prince.*

Razvan burst through the surface, emerging into a night filled with the sound of battle. Thunder cracked and lightning streaked across the sky, slamming into earth as bolts hammered into the crushing crowds of bats swarming over the ground. It looked like a living sea, bats walking on their wings, baring teeth at anything in their path. Flesh eaters, he'd seen the mutations in the caves Xavier occupied, placed there to guard, to sound the alarm and to provide blood from the animals they killed and dragged to the lairs.

Ivory emerged from the ground, shrugging, arms outstretched. The wolves leapt from her back and into the midst of the bats, snapping necks as they grabbed and shook their prey, fighting their way through the mass to the circle defending the prince. Ivory followed them, drawing one of her many homemade weapons, tossing it to Razvan and pulling another.

Razvan discovered the strange gun fired light, not bullets. He had never participated like this in a battle, with blood spraying across the snow. But he didn't hesitate, staying in Ivory's mind. She was a warrior through and through, wading through the bats, kicking them aside, spraying the bright light fed by a diamond across a wide path, severing heads.

"Keep the spray level with their necks," she advised, and then called out, "Gregori! We're coming in."

One of the bats seized Razvan's calf and tried to tear open his leg. Blaez, the second largest wolf, caught the malicious creature in strong jaws and ripped it away from Razvan, tossing the bloody body into a group of bats that tore into it with a viciousness that reminded him of Xavier.

Gregori slammed bolts of lightning into the center of the bats, opening the way for them. Razvan followed Ivory through the sea of bats, staying close to protect her back, his gun spewing the blade of light behind them in a wide arc. When the wolves hesitated, preferring to stay to the outside, Ivory hissed a command.

You will get eaten alive. Come! She held out her arms and the wolves leapt over the mass of furry bodies and merged with her back.

Ivory continued to wade through the bats, running toward the small group, fighting to keep from being overpowered. The group refused to just dissolve and abandon Gary, their human friend. It would be nearly impossible to protect him from the air.

"Get the prince off the ground," Ivory yelled above the din to Gregori. "The attack will come from under the ground. This is a diversion."

Falcon jerked Gary off the ground, no questions asked, as Mikhail rose as well. The hordes of bats went crazy, flying at them with renewed frenzy.

"I lost sight of Xavier's fragments," Gregori warned. "They're probably in the bats."

Ivory thrust one of her light guns into Sara's hands. "You have to sever them right at the neck or they really go psycho on you." She pulled a strange-looking object, much like a grenade, from a loop on her belt, readying herself.

"Have you seen these mutations before?" Gregori asked, continuing to use the thin whip of lightning to incinerate the bats.

"I study everything the mage does," Ivory answered. "There is a portal close. I must find it and close it or they will continue replicating. It is in the ground, not in a cave."

"You've seen these creatures before?" Mikhail asked.

Ivory nodded, her gaze scanning the ground. It was rippling beneath them, undulating, like a wave in the sea. "They get away from Xavier sometimes and they would be a huge threat this close to the village. They are major carnivores and attack in a group." She gripped the disc in her hand tighter as she saw dirt bubble up from the ground.

Gregori and Falcon were in constant motion, slamming white-hot energy through the mass with strike after strike. Mikhail slammed his fist hard, punching through one flying at Gary's face. All of the Carpathians and Gary had numerous bite marks and scratches from the continual assault.

"Give me one of those weapons," Razvan said. "You are not going alone."

Ivory frowned, her eyes still scanning the ground. "Going inside their lair is worse than the worm. Stay here and help guard the prince."

Now the ground bubbled ominously. Various sections sank several inches.

"Ivory." He waited until she glanced up to read the determination on his face. Razvan was not a man to back down. "Give me a weapon."

She tensed, seeing the ground shift in the sunken areas. One hand flicked to her waist and she tossed Razvan a duplicate of her grenade as she jumped, feet first, into the center of the spot where the sinking ground was the most active. Razvan followed her beneath the ground, shifting to vapor to go through the layers of dirt. The grenade shifted with his body, becoming nothing but molecules, telling him it was another of her homemade natural weapons. It had been oval-shaped and bumpy, not at all smooth.

A stench rose, a combination of fetid rotting meat, dead carcasses and sulfur. His stomach lurched, but he didn't hesitate to follow her deeper into the tube. Bats rose from beneath and he had to resist the urge to strike out at them as he dropped onto the rockier ledges where the colony dwelled. He kept his mind firmly in hers, following her exact movements. She was a warrior, well versed in the ways of Xavier, determined to defeat him and the mutations he set loose on the world. He had firmly joined her war, and what better way to learn than from the expert.

He couldn't help but admire her complete concentration and single-minded, no-nonsense purpose. There was no wasted talk, no wasted movements. Ivory was all business, flooding him with information as they dropped to the floor of the lair. The rock surrounding them was dotted with dark holes, the floor covered in bones, fur; old and new blood splattered the rocks and soaked the floor, pooling in thick puddles and hiding in crevices.

This is a slaughterhouse.

Once they escape Xavier's command, they start this behavior, swarming and reproducing, killing everything around them. They'll pick the bones from a horse clean in minutes.

I saw Xavier's first experiments. He fed them human and mage alike. Razvan tried not to remember the sounds of those dying in agony, but the hideous smells triggered the memories and his stomach lurched. *Once he threw one into my chamber. I was chained to the wall and it began to devour me from the feet up. I could feel every tooth as it tore into my flesh. I thought, if it ate me, I would cease to exist, but I could not stand the agony after a while.*

He didn't know why he felt compelled to make the admission, and was ashamed the moment he did. It had been long ago and he'd pushed those memories to the back of his mind until the stink of death and decay brought them crowding back.

Long ago, I had wolves gnaw on me, on my leg bone. Fortunately, they helped bury me.

Her voice was so matter-of-fact, he almost didn't understand what she'd said. She kept talking as if she hadn't revealed anything of importance at all.

What we are going to do is change the composition of air using our homemade grenades. The fire down here will burn hotter than anything you've ever felt, so remember, you cannot draw this chemical into your lungs and you have to protect yourself from the intense heat, even in this form. You will want to panic and go toward the surface, but the fire will race upward and we must wait until the chemical disperses. When you materialize to activate the grenade, they will swarm on us. The feeling is utterly horrifying. You felt one. Imagine hundreds.

Let's do it. The stench was getting to him, and the idea of exposing himself to hundreds, maybe thousands of the demonic creatures would be terrifying if he let himself think about it.

We do it on three. Materialize, pull the pin and count, and then throw it into the center of their lair. You have to hang on for five seconds. It will be a lifetime, believe me. Immediately resume this form and stay out away from rocks, but keep away from the center. Do not breathe, whatever you do, and do not attempt to surface, no matter how hot you get.

Razvan positioned himself to face her, hoping to block her face and the front of her body from the oncoming attack.

One. Two. Three.

Razvan took his solid form. At once his boots sank into the decayed, rotting bodies and, even as he pulled the pin on the chemical grenade and began counting, his arm swinging back for the throw, the bats swarmed over them, hundreds of them, the weight nearly driving them to the floor, teeth sinking deep and tearing at their flesh.

He heard the wolves roar, teeth snapping in return,

protecting Ivory's back. The five seconds seemed an eternity as the gas hissed into the air. The bats continuously issued a high-pitched shriek that reverberated through his skull, a call for more to join the frenzied feast. He felt the chunks of flesh being torn from his back and legs. He stepped closer to Ivory, shielding her with his body while her wolves protected her back.

They both lobbed the grenades at the same time and simultaneously shifted. The flash was deafening in the small confines of the rocky cavern, shaking the earth. The light was so bright, even without his body the intensity burned his eyes. The blast blew Razvan back and he had to hastily right himself to keep himself away from the walls.

In purging the lair of every occupant, they changed the composition of the air to gas, igniting it in a raging fire that rocketed up the walls. The rocks glowed orange-red, flames licking greedily inside every hole and tunnel. The extreme pressure hurt every molecule of his body. The noise was terrifying, the crack of the splitting rocks as great fiery chunks gave way, and the death screams of the bats as their furry bodies heated from the inside out and either burst or exploded. Some erupted into flames.

For a few minutes it was worse than any hell he could have ever imagined. Every instinct urged him to take Ivory and surface, but the fire was moving upward, ahead of them, purging every cranny and nook, every single hole and tunnel the creatures had constructed. It felt interminable, as if they were trapped in the center of a volcano. He fought the urge to take a breath while his body was still molecules.

Hovering protectively, he tried to surround her body with his to shield her from the worst of the heat, although the temperatures were so hot he doubted it mattered. The rock still glowed but the flames died down before Ivory began her rise to the surface.

Emerge as close to the others as possible. I will warn them and we will attack the creatures on the surface. It would not have done any good to kill them first without taking out the lair.

He had never admired someone so much in his life. She did what had to be done with no thought for her own safety. She was matter-of-fact about emerging into another storm of flesh-eating bats after her body had been torn up by the creatures. He couldn't feel the least reluctance in her, and something inside him opened and embraced his true destiny. He was meant for this woman. He was a match for her—her other half. He was born Dragonseeker, a warrior, not the evil monster Xavier had tried to shape.

Elation burst through him as he tore through the blackened ring of dirt, emerging into the midst of snapping teeth and fire raining from the sky. He had never felt so alive or free. He caught a bat in each hand and knocked their heads together, flinging them aside, and he was attacked from all sides, the sheer weight of bodies trying to knock him over as they did their best to eat him alive.

"Cover Gary. Cocoon yourselves in an airtight, heat-resistant bubble," Ivory said, then flipped a grenade to Razvan.

There was something very satisfying in being her partner. She hadn't included the other hunters or the prince in her fight. He was her lifemate, her partner, and, although he didn't have their experience, she trusted him far more than she did the others, and it was the first time since he had been apart from his sister that anyone had ever given him trust.

"Warn any coming to your aid to stay away. This is the only way I know to kill a colony." She knew they had seen the plume of fire bursting from the ground and probably even felt the heat. "This will be like nothing ever felt." Her gaze leapt to Gary in the midst of the melee. Gary was valiantly fighting. It was obvious he had been around the Carpathians, and even the wicked creatures did little to shake his faith in his friends.

"She is getting torn apart," Razvan snapped. "Do as she says *now*."

The sight of her with the bats slicing through her arms and legs was more painful than he expected. He fought his way to her side and faced her. "Pull the pin and count."

"Cover them, Gregori," Ivory reiterated. "No one breathe. You will have to do that for Gary. If you can, get any wildlife away from here."

"Do it," Mikhail commanded.

They pulled the pins and the gas hissed into the air. Razvan didn't look at the others, only at Ivory with her brave, calm face and the wolves fighting from her back. He didn't even feel the teeth slicing deep or see the bloody carnage the bats were leaving on the snow, he only saw and felt her. She gave him a half-smile, her eyes soft as they counted and lobbed the grenades into the center of the writhing mass and both dissolved.

He knew what to expect, but still, the explosion seemed worse now that it wasn't contained in a hole in the ground. A mushroom cloud of orange rocketed into the sky. The blast rocked both of them, the force blowing them back and away. The pressure raced through their bodies, feeling like great stones weighing on their chests.

There was a feel of power to shifting, an enormous rush to battle when one was in control of one's own body. Nothing dimmed that elation, not even the exploding trees or the masses of incinerated bats raining from the sky or the stench of foul flesh burning. For the first time in his life, he really felt as if he had done something that made a difference. Because of her—*Ivory*. He waited while the heat streamed around them, cooking everything in its path, his mind occupied with the woman who knew so much about Xavier.

Was it possible that she might be the key to ridding the world of such a monster? Was there actually a chance? The world around him was on fire, and yet for the first time in centuries, he felt hope. The roar of the flames and the snapping and crackling of the inferno mingled with the last gasping shrieks of the hideous creatures, and he could only hear her soft whisper in his head.

Life can have unexpected high moments.

A sharing. He recognized her willingness to share a small piece of who she was with him. Her love of battle. She *loved* the fight, the careful study of the enemy, the planning and preparation, the rush of adrenaline when her well-trained body and brain responded like a ballet dancer performing precise, complicated steps and emerging victorious. The feelings flowed from her into him, filling him with her, with her sense of purpose, with the realization that no other knew this complicated, talented woman the way she was letting him.

That realization humbled him, yet bolstered him at the same time. He had never felt as if he could measure up. He hadn't been strong enough to defeat Xavier, or even to get away or to save his child or his aunts. This woman, his life-mate, strong and enduring, offered him, at the very least, friendship.

You are right about those unexpected moments. It was definitely an unexpected high moment. While wind generated from the blaze roared around him, while heat blasted through his body and the world went up in flames, purging the last of the mutated bats, he felt at peace. He felt whole. And he was happy.

He felt her small, shared smile and held it to him, secreting it away in his heart—the heart she had given back to him.

When you go back to your natural form, I will be singing the revealing spell. The four splinters that were removed from you will need a host, and the bats are dead. He will have fled their bodies, Ivory cautioned. *He will be looking for another host. Warn Gregori to watch the rest of them.*

Of course. Vigilance was everything now. This was a chance to destroy a small part of Xavier. Even if it took one piece at a time to rid the world of him, it would be well worth it.

Razvan took his natural form and signaled to the others to do the same. "She is using the revealing spell. Watch for Xavier's dark spirit," he warned them.

Ivory shimmered into her physical form, watchful, already singing the revealing chant, sending the notes scattering across the charred field and into the sky. It was still raining debris. Smoke and ash swirled together and drifted on the slight breeze. Snow drifted from the heavy clouds, mixing with the falling remains, nature already attempting to cover the signs of battle.

I call to me all that is good to aid me in my
    desperate plight.
I plead for the song that I may sing to reveal evil
    stalking the night.

Light of sky, burning bright, find that which is
   dark and bathe it in light.
Evil one, I call forth the blight you left behind.

Light spilled across the remnants of the battlefield, illuminating four dark shadows sliding among the dead toward the small group of Carpathians shielding Gary. Gregori threw out his hand, fingers spread wide, and lightning jumped, sizzling and cracking, toward the four fragments. Three burrowed into the ground, but the tip of the whip slashed into the fourth, incinerating it.

The ground rolled and pitched. A shriek rose. Black blood bubbled up from the ground and a noxious smell burst from the center of the ooze. The shriek rocked the trees, sent leaves trembling. Gary put his hand over his ears to muffle the hideous sound.

Gregori tried following the remaining shards with the lightning tip, sinking strike after strike into the ground, but with no results. There was no following them into the ground itself. Three small slivers would be impossible to track, and all of them knew they would eventually find their way back to Xavier.

Ivory swayed with weariness. "The dawn will break soon, Razvan. I need to rest. Do you come back with me or stay?"

It was almost a challenge, he decided, studying her face. She didn't know if she wanted him to remain with her or join the others. He touched her mind and realized she had not been in company for so long that she found the contact with him—and so many others—overwhelming.

"We would be happy to provide you with shelter," Mikhail offered. "We have several safe resting chambers."

Razvan felt Ivory instantly recoil from the idea. She

trusted no one that much. She would never rest where others knew of her sleeping chamber. Razvan was her lifemate. She recognized him and yet was wary still.

"I think it best that we return to our own resting place," he said.

Ivory sent him a small grateful smile and nodded her head. "Xavier will not stop his hunt for Razvan. It is evident he has puppets in the area. I would make certain my children were protected both during the day and at night."

Sara slipped her hand into Falcon's. "We will double their protection."

Falcon clapped Gary on the back. "You look a little worse for wear. Thank you for going after Travis for us."

Ivory ducked her head, the color sweeping up her pale skin. "I did not mean to imply your friend was not valiant. I am certain he takes excellent care of your children during the daylight hours, but Xavier is desperate to find Razvan and get him back. He will need Carpathian blood. I doubt he can go long without a blood supply. No one is safe, least of all the most vulnerable."

Mikhail's piercing eyes moved over both Ivory and Razvan. "Perhaps our healer should take a look at your wounds before you leave us."

Razvan took a good look at his lifemate. There were scratches and bite marks up and down her arms; a few on her face and her legs had blood running down them. He was certain he didn't look much better. He didn't want to stay any longer. He feared his sister or daughter might come to the aid of their prince, and he had been through enough without facing them. He didn't know how he would feel or what he could possibly say to either of them, but, when he looked at Ivory's weary face, he refused to be selfish. She needed care, and her needs came first.

Ivory stepped back several paces. "These are mere scratches. My lifemate can attend to them. An inconvenience only." She inclined her head, a regal gesture, toward Mikhail. "I am certain we will cross paths again."

"Please do come and meet Raven, my lifemate," Mikhail invited. "She cannot travel at the moment and will be sorry she was not here. You are truly an inspiration to our women."

Gregori cast him a smoldering look before turning to Ivory. His strange silver eyes gleamed at her as she slid back into the shadows, and she knew he recognized the sudden dangerous stillness of a warrior in her. "If you have need, lady, call and I will come. I do not give my word lightly."

I guess you might want to rethink your position on women in battle, Mikhail sent telepathically.

The women are with this one for five minutes, old friend, and it will be anarchy.

Mikhail sobered. *What of Razvan?*

The boy has more honor than good sense.

That boy is older than you are, Mikhail was compelled to point out.

He has suffered greatly and he is no traitor. Less so than I am. There was a small silence and Gregori lifted his silver eyes to his prince and oldest friend. *When the woman, Lara, was so terrified of my eyes, I knew she had seen Xavier. We share the one lasting testimony, branded always for meddling with things best left alone.*

It was an apology and they both knew it.

Mikhail clapped Gregori on the shoulder, affection in his gesture. *It was long ago, as many things were, and in the end it came to good.*

That is what Razvan said.

Gregori stepped close to Ivory. She didn't back away, but

her eyes went as watchful and as still as her body, as if she half suspected he might attack her. He clasped her arms in the greeting of highest respect, one warrior to another. "*Kulkesz arwaval—joŋesz arwa arvoval*—go with glory—return with honor."

Without waiting for her hesitant reply, he gripped Razvan's forearms in the same respectful clasp. "*Kulkesz arwa-arvoval, ekäm*—walk with honor, my brother. We have only recently learned of Xavier's existence, and probably know far less about his ways than either of you, but, if you wish to pool our information, we would be grateful."

Ivory's uneasiness was more apparent to Razvan than ever. She edged away from Gregori and looked to the sky several times. Razvan took her hand and began moving a distance from the others with her.

"We will meet again," he said, knowing it was true. Right now, Ivory didn't want to face the fact that they had inadvertently become part of the Carpathian world when she had saved the child. Gregori and the others would look toward her, a warrior of their own, as an immense and invaluable vault of knowledge on their greatest enemy.

He could feel her withdrawing into herself. Her expression didn't change, but remained serene and distantly friendly. Inside she was quaking. He kept moving across the snow, leading her away from the others, making the responsibility for choosing to leave his alone. He cared nothing for what others thought. Long ago he'd learned to accept condemnation from everyone. He was the most despised Carpathian alive, worse than the vampires, and, although Mikhail and Gregori chose to welcome him, he saw distrust in the eyes of the others. He didn't want nor need acceptance from them—only from Ivory.

Keep walking away from the direction of our home. The snow will cover our tracks, but anyone will be able to track the blood scent. Just up ahead, we will have to close all wounds.

Razvan almost couldn't hear past *our home*. His stomach tightened. Home. Our home. The idea of it was comforting and frightening at the same time. He glanced at her through the thickening snow. Her face was turned away from his. She looked ethereal striding through the snow, like an ice princess, not the warrior he knew her to be.

They stopped beneath the shelter of several large trees. The high canopy kept the snow from falling on them while they examined themselves for poisonous parasites and took a few minutes to close every wound and scratch. The ones on their legs were the worst.

"The bats are more effective attacking from the ground," Ivory explained.

Razvan glanced at her. She studiously avoided his gaze. His heart gave a funny little wrench. She was nervous. The slayer, a warrior beyond measure, was nervous being alone with him. He hadn't considered that she might be more nervous than he was.

"Xavier wanted them to bring back blood," Razvan explained. "That was his original purpose, but they were so vicious he began to expand his ideas."

When they were both finished, Ivory insisted they look one another over a second time.

"You are very thorough," he commented.

"It is how I stay alive. How we will stay alive. You have to learn if you are going to stay with me. And you are free to go, if you wish."

Her lashes lifted and she flicked him a quick gaze. He couldn't tell from her expression whether she hoped he'd choose to go. He shook his head. "I will stay, and, Ivory, have no fear, I am a quick learner. I can play dumb if need be, but I am not."

"I have kept my lair safe for hundreds of years, even when I was slowly carving out the passageways. There are no traces of anyone around or near my resting place. I do not hunt close by. I never leave tracks. I am careful there is no scent. I do not go out every night. I live quietly and avoid people as much as possible." She looked at him, for the first time meeting his eyes. "When I do go out it is for one purpose only: to gather information on Xavier. If it takes a hundred lifetimes, I will find a way to destroy him."

He nodded his head. "I understand."

"I am not certain you do. It is my sole purpose for existing. I care nothing for society. I do not want friends. I do not know how to be civil other than for the purpose of obtaining information. Are you prepared for that?"

A slow smile welled up from the pit of his stomach and settled on his mouth. He saw her catch her breath, and then she looked away from him.

"I do not have friends, nor will society welcome me. I have more reason than any other to want to destroy Xavier."

"If you truly want to learn from me, then heed this. You cannot let this become personal. It is a duty, a sacred duty. You must pray and meditate until you are absolutely certain that you are on the right path. Will you give me your word of honor that you will do that?"

Razvan waited until she looked at him. "You have my word. Let us go home." He dissolved before she could find another reason to protest.

She led the way, choosing a route high enough that they were a part of the dark clouds moving in silence across the sky.

Razvan took note of the landmarks, the rising mountains, the lakes and streams and surrounding countryside. The snow was dazzling white, the air crisp and clean, refreshing after so many centuries of smelling blood and death, yet the wide-open spaces were disorienting. His life had been underground, confined to a small prison room unless Xavier was using his body.

Ivory's voice interrupted his thoughts. *We are coming up on the lair. Always approach it from a variety of directions, never the same one. Scan carefully. Better to sleep elsewhere for one night than lose our fortress to the enemy. There is a warning system in place. I have to reprogram it to allow you entrance. This system is made of gems,* Ivory explained. *I called the gems and asked for aid. Once I embedded them in rock, each about three feet apart, zigzagging down the crack, from one side to the other, the gems not only bring light to the lair, but they act as a warning system for me.* She hesitated and then corrected herself. *For us.*

He felt the rightness of her words, joining them together, but also the reluctance, as if she couldn't quite get around the fact that they were meant to be lifemates.

The safeguard is actually the way the gems work. They measure the weight of my molecules, with the wolves on me of course, as I am drifting down through the crack. If the weight is too heavy, or too light, the crack would close below and stop the intruder. If I am in the lair, I would hear the rocks closing and could prepare for an attack. Nothing can penetrate the rock from below us or either side—it is too thick. Not even the worms can drill through. In order to carry you in, I had to change it once already, and it was difficult with the sun so close on my heels.

How was I able to get out?

It only works in one direction; a warning system is not

needed in both. I would not keep anyone a prisoner. Again there was that slight hesitation. *In truth I have never thought to bring anyone down here.*

He thought it best to ignore her nervousness, and he did not have to feign his interest in her system. It was as unique and brilliant as the inventor. He waited while she disappeared into the crack and added a few more of her gems. The light worked much like an ancient mirror system, one prism working off another. He realized she used the gems for her weapons as well, that her experiments were sophisticated.

It is safe for you to come and go as you please.

Ivory floated down, avoiding the light spreading slowly across the sky, screened by the now-heavy snow. Once she hit the living chamber, the wolves leapt from her back and padded after her to the bed of soil.

"I do not do well, even under the ground, when the sun has risen." Again Ivory appeared uneasy. "I spent too many years in the soil trying to heal."

"I spent many lifetimes in the ice caves," Razvan assured, watching her curl up, the wolves surrounding her. He waited for an invitation.

Ivory gestured toward the side of the large basin. "There is plenty of room."

He envied the wolves pressed close to her, but said nothing, knowing she was being more than generous. He closed his eyes and allowed the breath to leave his body, his heart to slow and then stop while the soil poured over them like a living blanket. It was the first time he could clearly remember being totally relaxed and infinitely happy.

7

Ivory woke knowing three days had passed and the sun had already sunk from the sky. She was used to the way time passed so deep beneath the earth and the rhythms spoke to her, as she had become accustomed to them. It had been disorienting at first, which was when she'd come up with her prism system for bringing a small bit of light into her sanctuary. It rather shocked her that Razvan woke with her. The wolves would, of course, after so many years, but she had thought to go hunting alone and to give herself time to prepare for another in her lair.

She stared at his face, the lines etched there, the way his eyes seemed so compassionate and understanding. His life had been nothing but struggle and pain, yet he seemed, when she touched his mind, to be truly kind. Why, then, did her hands tremble? Why did she feel as if butterflies had taken flight and were winging their way through her body whenever she looked at him? She had absolute confidence in her abilities as a warrior, but had no idea how to interact off the battlefield.

Razvan's expression softened when his eyes met hers and he smiled. Her heart jumped in response. His smile was sweet and made him look years younger. "Good evening. You certainly are beautiful to wake up to."

She wasn't. She knew she wasn't. She was in her true patchwork form—her body put together in pieces and a little mismatched here and there. She rubbed at one of the worst offending scars, the one dissecting her collarbone, and was shocked to find the ridge lessened. The healer had done more than heal her wounds. The scars would never disappear completely, but he had helped them to fade to thinner, flatter lines.

"I am not, you know." She could feel color rising under her skin.

It embarrassed her that she no longer knew the civilities. Once, long ago, she had run a warm, happy household. Somehow, seeing that sweet smile on Razvan's face brought bittersweet memories rushing back. There had been so much laughter and love in her house. How could her brothers have turned their backs on everything honorable and chosen to give up their souls? They hadn't suffered the way Razvan had suffered, and he had endured the centuries of torment, being branded a criminal, despised by all those around him, his body used for vile things. Yet, still, he kept his honor.

She had told herself that her brothers had been grief-stricken over her disappearance, but she knew better. Everyone experienced loss. All five of them had turned together—unheard of in Carpathian history. She knew them better than anyone else, and she knew that meant it had been a conscious decision, not one made from too many years of lack of emotion or killing friends who had become vampire. The decision hadn't been made because they were desolate from grief or had waited too long for lifemates. She knew their decision had been reasoned out together. They wanted power. They believed they were smarter, stronger and more deserving than anyone else.

Her disappearance had been the excuse they needed to finalize something they had often discussed in the privacy of their home.

"You look so sad, Ivory."

She never thought to hide her expressions in her lair. She didn't hide her true form and now didn't know what to do or how to act. She gave a small shrug. "This is a little awkward."

"Only if you wish to make it that way. I will not intrude where I am not wanted."

Ivory shook her head. "No, do not feel that way, as if I would not want you here. I invited you. After all these centuries, I just am not certain how to act with company."

His smile widened, reached his eyes, warming them into soft velvet. "But then, I am your lifemate, not company. Act as you always have. I am here to learn from you."

That hurt, struck her in her belly like a knotted fist. He wasn't in her lair to be her lifemate in the way a man might claim a woman. She knew that. She wanted no part of that, yet she still felt slighted. It was the perverse reaction of a woman, not a warrior, and she was disappointed in herself. She had set the terms; he was merely abiding by them. She pushed at the fall of her heavy hair, more for an excuse to hide than because it was bothering her.

"I will get more at ease over time." It was all she could think to say.

Ivory watched the wolves as they gathered around him. In spite of his older appearance, he was a handsome man. Now that the earth had revived and rejuvenated him, his frame was filled out and muscular. His hair fell in a long wave nearly to the middle of his back. It was thick and dark, and she knew from three weeks of holding him and feeding him, running her fingers through that soft, thick fall, that many colors made up that heavy mane, not the least of which was gray.

Razvan, instead of towering over the pack and bullying his way into leadership, crouched down in the midst of the six wolves and allowed them to take their time pushing their noses into him and rubbing along his legs and back.

This is Razvan. My mate.

She included Razvan in the circle of communication, knowing when they went into battle together that leadership was essential. Raja had to accept him as her partner and therefore coleader of the pack. He would only do that if she named him mate.

Razvan glanced at her. Ivory willed herself not to blush. She tried to look as nonchalant as possible. Razvan seemed very large in the confines of the bedchamber. His masculine frame filled up the entire room. Every breath she took seemed to draw the scent of him into her lungs. Every breath he took made her ultra-aware of him, the way his heavy chest muscles moved beneath his thin, tight tee; the way his body looked in that brief moment before he'd donned that thin, tight tee.

Raja turned his head and looked at her, giving her an aloof glare, baring his teeth at Razvan. The Dragonseeker shrugged his shoulders.

"I know what it feels like to be displaced, old man," he soothed. "We will get along."

"Offer him your blood."

Razvan stood slowly, his eyes meeting Ivory's. "You feed them Carpathian blood?"

"You do not remember much of our first meeting."

"Some."

She took a breath, let it out, and then made her confession. "Many years ago, so long now that I cannot remember when it all started, a wolf pack helped me. They found pieces of me and would have consumed them, but I was able to touch their minds, and instead they buried the pieces of me together. In return, I found their descendants and I made certain they thrived. I did not spend much time above-ground in those days. My body just could not handle it. But when I did, the wolves were all that kept me sane. They were my only companions and all I had to trust."

She spoke in a soft, clear voice, as if she was telling a tale she had heard about someone else, as if the horror of those endless years had not been hers to bear. He had his horror locked away in his mind, but somehow hers seemed so much worse.

Something frightening deep inside Razvan lifted its head and roared in rage. He had long ago buried any aggressive feelings. Too many years of captivity, of being unable to do anything about it had pushed rage and anger aside, and then, finally, his emotions had faded into oblivion, so that he forgot the intensity, the sheer strength of feelings.

"That was a terrible time for me. I couldn't be out of the ground for very long, but I went looking for my brothers. I needed them. I could barely function. My mind or my body." She ducked her head and her hair fell around her face, hiding her expression. Her voice remained as steady as ever. "It took me twenty-two years to locate the first of my brothers. I had a few run-ins with vampires along the way and inadvertently began building a reputation for slaying the undead. They began to hunt for me. I still had to spend most of my time in the ground in order to hold my body together."

"You do not have to tell me this if it distresses you," Razvan said.

145

Ivory shrugged her shoulders and tossed back her hair, her eyes steady. "It matters little now. It was a long time ago. Over the next fifty years I searched for my family, only to find that they had all turned. It felt very much like they had betrayed me."

Ivory felt the lump rising in her throat, threatening to choke her, threatening to humiliate her. She shrugged a second time. "I had the wolves. You understand? They were everything to me. They do not have a long life span in the wild and so each new litter of cubs, each renewal, was my only family. I needed them."

Razvan wanted to hold her, to offer her comfort, but, when he took a step toward her, she moved away from him, back toward the other room as if she hadn't noticed. He followed her, moving through the pack of wolves, ignoring Raja's bared teeth as if the wolf was beneath his notice. He couldn't help but be intrigued by the story. He had no idea that wolves could carry Carpathian blood, and he doubted if anyone else had known it either.

"So these wolves are not the original pack," he prompted, watching as she picked up a comb and began running it through her hair. It was a soothing action, not one of necessity.

Ivory moved restlessly to her memorial wall. Her family wall. She touched Sergey's face, traced the beloved lines carved there. "No, several generations were born and died, but they were always with me. Eventually the vampires began trying to find my pack to kill them. They came to think the wolves protected me in some way. Believe it or not, the undead can be very superstitious, especially since they have an alliance with Xavier. He feeds them stories to make them believe he is stronger than they are."

Razvan watched the pads of her fingers move over her brother's face, stroke after stroke, the gentle, loving motion mesmerizing. He could only imagine someone loving him that much, missing him and wanting to save his soul the way he sensed she did her brothers'. He was dead to his own sister, much in the same way he knew Ivory had to have separated herself from her brothers now to keep her sanity, to keep from being overwhelmed by sorrow.

Feeling a driving need to hold her in his arms and comfort her, he did the only thing he could think to do that wouldn't earn him a blow. He stepped up behind her and held out his hand for the comb. "Let me."

There was silence. She held very still, her face turned toward her memory wall, her hand not moving, her breath not flowing. He could feel the faint trembling of her body. A wild creature held captive, unknowing whether or not to accept kindness. Very slowly, she held the comb back over her shoulder, not looking, not letting him see her face.

Razvan's fingers were gentle as he took the instrument from her and began a slow glide through her hair. "How did you come to have your present pack?"

Again there was a brief moment of silence while she tried to accustom herself to Razvan combing her long hair. She cleared her throat. "I still could spend little time aboveground. When I did, it was with the wolves or hunting. My pack had given birth to a new litter of pups. Six of them. Three male, three female. The entire pack was excited, and I more than any of them. The pack's good times were mine." This time her fingers traced the ancient Carpathian text. *Sív pide köd. Pitääm mustaakad sielpesäämbam.* Love transcends evil. I hold your memories safe in my soul.

He realized the importance of that simple statement.

147

She had no other contact, human or otherwise, that wasn't an enemy. The pack had virtually become her family and her friends, her very community and only confidants. She had seen the empty shell of her brother and needed the reassurance of her wall, her home, the words she had come to believe in. He felt the first stirrings of love for her, the beginning, and recognized he was stepping on a path he would not—could not—leave.

"Over the years, while living with the wolves, I realized a few had the ability to communicate with me telepathically. At the time the litter was born, the alpha male and female were both able to talk to me and I was not quite as lonely. I felt as if I had a family again."

She dropped her hand from the wall as if bracing herself. "One evening I rose and went in search of the pack. The vampires had gotten there before me. There was blood everywhere, fur and bones and carcasses strewn over the very meadow where they had done the same to me."

She pulled away from him, paced across the room. He could see her hands were shaking, but she put them behind her back as she turned and faced him. There was guilt and defiance mixed on her face. "I found the cubs in the den. All of them were dying. The vampires had inflicted wounds on them, but hadn't killed them outright, leaving them to suffer horribly before they died, or for other wild animals to finish them off."

She tilted her chin. "I saved them. I crawled into the den and I fed them my blood. I did not think beyond that moment. I just could not bear to lose everyone all over again. I had promised their ancestors that I would look out for them, but, because they had aided me, the vampires destroyed the entire pack."

"It was not your fault."

"Perhaps not, but it felt as if it was my fault. I stayed in the den to protect them, burrowing beneath the ground during the daylight hours and staying with them during the nights. I had to give them blood and, at times, I had to take theirs as I couldn't hunt. Raja was the first to turn. I had no idea it was even possible, but I knew the ramifications. No wolf pack could be Carpathian and let loose on unsuspecting humans. They would be immortal, or nearly so as we are. The first was an accident, but the rest, although it broke a moral law, was done with great purpose."

She met his eyes, expecting condemnation. Razvan shook his head. "It seems all of us have chosen a path that perhaps has not always been the wise one. You. Me. The healer. Yet our paths have merged and become the same."

Ivory shook her head. "You are a very different type of man."

"Am I? Perhaps I have been away so long I never learned what a man was supposed to be." He gave her a lopsided half-smile that stole her breath. She had never felt the strange girlish fluttering a mere smile from him seemed to generate, but the very feel surrounding him was one of peace and gentleness.

"I was not insulting you. I like that you are different." Maybe a little too much. She had a purpose—they both did—and it required full effort and attention. They didn't dare lose sight of their final objective, nor could she change the course she had set herself on.

His smile heated his eyes and changed the color to warm amber. She could get lost in his eyes if she let herself. Ivory squared her shoulders. "I made the decision to turn the pack based on my need to survive. They were all I had. I have tried to be responsible about it. They stay with me at all times, hunt with me and are given only my blood. They do not have litters, although Raja indicated that, should I have a baby, they would be able to provide a pack for my child." Again she found herself blushing, her gaze dropping from his. "As I did not think that would ever be possible, I did not give the idea much heed."

"So all six have been with you . . ."

"Centuries. They live here in the lair, hunt with me and fight with me."

Razvan nodded. "And I have come along and disrupted the peace of the pack."

"It is always difficult integrating a new member, but not impossible. Raja must accept you." Again she looked at him, her gaze steady. "You are my lifemate, whether we claim each other or not."

He didn't point out to her that the male of their species alone had the ritual binding words imprinted upon him before birth. He had been born Carpathian and human, but the words were there, should he choose to bind them together, with or without her consent. He believed the binding was given to the male because his half of the soul was darkness without his lifemate. Once his aunts managed to turn him fully, he had known he must find his lifemate to alleviate the darkness spreading with the passing years. The driving instincts of the Carpathian male were in him, urging him to stake his claim, where the man who was driven to protect those he cared about refused to take a chance with her life.

"Tell me what you think will aid Raja in accepting me." Should the alpha welcome him, then the others would as well.

"I have shared my blood with you repeatedly and called you my mate. We will feed the pack together. You offer your blood to Raja first. If he does not take it, no one will be fed this day."

"Perhaps I could reason with him rather than punish." He had been tortured and deprived of food until he was starving. He could not do that to another living thing.

Ivory padded barefoot into the midst of the pack, scratching ears and rubbing fur, her fingers massaging necks with affectionate familiarity. "The pack leader respects strength."

"Fighting or punishing is not always strength," Razvan said. "Xavier was the cruelest man I have known. Warriors came and went from every species. He defeated them all. Every one of them, yet I will never respect him, nor will I be like him."

There was quiet determination in his voice. Ivory sighed. Razvan hadn't survived imprisonment and torture by being faint of heart. He was stubborn, unswerving and relentless. She had been in his Dragonseeker mind and knew just how unwavering he could be.

"Raja knows I respect you." She pinned the pack alpha with a steely gaze. "I am certain he will accept you." Because, if the wolf didn't, she might have a few private words with him.

Raja snorted and then gave her a wolfish grin, his tongue lolling out of his mouth as if he might be laughing. Razvan smiled. With a casual tear of his teeth, he sliced open his wrist and offered it to the big male wolf without hesitation.

Ivory tensed. Raja leaned his head toward the welling blood and sniffed before giving a tentative lick. His mouth clamped on the wrist unexpectedly, teeth sinking deep.

She murmured the binding words softly in the ancient language.

Nó me elidaban, nó me kalmaban—As we are in life
*   we are in death.*
Elid elided—Life to life.
Siel sieled—Soul to soul.
Me juttaak, me kureak—Life to life.
Me juttaak, me kureak—We are bound together as
*   one.*

Triumph swept through Razvan. He was part of something. He belonged. Ivory's acceptance of him was far more reluctant than the alpha wolf's. The wolf respected her mate. Had fought in battle with him, saw no hesitation and that he was quick to shield and protect Ivory. Ivory might accept Razvan as a warrior—at least one to train—but as her mate, that was something altogether different.

Razvan hid a smile as Ivory turned away from them, frowning a little as she fed the females. She kept her back to Razvan, shutting him out as she talked to the wolves, allowing him to reach for the mind of the wolves himself. He found Raja to be very intelligent, a strong strategist and capable leader. His second in command, Blaez, was a very serious wolf. He liked Blaez's personality very much. And then there was Farkas, the male the vampire had attacked and injured so severely. Farkas's body had been repaired in the healing soil, but craved rich Carpathian blood to complete the process.

Razvan staggered when Farkas finally licked across the wounds to seal them. He sank down beside the wolf. "You do this every night?"

She shook her head. "We are very careful not to rise every night. It is probably unnecessary after all these years, but, without three consecutive nights in the soil, my body refused to function properly, so I still am cautious. In truth,

I have not had problems in a long while, but I do not care to risk it."

Razvan's brows drew together. "What kinds of problems?"

Ivory sank to the floor beside him as the smallest female closed the laceration on her wrist. "Nothing big. Walking. Running. Coordination mainly. My muscles were cut into pieces and they need to be strengthened."

"You should have told the healer."

A faint, haughty look crept into her expression. "I have never needed the healer or anyone else to survive. If I have need of the soil, it is there for me." She shrugged. "Besides, it is better for us not to be out much. The less we leave, the less chance of a vampire or hunter stumbling across the lair. I have much work to do here. We go out for a hunt and run, and then we stay in a few days. It has worked out well for us. I will need to go out to feed for both of us. It will take a few hours as I have to travel a distance from our lair."

"Not without me."

"There is no need for us both to go. Xavier is actively hunting you, using every resource at his disposal. You cannot leave traces for him to find you."

"Not without me," he repeated, his tone mild.

She narrowed her eyes. "That is so silly."

"So was refusing the healer's help, but you had your reasons. I have mine."

"You do not like anyone giving you blood," she guessed shrewdly. "You are Carpathian. You need blood to survive."

"I am well aware of that."

His tone never changed. Reasonable. Pleasant. Gentle even. She gritted her teeth. Nothing seemed to get to him, and she had deliberately needled him, wanting to shake him out of his stubbornness.

"It is just smarter for me to go alone."

"Perhaps. But we go together."

Her teeth snapped together at that mild tone. "Are you always like this?"

"I do not know. I have not been around any other than Xavier. I did not upset the woman who gave birth to Lara as I am upsetting you. But, like me, she was a prisoner and neither of us could make our own decisions. I am able to make this decision, for ill or not. I go with you."

She stuck her chin out at him. "I am your lifemate. It is my right as well as my duty to provide for you."

"Are you willing to provide solace with your body as well?"

Her heart jumped. Leapt. Took flight right along with a million birds in the pit of her stomach. Even her womb reacted. Which was silly, because he never changed expression, not on his face and not with the tone of his voice. They could have been discussing the weather. "No." The word came out a whisper. Maybe even a question when she wanted to sound absolute and distant. There was just something about him that moved her, called to her, a nameless need, a hunger in his gentle eyes, that stark aloneness that drew her like a moth to flame.

"Then there is no need to provide anything else. We work together toward a common goal. We both wish to pool our vast wealth of knowledge in order to destroy Xavier."

He was right. She knew he was right. It was *exactly* what she wanted, yet hearing him say it aloud in that calm, matter-of-fact voice made her want to weep.

"You brought me here to learn what I have learned of Xavier and to show me the ways of a warrior. I accept those boundaries."

"Good." She stood up. "That is excellent. We need to go." Her body gave a subtle shift and she stood in front of him in absolute perfection, her clothes revealing her smooth, petal-soft skin.

"Why do you do that? Why not be seen as you truly are. You are beautiful, you know. The lines are your body's badges of courage. A warrior's true tribute. I have never seen anyone so beautiful."

She turned away from him, not wanting him to see how his words affected her. She hadn't been told she was beautiful since she was a young woman, centuries earlier. Why did the warmth in his voice bring heat to her body when he seemed so unaffected by her?

"I do not want the vampires to know they marked me. It is a psychological game I play. When I discovered they were superstitious, it gave me the idea and I have continued to make them believe nothing they do to me can harm me."

His smile was slow in coming, but, when it did, she experienced a curious fluttering in the region of her stomach. She took a step backward and spun around. "If you insist on coming with me, I trust you will at least heed my warning to be cautious and leave no trail back to our lair. Xavier is going to send an army to retrieve you, everything he has in his arsenal."

"Which is considerable," Razvan agreed. "And he has your imprint now."

She stilled. Turned slowly. Her gaze locked with his. "What do you mean?" Her mouth went dry.

"You pushed him from my mind, my heart, my body and my very soul. To do that, you shared your light. He cannot fail to recognize you if you studied under him. He will work day and night to wreak vengeance. That is his

155

way, and I will not allow him to succeed. Until he is destroyed, you have me as your bodyguard." His gentle tone was still low, black-velvet smooth, but implacable.

Her heart fluttered along with her stomach, a feminine reaction she abhorred, which probably made her more caustic than she normally would have been. "I am a warrior, and you know very little about battle. I hardly think you are going to be of much assistance in a fight. If anything you will probably be a complete hindrance."

He bowed slightly. "Perhaps that is so. But I will be a powerful bargaining chip."

She went white beneath her already fair skin and her breath hissed out in a long, slow exhale. "Do you think that I would trade my life for yours?"

"No." He didn't look in the least ruffled. "But I would." He gestured toward the thin crack winding upward through the thick walls of rock. "Hunger is beating at me. Let us hunt."

She held out her arms for the wolves to leap onto her, shifting into the form of tattoos.

"Why did you want them fed first when we go to hunt?" Razvan asked curiously.

"Never take a hungry wolf with you when you are trying to leave no tracks. They are allowed to hunt game only once every few days to keep them sharp, but I do not risk wolf tracks or tempting them with human blood. In this form, we leave no tracks, yet they can aid me should I need it."

"I would not mind a wolf tattoo of my own," Razvan said. "It makes for beautiful artwork, as well as having eyes to watch your back."

The admiration in his voice threw her and she bit down hard on her lip to keep herself focused. She didn't want to like him as a person, only to see him as another tool in her war against Xavier, but he charmed her in ways she hadn't expected.

She let her breath out in a little rush again. "You are a frustrating man, Dragonseeker."

"I suppose I am." There was no remorse, only amusement.

Ivory turned away from him before her sense of humor got the better of her. The thing about Razvan, she decided as she began to ascend through the inch-wide crack that zigzagged the way up through hundreds of feet of rock, was that there was an inner peace that radiated outward from him. Nothing seemed to disturb him. But then, how could it?

He had asked Gregori what more could be done to him than had already been done. He didn't fear death. There wasn't much in the way of torture, physical, emotional or mental, that Xavier hadn't subjected him to. He had learned long ago that he couldn't control others or events, only his own reaction to what happened. There was a hidden strength in Razvan, a well of it, deep and pure, that she saw and felt every time she was close to him. But there was also a gentleness she hadn't expected from a man honed in violence and blood.

She had always believed she would need a fierce warrior in order for her to be physically attracted to a male, but she found inner strength appealed to her more than fighting skills. His strength and gentleness tempted her as no other. She looked too long at his eyes, those ever-changing eyes that seemed soft and deep where she might lose herself if she didn't take care.

The night was clear and crisp, snow glistening on the ground, turning everything overly bright. Ice crystals hung from the trees and dazzled her eyes when she scanned the ground.

Be careful not to disturb the snow as you come through the crack. The slightest movement can displace the flakes, and that might lead an enemy to investigate closer.

Ivory touched his mind to see if he was irritated by her instructions. He seemed just the opposite, soaking up her advice and following it carefully. He made no move to take the lead, following her across the sky inland, toward the valley, away from the region where Carpathians dwelled, toward a small farming community at the base of the ice mountains.

You are in his territory. Razvan did not have to name the mage. There was no distrust in his voice, only a mild question.

He will send his armies wide in search of you, thinking you will flee far from him. He prides himself on his long reach and he will assume you will fear him too much to stay close. This will be safer at the moment.

You have studied him.

I went to his school for a short time, Ivory informed him. *I loved the work and was good at it. Unfortunately, I also paid attention to him and realized he was not as he appeared to be. In those days, I was rather young and naive and did not know how to hide my thoughts and suspicions.*

Razvan's warmth flooded her mind, making her aware that the cold of the night had pierced her, or perhaps it was thinking of the past.

You have learned well over the years. I have observed him at work on a daily basis. I watched the madness in him progress over the years until his mind was no longer functioning properly. There is no reason. He has become a megalomaniac, believing himself a superior being to all who walk the earth. He is particularly bitter with the immortality of the Carpathians and is always experimenting to find a way to destroy them.

A ribbon of icy water cut through the valley, meandering through several wide meadows used for pastures and winding in and out of groves of trees. Ivory followed the same path, staying high, not moving fast, but drifting along, taking note of all movement—the animals, smoke coming from chimneys, any humans—she took it all in and shared with Razvan.

There is always a pattern to movement, she instructed. *Animals are important to watch, even the smallest of them. Mice will scurry into the underbrush at the first sign of danger. They see shadows from above. All prey animals do, and their instincts are good. You do not have to be connected to them to use them as a warning system.*

Razvan stopped drinking in the sheer beauty of his surroundings and began to pay attention to the things she pointed out. Ivory was the consummate warrior. When she left the lair, everything was all business. All survival. He needed to learn, and she was willing to instruct him.

He scanned the uneven terrain, seeing with new eyes.

Nature is your friend, your ally. Trees tell stories. Look at the area to the south. Just below the mountain near the small farm tucked into the shadow.

The grimness in her voice alerted him to trouble, but he couldn't see anything but glistening snow and dazzling ice and a few bare limbs poking out of an otherwise snow-laden tree. A few tracks in the snow led from a small house to a barn and then around to the back where several smaller buildings housed animals, but he couldn't see anything that might have alarmed her.

What am I looking for?

Something sat in that tree watching the house. It was no owl. If you look closely at the tracks, someone walked out of the house toward the barn and then around toward the shelter. The strides increased in length and depth, which means they began running. Whatever it is, it is still there. I feel the energy.

Razvan inspected the naked tree branches and then tried to open his mind to the energy fields surrounding him. Information flooded in. As they approached the small farm, the air lost its crisp, fresh scent and began to feel and smell foul. *Vampire.* His hissed the word.

Tell me what it feels like to you. Reach out very lightly. Let your mind expand to encompass his but do not enter his.

Razvan knew that if his touch was too heavy the vampire would feel his presence and be alerted. If his victim still lived, there would be no hope. The undead would kill and consume as much blood as possible to ready himself for an attack.

Vampires like their blood adrenaline-laced, Ivory explained. *They terrify the victims on purpose and keep them alive as long as possible. The blood is like a drug to them and they need the high continually. Can you feel the chaos in his mind?*

He could. The vampire's mind raced so fast it was like trying to board a runaway train. Even the sound was chaotic, as if the volume was turned up and down so that one moment noises roared and shrieked and then receded, only to start again.

He cannot keep the sound of the victim's heart under control. He is too excited. This one has recently turned. I doubt if he had time to have been recruited by the league of vampires or by Xavier. Usually at this stage they are left alone because they are too dangerous to approach. They cannot handle the highs they feel.

Ivory circled the house. *Two children inside. The vampire knows it, although the man tries to hide the information. His woman is in the barn. She thinks to fight for her man. She has armed herself with garlic, crosses and holy water, but has no real weapon other than farm tools.*

There was admiration in Ivory's voice. Razvan liked that about her. Her take on the world was very simplistic. A man and a woman fought together for their family, even against the worst kind of evil. Both knew they probably would die, but they hoped to take their attacker with them and give their children a chance to survive.

His first thought was to send Ivory to get the woman and her children to safety while he took on the vampire. He had no doubt that he could kill a vampire. He had a rudimentary knowledge of how to slay them, but she would have a better chance to save the farmer as well. He needed time to perfect his fighting skills, so he remained silent and left it to Ivory to tell him what she wanted to do.

I would not do what you told me to do anyway. There was a distinctly teasing note in Ivory's voice, although they both knew she was perfectly serious.

Deep inside, in spite of the gravity of the situation, Razvan found himself happy. Little moments like this, shared amusement, things he'd forgotten existed between people, made up joy in life. He'd forgotten that, and he bet Ivory had as well.

You are a bossy little thing, but I like that. I must be a little strange.

A little? She gave a snort and slipped into the barn through a crack in the window frame.

A woman frantically searched through several farming tools, dragging anything with a sharp blade out to a center pile. Tears ran down her face, but she worked fast, her breath coming in soft sobs.

"Shh," Ivory cautioned as she materialized to one side of the woman. "I am a Carpathian warrior come to aid you. Please put down your weapon and do exactly as I tell you. You will have to trust me."

Razvan instinctively stayed in the form of vapor, knowing his presence would only serve to frighten the woman further.

"With your help, I think we have a chance of saving your husband."

Ivory's voice was quiet and calm. She looked regal, a snow princess come out of the world of nature in her long silver wolf coat, so thick and luxurious falling to her ankles. Her hair cascaded in a long blue-black fall and her face looked serene and innocent. Her voice sounded like warm, melting honey. In contrast, she carried a lethal-looking crossbow and the belt at her hip was covered in weapons. But it was the double rows of tiny crosses embedded in her buckles that eased the woman's tensions.

The farmwife made the sign of the cross in the air. Ivory answered her with the same sign and the woman relaxed and tossed her curved scythe onto the pile of tools.

8

I vory walked from the barn toward the stable, her head up, her eyes glowing a strange whiskey gold as she approached the building. From his position inside the stable, where he now waited for her, Razvan could see her advancing, each confident stride carrying her closer. She took his breath away. She definitely had an otherworldly quality, as if the legend of the Dark Slayer had come to life and moved with grace and elegance through the snow.

The vampire toying with his victim looked up as the horses, nervous and stamping in their stalls, suddenly quieted. Pigs stopped squealing. The stables went eerily silent.

Ivory flashed a small smile toward the vampire. "I do not recognize you, but I see you have no table manners. Perhaps you wish to taste something much richer." Deliberately, her eyes on the vampire, she set her teeth into her wrist.

Razvan noted the vampire immediately lost interest in the human, dropping him to the floor, where the farmer did his best to crawl away while the vampire was fixated on the sight of those small white teeth sinking into a delicate wrist. Two beads of blood welled up, ruby-red, dotting her smooth, petal-soft skin. The fragrance of her drifted to the vampire mixed with the tempting scent of Carpathian blood.

Razvan watched as the farmer crawled toward a broken board in the wall. Instead of creeping through the hole in the wall, he reached to try to pry loose the board for a weapon. Razvan materialized on the other side of the wall and leaned in, finger to his lips. Taking a cue from Ivory, he sketched the sign of the cross in the air between them, knowing neither a minion sent from Xavier nor a vampire would do such a thing. When the man's eyes cleared and he nodded slightly, Razvan beckoned to him to slide through the ragged hole. As the man crawled into the snow, Razvan took his place, donning the illusion of the farmer's body and clothes.

The vampire shuffled closer to Ivory. He bowed, smiling at her. As further evidence that he was recently turned, his teeth didn't have the spiked points, nor were they stained black. He still maintained his rugged good looks. "What are you doing wandering around alone without benefit of protection?"

Ivory smiled sweetly. "What makes you think I am alone? Or without protection?" Keeping her gaze locked with his, she licked at the blood drops, closing the wound and depriving him of the treat he was so looking forward to.

The vampire shook his head. "You have no protection, lady, or I would feel them near."

Ivory made an elegant, derisive sound that wiped the smile from the vampire's face. "You did not hear me. Why, then, would you think you could hear my lifemate? You were so busy toying with your food, you forgot the most basic of all lessons. It is no wonder that you will not survive this night."

She poured contempt into her voice, yet she sounded very much the lady. Soft-spoken, nonthreatening, delivering the reprimand from princess to peasant. Razvan's admiration for her grew. She mesmerized the vampire without doing anything but talking. The undead had all but forgotten about the lowly farmer. He didn't view the human as a threat at all. Instead, he concentrated his attention on Ivory, wanting her rich Carpathian blood, a treat for a vampire who had recently turned.

The vampire scowled at her. "You dare to reprimand me when you walk the night alone? What are you doing here?" His voice turned wily and what he perceived as suave. "And such a beautiful woman, too. I have need of a lifemate."

"Your youth is showing. So impetuous and wrong. Only those newly turned vampires still believe they can force women to become lifemates. Too bad you will not have the time to grow experienced." She tilted her head to one side and studied him, her gaze sweeping him up and down. "You are new enough that you still have your looks. Looks are wasted on the young."

Before he could reply, her hand went to the loops on her holster and she flung six coated arrowheads into his chest in a straight line up and over his heart. Razvan rose to his feet and punched through the chest wall hard, the vampire blood burning over his arm and fist. He had so many scars that he barely felt the bite of the acid as he gripped the heart and began to extract it.

The vampire roared and slammed his head against Razvan's. He tried to dissolve, but the coated arrowheads prevented his chest from shifting to vapor. Raking at Razvan with talons, he tore the flesh from the heavy muscles covering Razvan's chest in an effort to dig through and get to his heart. Razvan yanked his arm back, using more strength than he had thought it would take. The heart was black, but still a normal size.

"Do not look at it. Incinerate it," Ivory said.

Razvan called down the lightning, careful to keep it from striking anything but the vampire and his heart. He bathed his arms and hands in the white-hot energy field. "Controlling the lightning is difficult. I almost missed and nearly hit you."

"I was prepared for it." She sighed and regarded him with worried eyes. "Hesitation can get you killed. You were on him fast enough, but you cannot count him dead until the heart is incinerated. You should have burned that first. A more experienced vampire would have repaired himself while you were still marveling at your work."

Razvan laughed aloud. Killing vampires was dirty work. The fetid breath and claws tearing into his chest and belly had been both frightening and exhilarating. He'd done it. He'd killed his first vampire. It hadn't been a perfect kill, but he had destroyed the undead and saved the farmer. It felt good to do something positive instead of waking up to find that his body had impregnated a woman, or delivered a poisonous blow to his sister or her lifemate. There was no way to tell Ivory how he was feeling, so he didn't try. He flashed her a smile and bowed.

"I will remember."

She was certain he would. He looked so happy standing in that bare, run-down stable with his clothes torn to shreds and his blood streaking his chest and arms and belly. She ran her worried gaze over him. Blood dripped steadily, but there was light in his eyes and in his mind. He made her feel humble with his simple pleasure in doing something she considered a job. He considered it good.

"Thank you for allowing me the experience. It is the only way I will learn to become an asset on our hunt."

Ivory shrugged, feigning indifference when everything

feminine and nothing warrior about her was reacting to that look in his eyes. "It was your plan," she pointed out.

He flashed a half-grin at her, shrugging modestly. "In the old days, before I realized Xavier was in my mind, I was good at planning battles. I kept myself sane, exploring his weaknesses, and everyone else's as well. The vampires. Carpathians. Even the Lycans. But one day I realized that whenever I discovered that Xavier had a weakness it suddenly would be found and shored up. I was aiding my own enemy."

She wanted to comfort him, to just wrap her arms around him and hold him close; instead she leaned down to casually pick up her arrowheads and place them in the small pouch at her side. Razvan wasn't asking for pity; he was stating a fact. But it struck like a blow, that boyish memory that had to hurt like hell. "You took the vampire down fairly easily. And that's what counts."

"I am grateful you let me practice on him. Thinking it through in one's head is not the same as actually experiencing it. Taking the heart was harder than I expected. I am strong, and yet you make it look easy when it is not. There must be a trick to it that I have not gotten yet. But I will. I do think I had an advantage in that I can barely feel the burn of the vampire's blood anymore."

To Ivory, it was heartrending that he thought the buildup of scar tissue from his vampire blood-coated chains was an asset. She wanted to weep for him. Instead she forced a casual response. "He was hardly worth messing up my fingernails." She waved her hand and the ashes blew from the rickety building. "Come here. Let me make certain there is no poison in the lacerations."

Razvan crossed to her side without hesitation. He caught her hand to examine her fingernails. "You are right.

He was not worth messing them up. You have beautiful nails."

To her consternation he brought her fingertips to his mouth and kissed them. "You forget to warm yourself." He blew on her fingers and then drew them into the warmth of his mouth.

Her heart nearly stopped and then began to pound frantically. He was lethal at close range. That gentleness that was so much a part of him surrounded her, mesmerizing her as surely as her voice often captivated those within hearing distance. She took a breath and drew him deep into her lungs. She was tall and she could nearly look him square in the eye, but his shoulders were far wider than hers, even though she was wearing her thick fur coat.

She felt safe with him. Which was silly, and disturbing. She had learned never to trust anyone, yet she had let this man into her life. She didn't need him. She didn't want him. But standing so close to him confused her. Hunters had a certain energy surrounding them; everyone did. His was different. His energy was peaceful, absolutely peaceful. Almost serene. Breathing him in gave her strength in a way she'd never known before. He had a quiet acceptance over his fate, and the lack of need to control everything and everyone around him. In his own way, Razvan was enthralling, charming her without even trying.

Ivory swallowed hard and kept her gaze glued to the deep lacerations running up and down his chest. One particularly long scratch led down to his belly and disappeared into the band of his trousers. She laid her palm over one of the worst lacerations and closed her eyes, feeling for the poisonous brew that would signal parasites. Even though, after the first time, she knew the wounds were clean and merely welling blood, she continued to examine each individual injury.

She liked standing so close to him. The sense of serenity was an aphrodisiac in itself. She had heard of the practices in the Far East that had spread throughout the world, and to her this man embodied the very spirit of Zen. He *felt* calm. Even the simple pleasure he took in learning was without ego or rush.

Ivory leaned forward without conscious thought, her eyes half-closed, and slid her tongue over the long laceration, the healing agents in her saliva immediately removing the sting and closing the wound.

Razvan went still. "What are you doing?" His voice went hoarse.

Ivory noted the change in his breathing. He wasn't nearly as calm now as he'd been a moment ago, and there was something enormously satisfying in that. Her palm slid down to the next scratch and her mouth followed. Every muscle was defined, jumping beneath her touch, his body radiating heat, smelling of the outdoors on a spring night.

His breath left his body in a rush. She felt the ripple in his taut belly as her mouth skimmed down his chest, lower, following the path of the laceration.

"What are you doing?" he repeated.

"Healing you." Ivory's voice had gone husky—almost liquid—betraying her.

He let his breath out in a long, slow exhale. "Listen to me, Ivory." Razvan caught her wrists in his hands and held her away from him. His touch was gentle, incredibly so, but his grip was unbreakable without a fight. "My body betrayed me over and over. I do not even know how many times Xavier used my body to bring himself not only pleasure with other women, but to deliberately have a child with them so he could use the child's blood."

"I do not understand what you are saying to me." Her eyes met his. Held there.

"I am saying this is dangerous. You are my lifemate and everything in me demands I claim you. Once I weld us together it is for all time. I would not do that to you when it is so dangerous. You seemingly purged Xavier, but I was weak enough once that he managed to place not one but four pieces of himself into me. He used me for abhorrent, vile crimes. There are children in the world who suffered horribly because of my body. I do not know them. I would not recognize them if I saw them."

"You would," she denied, believing her words. "You would recognize them."

"The healer and the prince tentatively accepted me, but only because I was with you. You would live the life of an outcast should you join with me."

Ivory shook her head. "You are so noble, Razvan, always putting others before yourself, but, in truth, you have not thought this all the way through." *What was she saying?* Ivory was appalled at herself, arguing with him as if she wanted him to claim her. When had her feminine nature become so perverse that she wanted him to want her, even though she would never accept his claim? What in the world had gotten into her? She must be far lonelier than she realized. She enjoyed her life. She had chosen her life. She licked her lips, tasting him. Craving him.

"I am sorry. I do not know what got into me." She turned away from him, but he didn't loosen his hold on her wrists, forcing her back to him.

"Do not do that. I would never reject the one person I want in my life. Though you have studied Xavier, you do not know how truly evil he is. If he knew you meant everything to me, that you are the reason I still live, then he would cease trying to find me and turn everything he has to acquiring you. I cannot allow that to happen. You are the one person I would trade my soul for. He cannot know that."

She strained away a second time and he pulled her back, forcing her gaze to meet his, his grip firm, but still as gentle as ever, disarming her.

"I would trade everything, even honor, for you. It is the one thing I have kept intact all these long years. I endured much for honor."

She nodded slowly. "Until I experienced the compulsion myself, I had no idea of the draw between lifemates."

He shook his head slowly, still holding her gaze. "It is more than the draw between lifemates—much more. I have been inside your head. I have studied your home and the drawings you so patiently carved into the rock. Everything about you appeals to me. Every moment in your company only makes those feelings stronger. Perhaps the pull between us is strong physically because we are lifemates, but the pull on my heart and soul is equally as strong."

She drew in her breath. "Thank you for that." She would hold his words to her. They were spoken in truth. She knew purity when she heard it. "We must feed before we return to our lair, and I should erase the memories of the farmer and his wife so they do not inadvertently speak of this and draw Xavier's attention."

"I touched his mind." Razvan brought up each of Ivory's hands and pressed his mouth to the sensitive skin on her inner wrists where he'd been holding her. "The farmer would have fought for you, knowing he was going to die. He is a good man."

"I liked his wife as well. I am glad we found them before it was too late. Very few vampires dare to enter into the territory protected by hunters. This is just outside the hunter's range. I come here often to check, and even here, probably because the vampires disappear when they come this way, this region stays fairly safe—at least until recently, since Xavier has expanded his territories."

Ivory stepped back away from him. She should have been shaken up by his rejection of her blatant advances, but, instead, she felt comforted and . . . cared for. She hadn't felt that way in more than a century. She found herself smiling up at him. His answering smile was slow in coming, but it warmed her.

Ivory paused and allowed her senses to flare out to search the night for other hidden dangers. A fox was close, searching for stray chickens that might have missed the lockdown for the night. A few mice hid from an owl circling overhead. She touched the owl several times to make certain it wasn't something else in bird form, but it was diligently hunting for a meal and not at all interested in what was happening in the human world.

She could feel Razvan's light touch as he followed her lead. The thing that stood out was his absolute lack of ego, which made for an extremely weightless touch, nearly impossible to detect. He would be a huge asset to any hunt just for that alone, but, if he could plan battles in the way that he said, the two of them would have an even better chance to stop Xavier.

She touched the few floating clouds last, careful to examine each one to make certain they were genuine. When she went to step from the stable, Razvan stopped her with a touch to her shoulder.

"You did not search below the earth. That is Xavier's

realm and he sends every spy through the tunnels the worms dig for him. In a recent battle, he went himself, using my body, to try to murder my sister and the prince. Another time he tried to kill Shea, the sister-in-law of the prince and her unborn child. I would fear the ground more than any other method of travel."

"I can sense the passage of the worms."

"He sends spies in very small forms now. Scorpions and insects have become his allies. He uses others from another realm, such as the shadow warriors he has drawn against their wills from the ranks of the dead, but other much more demonic creatures as well."

"He has never used insects to spy."

"He has always used them, he just mutates them. You are looking for his mutations."

Ivory let her breath out while she processed the information. "That explains a few things. You do know a lot about him."

"I have been with him since my fourteenth year. I have been present for most of his experiments, if not all."

Her eyes widened and her heart jumped. "He allowed you to watch him as he cast and wrote his spells?"

He nodded. "My sister was always good with spells. I have never been good. Once he recognized that, he did not fear my presence."

"But you have a good memory."

"I remember everything down to the smallest detail. That is why I am gifted when it comes to planning battles." He wasn't bragging, he was merely stating a fact.

Excitement coursed through her. "I really want to get this straight. You were present when he conducted his experiments and cast his spells? For his mutations? To bring the shadow warriors under his command? All of it?"

"He likes to brag. He needs admiration. He needs someone to know he is smarter than the rest of the world. He has few students. I can identify the mages helping him. Most fear him too much to be anywhere near him, and they should. He has no loyalty toward anyone. If he needs blood or a body for an experiment and he cannot get anyone else, he will lure an assistant to his death. I was extremely handy to have around. I had Carpathian blood he could drain from me, and he could brag."

A small humorless smile curved his mouth. "For years I was able to disguise my blood and my abilities, until he took me over so completely. I paid for the indiscretion of besting him, as well as for trying to warn my daughter and sister. But it was worth it to know he was not entirely invincible."

"I cannot imagine your life, or how you stayed sane."

Razvan's smile softened into the real thing. "No more than you, hacked to pieces and left for the wolves. Only you would have found a way to persuade the wolves to aid you. Your voice is an amazing asset, but it is your will that intrigues me."

"Some would say I am too pushy and obstinate."

"Some do not know you."

Again her stomach did that fluttery thing she was coming to associate as a very feminine response to him. It didn't upset her quite so much now that he admitted he was more affected by her than she had known.

She turned her attention to the ground, this time paying attention to the smallest insect. There was life beneath the snow, hiding in the richness of the soil and beneath the boulders and roots. She didn't detect even a small hint of evil, but she remained silent, allowing Razvan to examine the ground. He had lived his life with Xavier, and knew every secret experiment, knew his habits. Her excitement at the prospect of working with him, of tapping into such a source of knowledge was growing.

She believed in her own abilities. She had studied Xavier's ways and she believed she could unravel his spells and build counterspells to reverse his evil experiments if she knew the exact spell. If Razvan had really been present and could remember the exact wording, they would have a real advantage.

"I think we are safe," Razvan said, "although that fox is hungry and may decide you look a fine, tasty treat."

"Are you saying I look like a chicken?"

"Well, your feathers seem to be a little ruffled."

She found herself laughing when she never laughed. Razvan was just plain fun. Maybe having someone to share life with made things fun. Whatever it was, she hoped she could hold on to it, even though the prospect was a little frightening, just because she'd never really had much to lose before.

She moved ahead of him, striding across the snow. Razvan followed a step or so behind, gliding to her left. She realized he was allowing the wolves to guard her back and he was taking up a position on her weakest side. Very few would discern that she had a weak side. She practiced all the time, using either hand to throw, shooting the crossbow with either hand and generally working to make both sides even, but she just wasn't quite as quick with the left. He had a good eye for assessing an enemy.

Or a partner.

They were getting used to sliding in and out of each other's mind. From a warrior's point of view, that was a huge asset; from a woman's maybe not as much.

"Why?" Razvan sounded genuinely curious.

She flicked him an under the lashes glance, assessing his expression, but as always he had that same mantle of calm surrounding him. "This is not easy for me. I have unexpected feelings that I have no idea how to cope with." The admission was truthful because she could do no less than be entirely candid with him. He was honest and she needed to meet his integrity with honor of her own.

His smile not only encompassed her, flooding her with warmth, but it made her feel like part of something else—something bigger than herself. "That makes two of us."

The farmer stepped out from his house and into the snow. There was blood on his arms, defense wounds, Ivory saw. His wife came out and stood slightly behind him. The farmer looked very nervous.

Ivory smiled at them to reassure them. "He is gone from this world and we will erase all evidence of his passing."

"You are hunters," the farmer greeted, his voice neutral, neither welcoming nor rejecting. "There have been persistent rumors. We have never encountered a creature so evil." His eyes skittered back and forth, indicating his nervousness.

Behind him, hidden mostly from their view, his wife shuddered. Ivory looked at the small dwelling. Strings of garlic hung in the window. A cross was carved into the door. The farmer's fingers drummed against his thigh over and over.

Razvan stepped up, a casual movement, but slightly in front of Ivory. He bowed slightly toward the farmer. Ivory could feel the stillness in him. His eyes moved over and around the cabin, continually scanning around them. He had been perfectly relaxed before, but now he felt coiled and ready to strike.

Something is wrong. She kept her expression serene, but she went on alert.

I do not know what is wrong, Razvan mused. *Something. Something is off.* He paused.

Ivory opened her mind to encompass the farmer and his wife. As a rule, she could easily touch minds and do a quick read, but there were a few people resistant with barriers. A quick, light touch yielded nothing. The wife stayed slightly behind the husband, her face in the shadows. It would be peculiar and unlikely not to be able to read either of them, yet both minds were as if a clean slate.

Both? Razvan questioned. *The insects. None is near the house. Yes, they are going about their business, but not even an ant is near the dwelling.* He glanced toward the window of the little farmhouse. *Inside, Ivory.*

Ivory kept smiling, but her mind expanded further, reaching into the house to find the children. A boy and girl. Both terrified. Where was the threat coming from? Why hadn't either of them sensed it? *Only a master . . .* She broke off the thought, her heart thudding. She kept her eyes level with the farmer's. If she was right and a master vampire was in that room with the children, if the farmer realized she knew, so, then, would the vampire.

Only a master could keep his presence unknown, she explained. *He would control both of them and the children, too, to keep them from betraying his presence. He must have been recruiting the newly turned. A master will often use a lesser vampire as a pawn.*

Ivory steeled herself. It had to be Sergey. There wouldn't be more than one master in an area, not even related. They might have formed a coalition, but no master vampire's ego would allow him to be too long in the presence of another without serious infighting. She would have to face him again, unless she was lucky enough that he ran when he realized there were two hunters, not one.

She gripped her crossbow in preparation. *What we have to do for a meal is ridiculous.*

The fingers tapping on the farmer's thigh turned to a fist. He shuddered and reached for something positioned just out of sight behind a porch post.

The vampire has taken control of them. O köd belső—darkness take it. I do not want to have to kill a good man.

Razvan smiled at the farmer, but stepped back, forcing Ivory to do the same. *Are you adept enough to take them back?*

From a master vampire? Ivory hesitated. *I do not know. Probably not. Even with two of us, Razvan, we might not defeat him. To hear the voice of a master, you must listen with more than your ears or they can enthrall you. Put your arm around me. Stay to my left side and stay free of the coat.*

Razvan did as she asked without hesitation, sliding his arm around her waist while smiling amicably at the couple on the porch.

Ivory bowed slightly. "I hope that you both have a long and prosperous life."

He will expect us to attempt to erase their memories. As Ivory explained she took a step back, as if they were leaving. *When I go to do it, he will most likely strike at me, at my mind. If you join with me, we will be far stronger and we will have a chance, but we might not live through this. Now is the time to walk away if you wish to fight another day.*

But you will fight for these strangers. He made it a statement.

She was not going to allow Sergey to take any more from her than had already been taken. *I have to.* It was that simple. She no longer knew if she was driven by honor, but she could not walk away from these people and allow

Sergey to murder their children and turn them both into the walking dead. *I have to, but you do not.*

Razvan flicked her one telling glance of reprimand. *Tell me what you want me to do.*

She allowed a small smile in her mind to warm him, her only offering of thanks when they could both lose their lives. *Merge with me. He will strike hard and fast, hammering at me to get in, especially if I can manage to free the couple from him. You will have to hold.*

Ivory turned to the couple, lifted her hands to the sky and chanted.

I call to air, earth, fire and water,
I ask you to send me the voice of power.
Deep within these darkened souls,
Send forth my voice so that which is dark may be
    seen and unfold.
Allow what was hidden to now be seen,
So that I may cast out that which is unholy and
    unclean.

As Ivory chanted, Razvan felt the force of the vampire's attempted entry, battering at their shared minds. The blow nearly drove him to his knees, shattering all preconceived notions of power. The sky darkened and the ground shook. Pieces of the roof splintered off into large spears and hurtled down on them. The ground heaved upward, and scorpions poured out of the earth, blackening the snow, a moving carpet of lethal insects.

Razvan instinctively shoved Ivory away from him and took to the sky, going up and over the disintegrating porch roof. The rapidly gathering storm clouds burst, raining acid drops, so that everything the liquid dots hit sizzled and burned. Trees shrieked, the branches trembled, leaves and needles withering under the deadly assault.

Ivory spun away from the swarming insects, rushing the porch, yanking the man and woman up into her arms. The farmer dropped the pitchfork he'd grabbed, shocked that the vampire had controlled him. At least Ivory had managed to break them both free of the vampire's hold, but she felt it was due more to him orchestrating his attack then her strength pitted against his.

"My children," the woman sobbed.

Ivory tried to protect their skin as she carried them to the meager shelter of the trees. The acid rain poured down, burning through the wolf pelts so that the animals shifted and shrieked in pain. The woman screamed as drops sizzled over her arms, but Ivory, with a renewed burst of speed, moved them into the thicker canopy.

"Stay here. We will get the children free of him. My wolves will protect you."

She turned back to aid Razvan in the rescue of the children, streaming through the fiery burn of the rain while her skin burned to the bone.

Razvan streamed down the chimney, and into the tiny room. A boy of perhaps ten lay sprawled on the floor, blood smearing his mouth. The little girl, with a bone-white complexion and eyes too big for her little face, looked to be no more than five. The vampire laughed as he ripped at her neck, his teeth tearing into tender flesh.

The sight sickened Razvan, conjuring up too many memories, the feel of his own teeth tearing into childish skin. His stomach heaved. He had no experience fighting, but he had power and strength and determination beyond anything conceived of by the undead. It mattered not at all to him whether he lived or died, or how much suffering it took to extract the child. The vampire, on the other hand, wanted to live.

Razvan sped across the room like a human bullet, taking his human form at the last possible moment, slamming his fist deep into the wall of Sergey's chest while dragging the child out of his arms and tossing her toward her brother. She landed like a rag doll, broken and sprawled out across the sheep rug.

"Press your hand to the wound on her neck," Razvan snarled at the boy. "Press it hard."

Razvan stared into the vampire's hideous face, the stretched skin over the skull, the pitiless eyes, the jagged teeth stained with the fresh blood of the child. Sergey's lips peeled back in something between a snarl and a smirk. He bent his head and bit down savagely on Razvan's shoulder, the rows of teeth meeting through the muscle, ripping through sinew and bone, tearing at the flesh and devouring great gulps of precious blood. His hand clawed deep through the heavy muscled chest, burrowing relentlessly toward Razvan's heart.

Razvan turned his head calmly to look at the boy as if he wasn't being eaten alive by the monstrous demon tearing at his flesh. "Take your sister and go to the silver wolf pack. They will take you to the next village. Ask for a man named Mikhail. He will heal your sister and protect both of you. Run, do not look back."

His voice never changed, never trembled or showed pain. His hand, inside Sergey's chest seeking the blackened heart, was met with razor-sharp intestines, twisting and pulling around his fist, biting deep into the skin, acid blood pouring over him like molten-hot lava, but he was every bit as relentless as Sergey, refusing to back away.

"I do not mind dying, *hän ku vie elidet*—thief of life. What of you? Are you prepared for your final justice?"

The undead did not respond, and instead continued to rip and tear great chunks of flesh from Razvan's shoulder and neck. Ivory burst into the room, firing the crossbow, the first coated arrow hitting Sergey in his eye. She fired as she ran, hitting his throat as his head arched back. The third went into the open mouth, lodging in the throat. Sergey screamed, his voice so high-pitched the glass in the windows exploded. He jerked backward, taking Razvan with him, one arm shifting until it took on the shape of the beak of a hungry raptor.

As the beak clamped down around Razvan's arm, viciously slicing through flesh and bone, cutting it completely in two, the vampire hissed at him. "I will cut you in pieces and feed them to the wolves, and then I will devour those children."

Razvan staggered back. Blood sprayed across the room. Sergey gripped the stump of Razvan's forearm and yanked, drawing the fist from his chest and dropping it on the floor, before kicking it away in disgust. The vampire jerked at the arrow in his throat and hurled it toward Razvan with tremendous force.

Razvan moved with blurring speed, his one hand shooting out to catch the metal shaft in midair, reverse it and slam it down hard on the top of the vampire's foot, driving the arrow through the top all the way to the floor.

We have to slow him down. He will go after the children just for spite.

"Get away from him!" Ivory warned.

"Too late," Sergey snarled.

Even as Ivory leapt to cross the distance between them, Sergey whirled, a long sword in his hand. He sliced across

Razvan's shoulder and down his chest, carving more pieces. Razvan staggered and went down. Sergey slammed the blade toward his ankle. She met blade with blade, the force going up her arm and through her body as sparks flew and the sound rang in her ear. Razvan was eerily silent, but his hand gripped a knife of his own as he waited for an opportunity to aid her.

Sergey laughed, the sound cruelly malicious. "I will chop him up, piece by piece, as they did you, and I will feed them to your own wolf pack. I might let you live, sister dear, just to see you weep for the loss of your lifemate. You must learn who is strong and who is weak. You are on the wrong side. Join me. Let us cut him up together and I might spare you."

Ivory's heart pounded. Her body jerked in response to the sight of her lifemate's body in pieces. There was a hole in his chest and his arm was in two pieces, slices through his shoulder and chest and one leg, his blood a terrible fountain, pouring over the floor.

Ivory knew that the vampire was the vilest of all creatures. The one before her no longer even resembled her brother, although he tried to keep up the illusion with the hope that it would cause her pain and make her hesitate, throwing off her aim. He had deliberately chosen to tear at a child's flesh and to hack Razvan into pieces, bringing forth some of their worst nightmarish memories to make the battle all the more difficult. She gripped her sword harder and stepped between her lifemate and the undead who had once been a beloved brother.

"Kill me, then. But I am taking you with me."

9

The vampire jerked the remaining arrows from his body and tossed them contemptuously onto the floor. "So be it," Sergey said and thrust his sword straight toward her stomach.

Ivory parried, jumping to the side. Too late she realized the vampire had deliberately driven her away from Razvan. She lunged back, but Sergey struck again, slicing through Razvan's leg a second time, the cut deep enough to go through bone. Her blade raced toward the vampire's skull, but he dissolved and materialized across the room.

Stop thinking about me and fight him the way you always fight.

In the moment that Razvan spoke, every agonizing stroke of the blade flooded back to her, as the vampires chopped her into pieces much the same way Sergey was doing to Razvan. Methodically. Relentlessly. Mercilessly.

Do not try to save me. Think only of killing him.

I cannot defeat him. He was a great warrior. He taught me to fight. He is a master vampire. Even our strongest hunters rarely can defeat them alone.

Who better than you to fight him? You know his every move before he makes it. You have changed over the centuries. He will be expecting that young woman he taught, not the seasoned warrior you have become. He is preying on your emotions. Do not be tricked by one such as he. You are a great warrior, and you, better than any other, can defeat him.

Around them the house began to shake, the walls undulating and breaking apart so that debris rained down on the vampire. Ivory knew Razvan couldn't move with his agonizing, mortal wounds, but was buying her time to regroup, using what remaining energy he had, not to attempt to burrow into the ground, but rather to use his powers to aid her.

Ivory took a deep breath and let it out. Razvan may have been inexperienced, but he had the heart and soul of a warrior—like she did. Never had she seen another warrior so courageous, so stoic. She took another deep breath and let it out, allowing a mantle of calm to settle over her. Razvan was right. She could not allow her feelings to interfere with her primary job. She was a warrior first, a woman second.

She forced herself to look only at the vampire—to see only the vampire. As long as she could keep Sergey focused on her and away from Razvan, she might be able to keep her lifemate alive and slay the vampire. What weapons could be used against this master? Vanity was the one trait that not only all the undead shared, but her brothers in particular.

She changed her appearance subtly, very slowly, softening her features to take on a younger, more girlish look—as in the old days, long before the centuries had passed, when her brothers had loved and cherished her more than their own egos.

Sergey lifted his sword and touched it to his forehead in a mock salute, allowing her to see Razvan's blood running down the blade to the hilt. The ruby drops coated his hand and, with his gaze locked with hers, he licked at the blood.

Her stomach knotted, but she tilted her head to one side and laughed, a taunting, tinkling sound, like that of a young, giddy girl. "You have grown old, Sergey. I thought with all your intelligence and experience, you would become, at the very least, a master vampire, one so powerful it would take our strongest hunters to ban together to defeat you. Yet here you are, struggling to vanquish a woman, your baby sister."

His eyes glowed with fire. She could actually see tiny flames burning in the dark depths. She had been correct in thinking the way to shake him was through his enormous ego. Sergey swung the sword at her neck, slicing through the air with such force that, when she ducked and ran her own sword into his side, the momentum from his swing actually carried him away from her. He screamed, the sound a mixture of pain and rage.

The floor erupted beneath her feet, splintering, so that she nearly fell through. But thanks to her many lessons from her brothers, she was dancing out of the way of the falling floorboards. She could smell the rich soil beckoning from the various holes in the floor.

"Oh dear, you have gotten slow, haven't you? You are nothing more than a weak, withered shadow of your former self. In the days past, one look from you would have crushed me, let alone the might of your sword, but now you play games like the puny coward you are, the way a shriveled and fading old man might play chess with trembling fingers and a mind forgetting the moves."

Can you bring the rest of the roof down on him? she asked Razvan, hating for him to use up his strength, but needing a distraction.

Of course. There was no hesitation, but she was beginning to know Razvan and his iron will. He wouldn't hesitate, no matter the cost to him.

The roof crumbled with a thunderous roar, the wood and dirt once more falling on Sergey's head and shoulders. It wasn't nearly as effective as the first time, but it bought her the seconds she needed. Ivory tossed the sword to the ground beside Razvan's hand and jerked out the small, handmade laser. It was powered by a diamond she'd cut herself.

Sergey dissolved to avoid the wood and dirt raining from the roof as the house shook apart. He materialized just behind Ivory, but three wooden boards with jagged points came hurtling at him with breakneck speed, forcing him to dissolve again. Each time he flowed past Razvan the blade sliced another deep cut. Ivory timed him this time, letting loose a blast of white-hot energy that did some slicing of its own. The blade of light didn't cut all the way through his skull, but the letter T was very prominent.

Black blood splattered across the crumbling walls. A foul stench filled the air, as if a corpse was rotting from the inside out.

"The stamp of a traitor. Wear it proudly. It will not come off." Ivory inclined her head, the princess acknowledging something crawling beneath her feet. She ran toward him, firing the crossbow rapidly, the arrows running up his body and preventing him from shifting, giving her a straight line up his chest to the wizened heart.

Thin lips peeled back in a snarl, Sergey sprang to meet her, ripping at one of the arrows and slamming it home just over her heart as she plunged her fist into his chest. As her hand burrowed deep, his intestines wrapped around her fist and wrist, sawing away at her skin, opening deep lacerations, allowing the poisonous vampire blood to pour inside the wounds.

Sergey stood toe to toe with her, the black holes that were his eyes staring mercilessly down into her eyes. He twisted and dragged the arrow out of her body and plunged it in a second time. "Feel that?" he hissed. "Dear sister. Beloved sister. This is how much I love you. I will bring you to our side. We will rule the earth soon and you will be part of us, one with us. I do this for you."

The tone was very much that of the brother she had lost, but his face was a mask of evil, his eyes two hot coals glowing deep ruby-red. His breath was fetid in her face, burning her skin, singeing her eyebrows. She tried to keep her hand moving forward to find the shriveled heart, but the cuts were too deep and she was in danger of losing her hand. Gritting her teeth, she pushed harder, trying to move through those heavy muscles to gain the heart.

Sergey slammed his fist into her chest, intending to drive not only the arrow deep into her heart, but his own hand, using his strength and speed to outrace her for her heart. For a moment the crosses coated in holy water burned through his hand, straight to the bone so that he howled and screamed in rage, spittle running from his mouth. He flung back his head, enduring the pain, trying to push past that holy line of defense.

A flame burst from the sky above them, a fiery blast that slammed hard into Sergey's back. The vampire was driven forward onto Ivory's arm. Her fingers scraped the edge of the withered organ. Elated, she ignored the agony as the razor-sharp bands tightened around her hand and wrist and dug deeper.

Sergey screamed, the sound blowing apart the rest of the house, reducing the wood to spears, hundreds of them flying through the air from every direction at both Razvan and Ivory. With his last remaining strength, Razvan threw a barrier around Ivory's back and the top of her head to prevent penetration of the sharp spears. Half a dozen drove through his body, staking him to the floor.

Sergey swept Ivory's legs out from under her. She went down hard, slipping in the pools of blood covering the floor. Sergey staggered back, his face a twisted mask of hatred. Before he could slam his fist deep into her chest, she surged to her feet, leaping in the very motion Sergey had taught her as a young child.

Ivory smiled at him, deliberately locking her gaze with his as he had when he'd licked at Razvan's blood. She knew there was a gaping hole in her chest where he'd tried to reach her heart. Blood dripped steadily, yet she taunted him with a smile. She took a step and went down on one knee, still holding his gaze, watching his eyes narrow, watching the cruel thoughts move through his mind. Keeping their gazes locked, she drove her hand and wrist deep into the welcoming soil. She knew the soil intimately, knew the healing properties. She had lain companion to the minerals and elements for a hundred years.

She whispered to the earth in the ancient language, the language she knew better than any other, a language close to the earth.

Emä Maye, én, lañad, omasak Teteh. Jälleen jamaak—
  Mother Earth, your daughter stands before you
  wounded once again.
Maye mayed—Earth to earth.
Sív síved—Heart to heart.
Me juttaak elidaban és kalmaban—We are bound
  together in life and death.

189

Pusmasz ainam, juttad lihad—Heal this body, bring
*   together this flesh.*
Te magköszunam, sívam sívadet—I give thanks from
*   my heart to yours.*

She continued, her voice rising and falling with the ebb
and flow of the earth's blood.

Twist this root, break and bend,
Fit the wood to my hand.
Hone the edges, make them sharp,
To pierce deep within that which is aged and dark.
I name you need, fit to my will,
Your making is to stop the evil that would kill.

Sergey came at her as she had known he would, believing her distracted by her wounds, muttering to herself
beneath her breath. As he bent toward her, she jerked her
hand from beneath the soil, newly healed, all traces of the
deep lacerations gone. In her fist was a root, twisted and
sharpened to the finest blade, honed down to the finest ice
pick, and in one smooth, easy move she thrust it up and
straight into his left eye.

He slammed his fist into her throat, knocking her back
and down as he whirled away from her. As he came down
he viciously kicked at Razvan's head. Razvan was already
wielding the heavy sword, swinging it in a brutal cut at the
vampire's calf. Sergey barely moved his leg in time to avoid
most of the blade. The edge caught him enough to cut into
his tendon. The vampire leapt into the air to escape
another blow.

Coming down in a fighting crouch, her weapon already
blazing, Ivory added another letter in the word *traitor* to

his forehead. The laser cut the R so deep it dug into the skull itself.

"Before we are finished here, you will bear the mark of the traitor for our brothers to know that they taught me well. They will be amused that you could not dispatch a woman, your sister-child, so easily," she taunted.

Vampires were vain creatures, especially master vampires. Her brothers had always had large egos, believing they would do a better job ruling the Carpathian people than the prince and a better job of protecting the prince than the Daratrazanoff lineage. He knew when word of his defeat, of the damage done to his body, reached his siblings, he would be the laughing stock of the entire vampire world.

As if knowing it was all true, Razvan laughed, the sound low and taunting, echoing through the surrounding fields and sky.

Sergey shrieked, furious, blood and spittle erupting from his mouth. "You are already dead, weak one. You think I do not know how you crawled on the ground like a dog, following after Xavier for his scraps? You are less than a worm and deserve to die writhing in agony. You pathetic weakling. She will die a hideous death before she joins you in the afterlife."

Ivory put every ounce of contempt she had into her voice. "I will go to my lifemate and live in bliss while you walk through the fires of hell, snarling and spitting and crying like a child for blood. You are nothing, the undead, fodder for our brothers who laugh at your weakness and point fingers at your ineptness."

Sputtering with rage, Sergey clapped his hands together and his voice boomed like thunder, sounding as if it came from a great distance away, and surrounding her, echoing from the sky and coming up from beneath her feet.

Remove all sound from her throat!
Quiet the words that would be spoke.

Ivory instantly felt the effects, her throat closing, so that, even when she opened her mouth, no sound emerged.

He is using a spell Xavier often used on his underlings when he was tired of their questions. He is even using Xavier's voice, Razvan told her. *It is effective in frightening them into obedience because his apprentices believe he is powerful enough to remove their voices permanently.*

Ivory threw her hands into the air and double-time clapped.

Sound abound. Thoughts race by.
Air to lungs, let my voice cry.

She could immediately breathe better, and the air hissed from her mouth in blessed sound.

She replaced Sergey's spell with one of her own, turning his words back on him, although she knew it was temporary and wouldn't last long.

I call to the power deep within,
Remove the sound, quiet the din.
Take away that which is harmful, seal it tight,
Remove the offending orifice from my sight.

When Sergey tried to open his mouth, it was no longer there—a thick scar tissue of skin had grown over the opening, sealing it closed so that he couldn't speak. His face was blank from his nose down. His eyes, widened in alarm, spit venomous hatred at her. The arrows in his chest fell to the ground, eaten through by his acid blood.

He lifted his hands and electricity arced from his fingers, leaping at her.

Ivory dodged sideways, firing more arrows, using the same straight up-and-down pattern as before, marking the line over his heart. The hair on her body stood up as the electricity sizzled and snapped, but when the vampire snapped it like a whip, hurling the energy across the room at her, the force struck an invisible barrier and followed a vapor trail back to lash at Sergey.

Ivory made a second try for the heart, smashing her fist deep, but Sergey turned to the side, catching her wrist and snapping the bone, flinging her from him. As he followed her down, Razvan yanked a spear from his leg with his only hand, impaling Sergey as the force of his momentum carried the undead right onto the spear.

It missed his heart by inches, tearing through his gut. Sergey yanked the pole free and hurtled it at Razvan with vicious force. The warrior knocked it aside with the edge of his hand and retaliated with a weak sweep of the sword.

"You will be known to the vampire world as he who has no voice. They will ridicule you for all time, long centuries should you survive, because a woman defeated you along with her pathetic dog of a lifemate."

Sergey's eyes widened, spun, his nostrils flaring, black blood pouring from his wounds as he nearly exploded in his anger. He threw his arms out wide and energy surged, blowing out the remaining walls. The heavily laden clouds overhead spun and churned, twisting into a long thick spear of lethal ice.

Sergey ripped the arrows from his chest and dissolved, streaming away from them, leaving behind droplets of acid blood. Everywhere the blood fell, it burned through the wood and flooring of the farmer's house.

Ivory took to the air after him. Across the sky, storm clouds gathered in force, lightning rimming the edges, turning the once clear sky an ominous gray. The clouds boiled with activity, bursting upward like mushrooms exploding. The ice spear moved away from her, lightning sparking from its tip as it traveled across the sky.

Sergey must have sealed off his wounds, because the droplets ceased almost immediately. She could give chase, follow that telling spear. He was wounded, yes, but he wasn't really in such bad shape, and, without Razvan to aid her, she wouldn't fare nearly as well. The spell would wear off fast and Sergey would have his fangs back and a burning need for revenge. In the meantime, she would lose Razvan, if she hadn't already.

"Choose who lives and who dies!" Sergey's voice boomed across the sky.

The sound waves burst through her, nearly knocking her backward. Rage poured over her, filling the sky, squeezing hard on her chest. Obviously the spell wore off faster than she'd hoped.

"Give chase. Follow me, little sister, and you may have a chance to save the puny mortals and their disgusting whelps. If not I will kill and feed on them as well as your precious wolf pack. Follow me and your dog of a lifemate dies if he is not already gone from this world. Choose. And live with the choosing."

Ivory reached out to her wolf pack. They were carrying the two children and the two adults across the miles of rugged terrain on their backs, racing toward Mikhail's home deep in the mountains. The pass was still open, but, with the terrible storm brewing, she doubted if it would be for long. If they were forced to take a longer route through the upper mountains, they would be at a disadvantage as Sergey streaked across the sky to intercept them.

The vampire is after you. Call to the prince. Call to the hunters. I cannot aid you. She sent the warning to her beloved brothers and sisters. It was all she could do, she realized with a sinking heart. She could not allow Razvan to die.

There was a stirring in her mind. Weak. Flickering. *Save the children.*

She refused to argue, to answer. She would not let Razvan die. Ivory turned back, circling the farm once to make certain there was no feel of danger before she dropped down into the remains of what once had been a snug house. There was blood and flesh and bone, splintered walls and mud and debris. There was Razvan lying on the floor in a pool of blood, his arm and hand a distance away.

Ivory returned the pieces to his body. Five spears remained in his body, along with a large hole where the sixth had been. She drew a deep, shuddering breath. His sides heaved as he tried to drag in air. His eyes were closed, and all wound sites were sealed, although there was enough blood on the floor to make her think it was too late to seal anything off.

I need to know that you live. His voice came into her head from far away. *Heal your wounds quickly so I can leave you in peace.*

"You cannot go. I will not allow it. I mean it, Razvan, you must live." She bent close to him so that her breath was warm against his cold skin. "I need you. Do you hear me? I need you. You *must* live for me."

Remove the spears.

"I know they hurt, Razvan, but you will die if I do. Give me a minute."

195

I am already dead.

"No, you cannot think that way." Ivory knelt beside Razvan, pulling his head into her lap. She bent low over him again. "Listen to me. You cannot go from this life. We have not done what we know is possible together."

You ask the impossible.

She switched to telepathic communication, as it was easier for him. *I asked it of myself first. I know how difficult it is when no one else does. I know what I ask, know what I demand of you, of my lifemate. If you go, we go together. Bind us. Bind us now. It will give me what I need to save you.*

Razvan didn't open his eyes. His hand moved in hers, the fingers slippery with blood. *You wish me to live through this?*

We can defeat Xavier. We must defeat him. Bind us together. I will lead you now and follow you in the years to come. Bind us now, before you are gone from me.

Ivory forced back the burning tears, the terrible weight in her chest and the feel of her own wounds so little in comparison. He *had* to want her enough to live. Had to want to defeat Xavier enough. His will, so strong, had to match her own. Warriors, after so many centuries of loneliness, often embraced death. They could rest at long last, but she wasn't giving him up without a fight.

Razvan moved in her mind, searching. Whatever he found there, he came to a decision, even knowing the agony he would suffer. *I can think of no other I have met in my lifetime who I would rather have. If you accept me . . .*

Absolutely I do. Time was running out. He had lost too much blood. He had cauterized the wounds, so many, as Sergey sliced him into pieces, making his body a patchwork imitation of hers. But the blood loss was severe.

196

You are certain you wish to bind your life to mine with all it entails?

She answered without hesitation. *I am.*

So be it. His voice strengthened. *You are my lifemate. I claim you as my lifemate. I belong to you. I offer my life for you. I give you my protection. I give you my allegiance. I give you my heart. I give you my soul. I give you my body. I take into my keeping the same that is yours. Your life will be cherished by me for all my time. Your life will be placed above my own for all time. You are my lifemate. You are bound to me for all eternity. You are always in my care.* He opened his eyes and looked into hers. *Te avio päläfertiilam.*

Ivory felt the threads binding them together. The two halves of their souls merged as one. She pressed a kiss to his forehead, her voice a soft whisper. "I accept with my heart and soul your offer. I take your soul. I take your body. I take your heart. You are one with me. I take you into my keeping and bind you for all eternity with my strength and will and our combined determination. *Te avio päläferti-ilam*—you are my lifemate and I refuse to allow you to leave this world. Let your soul dwell within mine."

Razvan closed his eyes with his impossibly long lashes. A small satisfied smile curved his mouth. *I have given myself to you, lifemate. Do what you must.*

Long ago, when Xavier and Draven had sentenced her to die a horrendous death, it was not only her Carpathian blood and body, driven to repair itself and heal in the soil, that had saved her. It was a combination of those things, along with her will and Xavier's teachings. Xavier would have torn out his hair had he known how she had taken so many of his hexes and made them her own, putting her faith of a higher power into the weaving of each spell, twisting the curse into something for good.

This will hurt as much or more than the worst torture Xavier thought to put you through. Let yourself drift away, your soul and spirit in my safekeeping. She tried to warn him, choking back a sob. She knew from experience what she was asking to put him through.

She wept when she felt the flickering of warmth move through her mind, his life spirit a flickering dim light she now held in her soul. She began the work of removing all parasites from his body before closing off each wound and cauterizing it. All the while she worked, she switched between the Carpathian healing chant and the healing spell she had used on herself when asking Mother Earth to aid her.

I call upon the power of earth, she who creates us
   all. Hear my call, Mother.
I ask for clear sight—the ability to see that which
   seeks not to be seen.
Guide me, Mother. Take my hands make them
   your own.
Use them to mend that which has been broken,
   torn.
Guide me, Mother. Provide rest and healing to a
   tortured soul.
Embrace him, Mother. Heal him of all injuries.
   Guide him, Mother.
I call upon the higher power. Use me as your vessel.
   See through my eyes.
Look into my soul. Use me as a tool. Guard us,
   great one. Take us into your care. Nurture us as
   you would a child. Guide us with your
   knowledge.
So that we may arise once again to fight.

Her voice rose and fell as she called to the powers who had aided her centuries earlier in her need, rocking back and forth, heedless of her own wounds, caring only that Razvan, her lifemate, was spared.

Mikhail Dubrinsky, prince of the Carpathian people, heard the call of wolves long before they reached his house deep in the forest. *Gregori.* He summoned his second-in-command and best friend. *I have urgent need of you. Hunters, heed my call. I have urgent need of you.* He sent the command out on the common Carpathian telepathic pathway, summoning all who were close.

Safeguarding his home, Mikhail took to the air to intercept the wolf pack. They were still miles away, but the distress in their calls was profound. He sped through the thick canopy of trees, sending his senses out before him, trying to discern the danger following the wolf pack.

There was blood on the wind, and a foul stench that could only be attributed to the undead. Rotting flesh and poison. Humans.

Wait for me, Gregori demanded. *I am but a few minutes behind you. It could be a trap.*

I feel children. Blood. Terror. The wolves are calling. Which meant he wasn't waiting.

As Mikhail flew, another owl came up on his right, a second on his left. He identified both. Natalya, sister to Razvan, and her lifemate, Vikirnoff. Neither asked questions as they raced across the night sky with him toward the calling wolf pack. Overhead the storm clouds thickened, rolling and churning—boiling with anger. Flecks of white-hot energy lit up the edges of the cloud formations.

Ice rained down, sharp spears meant to slow the fleeing pack.

Vampire, Mikhail identified. *He pursues the wolf pack and whatever they guard.* He was already moving with blurring speed, and he pushed himself, forging ahead of the other two ancient warriors.

Mikhail. Gregori hissed a warning. *We do not know what we face.*

I believe it is clear enough. Mikhail ignored the rumblings of his bodyguard and slipped lower in the trees as the ice began to penetrate even the thick canopy.

A wolf howled, a child cried out. A woman screamed. Mikhail could hear them clearly now.

"Go, take the children. Leave us. You will travel faster," a man's voice rang out. "We'll try to slow him down."

The pack gave voice again, whether in protest or agreement, Mikhail couldn't guess. The wind rose to a howling shriek, blasting through the trees with hurricane force, uprooting several trees. As the large trunks struck other trees, they fell in a domino effect, pointing like an arrow in the direction the wolf pack had gone.

The force of the biting cold wind flung the three Carpathians back through the sky and into the path of the falling ice. Mikhail felt a sharp point pierce his arm and he dissolved instantly, although the wind pushed him farther from the pack. The storm increased in strength, dumping huge amounts of snow from the sky until the ice was so thick and dangerous they could not continue forward in the air.

Drop down, we will have to run to meet them from the ground.

Gregori growled at him, this time much closer. Vikirnoff said nothing at all as his prince hit the ground running, but he moved into a better position to protect the man. Natalya paced just behind him, watching their back-trail.

This wolf pack is unusual, Vikirnoff ventured. *They are using the ancient path of telepathic communication to call for aid. And they call us, not other wolves.*

These have to be the wolves that travel with Ivory Malinov, Mikhail explained.

He had, of course, given the news to Natalya that her twin brother was alive and had escaped at long last from Xavier. He, along with Gregori, had informed her of everything that had happened, and of Gregori's firm belief that Razvan's crimes had been committed when Xavier either possessed his body or his mind. The news of both Ivory and Razvan's appearance, and that they were lifemates, had spread through the entire Carpathian community.

He knew they were all suspicious of Razvan, particularly Vikirnoff, who had shielded Natalya so many times from her brother in the past. She had suffered emotionally, finally accepting the loss of her brother, and now both were distressed. He could only give his opinion that Razvan had been wronged these years, and was not the criminal and traitor the Carpathian world believed him to be—but he knew they would all have to make up their own minds about the man.

I do not sense a Carpathian traveling with them, man or woman. Vikirnoff kept exact pace with the prince, shielding him as they moved in and out among the snow-laden trees. *How can the wolves understand and call to us? How is it they can carry such heavy burdens on their backs and run with such speed?*

It appears they are Carpathian. Mikhail had no explanation for how that had come to be, but he knew Ivory had one. If she had converted the wolves, it had been a dangerous venture. Intelligent wolves craving human blood could be the biggest nightmare of all—especially if they bred. He would have to weigh the fate of that pack.

The ice rained down, but the group was at least afforded some shelter from the vicious wind and the stabbing icicles by the twisted branches overhead. Vikirnoff added a protective buffer, weaving the branches tighter so they formed a tunnel.

They carry humans on their backs, Natalya said.

Her heart pounded hard. A part of her was desperate to see her brother, desperate to believe he wasn't the monster she'd come to believe him to be, but the sane half of her whispered that none of the rumors could be true. As she ran with her lifemate and the prince, she found herself praying.

Beneath their feet the ground rolled. The weight of the heavy snow toppled a large tree, the roots springing up from the ground, forming a tangled barrier.

The vampire delays us, Mikhail said. *Gregori, swing around to the north. Come in from the other side with Falcon. His goal seems to be to reach the wolf pack before us. He must mean to slay the humans, but for what purpose I have no idea.*

I am put on this earth to guard my prince, not save the lives of mortals we do not know.

Mikhail sighed. *You grow more stubborn with each passing year, old friend. Vikirnoff is guarding your helpless chick. Come in from the north. Direct the others to come in from the other side. And stop giving me trouble.*

Gregori gave the equivalent of a telepathic snort. *I would not count on that happening anytime soon. The vampire races to close the pass. You cannot be caught on the ground if that should happen.*

It will not happen, because you will be stopping him. There was every confidence in Mikhail's voice.

You do not ask for much.

No. A chance to practice and hone your fading skills.

Gregori's amusement burst over Mikhail as the prince increased his speed. It felt good to be a warrior instead of a ruler, rushing through the forest in answer to a call of distress. His muscles stretched and contracted, and his body rejoiced in the exercise, running tirelessly, weaving in and out of the trees.

Overhead, a thick ice spear burst across the sky, shattering clouds of ice and snow, raining glittering sparks of gold and silver down on the trees as it arced above them and then fell toward earth out of sight. Everywhere the sparks touched, the trees froze, turning a ghastly white, the color spreading like a disease along branches and needles, down the trunks to the ground itself, where the forest floor buckled under the icy pressure.

The heaving ground cracked, jagged fissures opening, so they were forced to leap over the widening cracks as they ran. Sharp ice towers erupted from the ground. Trees cracked and splintered as the spreading cold snapped brittle branches.

Where's it coming from? Mikhail demanded. *We have to find the source.*

He is trying to slow down the wolf pack, Gregori hissed. *I have heard, but never seen, an ice spear that freezes everything in its immediate vicinity. You must be close to it. Break off and deal with it, and I will find the pack.*

We're too close to the pack, Gregori, closer than you are. You're better equipped to work your magic against an ice spear capable of freezing a forest. Break off and go after it.

Not on your life. Send Falcon. Nothing is going to stop me from fighting at your side.

For one, I am supposed to command. You do not listen to my orders.

Was that an order? I didn't hear an order in there anywhere. I've sent Falcon to deal with the ice spear.

Mikhail found himself laughing again. It was impossible to be frustrated with Gregori; he'd known him too many years, and Gregori's primary job would always be to see to the safety of the prince. He was still smarting from Razvan shoving a knife to Mikhail's throat. There hadn't been nearly as much danger as it appeared, but Gregori still didn't like that Razvan had gotten close to the prince.

The wolf pack raised their voices again and he lifted his head and answered as he raced over the frozen river. With each step they took, more jagged ice towers erupted, so they were forced to dodge as they ran, but Mikhail could feel the strength of the attack weakening. The vampire was close to the pack and wanted to direct his energy there. Not knowing what the wolves were capable of, Mikhail redoubled his efforts to reach them, taking to the air, avoiding the higher skies where the icicles could hinder them.

He caught sight of the running pack as they came around a bend in the river, streaks of silver with the burden of humans on their back, running tirelessly toward them on the ice. One child was slumped over the alpha's body, and blood streaked his thick fur. Out of the corner of his eyes, Mikhail saw a massive black cloud moving fast across the sky toward the wolves.

Get into the trees. Get off the river and away from the open, he warned.

Vikirnoff actually swerved into him before he could turn toward the riverbank, packed high with snow. Mikhail shot him a quelling look as he streaked through the trees toward the running pack. The two alphas with the children made it into the thick trees. Mikhail caught the little girl as Raja skidded to a halt beside him, tongue lolling, sides heaving.

The vampire had bitten into the child's neck and had not closed the wound.

Natalya dropped to her knees beside the girl. "Can you save her?"

The moment the two alphas were relieved of their burdens, they whirled around and raced back to defend the rest of their pack. The first strike hit perilously close to the wolf carrying the adult farmer. Blaez didn't even try to swerve. He ran steadily in a straight line toward the Carpathians.

Vikirnoff stepped out of the trees and faced the raging vampire. While Natalya and the prince worked to save the life of the little girl, he streaked toward the spinning black cloud. Gregori burst into view, coming up on the vampire's right, slamming bolt after bolt of lightning at the undead. Caught in the crossfire between two experienced hunters, already wounded, Sergey retreated, thrusting one last bolt of energy toward his ice spear, hoping to destroy the ground beneath the prince, wolf pack and humans.

Falcon struck at that exact moment, sending a fiery blast of heat through the brittle spear, shattering it, obliterating its potency.

Gregori! Mikhail called back the hunter. *Do not give chase. The wolf pack says we are needed at the farmer's home. Ivory and Razvan had been fighting the vampire. The fact that he escaped them bodes ill. Natalya, escort the family to safety with Falcon and see to it that the child is well cared for at the inn. Ask Slavica, the innkeeper, to put them up for me. She will take good care of them.*

I wish to go with you to see my brother.

I need you to do this for me. If the vampire doubles back, they will need the added protection.

Natalya hesitated, and then touched her lifemate's mind.

Tell me the truth, Vikirnoff. Does he need me for this task, or is he trying to protect me from what you might find?

Vikirnoff, Mikhail and Gregori were already in the sky, moving quickly toward the farmhouse, while the wolf pack circled back, running across the snow-laden ground.

He worries. The undead is a master vampire. Look at the havoc he has wrought on the earth. The wolf pack worries for Ivory. I feel their fear and Mikhail, as prince of our people, feels it doubly.

Natalya sighed. *It is done then.* She waited for Falcon to lift the two adults and she took the children, whispering a command to ease their fears as they raced for the village.

It seemed an endless journey to Mikhail. He felt the tear in the fabric of his people. The injuries were great. He knew Gregori, a healer of tremendous skill, would not fail to feel the agony the two fallen fighters were experiencing. The fact that the energy was not concealed told all of the Carpathians what shape to expect Ivory and Razvan to be in.

Still, none of them was prepared for the horror of that sight. The farmhouse was a pile of rubbish. It looked as if a massacre had taken place, a slaughter. Blood was everywhere, and in the midst of it all sat Ivory, her wounds massive, yet she sought to heal the man lying in her lap. Two spears still remained in his body, while four lay broken and bloody a distance from him. His body was hacked nearly to pieces, with his arm in segments.

As they neared, it appeared as if Razvan was still breathing and Ivory's voice sang the healing chant softly, interspersed with another song none of them had heard before.

This cannot be, Gregori whispered in awe. *He cannot still live. No one could live through that.* He listened to the ebb and flow of Ivory's voice, melodic and tuned to the very heartbeat of the earth.

Mother, dear Mother, I plead with thee now.
Daughter to mother, heal me and mine somehow.
I am his light, he is my warrior strong.
Challenged and scarred, he stood alone so long.
Mother, I beg you to look deep within, try to see
My soul gives light to his darkness, setting him
    free.
Lifemates we are, two halves of a whole.
Standing united, fighting evil, aged and old.
Mother, dear Mother, hold us close in your arms.
Provide us with shelter, with healing, hold off all
    harm.
Mother, please bring balance, darkness to light
Allow us to live, go forward to fight.

Ivory sang the words in the ancient tongue, the notes moving in and out of the rippling earth, twining with the ebb and flow of the sap in the trees and the heartbeat that was the earth itself. As she sang, the soil moved over their bodies, as if a living blanket, or the tide itself, always in motion, pouring over and around them, flowing into their wounds and encasing them in rich, black loam.

10

Razvan floated in a sea of pain. He had been there many times before, but nothing like this. His body felt as if all the parts weren't connected. He couldn't move. Maybe he was just afraid to move, to worsen the agony ripping through his body. He felt movement around him, as if insects and other nameless things crawled over him. Or through him. Even that wasn't enough to induce him to try to move.

He heard whispers, so low at first he thought he was hallucinating, but the voice grew stronger in his mind. Soft. Feminine. Determined.

I am with you. You are not alone. I watch over you and protect you. I will not leave you alone deep within Mother Earth. Do you feel her surrounding you? Holding you in her arms? Welcoming you? Feel her, lifemate. Feel her when all else seems lost.

He was certain he was hallucinating. Xavier would never allow him to sink into the rich soil to be rejuvenated. There was only pain and suffering. An endless life of it. He couldn't let go. He forced his will to obedience. No matter how much his heart stuttered or his lungs fought to draw breath, no matter the pain, he couldn't let go. He had promised—her.

He remembered her, although she might have been a dream, another hallucination. He considered that when he could get his mind to work through the waves of pain. He doubted he could have conjured her up even in his wildest imagination. He tried to picture her, but he found he couldn't think, so he just lay listening, trying to hear her voice again.

Far off he could hear a chant, spoken in the ancient language, voices raised, both male and female. It was impossible to sort through them to find one single voice, and he was certain she wasn't chanting with them. He felt her, not surrounding him, but merged with him, sharing his body. He didn't like the idea. If he felt so much pain, was she sharing that as well? He didn't know the answer.

Again his mind drifted, as if, because he couldn't do anything to prevent her from feeling the terrible pain, he didn't want to know if she was with him. He had spent too many years causing those he loved distress and he refused to think he was doing the same to her.

No, my love. I am with you by choice. I asked to be bound to you. I share your body willingly. Hear me, Dragonseeker, you must hold tight to me. Never let me go.

If he could have smiled, he would have. Where was he going to go? He couldn't move. He could only lie there, believing himself insane. The only consolation was her voice. He tried to remember if he'd dreamt it up when he was young.

After a while—and it could have been nights, or weeks, or even months—he became aware of a heartbeat. The sound was unusual, deep, echoing through his surroundings, so that it vibrated through his body, every muscle and organ, torn sinew and bone. Each beat shook him, yet soothed him. Each beat brought a twisting pain, but at the same time was strangely comforting.

After a long, indeterminate passage of time, he found he listened for that sound, enjoying the echo of it through his battered body. Now came a stirring of interest in his dark world. *What are you?*

I am Mother Earth, my son. You have become a part of me. My daughter begged me to accept you, to heal you. You are hearing the heartbeat of the earth moving through your body, making you one with me, with all of nature.

Now he knew he was insane. He was having a conversation with the earth. It was strange that it didn't bother him that he'd lost his mind. The pain was no less, but he had grown used to it, and he found the darkness and warmth a peaceful, restful place. He drifted further out on the sea of pain, letting it carry him as he had done so many times in the past.

His mind turned to his woman. Ivory. His lifemate. She was so beautiful she took his breath away. He knew if he'd met her a few hundred years earlier, their lives would have been so different. He had never dared to dream of her—never wanted Xavier to know for a moment that, somewhere in the past or the future, there was a woman who held the other half of his soul. It was such an intimate gift, the sharing of souls, and he would never taint that bond with Xavier's evil.

Had he not died and been buried to suffer in this place, he would have taken her to his secret garden, the one place he remembered from his childhood where life had been good and filled with joy. He had played there with his beloved sister, Natalya. They had laughed together so often, running free through the fields of flowers and skimming stones over the placid waters of the lake. He would have brought Ivory there to share his one fond memory.

He felt the brush of fingers against his palm. Warm breath on his face. *Take me there, beloved. Show me this place you dream of.*

He had not expected that his desire for her was so strong that he could conjure her up. He skimmed his hand down her face, shaping the angles, tracing the pad of his thumb over her soft skin. *I would take you there for our first courtship. It is part of me, the best part of me. Long before Xavier took my soul.*

He no longer has your soul. You gave it to me, remember?

Razvan searched his memory. He remembered her face. So beautiful to him that when he closed his eyes she was still there. Her body, covered in those thin white lines, badges of courage, a living embodiment of the strength of will she possessed. He wanted to kiss every line, follow the map of them over her body until he knew each white jagged line intimately. Her skin, soft beyond all imagining, called out for him to simply touch her, to feel how extraordinary she truly was. He loved the way she moved. Just watching her, the sway of her hips and her purposeful stride, brought him a simple joy he'd never thought to feel. The way her face softened when she knelt to greet her wolf pack made him wonder how she would look when she held their child to her breast.

Dragonseeker. She called his wandering mind back to her. *Do you remember giving me your soul?*

Yes. To save me, Ivory. I have sinned lifetimes and cannot save myself, but I have touched you inside where no one else sees you, and you can do it. Put me on your wall with your brothers and carry my soul into the next life.

You are already safe, fél ku kuuluaak sívam belső—beloved.

211

Her voice poured over him like warm honey, and he lay quietly, listening to the beat of the earth's heart and feeling every wound throb and burn in tune to the steady symphony. He thought about her words. *Fél ku kuuluaak sívam belső—beloved.* He wished he was truly her beloved.

I would have walked through the garden with you. I have always wanted to grow my own flowers. I know exactly what they would have looked like and I would have named them for you. Ivory. Hän ku vigyáz sielamet—keeper of my soul.

Show them to me, she entreated him.

Again he swore he felt those fingers moving against his palm, tangling with his own. He closed his hand tight to capture the feeling of closeness. He could drift along in the dream, or hallucination. Maybe he was on the other side, in a better place—although he could do without the agony rushing in waves over his body. He shoved the pain aside, settling deeper into the arms of Mother Earth and letting himself imagine the things he would show Ivory.

She looked carefree, with her long hair cascading down past her hips, a waterfall of silk that moved against his arm as they walked side by side. He liked that she was tall. He could see the length of her lashes, curling at the tips, two thick crescents that veiled her enormous eyes. He was thinking of leaning over and licking along the jagged seam of white that joined two pieces of her shoulder. Temptation was the way her skin was mapped into quadrants for him to explore.

I do not look like that. Embarrassment edged her voice.

Like what? He was puzzled that his dream woman could be embarrassed over his perusal. He could look at her forever—want to taste every square inch of her. He had a need to memorize every detail with the sensitive pads of his fingers, with his mouth and tongue, so he would forever remember the taste and feel of her.

As if these scars are sexy.

She ducked her head as she walked beside him down the narrow ribbon of stones that was the path winding through his garden. The long fall of hair hid her expression from him.

He stepped in front of her, effectively halting her, catching her chin in his fingers and lifting her face so he could hold her gaze captive with his. *Everything about you is incredibly sexy, especially the way you fight. You take my breath away.* The pad of his thumb rubbed over her full bottom lip. *Sometimes I spend far too much time thinking about each of those lines on your body and wondering where they lead. What pleasures they can take me to—take us both to.*

She blinked, her eyes going warm, then sultry. *You think of me as a woman, then, not just a warrior.*

How could I ever separate the two? Your traits make up the whole of who you are. His voice roughened with emotion. He searched in his mind for words to describe her, the way he saw her, but he could find little to express the way he felt, the beauty and light she brought to his soul, so empty and hollow and gutted by Xavier's evil.

Tell me. I need to know.

Words are not enough to explain a miracle, but I will do my best. You are tough, strong and skilled. Gentle. Kind. Compassionate. Fierce and formidable, with a will of iron. Sexy. Soft. Beautiful. Mysterious. Gentle and magnificent. You are all of these things. A miracle to me. A gift beyond any price.

Her lashes fluttered as she veiled her expression. The temptation of her mouth, the curve and soft texture, was too much to resist. It was a dream, nothing else, and it was *his* dream, the first one he had dared in a long time—since the betrayal of his sister. He hesitated, suddenly afraid. Could Xavier be tricking him? Was he now betraying the one woman who held his heart and soul?

No!

The warm honey poured over him again, stirring his body. His heart jumped, beat for a moment out of tune with the heartbeat of the earth. Pain slammed into him from every direction, taking his breath, his ability to think, his very sanity. He thought he screamed when he'd been so stoic, but he had concentrated more than he knew on the natural rhythm of the earth, allowing the heartbeat to keep the pain at a distance so he could tolerate it. For a moment he couldn't breathe, couldn't think. It was impossible to live with such pain.

Do not leave me! Her voice was panicked.

He'd never heard Ivory sound anything but cool and under control. The note of alarm in her voice steadied him. He realized he was drifting away from the scent and feel of her, distancing himself to prevent Xavier from discovering her, but there was need in her that he'd never seen before. She'd been injured. He remembered that much. Horribly injured. He didn't feel as if he had much strength left, but what he had, he would gladly give to her.

Ivory?

I am here, Razvan, with you. In you. I hold you tight, my heart to yours, my soul to yours. Do not leave me. Give me your word. No matter how terrible it gets, give me your word of honor that you will stay with me.

If you need me.

I will always need you.

He could barely conceive of the pure honesty in her voice. Could she really have need of him? He would never, no matter how difficult the circumstances, turn away from her should she need him. *I will be with you always, Ivory, if it is within my power.*

Her voice came again, close, gentle, that warmth that seeped into the coldest marrow of his bones and heated from the inside out. *Rest, then, fél ku kuuluaak sívam belső— beloved. Gain strength, but hold strong and endure for me.*

It was no small task she asked of him. He allowed the pain to consume him, to wash over and into him, to become part of him. It was the only way to survive. His will—and acceptance. He would survive for her.

He woke again after an indeterminate amount of time had passed. Like all Carpathians, he knew the difference between night and day; even deep beneath the earth he knew it was dark and the moon was full and high. Sound had awoken him. Summoned him. Voices raised in the ancient tongue—the healing chant rising and falling with both male and female voices lifting toward the night sky, burrowing deep into the richness of the soil to find his shattered body to surround him and provide strength and healing power.

He felt the presence of a male, white-hot energy surging through him, burning together parts that had been torn apart. Excruciating pain burst through his body and he heard his own cry, the sound strangled and anguished. Ivory echoed his cry, her voice resonating with suffering. He tried to move, to get to her, and at once gentle hands stopped him.

You cannot move. Stay very still or you will undo what small repairs have been made.

Ivory? Razvan recognized the healer's voice. *Save her first. I heard her distress.*

She is merged with you, holding you to this earth, and she feels what you feel. Do not move, just let yourself sink into her, hold tight to her.

Gregori came back into his own body swaying with weariness. Small droplets of blood beaded on his skin and he actually slumped against Mikhail, unable to hold himself upright after the healing session. "How is it they live?" he asked the prince. "It is impossible, yet they survive. Each night I come to them, I expect to find them dead, yet they still live. How is it they endure? No one can live through such pain, yet this is not the first time for either to suffer such torment." He opened his eyes and looked at his friend. "It is difficult for me to feel and see the absolute suffering the two of them endure."

Mikhail laid his hand gently on the healer's shoulder. No healer could be of Gregori's caliber without being empathic. Each time he shed his body and joined the couple to speed the healing of those terrible mortal wounds, he felt what they did.

"You are saving their lives."

Gregori shook his head. "I am aiding the swiftness of recovery, Mikhail. There is a difference. They have wills such as I have never seen in any Carpathian, male or female, in all my years of healing. Believe me, it is only their sheer will keeping them alive, not me."

Mikhail's voice was comforting. "Take my blood to revive you and then go home to Savannah and allow her to soothe you. Night after night, subjecting yourself to their agony is wearing on you. You cannot continue without some respite."

"As long as they continue, so will I." Gregori looked up at his father-in-law, his face lined with weariness. "His body is actually knitting itself back together again. Three of the six spear wounds should have killed him, along with the sheer volume of blood loss, but somehow the earth itself is putting them back together."

"Along with your blood and care."

Gregori shook his head. "I do not understand what I am seeing when I attempt to heal them. It is as if most of their bodies are encased in mineral, hardened and impassable, while I have access only to a single part each night. Some nights it is the same part. I can enter an arm or leg and concentrate there, but the rest of their systems are blocked off to me."

"I don't understand."

Gregori frowned and rubbed at his chin. "Usually when I heal, I can enter an entire body and flow through it with ease, moving through every part, but, when I enter Razvan or Ivory, only a small part of their bodies are accessible. It changes with each night."

"What could cause that?" Mikhail wondered.

"I don't know, but I'd like to find out. The soil has always aided healing. And when we're wounded and tired it rejuvenates us, but we've always used a healing spirit to go inside our bodies and repair from the inside out. Something is repairing their bodies, something other than me. It seems to be a slow process, but it is keeping them both alive. I think Ivory could have been saved, but she chose to bind her fate with Razvan's. She is fully merged with him and, wherever he is encased, so is she."

"A type of magic? Something Xavier might have come up with?" Mikhail ventured.

Gregori shook his head. "There is no taint of evil. Rather it smells ancient to me, as if they have awoken something from long ago, before our time, and it works to save them. And you know me, I don't trust things we've never encountered. We are a people who have seen much over time."

"True," Mikhail said, "but not all."

"I need to understand how things work. I would like to speak with Syndil. She has been cleansing the earth of toxins for us and is very connected to the soil. I have never seen this, and I don't understand how they are surviving, let alone healing. Nor do I have an explanation for how their bodies are segmented. Perhaps she can explain it to me."

Mikhail frowned. "I don't want her to feel the agony they suffer. It is difficult enough for the two of us."

"She might speak to the earth and hear the answer. Perhaps if I understood, I could aid them, reduce the pain in some way."

"I'll talk to her," Mikhail agreed reluctantly. "Both Natalya and Lara are anxious to help, but I've asked them to stay away until we are certain Ivory and Razvan will live."

"I have no doubt they will live, Mikhail," Gregori said. "I just do not know how."

"You realize Ivory did this once before on her own, centuries ago. There was no one there to hold her spirit, to keep her safe as she keeps Razvan to her."

"She must have been in the soil hundreds of years," Gregori said. "Her body didn't knit back together perfectly. I tried to ease the scars internally as well as externally." He ran both hands through his hair in a gesture of weariness. "She took great care, or perhaps it was Mother Earth, to make certain she could have children. It is the one area where she has no scarring of any kind, and yet there was evidence that, even across the womb, they had hacked her in half."

For one moment the air around them crackled with energy and then Mikhail took a breath, bringing himself under control. "I can't see how her brothers could ever have chosen to give up their souls knowing the vampires and Xavier conspired to kill her."

"They blamed Draven."

"It was an excuse and you know it. All of us have lived with betrayal and loss, with grief. They were not near the end; they made a deliberate choice. They have painstakingly pulled together vampires into a league to fight against us, and you know that has taken centuries of planning and even more time to implement. They have also allied themselves with our greatest enemy, the very mage who gave Ivory to the vampires."

"We will know what really happened when Ivory chooses to tell us." Gregori stretched and tried to stand. Dizzy from lack of blood he sank back down. "In the meantime, we can only hold to this course we are on and work to help the pair survive."

"They may be the key to destroying Xavier."

"I think you may be right, Mikhail."

The prince offered his wrist to his son-in-law. "Take what I freely offer. And Gregori, this time you heed what I tell you. You go home to Savannah and you rest. I have already sent her a message that you are on your way. I've asked Syndil to meet with you there."

"You sent word to Savannah?" Gregori glared at the prince. "She's going to fuss over me, and you know she's pregnant with the twins and needs to rest."

"She needs to feel as if she's helping her lifemate. Go home and rest. You said it yourself: these two will survive. Perhaps in talking with Syndil, she will find a way to enrich the soil even more in order to lessen their suffering."

Gregori made his way home, avoiding the two women and their lifemates waiting to speak with Mikhail. He didn't want to try to reassure them that Razvan and Ivory would live. He believed they would, but he didn't understand how, and he could barely function with the amount of pain washing over him each time he touched them. There would be no speaking to them, no getting answers, maybe even no recognition from Razvan for those women—he was too far gone. On top of the couple's pain, he didn't wish to feel the pain of a sister and daughter for the suffering of a loved one.

Savannah waited at the door for him, her beautiful face smiling, welcoming, her eyes so compassionate that for a moment he wanted to weep with joy that he'd been given such a miracle. He just gathered her silently into his arms and held her tight to him.

Savannah walked him inside. "You look tired."

"I am tired."

She tried not to be alarmed. Gregori never admitted to being tired, but this couple, so torn and mangled, fighting valiantly to live when anyone else would have chosen to go to the next life, had captured far more than his attention as a healer. She knew her lifemate well. He respected that couple, wanted—even needed—to find a way to end their suffering.

Savannah put her arms around him and held him, laying her head against his chest. Gregori's hand came up to stroke her hair.

"How are the girls behaving this evening?"

"Kicking a lot. We're getting closer. I don't think they're going to wait much longer."

"Maybe I should talk to them," Gregori suggested. "It is not yet time. They are too anxious and need to stay where they are safe."

Savannah laughed, the sound happy and bright, dispelling some of his tension. "I don't think you should talk to them again. You always sound gruff and stern, and the little one is a rebel. Whatever you order, she does just the opposite." She glanced mischievously up at him. "I have a feeling she's going to be a lot like you."

"Don't say that. I was a very bad child."

Savannah laughed again and Gregori found himself smiling. He dropped several kisses on her nose. "Have I told you that I'm madly in love with you?"

"Not recently."

"Well I am. I haven't quite forgiven you for twins, especially that they're female, but I'm so in love with you, sometimes I can't think straight."

The smile faded from Savannah's face. "Each time we go into the ground, I worry that the microbes will attack the babies again. And Lara is exhausted."

Xavier had found a way to use extremophiles to attack the Carpathian females and babies, very effectively reducing the population over hundreds of years so they were now on the brink of extinction. The pregnant women were terrified of losing their babies, and Lara, Razvan's daughter, could not be fully brought into the Carpathian world because, while the extremophiles could detect the Carpathians hunting for them, they could not detect Lara, as she was mage.

"She does a sweep on all the pregnant women each evening, and yet there's always a recurrence. Even though she makes certain the men are without the microbes, it doesn't take long before we're all infected again. She has to be converted soon. Neither of them complains, but it is difficult for Nicolas."

Gregori's fingers settled around the nape of Savannah's neck. "She has years before she will be in trouble, but yes, it is difficult on her lifemate. And if she gets pregnant . . ."

He trailed off with a small sigh. "I am hoping Ivory and Razvan are the answer."

"How can they be?"

"I don't know, but I think your father does. He was too calm, too certain that Razvan wouldn't drive that knife into his throat."

"He is sure of his skills, Gregori."

"That is true, although he should take more caution with his life. Still, it was more than that. He trusted Razvan when he shouldn't have."

"You can't know everything, Gregori," she said gently.

His brooding silver gaze slid over her. "When it comes to your father, I should. He is my greatest responsibility. Without him, our species would fade away, lost as so many others have gone." He spread his fingers over her rounded womb, holding his children to him. "We have to safeguard their legacy, Savannah."

"We will," she replied, leaning into him.

Gregori lifted his head. "We are about to have visitors. They've spared our daughters another lecture from their father."

Savannah's laughter warmed him. She hugged him. "They are very grateful to our visitors, especially the little one. She gave the equivalent to rolling her eyes."

His silver eyes slashed at her. "You are not encouraging them, are you? I thought I would not have to deal with that behavior for another twenty years or so."

"She thinks you are very bossy."

"I am bossy because I know what's best for her."

Savannah laughed again. "You argue with her and she isn't even born yet."

Gregori huffed out another breath, a man driven beyond endurance by his stubborn unborn child, but his fingers lingered with loving strokes. Savannah laid her hand over his and they stood quietly a moment, feeling the presence of their daughters, surrounding the twins with love.

The knock on the door was expected and Gregori opened it to Syndil and her lifemate, Barack. One was never far from the other, he'd noticed. He welcomed both of them with a traditional Carpathian greeting. "*Pesäsz jeläbam ainaak*—long may you stay in the light."

Syndil and Barack responded in kind and stepped into the house. "How are you feeling, Savannah?" Syndil asked.

"Very pregnant," Savannah replied with a small smile. "If I get any bigger I might pop."

"It is good to gain, especially with twins," Gregori said. "You are right where you're supposed to be."

"He monitors me carefully to make certain the babies are growing properly," Savannah explained. She leaned in to kiss Barack on the cheek, ignoring Gregori's sharp reprimand.

There is no need for kissing.

Savannah laughed again and rubbed her cheek against Gregori's shoulder affectionately.

"Mikhail sent word that you wished to talk to me."

Gregori indicated for her to sit. Barack sank into the seat beside her and took her hand.

"I am certain you've heard the news, that Razvan has escaped Xavier and that Ivory Malinov is alive. You were not raised in the Carpathian Mountains, and did not know the rumors of these two, but suffice it to say it is a shock to everyone to find out all we believed of them is wrong."

Syndil tangled her fingers with Barack's. It always surprised Gregori to realize this one woman who wielded so much power was so shy and humble. She walked on the

223

ground and new life sprang up after her. She danced and sang and toxic soil was restored to health. They had chanced on the knowledge, the prince spotting her healing an entire battlefield destroyed by vampire venom. She had been so quiet about her talent, so modest, no one would have ever known had Mikhail not seen her gift with his own eyes.

Syndil merely nodded her head, shifting just a little toward Barack. He moved closer to her, slipping his arm around her shoulders.

Gregori sighed. "I have no right to ask this of you. Indeed, it may be risky."

Barack frowned.

"The pair encountered a master vampire and took him on in order to save a family. While Razvan has little or no experience fighting, Ivory is an extraordinary warrior. Together they managed to hurt him and run him off, but at great cost to their bodies."

"You know I would aid you," Syndil said, her soft voice musical, "but I am no healer."

"I would disagree with that statement, Syndil." Gregori leaned forward. "You understand the earth better than most. You hear her talking to you, crying out when she's wounded, and you're able to fix every injury."

"That's different." Syndil waved a dismissing hand. "Not at all like healing a wounded Carpathian."

"I cannot do what you do," Gregori said. "I do not always hear our mother speaking to us. This couple, what is happening with them, I do not understand—and I've tried. I listen to Mother Earth, but she whispers and I can't comprehend what she is saying. They are suffering. In agony. Both of them." He hung his head and ran both hands through his hair in agitation. "I'm helping them, yes,

224

but so slowly, and each night that passes and I go to them, they feel untold pain."

"What would you have Syndil do?" Barack asked.

Gregori shook his head. Savannah perched on the arm of his chair and slipped her arm around him, her fingers sliding into his hair to soothe him. "Just tell them, Gregori. Let them decide."

"I have never seen anything like what is happening. Razvan's body was hacked up, literally. He had his arm chopped off and in pieces. He had six spear holes, three fatal. His wounds were horrendous. Slices all the way to the bone, in many cases cutting through the bone. The blood loss was unbelievable. Instead of attending his wounds, he aided her in the battle."

Barack sat up straight. "And he survives?"

"So far—yes. I don't know how. She also had many wounds, and yet she managed to merge with him in some way; I do not know how. They are separate bodies, but their hearts beat as one, their minds are one. Even that is not the issue. If I have access to his arm, the rest of his body is encased completely in mineral, as if he is part of the earth itself. When I share their bodies, I hear the earth whispering. I can hear the rhythm of its heartbeat, but I can't understand what she is saying to them. Could this be? Could Mother Earth be healing them? Not just rejuvenating them?"

Syndil was silent, turning his words over and over in her mind. Barack said nothing, waiting for his lifemate to give her advice. It was her realm of expertise and he was inordinately proud of her. He never ceased to be shocked that his quiet little Syndil was consulted by every Carpathian, and the prince and Gregori often asked her counsel.

"I believe so, yes. We have a connection to the earth, to

the very Universe. It's the reason we're able to shift and call down the lightning. It's why our bodies rejuvenate in the soil. If this couple has a deeper connection in some way, if Mother Earth claims one or both as her children, their bodies might be slightly different from ours."

Gregori's frown deepened. "We're all the earth's children."

Syndil shook her head. "Not in the same way. The earth is alive. There is a heartbeat, a rhythm, a pulse. She whispers and shouts and screams. She welcomes us home each dawn as her children, but if she accepts one of us as her own, as her biological child—I know no other way to explain it—she might send them everything she has, the very richest soil she can call, every healing element. Who knows what she is capable of doing for one she considers part of her."

The lines on his face remained as he sat back. "Why would she single out one Carpathian?"

Syndil, calm and serene, smiled at him, warmed him, enveloped him with her utter lack of vanity. "I would imagine the circumstances had to be extraordinary."

Savannah leaned closer. "Can you help her? Can you feed the soil where they are recovering, help to keep it rich to speed their recovery?"

Gregori brought her fingertips to his mouth. He hadn't wanted to ask Syndil. Anyone approaching that expanse of soil would be able to feel the agony radiating from the couple, and to ask a woman to share that experience was nearly more than he was capable of doing, yet, if she didn't help, it could well take years to heal such mortal wounds.

"Before you answer, Syndil"—now he looked to her lifemate, husband to husband, willing him to understand—"there are things you should know. The pain they suffer is unlike anything I have ever experienced in centuries of battles and healing. If you are empathic, you can't go there without being affected. Even if you don't touch them, just entering the area is an uncomfortable experience. I have no words to describe the suffering."

"And yet they live," Barack said.

"A seemingly impossible feat," Gregori said. "Yet they continue." His gaze moved broodingly over Syndil. "I do not ask this of you lightly. I would not want you trying to connect with them or helping me to heal them because to share their bodies right now is an agonizing task."

Even when he slept the sleep of Carpathians, that first moment of awakening was torture, pain flooding his body, wrenching at every organ and tearing great holes in his body, as if he shared some part of Ivory and Razvan deep beneath the ground. He knew it was a waking nightmare, but still, the dreadful dream lingered with him night after night upon awakening.

"I can't heal another human as you can, Gregori, but if the earth requires help in restoring minerals or any other particle it should need, I can and will do that. I wish I could be of more assistance, but I have only the one talent."

"And that one talent is much needed. Will you need help from others? I know Natalya and Lara and even young Skyler help you rejuvenate the soil where our women lie." Again there was a small frown he couldn't quite keep from his face.

The idea of Skyler, such a young girl, and Lara, who was already giving more than she should, enduring the pain, didn't set well with him. And Natalya . . . He sighed. Once she got near her brother, she would touch him whether they warned her against it or not. She was headstrong, and she had always adored her brother. If Syndil needed the other women, he would have to find a way without her to speed recovery.

"I can try, Gregori," Syndil offered. "I would like to see what the earth is doing to aid them. I may never get such a chance again."

"It is unique," Gregori agreed. "Thank you."

Syndil smiled at him and turned her attention to Savannah. They had become good friends over the last few weeks as Savannah fought to keep her unborn children alive. "How are you really feeling?"

"Exhausted, but very happy," Savannah said. "It won't be long, although Gregori talks to them nightly to convince them to stay in their safe environment as long as possible. We want them fully developed, with as much weight as possible. Even outside the womb, the microbes could attack."

"I hope we can allow Ivory and Razvan to rise before the babies are born," Gregori added. "I think they may be able to aid us greatly and give all of our children a fighting chance."

Syndil sat back. "There is no question that all of us need to aid them. Isn't it strange how, in the end, it is never the individual but rather the sum of all of us working together that makes things right?"

"It appears, Syndil," Gregori agreed, "that you are right."

11

Razvan woke to the sound of a woman weeping. He didn't open his eyes. He had heard that sound so many times—that same voice.

Natalya. Beloved sister. He whispered her name as his gut tightened into hard knots. He must have betrayed her once again. He didn't remember anymore, thank God. That was the worst of all torments Xavier could inflict on him—using him to attack his sister or his daughter or the aunts.

He felt Ivory's awareness as if she, too, came awake to the sound of that hopeless weeping. Nothing seemed quite as hard to bear with Ivory close—not the pain and not the terrible knowledge of the betrayal of mind and body. Natalya was the one person who had loved him all of his life. She had believed in him in spite of all the times Xavier had tricked and used her through him. Xavier had even used his body to try to kill Natalya. She had nearly killed his body—and he would have welcomed death.

You did not betray her, Dragonseeker. Not ever. Not in thought. Not in deed. Xavier used your body because you protected her.

Ivory was calm. Ivory was peace. Ivory had become his world.

Why does she weep? He could no longer trust what was

229

happening to him, his memories seemed to mix past and present together until his world was hazy and vague. His sanity was Ivory.

For you. For the torment you went through on her behalf. She understands now that you never betrayed her, that you saved her from Xavier. Ivory's voice was a soft caress, pride and respect for him surrounding him.

She had a way of making the world right when nothing really made sense. He didn't fight the pain swamping him. He simply accepted it, but he didn't want Natalya weeping for any reason.

Do not cry for me, sisar—sister. Even trying to communicate telepathically hurt, although he was either getting used to it, or he was healing enough to ease the worst of his suffering.

Razvan? Is it really you? They tell me you live, but when I reach for you, you are different.

I am your brother.

There was a silence. A sob. Natalya forced herself under control. *He tricked me, didn't he? Xavier tricked me. You tried to warn me, but I didn't hear you. All those years, and I believed him. It wasn't you at all. It was the personality he fed me so I would continue to create spells for him.*

Xavier is a cunning enemy.

I should have known. I should have fought for you as you fought for me. How could I not have known? You are my twin. My brother. How could he have fooled me?

I didn't want you to know. You would have tried to rescue me and you would have failed, Natalya. He is a monster. As long as you were alive in the world and safe from him, whatever I had to give up was worth it.

My love? My respect? My faith in you? The world branded you a criminal and I believed them. Was it worth it?

Your safety was worth any price to me. I do not regret for one moment placing myself in his hands to keep you from him. It was my choice. One I have clung to for many years. Do not take that away from me with regret.

He had never wavered in that decision, even in the most insane hours of his life. He knew what their grandfather would have done to her, and keeping her from Xavier's hands was the one thing, the *only* thing, that he had managed to do. And whether she—or anyone else—was proud of him, he was proud of himself.

Ivory's spirit moved against his, surrounded his, almost protectively, but she remained silent, not interfering in the exchange between sister and brother.

All those lost years, Razvan, years when you needed me.

He forced a smile into his voice, made certain she knew it was genuine. It was difficult to block the pain from his tone, but he did it to protect her. *I needed you free of Xavier, and that is what I got. During the time I was part mage and part Carpathian, the thought of you, my love for you, sustained me. Later, after the aunts turned me wholly in the hope that I might have the chance to escape, the Dragonseeker blood aided my resolve to protect you. You were there for me whether you knew it or not, sister. Do not weep. Do not regret. Live free the way you were meant to.*

I have a lifemate.

Xavier had tried to murder her lifemate. *Tell me about him.*

He is called Vikirnoff and he is a great warrior. You would like him.

What of my daughter, Lara? He nearly choked over her name.

A small child with enormous eyes, watching her mother's decomposing body, chained to an insane father

231

who tore at her little wrist to feed. Lara was one person he was not certain he could ever face.

You protected her as best you could. You endured torment and gave part of your soul to Xavier in order to save her, Ivory reminded. *She either understands or she does not. If she does not it will be sad for her that she chooses not to know so great a man.*

If he could have held Ivory close in his arms he would have.

We will dance to heal the earth, so that she can better provide her rich minerals for you. Lara is coming to aid us. Lara, Syndil, Skyler and I will dance and sing the healing song for you and your lifemate. It is the only gift we have to give you.

I do not know Syndil or Skyler.

They are wonderful women. Syndil is really close to the earth. When she walks barefoot, plants bloom behind her. She can take an area a vampire has virtually laid to waste and restore it to health. Skyler is young; she turned seventeen just recently.

There was a note, a hesitation in his sister's voice. Something she wasn't telling him. Something she didn't want to tell him. *Natalya, better to prepare me than to let me be shocked.*

Few things shocked him anymore, but he had the feeling she was going to deliver something he didn't want to hear.

Ivory moved against him again. Heart to heart. Soul to soul. *I am with you, Razvan. You will never be alone again.*

Ivory's voice was enough to make his heart sing. Love had been lost to him a long time ago. He hadn't believed he could feel such a powerful emotion for anyone, yet there it was. In him. Deep. How could he not love her when she gave him back his sanity? His life? When she embodied the honor and integrity he believed in?

Natalya took a deep breath. *We believe you also fathered Skyler. There is another woman as well, a lifemate to one of the De La Cruz brothers. Colby. She lived on a ranch in California before she met Rafael.*

He closed his mind to Natalya but there was no escaping Ivory, and the memory of a child in a mine shaft rose up. He had desperately tried to get to her before they had managed to kidnap her and take her back to Xavier. He'd brought the mine down on the vampire before Xavier had taken over his body again. He was grateful the child lived and prospered—but another one? Skyler? How many more? And from the hesitant tone Natalya used, young Skyler hadn't fared well.

Are you certain I fathered these girls?

Yes.

His heart again jumped out of rhythm with that of the earth and pain swept him away.

Razvan woke to singing and he knew time had passed. The voices were beautiful, soft and melodious, in tune with the earth. As they sang, the pain in his body eased considerably as if the earth could better absorb the terrible wounds in his body and knit him back together.

Isn't their song beautiful? Ivory asked. Her voice was hushed, as if she was afraid she would interrupt the tribute to Mother Earth. *They are gifted, these four women. And are they all related in some way to you? Sister? Daughters? I feel a part of you in them, though one, the strongest daughter of the Earth, is different and yet like you in some way.*

Razvan felt the melody deep in his bones. Peace had once again slid over him, the knowing that he could not change what fate had already decreed. Acceptance—his only recourse when the world around him made no sense.

Natalya says the young one is my daughter, but the one called Syndil I do not know. She is much older, older perhaps than I.

She feels as you feel. That same calm, at peace with herself in spite of the turmoil around her. She is . . . There was a frown in Ivory's voice as she tried to fit the pieces of the puzzle together. *The earth welcomes her as she welcomes me. As a daughter. A true daughter. There are only a few of us.*

Is she related to you, Ivory? Razvan could feel the strength in the woman Ivory was speaking of. The earth rejoiced and welcomed her. There was joy in the layers of soil beneath him, joy in the rock beneath the soil. *How do I feel that? How am I so connected to the earth? Through you?*

Mother Earth has accepted you as her son. She will come to your aid should you have need. She has found you worthy. There was satisfaction in Ivory's voice.

He felt humbled by the earth's acceptance of his torn body and wounded soul; not worthy, but he was grateful.

My body is healing. The dance is rejuvenating the soil and Mother Earth is pouring minerals into our bodies to speed healing, isn't she? He felt that connection strongly now. He heard the beat of the music and the stamp of feet, felt the pattern of the dance as they poured love and healing into the earth itself.

He realized they were all connected, not apart, and for the first time he understood the concept of the prince and why he was so important to the Carpathian people. He connected them in the way the earth did. Mikhail was the very blood of the people.

That's why Xavier wants him dead. To kill the prince might literally kill the species. We have to stop him, Ivory. Whatever else we do, we have to stop Xavier. We cannot be distracted by going after vampires or anything else; Xavier has to be stopped.

Ivory's mind slipped over his, mirroring that exact knowledge, in accord with him. It only mattered that they heal their bodies as fast as possible and then find a way to remove the threat of Xavier from the world.

Time passed. There was often the ceremonial healing of the earth, and each time brought renewed soil, working to repair the mortal wounds. And Gregori came to them nightly. They often protested, knowing they were taking his strength and blood, even his healing energy, but he was single-minded in his purpose, and nothing they said could stop him.

Razvan came to like and respect the man. He was stubborn, tenacious, determined to heal them as quickly as possible. Ivory had been leery of taking his blood at first, a natural reaction when self-preservation had been her way for hundreds of years, but necessity forced her to take what was offered. Gregori and Nicolas De La Cruz were the two Carpathians who came daily to take care of them. Often the prince came along and gave his blood, the richness and healing qualities like no other.

Nicolas had wept when he learned Ivory was alive and Razvan felt the mixture of joy and sorrow bursting through her. She had never thought that she would ever see the De La Cruz brothers again, family to her, adored brothers every bit as close to her real brothers as she had been, yet even they could not prevent the Malinov brothers from turning.

It was Razvan who held Ivory close, surrounding her with his heat, merging his mind and heart with hers to keep her from weeping uncontrollably, to steady her while she renewed her relationship with Nicolas, lifemate to his daughter Lara. It was Nicolas who fed her wolves for her and made certain they were well cared for. Most of the time the wolves snuggled beside them, there in the soil, sleeping the weeks away, waking only to feed when Nicolas arrived, and then sleeping again.

Razvan recognized Nicolas's face from Ivory's meticulously carved wall. Each stroke had been carved with loving care, and he felt that same deep love in Ivory each time Nicolas spoke to her. That man's voice was soft, gentle, almost as if she was still the young girl from centuries earlier. He didn't seem to recognize the fierce warrior in her, only her gentle side, as if he might be blinded to who she was by his love for the child from long ago.

On some level, he realized that it was Nicolas's lack of knowledge of who Ivory was that kept Razvan from the terrible possessiveness a lifemate would feel when other males were close to their female. Ivory loved Nicolas with the love of a sister, but it was Razvan who knew her intimately, her intriguing mind and the wonderful, intelligent brain that worked fast and accurately on any problem. Razvan spent a great deal of time in her mind, going over what she knew of vampires and learning how best to fight them. She was a wealth of information, and, as much as Nicolas loved her, he would never see her true value.

He sees me the way you see Natalya. She is a warrior and yet you wish only to protect her and keep her safe. There was amusement in Ivory's voice.

Her tone felt like velvet stroking over his skin. *Perhaps little sisters should never grow up, but simply stay young for their brothers.* He matched her teasing tone.

I am grown up. A woman. Her amusement faded to be replaced by something altogether different. *When we leave*

236

this place of comfort and healing—and we will soon to join the real world with its hardships and cruelty—I will miss our closeness. There was real regret in her voice. The thought of going back to her lonely existence after intertwining her mind so deeply with his was disturbing to her.

Hän ku vigyáz sielamet—keeper of my soul, you are also hän ku kuulua sívamet—keeper of my heart. We are bound together, lifemates for all eternity. When we rise, ready to fight our enemy, we rise as lifemates. I asked you if that was what you wished and your reply was clear to me. We do not separate. We face the future together, whatever it should bring.

Ivory sighed softly. *I am prepared to do that. I just meant* . . . She trailed off and he felt her searching for the right words to express whatever troubled her.

When she was silent for so long, he reached for her mind, his touch as gentle as a lover's caress. Once again he took her into another realm, his mind in hers, leading her away from pain and what they both knew they would have to face when they rose.

His hand slipped into hers and he walked with her, side by side, his body brushing against hers, walking into the night, taking her to his garden, the one place he was familiar with, the one place he loved and could share.

Flowers cascaded down the terraced rock and covered arbors of white. The fragrances mingled, rising above the mazes of shaped hedges and bushes. Trees formed small groves of oranges and lemons with taller evergreen towers on the corners of the stone-fence-wrapped garden. Weeping willows stood at the edges of the blue-green pond, while a few ducks swam lazily, dunking their heads beneath the rippling surface and coming up to shake the water from their feathers.

Ivory looked around her. "You grew up here?"

He brought her fingers to his chest, over his heart. "It was our mother's family home. We lived here for some time after she passed away. And then my father disappeared and Xavier took us away. But this was where we were together and happy."

"It's beautiful."

"I used to believe it was the most beautiful spot in the world, but I think you managed to create that in your home." Razvan looked around him and inhaled to drag the scent of lavender into his lungs.

"*Our* home," Ivory corrected. "It is our home now."

He felt the instant reaction in his heart to her words. *Home.* What would that be like, to feel as if he had a home, a woman to share his life with? They had a purpose for living, for suffering the fires of hell: to rid the world of its greatest evil—Xavier. For a short time he could simply be with Ivory, enjoy walking with her through a beautiful garden.

Ivory glanced sideways at him and then quickly averted her eyes, her long lashes hiding her expression.

Razvan stopped to push the long fall of silken hair from her face and back over her shoulder. "You are hiding from me."

Color rose, turning her pale skin to a soft rose. "Maybe. A little."

"I had no idea you were a little shy. You are such a fierce warrior and wholly confident, I thought you would be that way in all things."

She shrugged. "I have little experience with men—most of it long ago and not good."

He grinned at her, a slow, heart-stopping smile that revealed his straight white teeth, and suddenly seemed a little shy as well. "My body has a tremendous amount of experience, but not my heart—and not me. Truthfully, I feel like a young boy on his first date."

She lifted her chin. "It is my first date."

He regarded her steadily, his dark eyes drifting over the exquisite bone structure of her face. His gaze settled on her full lips. "Then we must make it memorable." He couldn't conceive of forgetting this moment, this one time with her, surrounded by the memory of his garden and so close to her that he could breathe the same breath.

She lifted a hand to his face, worn and lined, as if he still couldn't change that look, even in his dreams—even in his memories. He had forgotten what his face had looked like in his younger days, forgotten being a carefree youth. He could only give her what he was now, and hope that it was enough for her.

"You will always be enough for me," she whispered, meaning it. "I had stopped dreaming of my prince long ago."

"What was he like?"

She smiled, her eyes warming. "Tall, of course, with long, black, flowing hair and broad shoulders. He was a great warrior and he rescued me from my tower where my brothers had imprisoned me. He wanted me to ride beside him on his snorting, rearing steed, a sturdy animal that blew smoke through his nostrils and pawed the ground with impatience to rush headlong into battle." She laughed softly at a young girl's dreams.

Razvan made a face. "I am tall, but my hair is streaked with white, and I cannot say I am an accomplished warrior. But I would surely rescue you and take you off to ride beside me anywhere we went, including battle."

Her fingertips went to one particular thick white streak in his hair. She rubbed the silky strands back and forth between her thumb and index finger. "A warrior is not someone who merely fights, Razvan. You have the heart of a warrior and the soul of a poet. I find you fascinating." She dropped her gaze. "And tempting."

There was a moment when his breath caught in his lungs. Tempting? He tempted her? There was no shadow of evil inside his body. Nothing stood between them and she confessed to him that she was tempted by him? Ivory's stark honesty moved him as nothing else could.

His palm curled around the nape of her neck, drawing her closer to him. He could feel the warmth of her breath on his face, could see—not just feel—the softness of her skin. He had more discipline than any man walking the face of the earth, yet he could not stop himself from leaning his head down those scant few inches and closing the distance between them.

His lips brushed hers. Barely touching. Feather-light. His body reacted, clenching hard, tightening, every muscle, every cell coming alive, paying attention to that smallest of sensations.

Ivory didn't pull away from him. They stood in the middle of his garden, surrounded by cascading flowers of all colors, birds and butterflies, bees flitting from one bloom to the next, a place of absolute serenity, and time just seemed to stand still for them.

His hands framed her face and he tilted her head so his mouth could come down on hers again. She sighed into his kiss, her body somehow closer. He didn't know if he moved or she did, or maybe it was the earth shifting under his feet, but her mouth went from warm to hot to burning just that fast.

The sensation opened up an entire new world, one of pleasure, of intense sensation. Where his life had been pain and suffering, her mouth, soft and hot and enticing, swamped him with immeasurable pleasure. It wasn't just a physical sensation, but his mind was merged deeply in hers, feeding off her pleasure, heightening it as she heightened his. His heart was fully engaged, nearly overwhelmed with the feelings that had been growing stronger and stronger from the moment he'd first opened his eyes and saw her face, from the first touch of her gentle fingers as she pushed back his hair.

His tongue swept across the seam of her lips, not tentatively, but not pushing her beyond what she wanted to give. His hands were gentle, in contrast to the hard aggression of his body. Her mouth opened to his and he was inside that soft, scalding cavern of heat and fire. Flames licked at his belly. His groin tightened even more, swelling and hardening, and deep in his belly an inferno raged.

He took his time, as gentle as ever, savoring the reaction of his body as he explored her soft mouth, savoring her reaction, the small breathy moan that nearly drove him insane, the small movement that pressed her soft breasts against his chest and aligned the cradle of her hips with his. Little sparks ignited everywhere and the world seemed to spin away even further.

His hands slipped into that silky fall of hair cascading down her back. Each new exploration of her skin and body added to his rising pleasure, further intensifying it.

You are the most incredible woman ever born. He meant it. He let her see the truth of his statement in his mind, in his heart. He'd never imagined such feelings, of the strength of emotion and the intensity of his physical reaction to her.

His body had been used by Xavier, yes, but he hadn't been present, only witnessing the degradation at a distance. He had never experienced pleasure from the joining, only sorrow and regret when he could recall the emotions. And now that he had emotion in abundance, he felt distaste and shame at the memories, along with sorrow and regret. He hadn't expected . . . *this*—the wonder and beauty of love blossoming right here in his garden along with his flowers. Had he been in the real world he might have scoffed at the poetry singing in his soul, but here, in his dream, in his memories, the words were perfect, fitting the way he felt.

Her body shuddered against his, and her hands came up to grip his arms. He felt the sudden hesitation in her, the simultaneous urge to pull him closer and push him away. She was as unused to trusting, to sharing herself as he was—maybe more. The needs slammed into them like the vicious punch of fists, overwhelming her. It mattered little how gentle his touch was, the desire burned hot and unexpected, a firestorm out of control.

She stepped back, shaking her head, her fingers pressed against her trembling mouth and his dark eyes blazing with heat. She looked confused and a little shocked, as if she hadn't expected to feel anything other than physical pleasure—certainly nothing quite as intense as what had happened between them. It always surprised him that Ivory, so confident in herself as a warrior, was not as sure of herself as a woman.

He cupped the side of her face and ran the pad of his thumb over her soft, exquisite skin. Abruptly everything in him stilled.

"Ivory, look at your skin."

The lines that had been raised over her body, jagged and thick, were now white and smooth. They were still there, segmenting the seams of her body, but without the thickness that had marked them. The white lines cut through her body much like a jigsaw puzzle, and always would, but now they were smooth and soft, a part of her skin rather than raised scar tissue.

Ivory touched one of the lines just above the swell of her breasts. "This is the combination of the healer, the Carpathian blood and the soil. Amazing. I thought those hideous scars would be there forever."

"They were not hideous." He bent his head and brushed his lips over a smooth white line bisecting her body.

Ivory's womb clenched and she went damp. The brush of his hair against her skin felt like sin. How could he move her the way he did? Crawl inside her heart so that she felt weak when he was close? She had taken such care not to let anyone matter. Nothing could matter but destroying Xavier. It was her one purpose. Her only purpose.

She felt her fingers move in that thick fall of luxurious, striped hair. So dark the color made his eyes a piercing cobalt, so white it played over his lined face, making him look older and much more distinguished than most Carpathian males. She clenched his hair in her fist as her gaze drifted moodily over his face.

Razvan was so serene. Deep inside where there should have been rage at the atrocities committed against him, she found only peace and acceptance. His will was the strongest she'd ever encountered in centuries of battle, yet he felt no compulsion to force it on others. He stood there looking at her as if she was the very moon, a goddess, beautiful beyond comparison, his gaze hungry, his body urgently demanding hers, yet he didn't push her beyond where she was willing to go. There was no ego. No sense of demand in him, simply a quiet strength, a rock she found astonishingly peaceful and sexy.

There was a scant inch between them now. Whether

she had moved or he had, she couldn't really say, but it seemed necessary to taste him again. She ached to feel the heat, the sweep of his tongue sliding against hers, the fire that blazed the moment they came together. Her heart had simply melted and her stomach had gone jittery. She knew she was flirting with fire, but right then, at that precise moment with his hair brushing seductively against her skin and his body hard and hot, yet his soul so peaceful, the combination drove her past fear and into a frenzy of need.

She lifted her mouth and took his. For a dazzling moment, the world seemed to go up in flames, shifting away from them so they spun out of control, burning together, hot and wild, mouths fused together, minds welded tight, hearts beating the exact same rhythm. She hadn't known how lonely she was until his mouth moved over hers—until his mind moved in hers. She hadn't known her body could be so alive until she'd felt the skim of his fingers touching her reverently, exploring as if it was imperative to memorize every small inch of her body.

She hadn't known she could be so scared of losing someone again. She pulled away from him, but his hands held her close, not letting her escape too far. Unable to look at him, Ivory pressed her forehead against his chest.

"I had no idea I was such a coward."

He laughed softly. "You are far from a coward, *hän ku vigyáz sielamet*—keeper of my soul. You are an extraordinary woman." His lips brushed the top of her hair, lingered there for a moment, before he dropped his chin on top of her head and nuzzled her.

"I cannot imagine the Carpathian males being so careful with their lifemates' feelings as you are with mine."

He caught her chin and lifted her face to his. "We are not like others. We never will be. We make our own rules and we live by ourselves. Our world is different, Ivory. Never think yourself less because you are careful with your emotions. You are a warrior with a mission, a momentous task that few others would ever try to undertake. Never sell yourself short in any way. I take great pride in you and in the fact that I was chosen to be your lifemate. It is an honor like no other."

He meant it, she knew. She was in his mind and he meant every word. He made her feel special. It was an odd feeling after being thrown away by the Carpathian people, after the betrayal of her brothers when they made the decision to join the ranks of the undead and ally themselves with Xavier for power. It was odd to feel the intensity of Razvan's emotions for her: his pride, the honor he felt, the absolute unwavering devotion to her. He was a selfless man, uncaring what others thought of him, but fiercely proud of her.

Her heart did a jittery slide that seemed to go on forever, a slow turnover, and she knew she was lost. "I am more afraid of what is between us than I was facing the master vampire."

A master vampire who had once, long ago, been her very loved brother. Razvan curled his fingers around the nape of her neck and held her close to him, offering comfort when she didn't ask for it. She would never ask for it.

"I buried them long ago," she whispered, laying her head against his chest and letting the strength in his arms hold her up. Here, in this dream garden, with no one around, she could show weakness, just for a moment, because she knew Razvan accepted her exactly for who she was. "I carry their souls in mine, in the hope that, when I go to the next life, what I have done will count for them, and they will be given a second chance. Whether they take it or not is up to them. I had completely reconciled myself to their loss but . . ." She trailed off.

There were no words to express the overwhelming grief and wrenching sense of betrayal when her brother had used the illusion of his earlier self in an attempt to kill her. She knew he would have destroyed her as easily as he would the farmer and his family, Travis and Razvan. She had been completely unprepared for that terrible pain, the heartache she felt at seeing him again.

"I think it would be normal to feel that way. I was prepared for my sister to despise me, and I certainly feel I am prepared for my biological daughters to detest me, but that does not mean it won't hurt." He held her close, surrounding her with warmth. "You have a loving heart, Ivory. You guard it well, but those you let into your life are there permanently, regardless of what happens. I've heard the love in your voice and felt it in your mind each evening Nicolas comes to give us blood. It's the love of a sister and yet it has been centuries since you have seen him, and he has done many troubling things in his life."

"But he is such a wonderful man. He is so in love with Lara, your daughter," Ivory pointed out. "I could love him for that alone. He has not yet completely brought her into this world, although both of them suffer for it. They give so much to the Carpathian people, trying to save the babies."

"She has become sensitive to the light," Razvan agreed. "And she cannot go to ground, but she can live many years without too many problems."

"He worries she will get pregnant in her half-state. Did you catch in his mind exactly what she can do that no other can?"

"She is part mage, and they need a mage to hunt the

microbes invading the women's bodies. The microbes kill most of the children."

Ivory frowned and pulled away from him. She looked around the lush garden with its abundance of shrubs and flowers. Water wound lazily along the bed of a pretty little stream, coloring the rocks in sparkling golds and silvers. The ribbon of a waterfall zigzagged along the high rock face forming one wall of the garden. The water shimmered in a long drop. Butterflies flitted and birds sang even under the shine of the moon overhead. It was a dream world.

. They could stand together, close like they were, and she could feel the first thrill of love blossoming, the fierce physical pull between them, but even here, the real world crept in. Even here the snake that was Xavier crept in.

"He cannot reach us here," Razvan said. "He no longer has my mind."

"But he can. He colors the world in evil, Dragonseeker. Evil is such a little used word, yet he embodies it. There is no monster in the world equal to him. You saved Lara from him . . ."

"My aunts saved Lara. Even when they might have had a chance to escape, Xavier used my body to plunge a knife into Branislava's breast. They were already so weak, kept drained of blood to feed his insatiable need."

"As were you."

Razvan made no response, just kept pace with her as she went to the entrance of the maze. She took his hand again and drew him inside the labyrinth of tall shrubbery.

"Lara is still dictated to by Xavier. She cannot be wholly converted until he is destroyed." Ivory sighed. "We must find a way to rid the world of such evil."

"It is Lara's choice to remain in the half-world between mage and Carpathian. Her lifemate will protect her, just as

I would you. That's freedom, Ivory, true freedom, and thankfully her lifemate understands she needs that above all else. He must trust her enough to know that, when he tells her time is over for their safety, or health, she will listen to him and allow him to convert her and bring her fully into the Carpathian world. He will not let her give too much of herself, nor would any of the Carpathians want her to do so," Razvan pointed out. "Ivory." He stopped her again, standing in front of her to bring her hand to his mouth.

Very gently he rubbed his thumb back and forth over her knuckles—knuckles that had seen too many fights and would see many more. "We have accepted that we will hunt Xavier. And we will not stop until we destroy him. But we will live while we take this journey. Each night we rise, we will live. Every minute. Every moment. We will celebrate our lives and enjoy our journey, good or bad. He cannot have us. He cannot have those we love." He brought her knuckles back to his mouth and swirled his tongue over the scars there. "Do you understand what I am saying to you?"

Ivory took a breath. She felt herself falling forward into the very depths of his eyes, a very non-warrior-like thing to do, but in that moment she didn't care. A slow smile warmed her eyes to liquid gold. Razvan had just given her a key to the way he had survived. He would not ever allow Xavier to truly own him. Whatever path his journey had taken, he had accepted the consequences and was at peace with his decisions, no matter how difficult they might have been.

She brushed back that thick mane of silky striped hair, and then allowed her fingertips to trace the worn lines in his face. Her throat closed on an unexpected lump. "Do you wish for peace, Razvan? Should I have allowed you to slip into the next life?" The lump threatened to choke her. At times he looked so worn, his eyes old, his mind filled with too many memories—none of them good.

"I would not have wanted to miss being with you for the world. Perhaps I spent those long years with Xavier for just this purpose, Ivory. How do we know what we are meant to do? I had years to learn his ways and now each test matters. I do not forget. Ever. Anything you need is stored in my head. And I will quickly absorb all of your battle experience. We will make such a pair as the world has never seen."

He leaned forward and kissed her again, a slow, heartstopping kiss that robbed her of strength so that she clung to him, shaken by the intensity of her emotions. When he lifted his head, his eyes were warm with love. She saw it, stark and unafraid, a raw emotion he didn't bother to hide from her and it made her ashamed of her own fear.

"We will make a pair such as the world has never seen," she agreed.

12

Razvan and Ivory burst through the soil together, coming up out of the earth's arms after weeks of healing underground. The sensation of breathing air again was strange after so long sharing the soil and its healing properties. The moon was a full silver ball in the clear sky, glowing softly and casting light over the snow-covered terrain. Ivory, cautious as always, scanned their surroundings for any hint of danger.

Razvan followed her lead, reveling in his growing Carpathian knowledge. He stretched as he made a full circle, using all of his senses to gather information. He realized he saw and felt differently. He even processed differently. Before, as a Carpathian at full strength, he had been astonished at the flood of information coming to him, but now it was even more intense. It was as if the earth spoke to him, whispered her secrets, and ferreted out the smallest detail to share with him. He had changed some-how, beneath the ground. The soil shared something unnamed with him, allowing the trees and plants, the soil itself to pour a wealth of knowledge into him.

He turned his head to look at his lifemate. She was wearing her familiar fighting garb, the double-breasted vest and pants that molded to her long legs. Her hair was in the thick long braid that signaled business. He loved watching her move, all flowing muscle and soft curves.

"What?" She smiled at him with genuine warmth. There was happiness in her eyes, and, with a glow of satisfaction, he knew that he had brought it into her life.

"You are beautiful." He bent his head and took a tentative lick along his newly healed arm where the white lines clearly matched hers. "I bet if I were to taste you at this precise moment, you would taste of salt and sin." There was a high concentration of minerals in his skin, and he could discern the complex mineral recipe that had been used to heal both of them. He had been revitalized, with trace minerals flowing through his blood, and all of the elements pressed into his body to allow it to re-emerge whole again.

"I want to see your wounds."

Her gaze flicked to his face. "I do not understand."

"I know the vampire injured you, Ivory, and you took care of me rather than heal your wounds. I need to see what is left of the damage."

"Really, scratches. Nothing."

His eyebrow raised. "I recall his shoving an arrow into your breast right over your heart." As he spoke a ripple of pain crossed his face. "When you pulled your hand from his chest it was nearly severed." Razvan swallowed hard, his dark brows coming together in a frown. "He withdrew the arrow from your body, twisting it to do the most damage, and plunged it two inches lower, driving it deep. He was enormously strong and he punched your breast, right over your heart, with tremendous force. I heard your sternum crack."

Had he? She didn't even remember. She remembered Razvan had come to her aid in spite of his condition, sending a fiery blast at Sergey's back, shoving him onto her fist so she could get to the blackened heart. When Sergey had attacked by bringing down the house and forming spears that flew at her from everywhere, Razvan had used his strength to form a barrier around her, taking the brunt of the wooden spears in his own body.

"He broke your wrist."

How had he noticed when he had been so horribly mutilated? Ivory shook her head, unable to speak, not when his gaze moved over her body with brooding allure, touching her in places deep and secret and feminine.

He had to quit reciting the list of her injuries, so pale in comparison to his own. His voice was so gentle, she couldn't get it out of her head. The way he looked at her body when he spoke, as if her injuries were all that mattered to him, the healing of them, the fact that the vampire had hurt her. When she touched his mind, she felt nothing but his need to make certain, to see for himself, that she was wholly healed.

"Mother Earth and the healer aided me, and several Carpathians including the prince gave us blood to speed our healing process. I am fine."

"Nevertheless."

There was a note in his voice that fascinated, thrilled and repelled her all at once. She was unsure how to react to his demand and that confused her.

"What would you have me do?"

He held out his hand to hers. "Let me see."

She moistened her lips, feeling a little shaky, on unfamiliar ground, but she held out her hand to him so he could see the faint lines where the earth had healed the lacerations and knit the bone back together. She was unprepared for the feeling of his gentle fingers stroking over her skin. She felt his touch all the way to her deepest core, and then her heart stood still while his mouth moved over each of the faint white lines and his tongue swirled and stroked a velvet pleasure over her skin.

"You do taste like salt and sin," he said, and his voice roughened with hunger.

She pulled her arm away. "Are you satisfied?"

He shook his head, his gaze locked on hers. "Open your vest."

Her breath actually hitched in her lungs, burned there, raw and hot. Her womb clenched and spasmed, sending ripples of urgent need radiating through her body. His request wasn't sexual. It didn't need to be sexual. Her body didn't have to grow damp and hot with flames licking over her skin and turning her blood into a molten stream that thickened in her veins. She could just be cool about this, one warrior reassuring another. Her hands went to the silver buckles.

"Let me."

His voice was husky, maybe even shook a little, but it made her weak. So much so that she obeyed his silent command when his hands came up and covered hers to halt her unsteady fingers and gently push them aside. The pads of his fingers brushed against the swell of her breast, sending ripples of awareness through her body. His gaze remained locked with hers as he slowly unbuckled the vest and allowed her full breasts to emerge. Only then did he drop his gaze.

She heard him inhale. A sharp, sexy sound that curled her toes. She felt his breath warm her breasts, and her nipples answered by hardening into two tight peaks. She felt exposed, vulnerable, but she couldn't move, mesmerized by the look on his face, the stark, raw desire, the unrelenting hunger and admiration in his eyes. When he stroked his fingertips, feather-light, over the faint lines along the swell of her breast and then again lower, his thumb brushing along her nipple, lightning streaked from breast to belly and then lower, so that her thighs spasmed and her core grew hotter and wetter.

Razvan bent his head toward her. She wanted to stop him. She thought to take a step back, terrified of the feelings coursing through her body and the sudden terrible need that welled up out of nowhere, threatening her hard-won peace of mind. She had chosen him, but she hadn't considered that the physical and emotional pull between them would be so strong. She could barely breathe when he touched her, and she had no control over her body's reaction to him. She held her breath, waiting. Wanting.

His hair touched her first. Soft strands of black and white silk brushing seductively over her skin. Every cell in her body came to life. The breath burned in her lungs. Her fingers curled into fists at her sides as she struggled not to bury them in his hair and cradle his head to her. She was in his mind, and knew this inspection was as necessary to him as breathing. And now it was to her.

At the first gentle touch of his mouth she jumped, and, in spite of her every intention, she found her hands buried in that silky fall of hair. His tongue flicked out to swirl over each line and circle, to flick over her nipple, sending darts of fire racing to her belly and spreading even lower. Her hands tugged him closer even as a low moan escaped. His tongue slid along each line, his healing saliva providing a balm to the deep ache that was still there.

When he lifted his head, his eyes were so dark they were almost black, so blue they were like midnight and so hot with desire she thought she might melt. Her hands trembled and she forced her fingers to let go of the silky strands so he could stand tall. She just stood there while he slowly buckled her vest, enclosing her breasts behind the tight leather.

Ivory took a deep breath, shaken, but proud of herself for standing. "Are you satisfied?"

Razvan's eyes lit up with a male amusement and he deliberately shifted to ease the thick bulge in his trousers. "Not hardly, but I have assured myself you are healing well, and that will do for now."

The color crept up her neck. She shook her head. "You are crazy, but in a good way." She looked back toward the rich black soil, desperate to find something to divert her attention—to divert his attention from her. She gestured toward the ground where they could see the traces of excessive salt running like king's gold in deep veins through the darker loam where the wolf pack still lay sleeping.

"Are you ready for this? They have been attended to by others, Vikirnoff and Nicolas, Natalya sometimes, but they will be ravenous for us. Feeding is part of the ritual of sealing the pack together. They're like my children."

Razvan knew she needed the distraction to feel in control again. Emotions were difficult for her. His heart fluttered in his chest and he found himself smiling at her. Happy. Just to be alive. Just to be with her on this crisp, cold evening, with the moon spilling light over her blue-black hair, framing her face so that she looked as angelic as she did sexy.

"I am certain they will be happy to be out of the ground after all these weeks," he agreed. "Let us do this and bring our family back together."

He found he was as anxious as she to see the wolves. They had become family to him. He had spent so long in her mind that her deep affection for the pack members had transferred to him as well. "As children go, they are a fairly wild bunch."

Ivory laughed with him, sharing his humor over the pack. She stretched her arms and called softly to her pack. "Awake, brothers and sisters. We will run free this night. Come with me. Join with me."

She sent Razvan another quick smile that managed to raise his temperature and quicken his heartbeat. The soil boiled up into a geyser and one by one the six wolves leapt free, shaking their gorgeous silver coats and rushing to Ivory, nearly knocking her over. She sank to the ground, laughing, her arms surrounding them as they greeted her with more enthusiasm than manners.

Raja and his mate, Ayame, turned to Razvan and he sank down beside Ivory, surprised when the big male leapt at his chest and rubbed his body along Razvan's in greeting. He realized just as he had accepted the pack as family, they had accepted him as Ivory's mate. Joy swept through him. A family. Another gift from Ivory. He sank his fingers into the thick fur and roughhoused a little, ignoring the show of teeth, feeling the wolf's laughing intent.

Each animal took its turn coming to him and greeting him, being welcomed by him and reaffirming its position in the pack. He found he was particularly fond of Blaez, the second-in-command. He was quietly confident and very alert to danger, taking his cues from Raja, yet guarding the pack with a fierceness that told Razvan he would have had a pack of his own had his circumstances been different. He felt that same fierce protectiveness toward Ivory and the pack, and there was a sense of kinship when he stroked his hand through the thick fur and scratched the alert ears.

The pack was eager to feed, needing the bond, and he

waited for Ivory to make the decision on how she wanted them fed.

You feed Raja and Ayame and then I will. Next Blaez and his mate Gynger. Last will be Farkas and his mate, Rikki. If we start off that way, they will accept your leadership faster.

The offer of leadership in the pack was another great gift. He knew, after a century of being led by Ivory, they would always respect her and follow her, and she was now stepping aside in order to get the pack to follow his lead as well.

It is not necessary. I do not mind the present order. I may end up planning our battles but you will be leading us. I will protect you with everything in me.

She looked at him with soft eyes. "I mind. I want them to accept you as I have."

His stomach clenched in response, his groin thickening. But it was his heart that was most in danger. He drank her in as he offered his wrist to Raja, the rich beauty of her, not so much her physical body, but the light in her soul that shone over his.

The silver alpha wolf looked at Ivory and then obediently trotted over to Razvan and accepted the first feeding as was his due. Razvan fed the big male, all the while keeping his gaze locked on Ivory.

For so long he'd had nobody in his world, no one to send him warmth, to make him smile, to care whether he lived or died—and yet now there she was, sitting like some forest princess in the middle of her unusual wolf pack, willing to share her life with his, even if it was so he could aid her in destroying Xavier. He would take that—he'd take any reason at all, as long as she included him in her family.

"You are as essential to me as the air I breathe or the soil we rest in." He wanted her to know that he would have chosen her no matter what their destiny had been. He wanted her to know that, because of her, the sacrifices in his life had been more than worthwhile.

She shot him a look from under her thick lashes. "You are my lifemate, my other half."

He smiled at her, refusing to feel a sting at her reminder. She didn't have to feel the same way. "That is not what I am saying to you. I am not asking for anything in return, Ivory. I just felt it was important for you to know how I feel."

The alphas were finished feeding from Ivory now and the second pair took their place as the smallest ones fed on Razvan. He was beginning to get a little dizzy. Ivory hadn't been kidding when she said they would wake up ravenous and would want to bond with the ritual blood.

Ivory ducked her head and he saw her fingers curl deeper into Gynger's thick pelt. The tip of her tongue moistened her bottom lip, drawing his immediate attention. He'd made her nervous again, and that endeared his fierce warrior to him all the more. She wasn't the least bit comfortable talking about emotions. The wolves pressing close to her and winding around their mates seemed to give her the necessary impetus to answer him.

Her chin came up and her eyes reluctantly met his briefly before her long lashes once again veiled them. "You mistake my meaning."

That was all he was going to get out of her, but it was enough for him. The slow burn that started in his belly mixed with the blaze of love in his heart, making for a potent combination. He savored the feeling of wanting her. He had never thought he would feel that for a woman. He abhorred the crimes his body had committed and never thought to feel the powerful draw between lifemates for himself, yet every moment in her company strengthened his emotions for her and the urgent needs of his body.

He knew, deep inside, a beast had been awakened by this one woman. Only she could set that part of him free. Only she could tame that wild part of his nature. He watched her fingers move through the fur of the wolves and knew he wanted those same fingers stroking his skin. He had kissed her in their shared dream and he could taste her in his mouth, on his tongue, filling his senses with the wild rain of her, the scent and taste of a new storm washing the forest clean.

Laughing, amazed that he was alive and with her, he reached for the change, let it take him, the wonderful wrenching of muscle and bone, the stretch of tendons and sinew as his body bent and changed, as his skin itched and then fur burst through, his own luxurious pelt of black and silver, the markings distinct. His muzzle was elongated, his mouth filled with teeth and the delicious sense of freedom. His paws were large and moved over the snow and ice easily as he circled around his mate, pushing playfully at her with his nose.

The pack instantly pushed up against him, eager for the run, tails up and swishing as they nudged their noses against Ivory, wanting her to hurry.

"Okay, okay, you monsters," she acquiesced, laughing.

Through his wolf's eyes, Razvan watched her embrace the change, going to ground, the movement graceful and fast, so that one moment she was standing tall, elegant and beautiful, and in the next she was on all fours, a sleek, gorgeous wolf with a silvery coat. There was no mistaking her eyes; they glowed a soft amber as she looked at him, her mouth smiling.

The pack immediately went to her as they had done to

him, lowering their bodies in submission. She rubbed her body along theirs, accepting their homage, and then the pack went crazy, leaping around playfully, wagging tails held high, bowing toward one another and then pouncing, rolling in the snow and coming up laughing.

Razvan felt Ivory's laughter and then she lifted her head to the moon and howled for the sheer elation of it. Laughing, he joined her, adding his voice, claiming the territory, letting the pack sing their joyful music. The wild notes rang through the trees, lifted to the stars and moon and then there was silence as Ivory lifted her nose to scent the wind.

She took off running, streaking through the trees with the pack close on her heels, and Razvan discovered the sheer enjoyment of running in the pack. The wolf's body was made for running, the slight webbing between the toes allowing him to race lightly and easily over the snow. Because the wolf walked on its toes, he found his weight was evenly distributed, making the body more efficient for running. Razvan loved the new form, reveling in the way his muscles stretched and contracted as he loped along, covering large amounts of ground, easily springing over fallen logs.

All the while he ran, and the pack left evidence of their passing through the glands on their feet, marking the trail for one another and warning others away. At first Ivory set a fast pace, running flat out, letting the pack feel their bodies again, the flow of muscle, the wealth of information, the sound of the forest. He could hear the water trickling below the ice and the way the needles rustled in the snow-laden branches overhead as the wind blew just hard enough to send the limbs swaying.

The scent of rabbit and fox was heavy, as well as that of

an abundance of other forest creatures, all shivering in silence as the pack passed through their territories. Ivory swerved left, away from the Carpathian village toward the caves and sacred places the Carpathians used in their rituals. She didn't want her pack to run into any local wolves. As a rule she kept an uneasy truce between her pack and any others they encountered, but for now they were exercising their freedom and deserved to go unscathed through any territory they chose.

She was proud of them for their roles in saving the farmer and his family; at least, she hoped the little girl was still alive. No one had told her one way or the other, although she could understand why. They had all been amazed at the volume of minerals and elements the earth had encased her and Razvan in, a primordial mixture of everything needed to revitalize and repair them. The earth had done so centuries earlier for her alone, without the healing aid or blood of the Carpathians. It had been a struggle to find enough blood to maintain life.

She had been nearly insane those long years, merely existing without thought for anything but survival and, in the intervening years, she had accepted her solitary life. Now, Razvan ran beside her, his shoulder occasionally brushing hers, his heart beating in rhythm with hers. Every step through the snow, winding through the trees, fording a small, still-unfrozen river and skirting ice edgings was so much more fun.

I forgot about fun.

And there was that. Mind to mind. She wasn't alone anymore and never would be again. Once Razvan had bound them together she had merged her soul with his, her body with his, mind and heart, until they were literally one in spirit. He had experienced her life, just as she had experienced his. There was nothing they could hide from one another. She didn't know which was worse, the psychological damage Xavier had inflicted on Razvan or the torture. Once his aunts had turned him, she was certain that, as a Carpathian male, the worst would have been being used to breed children for Xavier to consume. And also betraying his sister, desperate to send her warnings, only to have Xavier corrupt each message until the mage had nearly trapped her.

As she loped across a field of white, Ivory moved closer to him, wanting to experience his first time as a wolf, wanting to be the one to give him joyful memories to ease the worst of his experiences. He stretched his neck and ran it along hers as he moved, and she felt him move in her mind, surrounding her will with warmth.

I am having the time of my life. I have never had such fun. I am not certain I would have known how to have fun without you showing me. I suppose one needs to have a companion to share this kind of adventure with to really savor it.

She liked the way he thought. Mostly she just liked his company. They played hide-and-seek in the trees and covered each other in snow. At one point Raja initiated a strange game of dog pile and Razvan seemed to be the one the wolves all leapt on, rolling in the snow and down an embankment, with Ivory laughing at him.

Razvan surged to his feet, reveling in the wolf's strength, shaking his body to loosen the snow clinging to his black undercoat and the silver tips of his fur. Ivory leapt from the bank and hit him with her shoulder, sending them both tumbling back down the slope, rolling so that the ice crystals clung to their fur. When they rose, they looked like two wolves carved of snow.

Razvan rubbed his body along Ivory's, helping to get the

snow off before turning and directing the pack back toward the Carpathian homes scattered throughout the forest. It was an amazing feeling to have the entire pack follow him. Ivory was just two or three paces behind, all of them trotting in ground-eating silence. The wind was in his face, the night air singing to him, smaller animals scurrying away to safety as he led the wolves through the forest, giving the pack their due, knowing who ruled there in that moment.

Both Ivory and Razvan needed to feed before they went to their lair, and he was eager to go, to get out of Carpathian territory. It was one thing to "see" his sister and daughter from a distance, to be told he might have a second and third daughter he knew nothing about. But to face them and watch them judge him—that was much more difficult.

It matters little to us, Razvan. I know who you are. And I know what is in your heart and soul. If they choose to look at you with suspicion . . .

As they should, he reminded gently, hearing the protective note in her voice. But it warmed him that she did know his heart and soul. She knew him better than anyone else, and, if he was strictly honest, he had to admit that having one person in the world know what his life had been, what his sacrifices were, mattered.

You are a miracle, Ivory. It is good to know there is one person who holds my true life in her memories. Why did it matter so much now, when he had accepted for so long that he was branded traitor, criminal, most despised and despicable Carpathian on the face of the earth. Just the thought that Ivory might believe he had bred children for the sole purpose of using their blood to feed his longevity made him ill.

Do not, Razvan. I have shared all of your life, even the most

263

hazy of your memories. Whatever your body was directed to do, it was not your spirit, the essence of who you are, that allowed it to happen.

He had to concede she was right. *But my choices led to him using my body.*

I have come to believe that fate hands us our destiny. Maybe I needed to endure the things in my life to be worthy of traveling by your side. Maybe you needed to endure your life in order to fulfill a great destiny. What we did shaped us and honed us into what we are now.

And what she was—was everything. He turned his face from hers, hiding his eyes as he continued up the trail leading to the prince's home. There was so much emotion in him for her that he didn't dare let her see, afraid of scaring her. She was so fragile when it came to accepting actual love. He tasted the word on his tongue, found it belonged in his heart. Yes, he was in love with his lifemate, and the emotion grew stronger with every minute spent in her company.

Razvan lifted his head and sent a questing call to the prince, announcing the presence of the pack. He knew Raven, the prince's lifemate, was pregnant and close to delivery. The entire Carpathian people anticipated the event and, no doubt, so did Xavier. That alone would make some of them suspicious about the timing of Razvan's appearance. It was best if they paid their respects and left as quickly and as quietly as possible.

Do you think Xavier will make a move against the prince's child?

I have no doubt, especially if the child is male. Razvan considered it carefully. *He will have to make his move. He hates the Dubrinsky family above all else. They represent the power of an immortal race.*

We can be killed, Ivory pointed out. *As such we are not truly immortal.*

When Xavier looks in the mirror, his flesh is rotting off the bone, and he looks at you, what do you think he wants? He stays alive now only by the blood of others, and yet every day he is slipping more and more. The blood cannot change his rotting brain. His entire life he has fought to defeat that family. He must do so now.

Then we must be ready for him. This might be our chance, Razvan, but we will need time to prepare for the battle. There was not so much eagerness as purpose in Ivory's voice.

That is probably why the master vampire was in the area. He searches for Xavier.

She drew in her breath sharply, skidding to a halt there in the deep forest. Razvan stopped immediately and turned back to her, shifting to his normal form. She followed his example, unknowing that her face was as pale as the snow beneath their feet.

"What is it?"

His voice was gentle. His eyes were gentle. Everything about him was, except for his strength, that deep, abiding, relentless strength that meant he would never stop. He didn't put his arm around her to comfort her—she would have pulled away. He simply put one hand on her shoulder and looked her straight in the eye, questioning. Not once did he invade to demand an answer. He stood there, simply looking at her, waiting for her to confide in him. She found him irresistible.

"As you know, Sergey was my brother. Long ago, in another time, he was my brother, yet he joined our greatest enemy. The very man who had me torn apart. He became the very thing that Xavier used to chop me into pieces and scatter me to the wolves. They laughed, Razvan.

I can still hear them sometimes when I first awaken from beneath the soil. I tell myself he is not my brother, but it was my brother who made this choice. He *wanted* to become vampire. He *chose* to go into league with Xavier. He did these things not to avenge me, but for power. Because my brothers believed the Carpathian people should follow them. They want power."

She didn't want that knowledge to hurt anymore. She wasn't that same naïve young woman who adored her brothers and believed the best of everyone. She knew Prince Vlad had sent her to Xavier's school, not to help her but to get her out of his son's sight. She looked at Razvan, unaware of the tears in her eyes. "It still hurts."

This time he did pull her close in that same gentle, slow way. He wrapped his arms around her and pressed her face into his shoulder and just stood, silently offering her comfort. She thought his compassion might diminish her somehow, but it only filled her with warmth and steadied her as nothing else could. She wasn't that young girl anymore, but she wasn't alone either. She had Razvan, and somehow he fit her like a second skin.

"I am all right," she whispered, pressing a kiss along his neck. The blood pounded there, calling to her. Her body stirred restlessly and she felt the instant answering heat of his. "It was a momentary weakness, passed now."

"Not weakness, *fél ku kuuluaak sívam belsö*—beloved. You are supposed to feel whatever you can. Regret, sorrow, pain, even betrayal. There is reason for sadness in that, for the loss of a loved one. Grief. You do not dwell on these things, but you must feel them. It is part of life."

She sent him a small smile, pressed one last kiss against his neck just to feel his warmth and take in his masculine scent. She stood there, her body leaning into his, her face

266

buried against his throat, and she knew she could face anything with him. "We certainly can say all those things have been part of our lives," she agreed, forcing a briskness into her voice to cover the emotion that threatened to spill over as she stepped away from him.

His fingers curled around her arm, slid down to her wrist and remained there like a bracelet. She couldn't look at him, not when her heart was so full. She felt silly and shy and out of her comfort zone. No one had touched her with such disarming tenderness. No one looked at her with such desire or love. She could only handle so much attention after being alone for centuries.

He cupped her chin in his palm and forced her head up, waiting until her long lashes lifted the veil over her eyes and their gazes locked together. She felt the rush of heat, like a drug pouring through her veins.

"You are a very dangerous man, Dragonseeker," she whispered.

His slow smile set off a burn, low and sinfully wicked.

"That is just as well, warrior woman, as you are the most dangerous woman I know." There was gentle amusement in his voice. And pure velvet heat.

He leaned his head down toward hers, taking his time in that slow, measured way he had. The way she knew he would stroke her skin. The way he touched her with the pads of his fingers, so light, but savoring, a slow burn that spread until the fire raged out of control, refusing to be dampened or extinguished.

She could feel her body tightening. Her breasts aching. Her womb spasming. His breath was warm and male. She couldn't close her eyes. She watched his face change as he came closer and closer to her. The way he looked, those worn lines softening, the wonder on his face and the building hunger in his eyes. She could see his long lashes, thick and full, the only really feminine thing about him, when his body was all hard muscle and strong, broad bones.

His breath took hers. Exchanged. He breathed for her. In her. He took her over, with that same slow, measured stroke of his mind. And then his lips were on hers and a heat wave rushed over her. White lightning streaked in her veins, electricity sizzled and snapped over her skin until she was lost, drowning in the pure fire of his kiss.

Ivory didn't know how it happened, but she found herself with her arms circling his neck and her mouth fused to his, her body pressing close. She felt a shudder run through his body, and hers trembled in answer. She wanted to stay there, just like that, in that perfect moment, with happiness and hunger singing through her veins. She tried to quench the desire rising like a tidal wave, swamping her, but there was no way to stop the rising need.

His lips left hers and trailed seductively from the corner of her mouth to her chin, to her throat; a burning fire at the swell of her breast. She felt the scrape of his teeth and she moaned, the sound breathy and a little desperate. His tongue swirled over the soft mound. Her breath caught in her throat. Another sound escaped. Her fingers fisted in his glorious hair as his teeth sank deep and the erotic pain burst into a swelling pleasure that spread through her body faster than lightning strikes to settle into a throbbing beat pulsing between her legs.

She wound one leg around his and cradled his head, trying not to cry at the pleasure crashing through her. He savored the taste of her like a fine wine, not gulping or tearing, but drawing the essence of her life and the exotic flavor of her into him slowly. His hands slid down her back and pressed her hips forward so that she could feel him hard and hot against her. Just as she thought she might drown completely, or sob and plead with him to complete their bonding, his tongue swept over the pinpricks.

His breathing was ragged, his eyes hot and a little wild. He simply tore his shirt open and pressed the back of her head with his hand. His fingers curled into a fist, bunching her silken braid, holding her against him, her mouth over the tempting sound of his heart. His blood ebbed and flowed, beckoning, a terrible temptation she couldn't resist.

She nuzzled against the heavy muscle of his chest, loving the feel of his strength and the depth of his response to her touch. With deliberate intent she stroked her tongue over his pounding pulse, wanting that Zenlike calm to go up in flames. She needed to know—absolutely know—that he not only wanted but needed her with the same growing intensity that she did him. She couldn't be alone in this desperate need.

His hand pressed her head closer, a silent command to take his offering. She did another slow swirl of her tongue just to hear that deep male groan, to feel the jump of his pulse and the hammering of his heart. She let the fire take her, sweeping up through her feminine channel to her belly and breasts, while her teeth lengthened and she drew the scent of him into her lungs.

He whispered something low and guttural, the sound more important to her than the words. His fingers were magical in her hair and against her scalp, the nape of her neck, and one hand swept over her buttocks, pressing tightly as he half lifted her. The strength in her body matched that of his will and she couldn't help the feminine thrill at the feeling of his hardness against her softness.

She took a breath, savoring the moment of exquisite lust

wrapped with terrible love so sharp it pierced her heart. Then she sank her teeth into his body, connecting them in the way of lifemates. Richness spilled into her. Every cell soaked him up, took him inside. The taste of him burst against her tongue like fizzing bubbles.

Razvan gave another throaty moan, even sexier than the first one, the sound vibrating through her body, adding to the swirling mix of emotions welling up with her physical reaction to him. He moved her like no other could, getting under her skin and into her bones, and now, the addictive taste of him nearly made her lose all perspective. She needed him, right there in the middle of nowhere with snow on the ground.

Not our first time. Our first time together I want to have hours with you, not a few minutes with our pack surrounding us and with danger at every turn.

Even his denying her was sexy. The velvet voice, the slow heat, the stark need he didn't try to hide from her. She let herself take one last taste and then she swept her tongue across the pinpricks and simply stood, letting his strength hold her up when her entire body was trembling.

"You are right," she said with regret.

"We need to go home soon." He whispered the words in her ear.

She liked the sound of that. More, she loved the husky note in his voice that told her he was every bit as shaken as she was. For an answer, she circled his neck with her arms and just held him, just absorbed him into her.

The pack grew restless, circling them and nudging at their legs in inquiry. Ivory found herself smiling. "The children are growing impatient, as children do."

To her consternation his hand slid down to her abdomen and rested there, fingers splayed wide. "You will look so beautiful with our child in you, should we ever manage to destroy our enemy."

Ivory had never considered the possibility of a child. Her entire life had been devoted to one thing—ridding the world of an evil monster. The idea that she might have a lifemate and a child, that she could someday live with a semblance of normalcy, shocked her. She wasn't entirely certain she could handle it.

Razvan laughed softly and leaned down to feather his lips lightly over hers. "Do not worry, my little warrior. There will never be normal for either of us, but we will make our own rules and our life will suit us just fine."

"Let's get this done then," Ivory said.

13

Mikhail Dubrinsky greeted Razvan and Ivory from his long, wraparound verandah. The house was large, nestled in the trees, blending into the forest so well that Ivory knew with a certainty that most people would never spot it unless the prince eased the safeguards around it. She was dressed in her warrior garb, with the wolves riding her body as tattoos. She preferred that to having him look too closely at her pack. Razvan stayed close to her, just a step behind, as if he was her guard, rather than her partner. She had tried twice to lag in her step to force him to walk beside her, but, once Razvan made up his mind about something, nothing stopped him.

"Good evening," Mikhail said. "*Sívad olen wäkeva, hän ku piwtä*—may your heart stay strong, hunters," he added in a more traditional greeting.

Ivory murmured a greeting, and glanced over her shoulder to look at Razvan. She couldn't feel nerves in him, or sense that he was in any way distressed over visiting the prince of the Carpathian people, yet he maintained his distance—that precise two steps to the side and behind her pace. His gaze moved restlessly over the house, the grounds, searched the trees and quartered every inch of their surroundings as if he was looking for a trap. His face was sober, mouth in a firm line. He was making her uneasy with the way he was acting, when they should have been safe so deep in Carpathian territory.

What is it? She sent a smile to the prince to cover the fact that Razvan had yet to speak.

I do not know, but he is not alone. We are surrounded.

Well, of course, she'd known there would be others. Gregori for certain would never allow a meeting with the prince and his lifemate without his presence. Now she was more than uneasy.

"You welcome us, yet your people seem to be circling into position," Razvan said.

His voice was hard, harder than Ivory had ever heard him speak. Now she knew why he had dropped back. He expected an attack, not from the front but from behind or either side. He wore a look that told her he meant business, and suddenly their friendly visit wasn't so friendly after all. In that moment she knew he was entirely capable of killing the prince should the Carpathian make a move toward her.

She took a small step back and away from Razvan, moving quickly from woman to warrior. Her bow came up slightly, the arrow angled just enough to cover the prince's heart. "We thought only to thank you for your aid," she said. "Nothing more. We will leave if we are not welcome."

The prince stepped into the open area, away from the long, smooth railing out to where she would have a clear shot at him. He kept his hands out away from his sides. "You are most welcome. My lifemate is inside and wishes to meet you. She cannot get up to greet you properly and had hoped you would have the time to visit with her."

He looked around the surrounding forest and sent out a call to the hunters surrounding his home. *These are my guests and they are welcome.* There was no mistaking the edge of anger in his voice. "Please, accept my apologies and come inside."

Ivory glanced at Razvan. "It is up to you. If you do not feel welcome here, I have no wish to stay." She did want news though. She needed news. If they were going to effectively hunt Xavier, they needed every detail the Carpathian people could provide.

Gregori came out onto the porch, his arms folded across his chest. "Every time I take my eyes off you, you make yourself a target," he said to Mikhail with a small grin. He lifted his gaze to the Dragonseeker. "When the prince wishes you to visit and guarantees your safety, it is a great honor."

Ivory's eyes flashed a single searing heat. "Only if one trusts the prince."

"Do you?" Mikhail asked, his gaze holding hers steady. "Do you trust me?"

Ivory was silent a moment, studying his face. He was nothing like his brother. And little like his father. She took a breath and felt Razvan move inside her mind. Supporting her. Holding her steady when the past was too close. She felt the brush of Razvan's mind in hers, strong and enduring and totally for her. No one else. Razvan's loyalty was utterly hers and belonged to no one else.

"Yes."

Mikhail stepped aside and gestured toward his front door with a slight bow. "Please enter my home as my honored guests." His gaze slid over Razvan. "Both of you."

Razvan moved up then, past Ivory, his senses flaring out

to inspect the occupants of the house. There were two women and several men inside. He halted at the door and glanced toward Gregori.

"Do you think we would prepare a trap in the very home of the prince with his lifemate present?" Gregori hissed, his silver eyes slashing at Razvan.

Razvan didn't flinch under the reprimand. "Tell me you would not be wary of so many distrustful people. Tell me you would not protect your lifemate." His tone was mild, but there was heat in his eyes. "I can feel their suspicion like a weight pressing down on both of us. We need only to give our thanks and leave. We ask for nothing from any of you."

A woman with striped red and gold hair burst from the inside of the house, skidding to a halt just outside the door, ignoring the restraining hand of her lifemate, a tall, imposing warrior with steel eyes and a grim mouth. "Razvan. Please."

Razvan blinked. Inside he crumbled. Went to pieces. His heart. His soul. For a moment his world narrowed to this one woman. The person he had given up everything for. His life. His soul. His sanity. Everything.

"Natalya." He breathed her name, unsteady.

His vision blurred as he stood feeling naked and vulnerable in front of her. It was one thing to talk to her from a distance, in a dream world where he lay beneath the ground safe from the recrimination that must be in her heart. But to have her stand in front of him, his twin sister, the one Xavier had systematically fed false information to and had tricked into giving him spells using Razvan . . .

Ivory surged into his mind. Into his heart. *I am with you.* Four words, but that show of unity meant everything to him. She meant it. Ivory stood with him, tall and straight, a warrior without comparison, utterly proud of him. Her fallen angel—her lifemate.

Natalya's eyes swam with tears. "Razvan, please don't leave."

He opened his mouth to speak, but nothing came out. He swallowed the sudden lump in his throat threatening to choke him. One hand came up of its own volition and touched that bright hair. Natalya flung herself into his arms, weeping. He closed his arms around her and held her to him, shocked that after so many years, after so much suffering, the bond between them had not been completely broken.

Ivory stayed in his mind, holding him just as close, easing the terrible weight of responsibility that poured into his mind. He had long ago dealt with and accepted his choices, but to see his sister standing alive and well, healthy and happy, was overwhelming.

He held her at arm's length and looked her over carefully. "You look good, Natalya. Young." So young. He was her twin, yet he was so much older.

You have earned every wonderful line. Ivory slipped her hand into his when he dropped his arms away from his sister. His fingers tangled and clung.

"This is Vikirnoff, my lifemate." Natalya rubbed the tall warrior's arm, the movement mesmerizing, as if she stroked a talisman that held her together.

And maybe, Razvan decided, that's what the man was doing. Ivory was certainly holding him together. "It is good she has you." He meant it. Whatever Vikirnoff might think of him, he was obviously fiercely protective of Natalya. And if the man felt one tenth of what he felt for Ivory, Natalya was in good hands.

Razvan brought Ivory's hand to his chest. She didn't feel comfortable with displays of affection, yet she didn't pull away. She stood beside him, her warmth enveloping him, steadying him, while he pressed her palm over his rapidly beating heart. "This is Ivory—*sívam és sielam*—my heart and soul." He brought her fingertips to his lips. "Ivory, my sister, Natalya, and her lifemate, Vikirnoff."

It was amazing to him to be able to stand there, free, in Natalya's presence, unafraid that he was providing bait for a trap that Xavier had set. But more than anything he felt pride in the woman at his side. He felt that with her he had everything. She had somehow turned a bleak, hopeless life into moments of pure joy—such as this one.

"It is wonderful to finally meet you," Ivory said. "Your brother speaks of you often. And thank you for aiding our wolf pack, as well as giving us blood when we were in such need."

Ivory followed Natalya and Vikirnoff into the house. Power surged through her the moment she entered. She glanced at Razvan to see if he'd felt that strong ripple of energy. He nodded silently at her, obviously uncomfortable that Gregori was behind them.

Raja has our backs, she assured.

"It was an amazing feat for the wolves to carry four humans through such treacherous terrain with a vampire close on their heels," Mikhail observed.

Ivory shot him a wary glance. "They are special. My family. Thank you for aiding them. Is the little girl still alive? We had no time to prep her for the journey. We had to send them out fast."

"I saw the destruction at the farmhouse." Mikhail went straight to the woman sitting in a large, stuffed chair, her feet resting on an ottoman. "My lifemate, Raven," he said and there was a wealth of love in his voice. "Raven, Ivory and Razvan."

"Thank you for coming," Raven said. "I'm sorry I can't get up, but do please sit down." She sent a quick glare at both her lifemate and Gregori. "It seems I'm being dictated to by both the healer and Mikhail."

"And I so enjoy the opportunity," Mikhail said, unrepentant.

Ivory and Razvan sat in two of the wide-backed chairs set in a circle. Mikhail sank onto the arm of Raven's chair and Gregori seated himself opposite Razvan, his restless eyes moving constantly to sweep the surrounding forest through the windows.

"I think you have enough guards out there," Ivory said. "I counted seven. Did I miss any?"

"Guards?" Raven echoed, looking from the prince to the healer. "What guards?"

It was Natalya who answered. "My brother has been considered the enemy for so long, many, including me, thought him a traitor, and it is difficult for others to believe he isn't."

"You are pregnant with the prince's son," Gregori pointed out gently. "Many think it is a suspicious coincidence that he has arrived when you are close to giving birth."

"But Mikhail would never invite anyone into our home he was not certain of," Raven said. "That's utterly ridiculous."

"And they are suspicious of me as well," Ivory pointed out, unwilling to let the prince get off too easily. "Because I am a Malinov."

"Long thought dead these past centuries," Gregori said. "Yes, some are suspicious, but I have been in your mind, healing you and Razvan. I know what you went through to save the farmer and his family."

"Tell me about the child," Ivory persisted.

"She lives and is well," Gregori assured. "Falcon and Sara took the family in until the child was healed. They are living at the inn now, and we will help them get started again. Just about everything they had was destroyed. Fortunately, the vampire didn't kill all of the animals, as often happens. You must have come along and interrupted him before he could do too much damage to the farm."

"Have you erased their memories?" Ivory asked.

Mikhail leaned forward, frowning. "The parents were easy enough, but the children still have nightmares. Gregori is working to help them. Some are more resistant than others. I'd like you to tell me about your wolves."

Ivory stayed very still. Razvan was just as still inside as she was, sensing this was no idle question. "I made a promise to the wolf pack that helped me and I have always kept it. The summer the pups were born, game was plentiful and it had been a mild winter. The pack had two litters of pups, which sometimes happens in a good year. I helped with the hunting, so my pack was well fed and the alpha pair and the next in the hierarchy mated. The vampires hunted my pack and destroyed them, hoping to find me running amongst them."

Her hand trembled in her lap and Razvan laid his over it, his thumb sliding back and forth in a soothing gesture. Ivory didn't look at him, but she opened her mind to his and let him comfort her where no one else could see. It had been one of the worst moments she could remember, finding the pack dead and dying.

"The pups are all that remain of my original pack. They were badly hurt, but I was not entirely"—she searched for the right word—"sane . . . in those days. I could still barely stand the moonlight and spent most of the hours beneath the ground. I needed the pack for my own survival. I couldn't let them go, and I crawled into the den with them and gave them my blood repeatedly. Sometimes I had no choice but to take their blood. It was a long time—weeks, I do not really remember—before the first turned."

She remembered that moment, the animal screaming in pain, and her shock at what she'd done. "I was careful to make certain they learned to hunt only with me. I feed them and care for them. They do not breed." She lifted her head and looked the prince straight in the eye. "They are my family. We have hunted the vampire for centuries and they have saved my life countless times." She conveyed in that one brooding look exactly what she meant—that she would fight to the death for her pack.

"You can see how they could be troublesome if they began to prey on the human race for food," Gregori said.

She flicked him a cool glance. "No more than when one of us does. We would have no choice but to hunt the wolf and destroy it."

Mikhail held up his hand. "We just needed to know, Ivory. The pack is most unusual, but you seem to have it all well in hand."

Razvan stirred. "It grows late and we have not fed. The pack is fine, but we must hunt before we return home."

He savored the word *home*. Let it roll off his tongue. The confines of this house were too stifling. He couldn't really remember when he had been in a home, certainly not with so many other people with all eyes on them. Ivory was hiding it well, but she was equally uncomfortable. Neither of them was good at social skills, having been alone for so many years.

"We can feed both of you," Mikhail said. "I really brought you here for a purpose."

Ivory settled back in her seat, but Razvan noticed that her fingers circled her crossbow, and he felt the ripple of awareness in the wolves. "Of course you did."

Mikhail smiled easily. "Our children are dying before they are born, Ivory. I have no time to waste on the niceties. Our greatest minds have tried to find solutions to the problem and finally, recently, we had a breakthrough. We discovered the source of our miscarriages is Xavier. He mutated extremophiles, microbes that attack our unborn children. The microbes are in the soil. Even should we move locations, and of course we considered that, he can contaminate soil anywhere we go. We have to stop him."

"That is our goal," Ivory said.

"Gregori informed me he believes both of you are set on destroying Xavier. He believes, if anyone can do so, you two have the best chance. I have a great deal of faith in Gregori, as well as in my own instincts. We would like to aid you in any way possible."

"No," Natalya interrupted. "No, Razvan." She shook off Vikirnoff and stood, hands on her hips. "I've just got you back. You can't go near that man. Not for any reason. You know he's hunting you. You know he is."

Razvan sighed. When she was a child he had never liked it when Natalya was upset, and it was equally bad now that she was a fully grown adult. "I know him better than any other, Natalya," he said, his voice gentle. "Ivory has studied him and has actually worked with him at one time in his school. She is good with his spells, turning them around. Mikhail is right in that Ivory and I have a better chance of stopping him than any other we know of."

"But it isn't right. You've suffered enough." What she really meant was she'd given him up for years, and it wasn't right for either of them. She wanted him back.

Vikirnoff held out his hand and, after a moment's hesitation, she took it, leaning back against him, obviously trying not to cry.

"Ivory's and Razvan's great sacrifice may be the very thing that saves our people," Mikhail said. "Both knew our enemy in the years we thought him dead. We have only Lara to keep the unborn children alive, and she cannot continue forever. We have four women—Syndil; you, Natalya; Lara and Skyler—who can cleanse the earth. Our species is very fragile right now. Should we manage to remove the threat of Xavier, we still will be fighting the odds to continue. We need Razvan and Ivory. We need every warrior we have to fight in any capacity they can."

"I do not understand what you mean about these extremophiles," Ivory said, frowning. "Before, when we were beneath the ground, I caught images of these things in your minds, but I do not understand exactly what these things are used for. Xavier has bred parasites to enhance the vampire's communication as well as to identify his allies. What do these microbes do?"

"They are in the soil and enter the male's body while he rests," Gregori answered. "During sex he transfers the mutated microbes to the woman, who then transfers it to her unborn child. It is a vicious circle we cannot seem to stop."

"And you are very certain Xavier is the source?" Ivory asked.

It was Razvan who answered. "I witnessed his experiments, all of them. I was present when he cast his evil spells, twisting and corrupting nature for his own dark purpose. He had pools of blood and liquid poison."

Ivory's head came up as if scenting a fresh trail. "You actually *heard* his spell? He let you? You were there with him?" She tried to quell the exhilaration bursting through her.

"I told you I am not good with spells. That was why he wanted Natalya. She is."

Natalya started to interrupt, to say something, but Mikhail silenced her. *Let them speak together.* He could see—feel, even—that Ivory was suddenly excited.

"But you have an extraordinary memory," Ivory pointed out. "I have seen it, and you do not forget the smallest detail." She looked to Gregori for confirmation, knowing the healer had spent a great deal of time in Razvan's mind. "We have talked about this, Razvan. If you can remember the precise, *exact* words of his spells, I am certain that I can unravel them. He used apprentices for the base of most of his spells, and then, when they were getting too good at what they did, he got rid of them, because he feared them."

Razvan's hand moved against hers, stroking over her wrist, over the thin white line where a cut had been. *I have said I can remember, and yes, I recall even this one, but the remembering will not be easy.* He didn't want to relive those days of torture, the sounds of screaming, helpless victims, of women he couldn't help, of his own role, whether knowing or not. *If it is your wish, I will do so,* he said.

Ivory touched his mind and found that same serene peace in him, the calm of complete acceptance. If she asked him to go back in his memories, she knew he would without hesitation, and love for him shimmered in her heart. Her pride in him rose in her soul. No matter what the others saw when they looked at his worn face, she would always see a hero.

"If you had the spell he used, could you take command of these extremophiles?" Mikhail asked Ivory.

"I might be able to, with enough time. I would have to study the spell. Xavier likes complex spells. And he would need a very complex one for the killing of an entire species and the mutating of another." Ivory shrugged. "I have no idea how long it would take, but so far, when I have studied one of his spells, I have been able to reverse it." Her chin lifted. "I was a very good student."

Now Razvan's thumb pressed into the sensitive skin of her wrist, stroking a caress over her jumping pulse.

"If we have to move from the mountains, we will do so," Mikhail said, "but I doubt if that will solve the problem. Eventually it will spread across our country into other lands. It would be far better if we could eradicate it."

Ivory nodded. "Xavier will make his move against you very soon." She looked at Raven. "You already have a daughter and now, with a son, he cannot afford to let you or your children live. He will come after her."

Mikhail slipped a comforting arm around Raven's shoulders. "We are prepared."

"Is that why your warriors surround this house?" Razvan asked.

Mikhail nodded. "We are all uneasy. The attacks are becoming frequent, picking us apart, one by one, going after the children during the day, using their puppets. They wear us down. It was a shock to have the two of you show up. And, of course, as mentioned earlier, the timing is highly suspicious."

"But not to you?" Again Ivory met his gaze. Steady. Challenging.

He sent her a small smile. "The weight of my people has been on my shoulders a long time, Ivory. I do not have my father's gifts, but I have good instincts. I have to trust them. Few things are certain in this world. I choose to go with my instincts about the two of you and with Gregori's opinion. The combination has rarely failed."

Gregori gave an inelegant snort. "*Never*, you mean. I do not make mistakes when it comes to your safety."

"I do believe Razvan managed to hold a knife to my throat with you not twenty feet away," Mikhail pointed out with amusement.

Ivory realized the relationship between the two men was one of close-knit friendship and camaraderie.

"I paid him a great deal of money to do that," Gregori said. "I wanted you to realize, as our prince, you shouldn't be chasing vampires all over the country and Razvan agreed to help teach you a lesson."

Raven laughed. "You two are impossible. I can feel our guests' hunger. Perhaps you should do something about that so we can visit," she suggested.

"We are capable of hunting," Ivory said, trying not to sound stiff. It was one thing to take blood when she was helpless, something altogether different when she was fit. She was a warrior, not a child.

"There is no need," Mikhail said. "I offer my blood freely."

The prince smiled at her. Easy. Friendly. Making her stomach knot up. She didn't have friends. She didn't know how to have them. What did he want from her? What was he expecting? The room felt too small. She could barely breathe the air.

It matters little what they want from us, Razvan reassured. *We need nothing from them—they need us. Anything we choose to do is our decision. We have no sworn loyalty to this man. We are set on a path and we will continue down it. There is no harm in listening to him. His blood is pure and carries more power than any other. If you do not wish to feed from him, I will do so and feed you later.*

She heard the cool resolve in his voice and her stomach settled. She had stayed alive by being aware of everything around her, of avoiding others and taking great care to put herself in the most advantageous position should she need to fight. Razvan was doing the same.

Ivory had carefully chosen the chair they were seated in so that no one could slip up behind them or get too close from either side. Raven and the prince were quite vulnerable right in front of her. She knew the prince had deliberately seated himself in a position of weakness to take the edge off her sharply honed wariness of such situations and, while she appreciated it, she still wanted to leave.

It was difficult to maintain composure when too many hearts beat, the sound of blood roared through veins, emotions seemed too raw around her. When she'd been alone for so long, being crowded into a room—albeit a spacious one—still was uncomfortable. She forced a smile at the prince, inclining her head like a princess. "We thank you for your generous offer."

It was Razvan, more than her, who was uncomfortable with the feeding process. He didn't like taking blood from a wrist, and she felt his instant aversion to the idea when the prince so casually offered his wrist. She took the blood without hesitation, willing to draw attention away from Razvan.

"I offer you my blood, Razvan," Natalya said into the silence. "I wouldn't mind experiencing the bonding process with you all over again."

Razvan went absolutely, utterly still. Ivory felt his instant rejection, his complete withdrawal. His skin went to a pale white, almost transparent, and the lines in his face deepened.

"I am not the prince, but, as your sister, I offer to you freely."

Every muscle in his body tensed, although he looked as calm and serene as ever. He simply stood and glided away from Natalya, putting distance between them, though a slight smile softened his mouth and his eyes were sad. He inclined his head toward her in a gesture of respect.

"You honor me, little sister, but I cannot accept such a gift."

His stomach churned and bile rose. Ivory slid her tongue over Mikhail's wrist to close the wound and straightened slowly. Razvan looked calm, but she could feel the tension mounting in him.

Gregori frowned. He had given a tremendous amount of blood to Razvan over the past few weeks and had been inside his mind and memories. He sensed the usually serene man was distressed. He rose and walked over to Razvan, blocking the others' sight of him. "It is best for him, Natalya, to take a healer's blood. He is better, but not completely well. His bones must knit stronger than ever."

Razvan said nothing. He didn't trust himself to speak. He simply accepted the healer's offer, grateful the others couldn't witness his shaking hands.

I am with you. You are not a monster, tearing into someone's flesh to get blood. Ivory kept her voice low and steady, reaching to surround him with her presence.

Razvan made no reply, but he did allow her to slip seamlessly into his mind to see the images swirling in chaos. For a moment horror gripped her, as it did him—as it did Gregori—as they shared the sight of a child's wrist being torn into by sharp teeth.

"Xavier has much to answer for," Gregori said quietly.

Razvan again said nothing, but the understanding went a long way toward settling the knots that had pulled tighter and tighter in his stomach. He closed the pinpricks on the healer's wrist and gave him a slight bow of appreciation. Gregori ignored his formality and clapped him on the back.

"It isn't as if we do not know each other," Gregori said.

"Mikhail." Raven's voice was thoughtful. "Have you noticed the resemblance in Syndil and Ivory? They could be sisters."

"I do not have a sister," Ivory assured her. "I had five brothers."

"But you do look alike," Mikhail agreed. "And you have a special affinity with the earth, as Syndil does. She's an extraordinary woman. You will want to meet her."

She was not going to get sucked into the Carpathian community. She could barely function here, unsure of herself, not at all confident, as if everything was off-kilter.

I feel the same. Razvan's voice was gentle in her mind.

What is wrong with us when they are being so kind and welcoming?

We have been too long away from others, he reassured her. *Too long in our own company. We need the open spaces and the quiet of our own lair.*

She was desperate now to end this meeting and go home, but there was something on Mikhail's mind and he wasn't going to let her leave until he told her.

Razvan took her hand. Both were standing now, the first step toward a graceful exit. Before Ivory could make her excuses, Mikhail spoke again.

"Some time ago, Natalya came to us, to these mountains, to look for answers. Her father stole a book."

Razvan drew in his breath sharply, his fingers tightening with sudden strength around Ivory's. "Our father died for that book. Xavier's master spell book. Xavier sealed the book in the blood of each species. Mage. Carpathian. Lycan. Jaguar and human."

"There was no Lycan blood present," Natalya said. "I saw the vision on my quest to find the book. It was sealed with the blood of the three and must be opened with the blood of the three." She looked to her lifemate. *Vikirnoff, why would he lie about this? You saw the vision as I did. Xavier poured the blood of the three. Why would Razvan insist that there were others?*

I do not know. But Natalya heard the suspicion in Vikirnoff's voice.

"He murdered a woman from each species and sealed the book," Razvan said. "I saw him. Whether you choose to believe me or not is up to you."

Mikhail paced across the room. "Lycans hide better than any other species. Their blood is powerful and different. Xavier would have known that. He studied blood and he would never have left them alone. Lycan blood might hide itself, but not human blood."

"Then what happened to the Lycan blood?" Natalya asked. Suspicion crept into her voice in spite of herself. "I saw Xavier perform the ritual."

Ivory flicked her a quick glance and shrugged. "It is probably there, hidden. A secret to help in the protection of the book. If Xavier knew the properties of the Lycan blood, he would know it might hide from others. He could rely on that to keep his book from being opened and used. As for the human blood, Xavier would have no problem hiding anything if he so desired. As for your vision, it is possible he prepared for someone to access it. Xavier put safeguards on everything he did."

Natalya shook her head. She had gone through a horrendous ordeal to recover the book, including watching the death of her father.

"You actually held the book in your hands?" Razvan asked his sister. "You found it?"

She nodded. "Our father left me a message, a way to find it. I brought it to Mikhail."

"I want you to take the book, Ivory," Mikhail said. "No one knows where your lair is. No one has had any idea of your presence for these long years, yet you cannot be that far from our territory. The book must remain hidden and away from Xavier. I entrust you with the book and any knowledge you may gain from having it in your possession."

A gasp went around the room. Even Natalya shook her head. Vikirnoff actually stepped forward aggressively.

"The book was entrusted to you, Mikhail," he objected. "No one else. Forgive me, Razvan, but someone must have a clear head in this matter." Vikirnoff swept his hand toward Ivory. "This woman's lifemate was possessed by Xavier for years. He's been used by Xavier to spy, to trick, to lie and to cause great harm. How do we know he is not tricking all of us even now? Would you take a book so dangerous and put it into the very hands of the man who spent several lifetimes with him? We just met this man." He looked at Gregori. "We have no choice but to take this to the council."

Mikhail drew himself up to his full height. In that moment, he took Ivory's breath away. Power surged in the room, enough that the walls expanded and contracted and there was a shiver of movement beneath their feet. Even his hair crackled with energy.

"I do not ask the advice of the warriors' council, nor do I need to. If you cannot be civil to a guest in my home, then you may leave."

He didn't yell or shout. In fact, his voice was pitched low, but it carried enough weight to take someone down instantly.

Vikirnoff opened his mouth and then closed it, swift impatience crossing his face. "I go on record stating that this is a poor idea and the decision to hand over the book should wait. Until we know these two better, we cannot trust them."

Natalya stood, torn between believing in her brother, and remembering the numerous times it was her brother who had tricked her into giving him information Xavier needed. She shook her head and followed Vikirnoff out of the house.

I am sorry she hurt you, Ivory said, trying to comfort Razvan.

She has reason to worry, Razvan replied gently. *Do not be upset on my behalf.*

"They should have asked if I wanted the book," Ivory said. "I do not. But I thank you for your confidence in us." *Of course I am upset on your behalf. She hurt you whether you acknowledge it or not and you do not deserve that.*

"The book may be of some use to you as you try to find a way to reverse Xavier's spell on the extremophiles," Mikhail said, seemingly unaware that they carried on a private conversation, although Ivory was fairly certain he knew.

Do not blame her, Ivory. She was put through so much over the years. Alone and frightened, with Xavier constantly on her heels. For my sake, do not blame her.

Ivory sighed. She would do anything for Razvan right then. If forgiving his sister and her lifemate meant so much to him, then she would oblige. She sent Razvan a small smile before turning her complete attention to the prince.

"I cannot undo the extremophiles' mutated state, although I might be able to redirect them," Ivory told him. "But that book will not help. The book is one for twisted spells and is so dangerous any wielder trying to use it, including Xavier, will only become as corrupt and twisted as the book itself."

Razvan took her hand, loving her all the more for her support of him. "She is right, Mikhail. It is a work of evil. The blood sealing the book was the blood of the women he killed. In death he sealed it. And in death it would have to be reopened. Destroy it, though it will not be easy. Never let anyone touch it but you, and destroy it as soon as you can figure out how. You cannot risk the contamination."

"He would have put other safeguards on it as well," Ivory added.

"You are certain this is the best course with the book?" Mikhail asked. "If the book has information containing Xavier's spell to kill our children . . ."

"I know it is logical to think you might use the book to reverse it, but that book is nearly as great an enemy to you as Xavier himself. Should that book end up in the hands of one of my fallen brothers, you will know war such as you have never seen," Ivory said. "Destroy it." She sighed heavily. "It will not be an easy task, and one I suspect you will not be able to do alone. Look to Razvan's aunts. I know they still sleep, but, when they awaken, put the matter before them."

"How do we reverse Xavier's spells if we cannot use the book?" Raven asked.

"Razvan will remember the high mage's spells and I will document them," Ivory replied. "In that way we can have a safe record. As long as Razvan lives and remembers, we can probably re-create the entire book without the corruption."

"You believe you can do this?" Raven asked. She pressed both hands protectively over her unborn child.

"I wish to have children some day," Ivory said, although, truthfully, she didn't believe she would survive the coming battle. "I will do this, no matter how long it takes."

14

The night welcomed them, the wide-open spaces, the sky heavy now with new clouds. Ivory inhaled deeply, drawing the night air into her lungs, and laughed just for the sheer joy of being outside where she felt alive. Where she could breathe.

"Let's never do that again," she said.

Razvan grinned at her. "Good idea. You were the one with the good manners, insisting we thank everyone." He stretched his arms to the gray clouds and inhaled. "I do believe it is going to snow on us."

"Shall we take the children and go home?" she asked, her slow grin matching his.

"Are we flying? Running?" He arched a brow at her.

Ivory took a slow, careful look around her. "I think we will walk for now."

Razvan sent his senses flaring out into the night, trying to pick up on what she felt. He didn't doubt that some of the Carpathian hunters might follow them to make certain they were not meeting with Xavier and reporting everything they had spoken of.

"They think I am a spy," he said. "Does it bother you?"

"Actually," Ivory corrected, "they think we are both spies." She sent him an amused grin. "I have spent more than one human lifetime thinking of the Carpathian people as betrayers, and yet they think me the spy."

"Because you are with me," he pointed out. "If you like, when you wish to visit or speak with them to gather information, it will not hurt me to have you go into the village alone. I can spend the time with the pack on the outskirts, waiting for you."

She shook her head. "It is not simply because of you. I am a Malinov. I cannot blame them. The timing is very suspicious. I would be suspicious." But she wasn't happy with his sister. Natalya should have believed in him. She was afraid to believe, more than she disbelieved. Ivory didn't voice her opinion because Razvan simply accepted his sister's suspicions as he did most things, but, if she had an opportunity, she might just have a word with the woman.

Razvan laughed out loud and enveloped her hand with his. "I am still in your mind."

She blushed, realizing she was still in his as well. "It feels so natural. I did not mean for you to hear that."

"I do not mind you wanting to stick up for me, but truly, Ivory, it is not necessary. I have learned to live without Natalya's admiration these long years. I do worry for my daughter, Lara. I hope we can alleviate her problems by eliminating Xavier, but I have no wish to disrupt her life or Natalya's, or even the aunts'. I am fine the way I am. Happy the way I am."

He tucked her hand against his chest as they walked, bringing them close together. "Lara did not come to see me, which you and I both know means that she was not ready to face me. I am uncomfortable in the presence of so many. Emotions, which I am unused to, can be difficult. I need peace in my mind and, with the combination of their doubt and guilt pressing on me, I found myself having to work at keeping my mind calm, which hasn't happened in more years than I care to count."

"They are fools, Razvan, not to understand what you suffered for them. For all of the Carpathian people."

"My aunts will tell them once they emerge from the healing ground. They were kept too long starving and Gregori has long been trying to aid them to recovery," Razvan said. "When we shared minds, I could see them very clearly." He smiled, and this time his eyes held affection. "I observed them as women, as he saw them, not in the form of dragons as they were held captive. It was . . . *astounding*."

Ivory walked through the snow, swinging hands with him, wishing she'd paid more attention to the various people in Gregori's mind. If they hadn't pertained to battle or seemed significant to her, she had tried to be careful of his privacy. Now, she could scarcely recall the two women who had saved Razvan's life by turning him fully Carpathian. They had Rhiannon's blood flowing in their veins—Razvan's grandmother. Rhiannon had come from such a powerful Carpathian line.

"Dragonseeker," she murmured aloud. "How often that name was whispered in awe and respect. You carry that line and you stayed true to it."

The first flakes began to fall. Small crystals of enormous beauty. Razvan watched them as they walked, their tracks light and then, when Ivory wished it, nonexistent. They still left their scent behind, making certain that anyone who might wish to track them would see the wide curve of a new direction.

Razvan walked along beside her, feeling content, occasionally scooping snow into his hand and packing it to form a ball just to throw it at a tree trunk as they passed.

It made him feel a bit like a kid again, carefree and happy, just as much as when he'd run with the wolves.

"You take every moment," Ivory said, "and you live it right then."

He shrugged. "I found that in order to survive I had to live in the moment. I do whatever I am doing with everything in me. I enjoy it, or endure it or survive it." He looked around at the drifting snow and the heavily laden trees with their crystal formations. "This is paradise to me."

"Walking through the forest in the snow, hoping to throw off anyone tracking us?" She laughed, shaking her head. "You really are a little bit peculiar. I like it, but you are still weird."

Razvan's laugh was joyous, the sound deep and pure, sliding into her body and making her heart sing. It made her feel like a bit of an idiot, but she didn't care; she kept the silly smile on her face anyway.

"We have everything we could possibly want right here in this moment. You. Me. The pack. Look around you. The snow is beautiful, the trees unbelievable. We are happy. Whatever comes later, we have these moments right now. Right here. We may as well make the best of them because we will never get these moments back."

He lobbed a snowball at her. It landed in her hair and broke, covering the blue-black strands with flakes. He sprinted away from her.

Ivory gasped and went after him scooping up snow on the run, packing and throwing with the tremendous speed and accuracy born of throwing her arrowheads.

Razvan dodged, looking over his shoulder at her, laughing. She was so beautiful to him, running in the snow with her long strides, her muscles rippling beneath the smooth expanse of skin. Just the way she moved was pure sin. Her eyes were enormous with excitement. Crystal flakes landed on her lashes and she batted the two thick crescents to get the snow off. The gesture was feminine, sexy beyond measure yet totally unintentional.

He took advantage and reversed direction, running at her fast, hurling three snowballs to distract her, uncaring where they hit, watching her mouth, that beautiful bow of a mouth, curved and soft and so tempting. He dropped his shoulder and caught her low, lifting her and taking her down in one smooth move.

They landed in the snow, sinking into the icy powder. Razvan caught her wrist before she could stuff another snowball down his shirt. She laughed up at him, looking good enough to eat. Before he could take advantage and kiss her, she pushed up with her heels, loosening him enough to roll them over so she was on top, trying to pin him down. They wrestled there in the snow, the flakes rising like a whirlwind to meet the ones falling from the sky, their laughter stirring the needles on the trees. The wind carried the sound on the stillness of the night.

They lay side by side, throwing arms and legs out, like two small children, making snow figures on the ground and then leaping to their feet for another wild battle with snowballs flying furiously.

Ivory finally leapt on him, arms circling his neck, her legs wrapped around his hips in an effort to stop the crazy game before she laughed so much she cried. "You are so crazy, Razvan," she said, holding him tightly. She buried her face against his throat, afraid she really would burst into tears at the emotions welling up, threatening to overwhelm her.

She knew he thought her some kind of miracle, but, in truth, to her *he* was the miracle. She had no idea how to have fun, and she had no idea how he did. There had been no fun in his life, only cruelty and torture; she at least had played with her pack, but it was Razvan who brought fun into her world again.

"Ivory?" His voice was gentle with inquiry.

She refused to lift her head, only held him tighter, keeping her face pressed against his throat, listening to the wild beating of his heart and feeling the reassuring throb of his pulse.

Razvan tightened his arms around her, rocking gently as if comforting her, but he said nothing at all, not asking for an explanation to the end of their game. He simply accepted. She closed her eyes and savored him. It wasn't the physical strength Razvan possessed in abundance that drew her to him, it was the sheer strength of his character, the absolute well of determined spirit deep inside of him. He was so steady. A rock. For her.

She lifted her head and smiled down at him, not realizing her heart was shining in her eyes. "You are mine, Dragonseeker. *My* rock."

His slow, answering smile nearly stopped her heart. "That I am, *hän ku kuulua sívamet*—keeper of my heart. I will be your everything."

Ivory allowed her feet to drop down into the snow. "Let's go home." More than anything she wanted to be home with him. She wanted her private sanctuary to welcome him, to feel as if he was as much a part of the pack—of her home—as he was her heart.

Razvan held out his hand to her. She glanced up at the sky, scanned the trees, hesitating. She was a warrior first. She could never lose sight of that.

"You will never be diminished by what is between us," he said softly.

Something in her settled. She couldn't imagine being diminished by Razvan. If anything, she would be better, stronger, *more*. She looked at his upturned palm. His hand was large. There were scars up and down his wrist and forearm. Her heart fluttered. She placed her hand in his and watched his fingers close around hers, binding them together just as the ritual words had done.

Do you remember? She couldn't ask aloud; it meant too much. She was very spiritual and believed, whether anyone else did or not, that they had been created to be together, and those words imprinted on him from birth had made them one.

Razvan brought her hand to his chest and stepped close, brushing the snow from the strands of hair tumbling around her face, pulled from her thick braid in their wild battle. "I remember every word, Ivory, and I meant them. I wanted the binding between us. It was not desperation. And it was not the need to save me."

He bent his dark head in that slow way of his. He still had snowflakes on his lashes. As he moved, a thick heat slipped like molasses through her veins. His mouth closed over hers and the snow melted around her, she was certain of it. She swore she could see steam rising from the ground and feel molten liquid gathering like thick magma in her most feminine core.

She leaned into him, melting like the snow. She felt on the edge of a great precipice, teetering, knowing she was going to fall and it was far too late to save herself. In truth, she didn't want to; she already craved the taste of him, the heat and white lightning arcing through her body, sizzling in her mind, shorting out her brain for way too long when they were out in the open.

When he lifted his head she took a moment to drown

in the intensity of his desire. Taking a deep, shuddering breath, Ivory stepped away from temptation. "You are the most lethal man I know."

"I will take that as a compliment." He kissed her again. "You like lethal."

He knew how to kiss. Long and slow and delicious. A slow, burning heat that scorched from the inside out. She found herself smiling up at him all over again as he lifted his head. "Yes, I suppose I do." Although she was scared to care that much about anyone ever again.

They walked through the drifting snow for several miles until the flakes began to look like a white blanket falling from the sky. It might have been the muffled world they found themselves in, alien and white and so quiet that even their breathing seemed too loud in the vast silence, but Ivory began to feel uneasy. Another mile and her wolves stirred. She felt the itch spread over her skin as Raja lifted his head out of her back and bared his teeth in a snarl.

I know, she soothed. *We have company.* Ivory glanced at Razvan. "We are being followed." Her voice was a thread of sound, as muffled and as quiet as the snow.

A small, unexpected smile of amusement lit up Razvan's face. "Well, I guess we get to have a little fun."

She frowned at him. "Fun? Razvan, it is not the undead who are following us. We cannot have anyone finding our lair, nor do we want to engage them in battle if they are Carpathian as I suspect they are."

His grin widened. "I was fairly certain someone would try to follow us. I have been giving it quite a bit of thought as we walked, working out a plan."

Ivory's amber gaze narrowed as it drifted over his face. He looked younger. Happier. She had done that but . . .

"Trust me, Ivory. I am not the experienced fighter you

are, but I am very good at planning battles and strategies. This is a situation made for me."

She sent her senses racing out into the night, seeking information, looking for any blank spots that would indicate vampire. The hunters were well hidden, so much so that she wasn't entirely certain she was right, but Raja was never wrong and he had issued his warning.

"What do you want to do?"

"We should make our way to the valley of mists. That is where we will disappear altogether and leave those following behind. But in the meantime, I think a little lesson is called for, don't you?"

"Lesson?" she echoed faintly. There was way too much amusement in his voice.

"They need to learn a little respect for my woman. You are a warrior, equal to them, and yet they treat you as if you are an amateur. They did not even give us the respect due by confronting us face-to-face. It might be a good thing for all of them to know they are not as good as they think they are."

"I do not think these are children following us, Razvan. They are experienced Carpathian hunters, possibly ancients who have thousands of battles under them."

His cocky grin made him look boyish when there was nothing boyish about him. "Perhaps, but then again, we may make them remember their childhood."

"What do you all think you are doing?" Gregori demanded as he came upon the small group of Carpathian hunters.

Vikirnoff had the grace to look uneasy. "We are not children to be reprimanded, Gregori," he answered.

Gregori's eyebrow shot up. "No, you are not. You are an

ancient hunter, Vikirnoff, one far more experienced than me. Nor did I come to reprimand you. I asked what you were doing merely to see if you needed aid of any kind."

The others looked at one another. It didn't surprise Gregori that Vikirnoff's brother, Nicolae, traveled with him. The brothers had been guarding one another's back for hundreds of years. The other four hunters were also ancients, returning to the Carpathian Mountains to establish ties with the prince. It occurred to Gregori that all of these ancient hunters did not really know Mikhail and had every reason to worry about his judgment. They were far older and more experienced than the prince, and were used to relying solely on their own judgment.

Tariq Asenguard had come from the United States. Over the centuries he had amassed a huge personal fortune, which he often fed to the other Carpathians. He owned several businesses. Tall, like most Carpathian males, he wore his hair long, but his eyes were midnight blue, almost gemlike. Tariq was a man used to going his own way and the thought of an ancient book in the hands of Razvan and a Malinov was enough to set him traveling fast to see for himself just what the pair was up to.

Andre moved through countries like a ghost, drifting in only to pay his respects and pledge his allegiance. A man of very few words, he stayed aloof, as most ancient hunters did, his eyes restless, the urge to continue moving, the drive to find his lifemate ceaseless now as he neared the end of his tolerance. He was one of the single males Gregori kept a firm eye on, as both Tariq and Andre seemed very close to turning.

Mataias, Lojos and Tomas were never far from one another. Like most siblings raised together, they had formed a bond to see each other through the darker times.

They came from a long line of famous warriors, a respected family that always produced multiple children, yet rarely gave birth. Two daughters had been born after the boys, both living no more than their second year. A master vampire had claimed their parents while their mother was pregnant with another set of triplets. The brothers had hunted the vampire across two continents, never ceasing in their pursuit until they had destroyed the undead, exacting justice for their parents and siblings and earning themselves quite a reputation.

Gregori folded his arms across his chest and regarded them all, making certain not to show amusement or exasperation. These men were some of the most respected ancients. They were experienced hunters, every one of them. Yet what they were doing was very foolish and more than a little dangerous and they all should have known better.

"Have you considered that you are following a couple that your prince has promised safe passage to?" he asked, keeping his voice mild and nonjudgmental.

Vikirnoff shrugged, equally casual. "This is an uncertain road. We would be remiss in not guarding the prince's guests."

Gregori's eyebrow rose even higher. "I see. You don't mind if I just tag along and make certain you're all safe, right?"

Swift impatience crossed Vikirnoff's face. "I doubt we'll need protection, but you're welcome. Just make certain you mask your presence. I gave both of them blood so I will have no problem following them."

"That will be interesting. I also gave them blood. Between the two of us, we should have no problem."

Andre and Tariq exchanged a long look and then peered through the snow. It was coming down faster and faster.

"Is there something about this couple we should know, Gregori?" Tariq asked. He still held a faint European accent beneath the American one.

Gregori shook his head. "I am certain none of you would have come on such a mission without a clear idea of who you are chasing."

"A woman," Andre said. "Just a woman and her life-mate. One fairly unskilled."

Gregori followed the others through the snow. "To be fair, they did encounter a master vampire and saved four humans."

Andre gestured around him. "They play like children in the forest, while they carry a book of immense importance."

"Do they now? A book of immense importance?"

Vikirnoff glared at him. "Enough, Gregori. You choose to be amused by this situation, but you did not see the things I did when Natalya recovered that book. It is dangerous. Too dangerous to go unguarded with people we do not know and with enemies closing in around us."

"Oh, I assure you, Vikirnoff, amusement is not what I am feeling." Gregori strode away from the man before he cursed him for being bullheaded. He dropped back, allowing the others to take the lead, knowing the seven hunters were underestimating their prey. In fact, chasing the pair into their own territory was probably the worst idea anyone had had in a long while, but he refused to waste his breath.

Nicolae held up his hand and all of them crouched low, spreading out and automatically blurring their bodies to make it much more difficult to see in the thick snowstorm. A slight breeze blew through the trees so that they caught glimpses of figures up ahead in the meadow—many figures. Big. Tall. Short. Stout. Arms stuck out in strange sticklike shapes, the fingers outstretched as if seeking something.

"What is it?" Vikirnoff asked. "That's not them."

"Ghouls? An army of ghouls?" Andre suggested.

Gregori rolled his eyes. "I very much doubt it."

As they stared, trying to peer through the heavy veil of snow, the figures shifted, moving busily around, stooping, shaping, building a low structure.

"A wall?" Tariq whispered.

"It's going up fast. Too fast to be anything but magic," Mataias warned. He signaled his brothers and they separated, coming around the meadow from three different points of attack.

The hunters crept closer, using the trees to mask their presence, all senses alert. Whatever was guarding the couple gave off no scent, no spoor whatsoever. It was as if the couple was gone, and the land itself was pristine with snow.

"A fortress," Lojos hissed in warning.

The attack came swiftly. Missiles whistled through the air, a bombardment, the air heavy with white-capped balls that hit with deadly accuracy, slamming into the Carpathians, the trees, and everything else in the battle zone.

"Acid!" Tomas hissed in warning.

The men dissolved and burst onto the battlefield, each in front of one of the attacking ghouls, punching through the chest to get at withered hearts, others slicing through necks to take the heads from the vampire's puppets.

Gregori folded his arms and leaned against the broad trunk of a tree and watched the frenzied, chaotic fight, the battle raging furiously as the ghouls continued hurling the missiles and others continued rapidly building until the structure began to form a roof, now surrounding them on all four sides, confining them within its walls.

"It is a trap," Tariq warned the others. "Above you."

The seven Carpathian hunters somersaulted away from their opponents, each trying to study the structure rapidly enclosing them.

Gregori shook his head, rolling his eyes while the minutes ticked by and the ghouls grew more plentiful and the missiles doubled.

Vikirnoff worked his way across the battlefield to his side. "Do you mind helping?"

"I would feel a bit ridiculous fighting snowmen, but you go right ahead," Gregori said with a small elegant bow toward the ancient hunter.

Vikirnoff looked around, a frown on his face. Everything slowed a bit as he tried to see with all of his senses. The ferocious battle continued, but now the ghouls were white and flaky and suspiciously round in body and head. The arms appeared to be nothing more than branches and old twigs. The missiles were snowballs, splattering against their chests and faces.

Vikirnoff took a breath and let it out. The scene cleared and completely focused. Color swept up his neck and flooded his face.

"I believe you just got spanked," Gregori said. "And by a girl."

"*Terád keje*—get scorched, Gregori," Vikirnoff snapped. "It is an illusion," he called to the others. "She is good with magic. A delaying tactic only. They know we follow them."

The fighting slowed and then halted as the hunters slowly realized they'd been duped. Around them, snowmen lay fallen, slashed, heads rolling with grinning faces laughing up at them.

"I cannot believe we fell for this," Tariq said. "She is better than I gave her credit for. I did not, for one moment, feel a surge of energy."

The hunters looked at one another. It was Lojos, renowned for being a great warrior, who voiced his appreciation. "Not only was there no surge of energy, the illusion was absolutely seamless. This is no amateur. Even the skill of the snowmen fighting was superb." If he could have felt admiration it would have been in his voice, but his emotions had long since faded and all he could do was voice his acknowledgment of the expertise.

"Pick up the trail, Vikirnoff," Mataias said with relentless purpose. "There is not even a faint trace left behind. We will have to use the call of your blood to track them."

Gregori smirked a bit. "Yes, Vikirnoff. You use that. I am certain you will have no problems finding them." The snow was coming down so hard that he almost failed to see Vikirnoff's face, but it was well worth the extra effort to see the hunter's exasperated expression.

"If your lifemate had been duped repeatedly by someone, you would not be so quick to trust him, Gregori," Vikirnoff accused.

"Perhaps not, but I would trust my prince."

Vikirnoff stalked away, leading the group of hunters across the meadow thick with snowmen and back into the forest. The scent was so faint, even with the call of his own blood, as if somehow it had been diluted. Wary of traps now, they had to move much more slowly, spread out in a standard search pattern, all senses alert. There were no tracks, no visible signs of Razvan and Ivory's passage. Twice Vikirnoff had to backtrack and wind his way deeper into the forest where the trees were taller and closer together.

The canopy wove an umbrella overhead, blocking the worst of the snow so that the layers on the ground weren't quite as deep, although the branches overhead were piled high and every open space had high drifts.

Tariq clawed a spiderweb from his face as they infiltrated the darker recesses of the forest. The webs here were much more abundant, as often happened in less-traveled areas.

"It does not appear they came this way," he cautioned. "The webs are intact."

The hunters halted, maintaining at least a five-foot distance between one another. They inspected the numerous spiderwebs that stretched from tree to tree. Sparkling like diamonds from the ice crystals coating the intricate strands, the webs actually draped over many of the trees and stretched between them in labyrinths of artfully connected roadways. They had seen the ice spiders' elaborate webs before, mostly in caves deep beneath the ground, but once in a while they were treated to the rare sight during a prolonged cold winter.

"These webs have been undisturbed for many weeks," Andre added, stepping close to one of the larger ones to study the insects trapped there. Even a few hapless lizards and birds had been snared by the strong webs. "I doubt they passed this way."

"Perhaps as mist?" Mataias suggested. "They might have slipped through."

"Not an ice spiderweb," Lojos objected. "Everyone knows you cannot simply slip through."

"Ice spiders are small, but ferocious," Tomas reminded. "If you stumble upon a colony in the caves you had better fear for your life. This looks like a colony."

"Without a doubt," Nicolae agreed. "If we go into the

middle of that, we had better be prepared to burn them out. Even with everything wet, we could destroy this forest."

Vikirnoff glanced uneasily at Gregori. The healer made no suggestions, he simply stood off to the side and watched them puzzling out the trail. There was no expression on his face, no indication of what he might be thinking.

"Watch out for an ambush," Nicolae cautioned, "but look around. They had to have come through here. If they found a passage, so can we."

"Do not disturb the webs," Vikirnoff cautioned as the hunters began to cast for signs.

The blood spoor was faint, and Vikirnoff was certain the couple had come through the ice spiders' territory. The webs appeared to encompass several miles of forest, a thick barrier stretching like fences through the trees. If the couple had skirted around rather than going through the colony, it would have taken them much longer, and the blood scent didn't lead that way. To avoid trouble with the dangerous and very aggressive spiders, they would have had to find a way to go through the area without tearing the webs. The spoor was so faint already, he was afraid if they chose the longer route they'd lose the couple altogether.

"I believe I've figured out what they've done," Lojos said. "They had to have repaired all damage to the webs as they passed through. If they could weave quickly enough and keep each web intact enough not to rouse the ire of the spiders, they might have made it through without a battle."

Tariq nodded. "That is the only logical explanation. Spread out. No one is good enough to repair an ice spider's web exactly as the spider weaves it. They will have left signs."

Vikirnoff sent an elated look toward Gregori, who

merely shrugged, which irritated the hunter even more. The seven ancients spread out through the trees, stepping close to the webs, almost pressing their noses against them in an attempt to find any signs of ragged edges where the crystals clung to the silken strands.

Vikirnoff glanced at Nicolae, his frown deepening. "I do not see anything here, but no one passes through the heart of ice spiderwebs. They can go on for miles and it would be far too perilous. Not only is it too dangerous, the caution they would have taken would certainly have slowed them down."

Looking at his brother, he moved from the outer trees toward the center of the forest. He took a step and his foot sank about four inches into the snow in spite of making his body light. At once silken strands whipped up and around him, enclosing him in a net that sprang from the ground high into the air, the web tight, without the tiny holes allowing vapor to pass through.

Vikirnoff struggled, but, as with all ice spider traps, the web tightened the more he struggled, rolling him until he was trussed up like a turkey. He forced himself to go still, fury eating at his usual calm. He found himself high in the canopy, dangling several hundred feet up in the air. His brother glared back at him from the net where he was wrapped like a mummy and trapped within the silken, crystalline net. Around them the other hunters had met the same fate.

Vikirnoff didn't dare look at Gregori. "Get us down," he bit out.

Gregori sighed. "If I move, Vikirnoff, I may step into one of the numerous traps laid out. I have to study the situation first. It will do no good for me to wind up the same way."

"Spiders could never do this," Lojos said. "Magic is at work here."

"You think?" Nicolae was sarcastic. "We are being made fools of."

"Or perhaps you are simply being fools," Gregori offered.

Vikirnoff snarled at him. "Say what you like, Gregori, but, if they have nothing to hide, they would not have gone to such lengths to hide from us."

As he spoke the branches overhead stirred, flakes raining down as spiders scurried along the intricate webbing. One began to lower itself toward Vikirnoff, drawn by his voice.

Gregori, placing his feet carefully in the obvious minefield of snares, moved closer, should his aid become necessary.

The spider stopped level with Vikirnoff's eyes. They stared at each other for a long moment. Vikirnoff could see the fangs dripping with venom. The spider began to weave another web, this time forming words as if programmed. It took some time for the spider to connect the silken lines.

Fear not. I have arranged for safe passage through spider territory.

Vikirnoff felt his gut tighten. Safe passage. As if they were children unable to make it through the ice spiders' realm on their own. The blow to their pride was deliberate. A slap in the face.

Vikirnoff was tempted to roast the entire colony by calling down the lightning.

"I wouldn't do that," Gregori said. "If Ivory or Razvan used magic and befriended these spiders, chances are they left protection behind for them. They traded something for your safe passage."

"We didn't ask for their help," Vikirnoff snarled, his teeth snapping together.

Above their heads the trees came alive as thousands of spiders shifted and moved. Vikirnoff wished he'd never set out on the journey in the first place but he wasn't about to tell Gregori that. Forcing back his anger, he inclined his head to accept whatever agreement Ivory and Razvan had made.

"Hopefully you are right about them and they haven't traded their safe passage by giving us to the spiders for their winter food."

"I would not allow that to happen."

That was almost as hard to swallow as the couple arranging safe passage. Vikirnoff swore silently. They had no choice now. They had to continue forward, and he knew the healer wore that particularly annoying smirk.

They were lowered back to the ground almost at a snail's pace, making Vikirnoff want to scream in frustration. Another delaying tactic. And then each was rolled out, one by one, so the silken strands binding them could be preserved, another absolutely humiliating torture for experienced hunters. And if Gregori mentioned spankings again, he'd kill the man and damn the consequences. While the hunters were being rolled out like sausages, an opening was prepared through the webs, so, when all seven hunters were once again standing beside Gregori, there was a way through the thick forest.

Uneasy now, the group continued to follow Vikirnoff as he set out to track Ivory and Razvan through the dark interior and back out the other side. They found themselves in the worst possible place and the spiders worked quickly to close the passage behind them.

The Valley of Mists lay between two tall mountain

peaks, rising abruptly at near vertical angles. The gorge was narrow and treacherous, nearly always entrenched with thick, icy mist, the particles small enough to nearly freeze lungs when inhaled. No one, not even Carpathians, could see through the heavy veil of mist that hung like clouds. Snow and ice often calved off the angular cliffs, and avalanches were frequent in the area.

The wind often came in off the highest peaks on a spiraling downdraft to howl through the canyon at breakneck speeds, carrying voices, wreaking havoc with auditory senses. Few animals could live in the valley; snow leopards reigned, but even they stayed away from the base of the mountains where the snow and ice sloughed off with thundering force.

The hunters heard the sound of a woman's laughter and figures moved in the mist. Tomas glanced at his brothers and they moved forward only four steps into the valley and disappeared.

Vikirnoff looked at Gregori. "They chase ghosts, don't they?"

Gregori shrugged. "I would imagine they do."

Vikirnoff closed his eyes and sent his mind seeking the blood trail. It was lost in the mist. Not even the faintest trace remained. "They probably dissolved into mist and are mixed in this thick soup. I could spend months trying to trace them."

"You will not find them," Gregori said.

Tomas, Mataias and Lojos returned. "We are chasing phantoms. They play with us, but they are no longer here."

Vikirnoff shook his head. "I hope your prince knows what he is doing, Gregori."

"*Our* prince," Gregori said. "Each of you swore allegiance." This time there was no amusement. None. The silver eyes glinted at each of the hunters as if marking them. "Ivory and Razvan refused the offer of the book. Mikhail tested them in every way and they passed each test. I cannot say the same for any of you."

He simply dissolved and streamed away, up and over the forest with its spider colony, back toward Carpathian territory, leaving the others to follow.

15

"I think you have a devious mind," Ivory said as she once again resumed her physical form, standing in the memory room of her lair. "Leading the hunters into the Valley of Mist and then going beneath the ground rather than through the mist was a stroke of genius. There was no way they could track us, not even through the call of blood."

"The earth welcomes us and covers all tracks. I knew they could never follow our scent, even with the call of blood." Razvan grinned at her. "I would have liked to have been there when they realized they were trapped in an illusion and fighting with snowmen, not ghouls." He burst out laughing.

She stretched her arms wide to allow the wolves to take their normal shapes. "We did not make any friends."

"We do not need friends. In any case, if they are without emotions, they could care less one way or the other." He frowned. "I do not envy Mikhail his job."

"Especially trying to destroy that book. He has no idea of the evil things inside of it."

Razvan was silent for a long moment. "I should have spoken with him more about the book and its destruction. I dislike the idea of my aunts having to deal with anything involved with Xavier, but they, better than anyone else, would know how best to destroy the book."

The concern in his voice moved her. The man had more compassion in him and more drive to protect those he loved than any person she'd ever met. Ivory turned toward him, her gaze drifting over him slowly. He took up a lot of space there in the confines of her home. His shoulders were broad and his physique very masculine. There was little soft about Razvan, although he had the calmest, most serene nature she'd ever run across as a rule. He glanced up and caught her looking at him.

Her heart leapt. There was stark, raw hunger in his eyes, glittering at her, devouring her, drinking her in. Her mouth went dry. They were alone. She moistened her lips. Wanting him. Even needing him. Fear gripping her.

"Razvan." His name came out husky, her voice shaken.

His smile was slow, his voice as thick as molasses. "Ivory."

The way he said her name made her body go hot and damp and her heart pound more. There would be no going back. It was all or nothing with him, she knew that about him. Once he touched her, claimed her, made her part of him, she would be lost. Completely. How much of her would disappear? She ached for this. For him. She was on fire for him. Almost desperate, when desperate wasn't part of her makeup.

She held up a shaky hand before he could take a step toward her. "If you ever betrayed me, I would kill you. I would, Razvan. You have to know that. There would be no forgiveness. I have not trusted another person in centuries. Others do not matter, but you—you would matter."

"I would expect nothing less from my woman."

A slow, sexy smile curved his mouth and burned in his

eyes. Hunger stared back at her. Desire. Lust. All things she could cope with. But there was love, pure and honest and so real it took her breath away, shaking her to her very core. Something inside her welled up. Burst. Opened to him. For him. This one man. If she took him in, her love for him would consume her. She had so much to give, but she'd been alone for so long . . .

He held out his hand to her. "I have been alone, too."

She wanted to make him understand the enormity of the decision. Did he know what it would cost her? Did he know how terrified she was? Did he have any idea how bad she was going to be at a relationship?

His smile widened, giving her a flash of his white teeth. He leaned down and brushed a gentle kiss over her mouth. There was no way to save herself from her treacherous heart. She had already committed to him. She had fallen for his smile. His gentle nature. His iron will. Everything about him drew her. Even his stubborn streak and that absolute boyish sense of humor. *Everything*.

There was more danger to her here, in this man, in this moment, than from the most powerful master vampire imaginable, or from the most ferocious of battles. Loving him too much, as she would—maybe already did—might destroy her. She could put her physical body back together, but not her heart, not her soul—not the very essence of who she was.

"Trust me, beloved. I know I am asking more than any other has dared to ask, but look into the soul we share and trust me."

Ivory kept her gaze locked with his. His eyes. His gorgeous, wild, midnight-blue eyes that held so much. All for her. Only for her. So much hunger. So much desire. So much love. Her mouth trembled as she placed her hand in his and let him lead her into their bedchamber. Her heart pounded so loudly she was certain he could hear it.

Razvan closed the door on the wolves, leaving them settled in the larger memory room. He waved his arm to set lights flickering on a hundred miniature candles set into small indentations in the rock wall. The flames danced, throwing shadows across Ivory's face. Her skin looked porcelain, rose-petal soft and inviting. Her eyes were enormous, burnished gold, liquid and frightened like a wild creature trapped by a predator, looking at him with a mixture of longing and innocence that was both intoxicating and irresistible.

He reached behind her and pulled her thick braid over her shoulder to release the tie, his fingers tunneling through the silky strands to loosen the tight weave so that her hair tumbled around her face and cascaded down her back. The texture of her hair, so soft, the strands running through the pads of his thumb and fingers, brought the smoldering embers into a slow burn. She didn't flinch or turn away from him, nor did she lower her gaze from his.

There was courage in Ivory, an abundance of it. Courage he knew was a huge part of who she was. Ivory didn't give up. If she committed herself to him, she would give everything to him, hold nothing back. He loved her all the more for that trait, that absolute unswerving characteristic that made her a dangerous hunter, but would also make her a fiercely loyal partner and a fantasy lover.

He wanted to take his time, explore every inch of her, every secret shadow and hollow, every intriguing, mysterious feminine curve. He could barely breathe with wanting. His hands moved to the buckles of her vest. He knew each buckle intimately, having committed them to memory earlier—the leather straps with the double holes—the tiny crosses embedded in the steel of each metal clasp and the three metal rivets on each side of the buckle and strap, also embedded with a cross—the cross that represented her faith and shining soul.

Of course either of them could have removed her clothes with a single thought, but he wanted the pleasure of unwrapping her. He wanted to take his time and offer her every single moment of pleasure he could give her— build her need from a smoldering ember into a raging firestorm.

She didn't move, but he felt her sharp inhale and her breasts rose and fell against his knuckles as he worked the straps apart and pushed the material off her shoulders for a slow unveiling of her magnificent body. Her breasts spilled out. Soft. Enticing. So tempting he cupped the soft weight in his palms, all the time watching her face.

He saw the swift pleasure overtake her, the flush of color, the slight glazing of her eyes as his thumbs brushed over the taut peaks of her nipples. Holding the twin soft mounds in the palms of his hands felt like a miracle, the sensation beyond his fantasies. He'd given up those dreams long ago—so long ago he couldn't even remember if he'd ever had them—yet she stood before him, her soft feminine curves a gentle weight in his hands and her enormous eyes looking at him with such trepidation . . . and anticipation.

He brushed a kiss over her forehead, then down to the corner of her left eye. A small shudder went through her body. He kissed the tip of her nose and the corners of her mouth. Her lips parted slightly. Hunger welled up in her, swamping him so that for a moment his mouth hovered a scant inch from hers while he fought for control.

He took her breath first, drawing it deep into his lungs,

and then he took her mouth, his lips settling over hers, absorbing the shape and texture, the soft firmness, the building heat. His tongue slid along that slightly parted seam, the small invitation.

Ivory's breath caught in her throat. He was leading her down an unknown path of temptation, and she was just too far gone to resist. His kiss was sinful, his mouth a wicked excitement that filled her with such need she couldn't stop her response. He whispered something, sexy, nearly imperceptible, as his tongue swept into her mouth, exploring the hot recesses, running seductively over her teeth and claiming her body for his own.

She knew that was what it was. A claiming. Taking her body and making it his own. His thumbs brushed across her nipples and she nearly cried out, the sound strangled by the lump rising in her throat. Streaks of fire raced from her breast to her clit and her womb clenched. He kissed her over and over until she felt delirious, but one part of her was always focused on his hands. On waiting. On needing.

She stood there with him fully clothed, his dark, streaked hair pulled back so that he looked in control, while she was naked from the waist up with her hair tumbling in every direction, a wild, wanton bundle of nerves that finally understood that her destination was this man. This journey she took with him, no matter how frightening, wasn't being taken alone. He had allowed her to lead the way in her field of strength. He was asking her to give herself up to him, just as he had done for her.

He wanted her trust. Wholly. He wanted her to give him everything she was or would ever be without pride or ego, trusting he would cherish her gift for all time. His kiss had been a match, lighting something deep inside her that flared up now, something feminine and alive and needy beyond belief. She wanted to please him. She wanted to be his solace. His pleasure. His everything.

Her tongue slid along his, dancing and teasing, as she pushed her aching breasts deeper into his palms, needing that next brush of fire. His kisses were addictive, burning hot until she knew passion was spinning out of control and her mind was hazy with desire. He bit at her lower lip and the sting sent a lightning strike sizzling through her belly straight to her feminine channel. Even her thighs quivered, her body going into meltdown.

His teeth scraped along her chin, his tongue swirling over the small dip there and traveling down to her throat. He took his time, even though she was melting right there on the floor. His mouth moved over her throat, those wicked teeth scraping gently, sending a sinful lash of spiraling heat sliding from belly to thigh.

She could barely breathe, waiting. Knowing. In the grip of a desire far too strong to ever withstand. He lowered his mouth and took her breast with the same slow heat he'd taken her mouth. His warm breath came first, so that she felt him all the way through her breast and deep under her skin. Her breath just stopped as she strained toward him. His tongue flicked her nipple and she whimpered. Then his mouth drew her deep, suckled, and she cried out, throwing her head back, her arms cradling his head to her, holding him close. Her fingers curled into fists, bunching his hair while her toes curled in a matching reflex.

Desire punched low and fierce, as he captured her other nipple and began to roll and tug to the rhythm of his mouth. Another cry escaped as white lightning ripped through her body, straight from her breasts, through her abdomen to her very core and even lower still, spreading down her thighs until electric sparks crackled around her.

Blood roared in her ears, pounded in her heart and through her veins as he drew the nipple tight against the roof of his mouth and stroked and caressed. She needed him in a way she'd never needed anyone in her life. He was like the brightest star, the moonlight spilling silver across a new snow. He made an ugly world beautiful and decent and made her remember she was a woman.

His mouth was like black velvet, dark and intoxicating, his hands shaping her breasts while his teeth and tongue built the fire in her hotter. When he lifted his head she could see ravenous hunger, yet, with those same unhurried movements, his clever fingers skimmed her bare belly. He caught her rib cage between his palms and bent his head to trace a trail of fire over each rib and down to her belly button, where his tongue swirled until she clutched his hair to keep herself upright.

His eyes met hers and his hands dropped to the belt at her hip, pulling the slider apart and dropping weapons and holster onto the floor. She felt the brush of his fingers against her lower belly as he tugged on the leather ties and unfastened the opening. She was tempted to just get rid of her clothes herself, her body on fire with need, but there was a warning in his hot eyes, a look of possession that she found just a little thrilling—okay, maybe a lot. He enjoyed unwrapping her and she wanted to give him that joy. She found herself feeling unexpectedly sexy as he tugged her trousers down her legs and one hand at her hip urged her to step forward out of them.

She held her breath. She was totally naked, every line and curve exposed to his hungry gaze. He just stood there, hands on the curve of her hips, his gaze moving over her, absolutely, wholly focused on her in that way he had, as if he saw nothing else, was aware of nothing else. Only Ivory.

She put her hand on his chest, right over his heart, and felt it beating hard. Stark desire radiated from him—for her.

She'd never had a man look at her like that. Certainly Draven had wanted her, but not with love carved into every line of his face. Not with his body shuddering and his heart hammering. He had never looked at her with such a fever of need, with his mind open to hers and his heart given fully to her. No one had ever made her feel as if she was the most beautiful woman in the world, wholly desired, completely loved—until now.

"Ivory." Her name came out strangled in his throat. A soft symphony that brushed her skin just as effectively as his hands.

He brought her to him again, taking her mouth, this time in a fever of need, scorching her with his searing heat as he pulled her closer, so that his heavy erection pushed against her soft belly right through the material of his trousers. She heard her own strangled moan as his mouth fastened on hers, this time without that slow burn. This time wild and so hot it scorched her. He had driven her out of her mind so that need was the only thing she knew, and she melted into him, nearly blind with hunger for his touch.

His tongue tangled with hers as his hands came back to her sensitive breasts, fingers tugging and rolling her nipples until she was panting, gasping, little whimpers escaping. His skin felt hot beneath his shirt, as her nails dug deep into his shoulders. A shudder went through his body. His mouth was addictive, that dark, rich taste of sin and sex she found intoxicating. His body was hard and powerful, moving against hers, controlled, aggressive now, inflaming her more. She could feel each defined muscle rippling beneath his skin, his body tense with need as his kisses sent electrical sparks sizzling through her veins directly to her feminine channel so she was damp and needy, and moaning into his mouth.

She couldn't stop touching him, his hair, his neck, his throat, sliding her hands over his arms and the muscles there, dragging husky male groans, throaty and raw with passion for him. The sound inflamed her more until she thought she was burning up, her body moving almost compulsively against his.

He made a sound. Dark. Dangerous. Intoxicating. He simply drove his hips upward, against the junction of her thighs, pressing tightly while he rocked her there. The urgent movement was incredibly sexy, sending a shaft of desire, sweet and hot, piercing through her core, and she buried her face against his neck, stroking with her tongue, nipping with her teeth, reveling in the way his body shuddered in reaction.

His fingers found her inner thigh. Stroked. Took the breath from her body. His leg forced her thighs open to him, the rough material rubbing over her skin as she bucked helplessly into him, nearly sobbing with need.

"Are you wet for me, *fél ku kuuluaak sívam belső*—beloved?"

His voice was a black velvet seduction in her ear. A blatant, wicked temptation.

"Are you?" He sounded like pure sin.

She tugged frantically at his shirt, desperate to get at him, as need clawed at her. She ached, her feminine sheath coiled tight with building tension, frantic for release, for him to fill the clutching emptiness. She managed to shove his shirt off his body and couldn't stand anything between them, not even for another second. She stripped him with magic, with frenzied, almost violent haste.

One hand fisted in her hair, dragged her head back to expose her throat to rake gently with his teeth. He bit down and her womb clenched. He trailed fiery kisses over her neck, and then his mouth was ravaging her breasts, his teeth and tongue sending molten fire racing through her blood. His hand slipped over her thigh, caressed and stroked the soft inner skin, moving higher, knuckles brushing the damp mound at the junction there.

Ivory inhaled sharply. Went still. Her breath caught in her lungs. Just stayed trapped there, burning and raw. Razvan pulled his head back and stared into her eyes. She drowned there. Holding her gaze captive, he plunged his fingers into her tight, wet channel. Ivory's eyes widened. She heard the surprised wail escaping her throat, dizzy with shock.

Razvan thrust into her mind so he could feel her response, her reactions guiding his every move. She didn't know if she could stand feeling both of them, the ravenous hunger, the building fire leaping between them.

Still looking at her, Razvan dropped to his knees. He lowered his gaze in a slow, possessive study of her body, watching her flush with arousal, all the while his fingers plunged deep. Her scent called to him as she rode his hand, almost sobbing. Very slowly he removed his fingers and licked at them, savoring the exotic taste of her. She moaned and the sound vibrated through his heavy erection so that he pulsed with urgent need. He ignored his own body's reaction, desperate for the taste of her.

Desperate. He was desperate for her taste. That alone was enough to undo her, that this man, kneeling at her feet, looking like a fallen angel, could be so desperate for her taste, for the hot cream spilling out to welcome him.

He kept her thighs spread with his hands and took her

with his mouth, his tongue sliding through the satin-soft heat. She shuddered. Caught his hair with both fists and yanked, the biting pain thickening his shaft even more. His name was strangled, cut off as she lost her ability to breathe when he licked at her like a hungry wolf.

The rasp of his tongue was too much. Her knees weakened and her body coiled too tight, burned too hot, clenching and rippling with shocking intensity. She cried out his name again, trying to say *stop*, but not wanting this to ever end. It mattered little; he was beyond hearing, his blood thundering in his ears, the taste of her driving him wild. He ate at her like a starving wolf, his tongue stroking, lapping and then suckling her clit, plunging deep and then flicking at the hard nub while she bucked and thrust against his mouth in a mindless, fiery explosion.

Ivory screamed. She'd never screamed in her life. Not when Draven caught her. Not when the vampires had attacked. Never. Not once. But the pleasure bordered on ecstasy, roaring through her belly and rippling through her womb, wave after wave, so that she clung to his shoulders for support while the tidal wave burst through her.

Razvan lifted her then, cradling her in his arms, taking her to the soft bed in the chamber, weaving and floating a silken sheet to lay her on. He came down with her, spreading her legs a second time, his mouth latching on to her, tongue stabbing deep to drive her up a second time. She wept, digging her nails into his back, trying desperately to hold on to sanity as he took her up fast. She heard herself pleading, for what she didn't even know, and then he was rising above her, his face a harsh mask of desire in stark contrast to the unashamed, fierce love in his eyes.

She felt him press the broad head of his erection at her entrance, and time stopped. Sound stopped. There was only the sensation of his body demanding entrance to hers. There was white lightning flashing over her skin, through her body, streaking through her bloodstream as he began to invade, his thick shaft pushing through the tight folds of her body. Between her thighs, his shaft was like a hot brand, where he stretched her slowly on an exquisite rack of pleasure.

His voice was harsh as he murmured to her in the ancient tongue, somewhere between swearing and praising, maybe both. Her blood, thundering in her ears, drowned out the actual words. He was trying to ease into her, to allow her body plenty of time to accommodate his length and girth, but she couldn't stay still, not even when his hands pinned her hips and held her. The pleasure was too much. She thrust upward, using her heels for leverage, just as he eased forward again.

A lash of pain accompanied the pleasure pouring over her as his body thrust deep into hers. His fingers tightened on her hips—dug in—forced her to be still.

"Stop, Ivory. Do not move." His breathing was as harsh as his voice, ragged and uneven. "We're both going to go up in flames. You are so tight."

She could see his white teeth snap together as her muscles gripped and squeezed. That smooth control had slipped. She loved that she'd managed to shake his calm. She could feel the pounding need in him, the dark hunger, see the lengthening of his teeth, just that hint of danger that made her heart jump and her body flood with more liquid cream. She dug her nails into him, her breasts heaving, desperate for more—desperate for him to move. "Please, Razvan. *Please*."

The urgency in her took him over the edge. He caught her hips and dragged her legs over his arms, levering himself to ride over her clit, and then he plunged deep, the friction nearly intolerable, the pleasure so intense she was afraid of losing herself completely in him. He reared back and began a harsh rhythm, deep and strong and fast, so deep he pierced her womb, the hot length of him filling her, binding them together.

His mind moved in hers so that she felt the fire streaking through his body, the way her tight sheath dragged and milked at him, scorching hot, velvet soft, an exquisite pleasure-pain that shook him to his soul. The tension in her body built, coiling tighter and tighter, until she was frantically writhing beneath him, her breath coming in wild gasps, her head tossing back and forth, her nails raking at his back.

"Razvan." She sobbed his name. A plea. A demand. She needed . . . Needed!

"I know, Ivory," he bit out softly between his teeth. "Give yourself to me. All of you. Let go, *fél ku kuuluaak sívam belső*—beloved. I will catch you."

She felt consumed with fire. Terrified she might disappear in the flames. The tension wound her so tight, yet she couldn't let go, couldn't bring herself to take that last leap of faith. She sobbed again, clutching him tighter, not wanting this moment to end, but fearing, if they didn't stop, she would be lost.

He pounded into her, his shaft a steel-edged sword, piercing her womb and her heart, taking a part of her into him, just as a part of him was deep within her.

"It is already too late," he whispered, and his voice was that of a dark angel. A whisper of velvet, a lash of heat.

It was too late to save herself; her body was already lost, would forever need his. He had driven her so high she had to fly. He dragged her closer and leaned over her, his body still surging into hers, over and over, a piston that never stopped, never slowed, until she thought she might scream again with the wonder of it. She felt her body tighten. And tighten. Gripping his. Squeezing. She could hear the sounds of their bodies coming together, the hard slap of flesh; felt the power of him moving within her. His body tilted one more time and he dragged the long length of his hard shaft over her sensitized clit.

Her body went rigid. For a moment she couldn't breathe. Couldn't think. Her body tightened around his thick shaft, clamping down almost painfully as the rippling sensations began building into a giant tidal wave, spreading through her body like a flash fire, white hot and powerful. Wave after wave. Never ending. A shock that put her system on overload. She wept with the force of her release, the beauty and wonder of it, as she felt her body take his, forcing him with her, hearing his hoarse shout as his hot seed emptied into her.

She felt his bite, the pleasure-pain of it, and her body clenched and rippled again and again as he took her blood in an erotic exchange. She arched her back, thrusting upward with her hips as her body continued to clench around his, squeezing down on him, milking every drop from his body. He swept his tongue across the swell of her breasts, closing the pinpricks and looked down on her with his sexy eyes.

Just his look made her body react again, another wave washing over both of them. She raised her head to capture his mouth with hers, kissing him, holding him to her as she kissed her way down his throat. She felt his shaft harden again that fast, filling and stretching her as she licked at his pulse. A harsh groan escaped him.

Her teeth nipped his skin and she felt the instant jerk of

his erection. She bit down and he slammed his hips hard, burying himself deep, holding her bottom with one hand, forcing her to accept his wildly plunging body. She felt the taste of him exploding inside of her, filling her with his essence. She'd never felt so complete. So loved. She swept her tongue across the pinpricks on his throat and let her body go up another time, this time without resistance.

She could hear her own soft gasps, smell their combined scents as the waves broke over her again and again before he found his own release.

They lay together, their arms around each other, their bodies joined, neither wanting to move. It was several minutes before Razvan found the strength to move, rolling off her to stare up at the glittering ceiling, his fingers linking behind his head.

"Give me a few minutes and I will carry you to the pool."

He turned his head, his smile tender, sending her heart somersaulting. He looked different. Younger. Happier. That same serenity was there, but this time there was love looking back at her with pure, undiluted happiness and joy. She wished she could share her emotions with him aloud, but she contented herself with surrounding him with the deepest feelings she had for him, overwhelming love, so much she couldn't give voice, even telepathically.

His fingers moved over hers, stroked small caresses until she linked her fingers with his. "Thank you, Ivory."

"For what?" A smile escaped. "I think I should be thanking you."

His smiled widened. "You have given me the most beautiful experience of my life. Whatever else happens, I will always have the memory of you giving yourself to me."

"I was afraid," she confessed in a low voice.

"I know you were," he said gently, "which made your gift all the more treasured."

"Are you really going to carry me to the pool?"

"Don't sound so scared," he teased. "Somehow I will manage to find the strength. I promise, I will not drop you."

She tightened her fingers around his. "I know that. I just might feel silly."

"No one is here but us, Ivory," he pointed out, his tone more tender than ever.

She felt her heart twist again. He could do that so easily to her. Move her. Make her melt. It wasn't his incredible body or the way he took her to such heights, it was that enduring love he seemed to have for her. A rock. A foundation. Strong and accepting that made her feel as if she could always count on him.

"I know."

"Do you think I will think less of you?"

She was silent, contemplating his question, turning it over and over in her mind. She just felt ridiculous feeling about him the way that she did. Why couldn't she let herself go in the way that he did?

"I don't think I know how to be a woman." She didn't know how else to say it.

Razvan turned on his side and propped himself up on his elbow. "Ivory, you are *my* woman. You do not have to be like any other. I do not want any other. There is no comparison. Be who you are. Make no apologies, certainly not to me." A small smile curved his mouth and he leaned forward to brush kisses over her mouth. "I love the way you are, that little reluctance you have to tell me I am the greatest man in all the world."

His soft laughter stroked over her skin. He sounded so

boyish, carefree even, less inhibited for the first time in his life.

He managed to climb to his feet and lifted her, cradling her in his arms as if she were as light as a child. "You have worn me out, warrior woman."

Ivory couldn't help laughing. "If you were truly the greatest man in all the world, you would not be worn out. You would be ready to service my every need."

His eyebrow shot up. "I believe that is a challenge." He fastened his mouth to hers as he took her through to the next room where the water spilled out of the rock wall into the smooth basin. "I am more than up for servicing your every need." He whispered the words against her mouth, his tongue flicking over her lips, savoring her taste.

"Really? I am not quite as certain." She used her haughtiest tone.

He dropped her into the water. She came up sputtering to find him standing there, hands on his hips, the water lapping at his thighs.

"That was so mean."

"You deserved it."

"Maybe I did," she agreed, laughing.

He was teaching her how to have fun. To play. To take each moment they had together and live it well. In the spirit of learning, she sent up a plume of water with deadly aim. The water shot over his face and splashed down his chest.

"I thought you might need a little cooling off."

His eyebrow rose. Amusement lit his eyes. "I think you just declared war."

She stuck out her chin. "I think I did."

The water fight was fast and furious. Water geysered nearly to the ceiling and splashed against the wall. Twice he launched himself at her, bringing her down like a crocodile might its prey, rolling her under the water before she could wiggle away from him and surface to attack again.

She threw herself at him, arms circling his neck, and body slammed him, taking them both under, and, when they came up, they rested on the side of the warm pool and let the bubbles fizz against their skin.

She rubbed her arms and glanced upward as if she might be able to see the sky. "I can always tell when the sun is about to rise. My skin prickles and becomes uncomfortable. Most Carpathians can stay out in the early-morning hours but I cannot."

"Not at all?"

She rested one hip against the smooth basin and wrung out her hair. "My skin is so fair, all the years spent in the ground away from even moonlight while I was healing, and I get burned. More like a light sunburn, I guess, but I blister fairly easily." She smiled at him as a memory came to her. "Once, I found a bottle of sunblock a hiker had dropped. I tried it."

He tucked her hair behind her ear. "I take it that didn't go very well."

"Not really, no."

"Have you tried staying up longer while you are here, underground?"

She rubbed her arms again, shivering a little. "Sometimes when I get working on experimenting with new chemicals to hold the vampire in place, I do not feel the sensation for a while, but most of the time, I am so uneasy, I just go to ground."

"Your formula to coat your weapons is brilliant."

She sent him a quick, pleased smile, a little shy when he gave her compliments. "I am still working on it. It needs to last a little longer before their blood eats through it. The more time I give myself, by preventing them from shifting, the more of an edge I have."

"*We* have," he corrected.

She nodded. "We have," she agreed.

"Is your skin hurting now?" Razvan asked, clearly prepared to carry her back to their bedchamber.

"Not really. It is close to dawn though. Very close."

She liked being with him. She hadn't thought she would. She had been alone for so long she thought it would be uncomfortable to share her space with him, but she enjoyed his sense of humor. He was an intelligent man, quick-witted yet he lacked an ego, which might have made it difficult for someone like her to be with a partner. He was peaceful, and she often found herself wanting to just stand beside him, to feel the way his serenity radiated from him to surround and hold her. Truthfully, she found him sexy and rather intoxicating.

Razvan smiled at her. "I am reading your mind."

She tossed her head. "Do not read too much into whatever I was thinking."

Razvan lowered himself into the water, ducking his head and then coming up fast right beside her, his hands skimming up her thighs, over the curves of her hips, along her tucked-in waist and higher up along her rib cage until he was holding the soft weight of her breasts in his palms. "I think you should read my mind."

Before she could reply he dipped his head and drew her nipple deep into his mouth. It mattered little that he had already made love to her twice, that her body had been sated. She instantly felt the heat swamping her. His wet hair slid over her abdomen and teased her mound as he tugged and teased and suckled.

She held him there for a moment, savoring the pleasure filling her and then she dipped her fingers beneath the water and found his erection already growing firm. At the touch of her fingers his shaft jerked and pulsed. She smirked, realizing the power of her touch as she caressed his hard length with strokes before wrapping her fingers around him to enclose his hard flesh in a tight fist.

Razvan lifted his head and looked at her with dark, hungry eyes. "What are you doing?"

"A little exploring of my own."

He leaned back until his hip brushed the wall of the basin to steady himself. Her touch left him weak, his body shuddering with need.

"You could always sit," Ivory suggested, her voice silky, "as this may take some time. I am very thorough when I explore."

Swallowing hard, Razvan sat up on the very edge of the smooth rock, allowing his legs to dangle in the pool. His erection throbbed against his stomach, rock hard and growing by the moment. When she cupped his balls and leaned down for her first tentative lick, his breath exploded from his lungs. When her mouth took him, he was lost in her body, in her mind, in everything she was to him.

Razvan fisted his hands in her hair and held on, knowing this was the beginning of a wild ride with his beloved lifemate.

16

"**W**hat is this?" Razvan looked over Ivory's shoulder, his body deliberately close to hers, his chin on her shoulder as he watched her work.

He had awakened that evening with the feeling of her fingers caressing his skin. The wonder of having Ivory in his life, in his bed, his soul merged with hers, was beyond anything he could ever have imagined. Their lovemaking had been gentle and tender and then turned ferocious and wild.

Hunting had been fun together. They had watched the rising moon burning across the snowcapped mountains, pouring silver across the midnight-blue skies to spotlight the sparkling snow layered across the meadows and hanging in the trees. They flew through the sky together, high above the trees, wing tip to wing tip, the wind ruffling feathers, both caught up in the freedom of the owls soaring, wheeling and dipping, performing acrobatics just for fun because they could.

Somersaulting with her, talons linked, Razvan knew that everything he needed was here, in this one woman. She had saved him with her smile. With her inner beauty. Her soul. She had become his own personal miracle. He wasn't altogether certain the earth had healed him. She had. With the colors she had provided, bringing life to his world. With the joy she had restored, so that each moment meant something to him. She had replaced the shadows in his eyes, in his heart, with love. She had replaced the darkness in his soul with light.

He swallowed hard, his chin nuzzling her shoulder as he peered at the book she had open as she studied her books in her workroom. He could see she had written in the ancient text and he read the words to himself, frowning over them.

The mage walks forth as the Hell Gate closes
Lightning strikes with his first order
Energy spirals from his fingertips
A spell does form upon his lips
Tall and dark, handsomely slender
His silver eyes burn like lighted embers
A power, a presence one cannot explain
A drawing feeling that will not leave the brain
A longing, a yearning that burns like fire
To be wanted and taken with heated desire
The mage walks forth unfolding his arms
His victim comes quietly, succumbed by his charms
The embers of passion burst forth in flame
As the mage draws heart's blood from deep within
Consuming all, leaving no remains
The victim languishes in untold pain
The mage, having taken body and soul,
Now turns from the broken to seek one who is
    whole
The pattern is set, the ending the same
The mage needs heart's blood to be whole and
    remain.

Razvan's stomach lurched, and just like that his world spun away from him, collapsing into images of blood and screams and death. He dropped his arms and stepped back, turning away from her. "Why would you write such a vile thing? Why would you give him such honor as to set him down on paper and give him to history?"

Ivory turned at his low tone, caught his arm and stepped in front of him. His eyes were filled with horror. Nightmare memories. His were not the nightmares that evaporated because the mind played tricks, his were made of true memories that would last an eternity. She had inadvertently conjured up the images of his past.

"It is not to memorialize him. I have to hold his image when I work. The image I saw, so that I know him, so that I am never tricked as I work on his spells. He is evil. He will always be evil. He chose to be evil. And I have to keep my mind clear at all times. Razvan, I am sorry I hurt you with the image of him, but it is my protection."

He wrapped her braid around his fist but he remained silent, drawing in breath, matching the rhythm of his heart to hers.

"When I work with his spells, Razvan, it is dangerous. I cannot tell you how dangerous. You said you were not good with spells. Well, I am, but, to be so, I have to form the words in my head, conjure up the images to go with them, and I cannot make any mistakes when I am working with his spells."

He took another deep breath, visibly fighting to get his control back. "I still do not understand."

She gestured around the room. "This is my fortress. Solid rock. He cannot come here. He cannot trace me through the solid rock, but if I make a mistake, if I forget for one moment who and what I am dealing with, then I make myself vulnerable."

He frowned. "Even here?"

"He is utterly evil. The first line says it all. 'The mage walks forth as the Hell Gate closes.' He is not entirely earthly. He has visited hell and returned, needing the blood of others to survive."

His frown deepened. "I lived with him for hundreds of years. He is evil, yes, but he is not a demon. He is mage."

She nodded. "Yes, he is mage. There is always a balance in the universe. Where there is good, there must also be evil. One can use the earth's natural elements to weave for good. It is done all the time for healing and other things our people need. One can also weave spells for evil, calling upon demons and bargaining with them."

"I know that he does that. I have seen foul creatures in his caverns, but I have never seen portals to another world or another realm that even a mage can walk through."

"No, I am certain he would not be foolish enough to allow anyone to know what happened. He wants to appear all-powerful to everyone—even to himself. He needs that illusion. As far as I can tell, as far back as when I attended his school, he was using apprentices to write spells and then he used those spells as the base for his own. He can no longer come up with new spells, I am certain of it. Each mage has a rhythm, a twist in how they cast and what they use, a signature, if you will. Xavier's spells cover a multitude of other mage's spells."

Razvan ran agitated hands over his face and then through his streaked hair. "What else have you learned by studying him?"

She ran her hand down his arm to soothe him. "I know it is disturbing to speak of him."

The feeling of her fingers on his skin shook him. As long as he lived, he would never get over the wonder that she had been chosen for him. "Your description fits him so well. I lived with him and thought I knew him better than anyone living, yet . . ." He gestured toward the book and her flowing, obviously offensive words. "Yet you managed to convey the very essence of him."

"I hope you are right, Razvan. I am staking both our lives on this." She took his hand and tugged until he followed her out of the room. They sank into the chairs in the memory room. "I have to know you are with me on this, Razvan. It will not be easy and I cannot have you hesitate when we confront him."

He leaned back in the chair and regarded her steadily. "You never have to worry that I would hesitate. We are in this together. It is my choice. I made it when you asked me to live. I knew then we would go after him."

She allowed herself a sigh of relief. She shouldn't have doubted him. He had the courage to be whatever she needed. He found no shame in following her lead. No hesitation in accepting their destiny. He was more of a man than any other she knew.

"You know what I think, Razvan? I believe Xavier has to find another body. He was not merely possessing you, leaving pieces behind in you to stay in control. I believe he was looking for a host body and a way to enter it, to claim it completely and make the body his own. He wanted to be Carpathian. You were born with Dragonseeker blood running in your veins, known to be one of the most powerful lineages, if not the most powerful. He coveted that bloodline. That is why he went after Rhiannon. And that is why he drank the blood of her children and grandchildren. He craves a body from the Dragonseeker bloodline."

"No Dragonseeker has ever turned." There was no pride in his voice. It was merely a statement. "I would not allow him to make me the first."

She smiled at him, her smile lifting him back from the shadowy place that he had dropped into. "No, you did not. And you saved all of us. No one will know what you did, but I know, Razvan. If he had acquired a Dragonseeker body as was his goal, there is no way to judge the harm he would have done."

He took her hand, played with her fingers, shaking his head a bit. "It is my stubbornness."

"It is your immeasurable courage," she corrected. "It is not as if anyone could have endured as you did."

He brought her fingers to his mouth and bit gently. "You will make me blush."

She doubted that. He had no ego. None. He simply accepted his life and lived in the moment, focusing his entire attention on what he was doing and giving his best to whatever task was at hand. She did a little blushing thinking of how he focused so completely on her when they made love. Nothing else was in his mind but giving her pleasure. It was an intoxicating, exhilarating experience, and one she was already addicted to. She lost herself in him so completely, and found herself wanting to give him that same complete focus.

"My entry in that diary is the formula with which we will defeat him."

Everything in him stilled. "We are going to bait a trap."

She kept her eyes steadily on his. "Yes, we are. He needs a body. And he needs heart's blood. Dragonseeker blood."

"You are going to ask me to put myself in his hands once again."

His voice was strictly neutral and his mind was firmly

closed to hers. Her heart contracted. There was no expression. No condemnation. No judgment whatsoever. He merely waited for her answer, his fingers still on hers. Sometimes, like now, his courage terrified her. His belief in her shocked her.

"You would put yourself into his hands if I asked you to, wouldn't you?" she said, her stomach knotting.

"Yes."

She shook her head. "I could not *ever* conceive of putting you anywhere near where that evil mage could get his hands on you."

For the first time he stirred and something crossed his face so swiftly she couldn't quite catch it, but it made her nervous. "Just what or who is the bait?"

"I now have Dragonseeker blood running in my veins. When I open them and leave tracks, he will be unable to resist. I am a woman and he will think me easily controlled."

He sat back in his chair, his lips drawn into a tight, implacable line. Tiny embers smoldered in the depths of his eyes, but again, he went silent—waiting.

"I have thought this through, Razvan," she hastily explained. "It is all there. He will come for me, darkly handsome, taking your form, using his mind to draw me to him. He will want to seduce me, and he will open his arms to bring me in close to him."

"No."

"You know I am right. This is the way."

"No." Razvan rose and called to the pack. "I am taking the wolves running. Would you care to join us?"

"We need to discuss this."

"There is no discussion. Are you coming?" He moved away from her with swift, long strides, snapping his fingers and calling to the pack.

Ivory stood for a long moment, unsure whether to be angry or happy that he would be so protective. No one had wanted to protect her, not since she was a young girl and her brothers and the De La Cruz family had surrounded her with love. Ten men doting on her had made her feel like a princess—a smothered one at times, but still a princess. Razvan had gone through so much with Xavier. He just needed to get used to the idea.

She was astonished when she saw him spread his arms as she did, and Blaez and Rikki leapt onto his back, merging into his skins as tattoos. For one moment she found herself a little upset. The pack had never been divided. They were her family.

"The pack is not divided," Razvan said. "We are a family."

He was back to his usual calm. Matter-of-fact. Or maybe he always had been. Even saying an adamant *no* to her, he had not raised his voice or sounded upset, just implacable.

She nodded in agreement. "Yes, we are. It is a good thing for both of us to carry the wolves. They will guard our backs."

He flashed a small, tentative grin, removing the years from his face until he looked almost boyish. "It is amazing to be so accepted by them."

She felt that peculiar wrenching in the vicinity of her heart that he often produced in her. His simple pleasure touched her. "Where are we going?"

"I want to go to the place where you found the soil for our bedchamber."

"The cave of gems."

He nodded. "The soil is pure, so we know that Xavier has not had a chance to spread his poison everywhere. I would like to find how far the infection has spread, how large of an area there actually is. I cannot believe this would be the only place. Once we know how to look, we can send word to other Carpathians to check their soil."

"You believe we can cleanse it?"

"I absolutely believe *you* can," he said.

She tried not to feel a ridiculous glow, but there it was, a silly ember that spread through her body like heat. It truly was frightening how she reacted to him. Embarrassed, she held her arms out and allowed the remainder of the pack to merge with her skin before scanning above them to ensure there was no way anyone could observe them leaving their lair.

They went out into the night, streaking fast through the dark, clear sky. Stars glittered high overhead, spreading a fantasy blanket over them, wrapping them in beauty that never failed to move Razvan. Ivory felt it through him. The wonder. The majesty. The miracle.

She had never looked at her surroundings that way, but, with Razvan, she saw everything through new eyes. He felt as if he was sailing across the moon, sliding down a comet, playing hide-and-seek through the constellations. He raced through the scattered bits of vapor rising off the ribbon of a river and she experienced all of it with him. She had flown as an owl thousands of times, but never once had it been so fun or exhilarating.

The owls glided on silent wings over the snow-covered ground as they crossed above a meadow, the female moving into the lead, dropping low to gain the protection of the forest for as long as possible. They flew fast, banking sharply around the trees and through the branches, so soundless the rodents still scurried below, unaware of the danger above them.

They broke from the forest just as the floor dropped

away to a valley running between two long mountain ranges, far from the ice caves of Xavier and miles away from the Carpathian village. The owls changed color to make it more difficult to be seen. Razvan went snowy white, while Ivory was darker white with a few dusky spots on her wings, indicating a female.

Let the owl guide your thoughts, Ivory cautioned. *Anyone scanning might find one of us within the owl's body if we are not careful.*

She had been careful every day of her life since the moment she had clawed her way out of the earth a century after the brutal attack on her. He didn't respond, although he wanted to. He found the warrior in her sexy. Instead he brushed her with warmth and then simply let go of his self, merging deeply within the owl so, should an enemy be seeking them, their adversary would never suspect anything but owls winging their way across the valley.

The moment he allowed the owl completely to the forefront, he was astonished at the bird's ability to hear and see. The thick white plumage, soft and dense, extended to his toes, covering and insulating his body. Soft fringe on the flight feathers muffled the sound, allowing him to soar ghostlike across the sky.

Ivory dropped low, skimming close to the ground now, and Razvan followed, enjoying every second of the silent flight, watching the wind ruffle his mate's feathers as she glided along mere feet above the ground, making them smaller targets. She suddenly rose sharply, wings beating powerfully to bring her high, up toward a peak and then plunging over the other side, talons outstretched as if hunting prey.

Just before they hit the ground, Ivory moved in his mind with a sharp command. *Shift.*

He landed on his feet, crouching low instinctively on a small outcropping nearly at the very base of the mountain. Ivory did another slow, careful scan of the area and Razvan followed suit.

"This place is sacred. I was directed here by Mother Earth, to this place of immense power. There are magic metals here, and gems for any occasion. The soil is rich and has never been used by any other than me."

He bowed low, a gesture of respect. "Thank you for bringing me."

"You are my lifemate." Ivory said it casually, but inside her stomach knotted.

This was her favorite place, just as his garden had been his. She wanted him to feel the same way about it as she did, to love the spectacular cave, the feel of the soil, to see the beauty of the gems and realize the richness of the metals. Most of all she wanted him to realize the honor they both had been given by their earth mother. No one had ever walked inside the cave before her, and no one would find it after her.

Ivory couldn't believe how nervous she was as she floated just above the stones covering the entrance. She wanted to leave no tracks, and disturbing the snow would do so. She made certain she took a detailed picture in her mind so everything could be arranged exactly as it was before they moved the twin stones opening into the long narrow tunnel that led to the caves beneath the ground.

Razvan realized what she was doing and immediately followed suit. He had a photographic memory. If she wanted the area pristine, he would make certain it was left that way when they were gone.

Ivory floated the two small rocks away to reveal a crawl space low to the ground. They both shifted into vapor and poured into the narrow opening. Ivory wove safeguards to hide the entrance while they were inside and then proceeded along the curving tube, following its direction down into the warmth of the earth. The crawl space was no wider than a small man's shoulders, but, in their present form, they traveled fast.

The tunnel began to widen and the ceiling became high enough for them to stand, but Ivory, conscious of disturbing the natural balance of the ecosystem, remained as vapor until she got down into the cave itself. The cave was quite large and wide, terraced with many levels.

She left off her shoes when she shifted to her natural form, letting her feet sink into the rich soil just to absorb the feeling.

"Hurry, Razvan, like this. It is so wonderful—like heaven."

She flashed a quick smile his way, but Razvan could tell it was a bit tentative. That always moved him. His confident warrior always became a little nervous when she was having fun or being a woman. He stayed just inches from the soil with his bare feet. "I do not know about this, Ivory. I have been in heaven, you know."

She looked up with a small frown, realized his meaning from the look in his eyes and then she blushed. He loved that—the sweep of color moving up her neck and creeping under the porcelain of her skin when he teased her.

"Put your feet in the soil," she said, shaking her head at him.

He floated to just in front of her, keeping his feet hovering above the enticing richness of the dark loam. His body bumped against hers. "I cannot quite settle. I am new at this, you know."

"You are always up to something when you give me your

little-boy smile." The one that melted her entire body and left her weak and breathless and ready to do anything he wanted right there on the spot. In a kind of desperation, she gripped his arms and yanked him down. His body slid along the length of hers, sending a shiver of excitement spiraling through her.

Razvan's bare feet sank into the rich soil nearly up to his ankles. His fingers curled around her arms as they stood with only a breath between them. "Ivory!" Excitement shook him. "This is such a find."

Pleased, she shrugged. "It is not really my find. I was given the location by the earth when I was deep beneath the layers and fighting for my life. I crawled here. Inch by inch."

She swallowed the dark memories of those difficult days and leaned into him, unconsciously seeking the shelter of his heart. She hadn't realized until that moment how much she already relied on him. It both frightened and elated her that Razvan had become so important to her so quickly.

"I would crawl as far as I could when there was no moon to burn my skin," she explained. "In the first attempts to rise for a few hours and start the trek, even the smallest light hurt my skin. The pack would guard me and then I would sink beneath the soil and recover until I could manage to gather the courage and endurance to go farther."

His arm swept around her and he brushed kisses over the top of her head. She wasn't asking for sympathy, she simply was giving him the facts. Everything he was rebelled at the images of her crawling on her hands and knees, dragging herself over the rough terrain on her belly, using elbows and knees to propel herself forward. He hadn't been there to aid her and the thought of her enduring such agony without him to help her left him sick.

He traced the thin white lines segmenting her body, the one around her throat, the one over her upper arms and down the swell of her breast. He tipped up her chin, using two fingers, waiting until her lashes lifted and he was looking into her eyes. "I love you."

Her womb clenched. Her heart stilled. She could see it in his eyes. Feel the emotion surrounding her, swamping her, lifting her up. Her mouth opened, but nothing came out. He shook her with his love. His slow smile made her tremble and she veiled her eyes again as his mouth descended to take possession of hers. The earth trembled beneath their feet.

Ivory tangled her fingers with his as he lifted his head. "I want to show you something. This place is a treasure trove of gems, but, more importantly, metals."

Razvan looked up at the terraced walls with the veins of silver and gold. Along the walls and scattered throughout the dark soil, he could see evidence of sparkling gems.

"Iron. Not from ore, but from a meteorite. It is in its purest form, straight from the skies, Razvan. The protection properties are tremendous. And lead is here as well. I have been experimenting with lead to aid in lengthening the endurance of my coating with protection spells. I can make our weapons of natural metals that do well with magic so we can easily transport them. The coating is essential when we fight vampires."

"Amazing," Razvan agreed. "This place is beyond important, Ivory."

"It was entrusted to me and I have to keep it safe."

"I agree." He crouched down even as he was looking around at the various properties she pointed out to him. Scooping up a handful of soil, he let it slide through his fingers. "This soil is not contaminated."

"Why would it be?" Ivory said. "Xavier has no idea it exists. No one does."

"The microbes are in the ground, Ivory. They do not stay in one place. They spread. That is what he sent them out to do, spread to far lands and contaminate. That, coupled with the fact that they are nearly impossible to destroy, is why Xavier used them. You can bet he sent his microbes across the sea to every continent. Xavier is a very thorough man."

"How do you know they are not here?"

"I lived in the ice caves in the middle of the experiments for more centuries than I care to remember. I feel them."

"Like Natalya said Lara does." She spun around to look at him. "But she is still mage; they believe she feels them because she is mage."

He shook his head. "No, she can hide her presence from them because she is mage. That is why they cannot convert her. She is the only one who can at this point."

"You are thinking that you can find a way to aid your daughter."

He nodded. "*We* can find a way," he emphasized. "I cannot do it without your help. She cannot be converted and lives a half-life in order to keep the unborn children alive. If we can find a way to rid the soil of the mutated microbes, she can be converted."

"Razvan . . ." Her voice was gentle. "It is most likely the microbes have not found their way in yet. It is probably only a matter of time. As I understand it, extremophiles can live under pretty much any condition, no matter how harsh. If there was a way to destroy them . . ."

"You said yourself, you can reverse what he did."

"Yes, but not destroy the ones already in the ground. I can stop them, but it will take time. Years even."

Ivory hated to disappoint him. He was looking at her as

if the moon waxed and waned with her. She laid a hand on top of his head. "We will find a way to help her."

"It is here, Ivory. The answer is here," Razvan insisted. "In this cave. Life began in microbe form. There is something in this soil that protects against the invasion of the mutated microbes, I am certain of it."

She sank down beside him, feeling the healing earth move around her as if to cushion and blanket her with its warmth. Whenever she came to the cave she felt as if she'd come home. She'd spent a lot of time beneath the ground here, covered in the rich soil, absorbing the healing properties through her skin.

She scooped up a fistful of dirt and allowed it to run through her fingers like water, feeling the individual properties as the substance moved over her skin. Was it only her imagination because she wanted to do this for him so much, or did she really feel as if there was something different, an element in the soil she was missing?

"You said there is always a balance of good and evil, Ivory," Razvan reminded.

"Yes, but I deal with what is natural. Xavier twists what is natural into something evil. The microbes started out good, not evil, or at least neutral. They were not put on this earth to harm Carpathians. Xavier changed them for his own evil purposes. Had they been naturally poisonous, I would have no doubt that the cure would be close to them, as is always the case with nature. I can reverse his spell. I am certain I can, given the time to study it. But to find something to destroy what he has wrought . . ."

"It is here," Razvan insisted stubbornly. "I feel it."

She looked around her. She had utilized the precious metals and called the gems to her for her weapons and her warning system. She had used the soil for her bedchamber, painstakingly transporting it until she had a full basin. Occasionally she replenished the soil with new, fresh earth, although the healing properties had always remained as powerful as within the cave itself.

She believed in feelings. Ivory was very tuned to the earth after spending so many centuries deep within its rich beds of healing soil. If the metals and gems were the very veins and blood and bones of the earth, perhaps the organisms were her heart and soul.

Razvan had experienced the same connection to the earth. Mother Earth had accepted him, attached her veins to his and encased him in her gems and minerals to save his life. She flowed in his veins in the way she did Ivory's. Perhaps, with his newfound life, he was closer to the soil and could feel the minute differences in ways Ivory hadn't explored yet, but that still didn't make sense. She'd spent centuries in the earth, hooked to the ebb and flow of the earth's lifeblood and she couldn't detect what he thought he felt.

"Clear your mind of everything," Razvan suggested. "Sit like this." He lifted his left foot and placed it on his right thigh and tucked his right foot onto his left thigh.

Ivory sat facing him, assuming the position without question.

"Spine straight, relax your shoulders. That is right." He nodded his approval. "You want to make an oval with your hands, left hand on top of right, with your thumbs together and your middle joints of your middle fingers together. Let go of yourself. Similar to what you do in healing, but mind and body as one, and just let information flow into you. Take it in and let it out. Do not try to hold on to anything. Just be still. Breathe. Match the flow of my breath and then let yourself forget that, too."

Ivory did as he asked, giving herself up to the moment. To the cave. To the earth. It was not only the connection to the earth, she decided later, it was this—Razvan's stillness, his peace, the way he was one with everything around him—that allowed her to first feel the presence of the organism.

She drew in her breath and slowly lifted her palm, using her body like a divining rod. She slowly turned and found that she'd picked up the existence of the life-form in every direction, as if the soil was saturated with it.

"It is everywhere," she said, letting her breath out, a little shocked at the widespread dispersion. "I have to figure out what it is."

"Can we take a sample?"

"We have an entire basin full," Ivory reminded. "We sleep in it every day."

Razvan frowned and ran the soil through his fingers again. "I think we should take a new sample, to make certain it was not contaminated in any way by us."

"I always ask permission before I take anything from this cave," Ivory warned. "If the answer is no, we go with what we already have. The earth has been more than good to us and we cannot allow greed to creep into our hearts, not even for a good cause."

"The earth is a mother, Ivory, she saved us. She will want to save the children of her people," Razvan reasoned.

Ivory smiled. She loved the way Razvan had such faith. Where had it come from? He had been tortured by his own grandfather. His people had believed the worst of him, yet he still had faith in the goodness of the world.

Razvan caught her looking at him with that look on her face she reserved only for him. Tender. Loving. Proud. She probably didn't even know she had that particular look, but it made him soft inside whenever that expression crossed her face, no matter how fleeting. It was enough for him that she knew him and understood why he did the things he did. No one else had to know, only Ivory.

Ivory lifted her hands and closed her eyes, using a melodic voice to plead their case. She was startled when Razvan joined in, harmonizing in his deeper male voice.

Mother, oh Mother, we come to you for aid.
Hear our children, hold them close, never let them
    fade.
Mother, oh Mother, our children are dying
Catch our tears, we plead with you, stop our
    crying.
Listen to our plea, see what is in our hearts.
Hold us together, don't let us fall apart.
We ask for the life in the soil to bring strength to
    our young
Heal their wounds, protect our special ones.

Around them the ground shimmered and the gems sparkled bright. Above their heads columns of stalactites hummed, vibrating with the tune of their harmony.

Ivory bowed her head in gratitude and Razvan slid his hand almost lovingly through the soil before they lifted their voices in thanks.

Mother, oh Mother, you are great indeed
Your gift is so precious, we're humbled by thee.

Razvan scooped up handfuls of the precious material and, forming a silken pouch, poured it into the bag. "How much will you need?"

"Enough to conduct several experiments just in case it is not an easy answer." She couldn't keep the excitement from her voice. Usually there were no easy answers, but this time, they might have just gotten plain lucky. If there was a life-form that kept the mutated microbes at bay or, better yet, actually destroyed them, she should be able to find it fairly quickly. It wasn't as if she had a lot of combinations to choose from.

Razvan's fingers settled around her wrist and he pulled her to him. "You are a miracle to me, Ivory, whether you think so or not. This place"—he swept one arm in a circular motion, taking in the giant cave—"this may save my daughter. She has been through so much, and, as always, you seem to be the key to my happiness. If I can ease her suffering and that of her lifemate, I will feel as if I at least partially redeemed myself."

"Xavier possessed you, Razvan," she reminded gently. "I shared your memories and saw what he did. The fault was not yours."

He shrugged and tucked stray tendrils of hair, which had pulled loose from her braid, behind her ear. "I should have been more careful in my wording of things. I grew up with a mage. I know that words carry power, yet I continued to make mistakes that cost those I loved dearly."

"You were fourteen years old the first time he took you, and you gave up your life so your sister would be safe. You were a child, Razvan," she said.

His smile was gentle. "You are so fierce in your defense of me, *hän ku kuulua sívamet*—keeper of my heart, yet you should be called *hän ku meke pirämet*—defender."

"I am the keeper of your heart," she said, "and I will defend you to the death, Razvan. You are an extraordinary man and I am proud to be your lifemate." She ducked her head, embarrassed as always when she showed too much emotion. "We should go back to our home so we can study the soil and see if we truly have your answers."

He caught her chin and took a kiss. Just one. But he savored her, the taste and texture of her, savored the scent and feel of her. When he lifted his head he smiled. "*Päläfertiil*—mate."

Just the way he said that single word made her weak inside. Soft. Tender. Sexy. She smiled back at him. "That I am."

17

"The life-form had to have first been in the meteorite," Ivory said and slumped down, her arms cushioning her head. "I should have known. It is iron rich."

"How did it survive coming to Earth?" Razvan asked, rubbing her shoulders.

"I have no idea, and frankly, I do not even care at this point. The soil is teeming with them and, so far, every time you have brought me contaminated soil, they rush to surround the mutated microbes and destroy them while leaving everything else intact." She turned her head to one side to look up at him. "Do you know where the microbes are produced?"

"Xavier's largest factory was destroyed and he moved to his fortress deep under the mountains. I can find it. But the microbes are not in the soil there. He leaks them down a glacier to feed the water systems and spread to the soil. The last time I hunted for us near the village just below the glacier, I overheard the local midwife speaking of the high rate of miscarriages. I fear the contamination has spilled over into humans. If the microbes infected their gardens, they could begin to suffer the fate of our species." He massaged her neck with gentle fingers. "You need to rest, Ivory."

She had been working steadily for three weeks straight, never leaving the lair, not even for food. Razvan had hunted for the pack and for Ivory. He had taken the wolves running nightly and had gathered soil samples from dozens of places, bringing each back to her, but Ivory refused to go with him, preferring to stay and conduct her experiments. She looked pale and worn, with dark circles under her eyes.

"I have a bad feeling, Razvan," Ivory said. But she gave a small sigh of pleasure as his fingers worked their magic, easing the knots out of her neck. "It has been growing in me for some time now and I feel the need to get this done fast."

He was silent and she looked up at him to catch the expression on his face. Ivory sat up quickly and turned to face him. "You have felt it, too."

He nodded. "Growing stronger all the time and the pack has been strangely restless."

"Something is wrong."

He didn't want to agree with her, not when she was so worn, but his every instinct told her she was right. "We have to go to the prince with what we have," he said.

She bit her lip. "I think I am right, Razvan, but I am always so meticulous. I would repeat the experiments a thousand more times and document more evidence. I am still working on the spell to change the existing mutations for when we find his factory."

She pushed her hand through her hair in agitation. "There is still so much work. You cannot just rush this kind of thing. If we make a mistake, we could do as much harm as Xavier, no matter what our intent."

They stayed up into the morning hours when her skin hurt and blistered, despite being so far beneath the ground—an aftermath, he knew, of spending more than a century beneath the earth to heal her horrendous wounds. She sank into the sleep of their people. Ivory often woke before she should, agitated and on edge. Her body was unable to move while her mind raced with worry. Razvan made love to her often, easing the tension in her, but she couldn't stop the obsessive drive that kept her working nonstop. Even the soil couldn't seem to rejuvenate her.

He pulled a brush from the table and began to run it gently through her hair, knowing she always found that soothing. He did as well. The feel of the silken strands against his skin served as a reminder to him of the absolute wonder of finding her when there had never been a moment of hope of such a miracle.

"How close are you to reversing the spell?"

"I will not know until I try it, Razvan." There was a hint of despair in her voice. "I am beginning to see the enormity of what Lara and Nicolas have faced. They do not dare convert her and bear the death of our children on their souls, yet how can they continue without a life of their own?"

Razvan's smile above her head was tranquil. "You endured. I endured. Such is life, Ivory. We hope our children do not have to struggle as we have, but living life well and handling adversity shapes character. I am proud of Lara for her choices and would not take away from her the chance for service to others. She has many years she can continue to live well before it is necessary to convert her. If we fail, she will endure as we did. At the end of the day, we can only say we did our best. We cannot control others, just ourselves."

Ivory felt his quiet stillness, the peaceful calm that kept him so composed in difficult situations. She allowed that serenity to seep into her and soothe her own turbulent mind. With each stroke, the brush seemed to pull more of the tension out of her soul. Razvan was right. They could only do their best and that was what they had done.

She realized, as he divided her hair into three thick strands and began a tight weave, that she had wanted to show the Carpathian people that Razvan was no criminal to be mistrusted, but was, in fact, a great man who had sacrificed for all of them. Razvan didn't want that. He didn't care about others' opinions. He simply was. That was how he lived his life. He did his best and didn't try to control others.

She took a deep breath. "Okay. I say we go then, find out what is happening and let the prince make the decision to try a larger experiment or keep working. I also need to try the reversing spells on microbes that are out in the field. There is no point in attacking the factory if we cannot permanently stop his work."

"The more Xavier is harassed, the less time he has to do damage," Razvan said gently. "If this does not work for us, then we can buy ourselves time by taking down his fortress and making him move again."

She started to turn her head to look at him over her shoulder, but he tugged on her hair, preventing her. Ivory frowned. "We cannot take a chance on losing him. If he disappears . . ."

"I can find him. Anywhere. Anytime."

She waited a heartbeat until her pulse settled. "How?"

"He took my blood for well over a hundred years, Ivory. He left pieces of his dark, depraved soul within me. I will draw him as no other."

She clamped down hard on the surge of bile rising suddenly at the idea of Razvan in Xavier's hands. "You would use yourself as bait."

"Of course. To draw him to us. He would come."

His hands were steadier than hers as he secured the tie on her braid. She knew because she reached back and laid her hands over his. "No." A single word. *His* single word to her. Now she knew how he'd felt when she'd suggested using herself as bait.

He didn't argue, but then she was getting used to his ways. That didn't mean agreement. He simply bent down and kissed the side of her neck, right over her rapidly beating pulse.

"I mean it, Razvan. We will not destroy his present fortress, even if we need more time."

His smile was placid, gentle, even tender. His palm cupped the side of her face. "As we do not know if you have succeeded, there is no reason for discord between us."

She bit his fingers hard and glared at him. "Just so you know, there will be discord between us. A lot of discord. More than any man will ever want to have in his life."

He burst out laughing, sticking his fingers in his mouth to ease the sting. "I will remember that."

She gave him a sniff of annoyance and gathered weapons. Razvan had divided his time between helping her, caring for her and working on his proficiency with the various weapons she had. He was a quick learner with astonishing reflexes, and was very disciplined about his practice. He spent hours with the crossbow and sword each night. He practiced tumbling and hand-to-hand as well as throwing the arrowheads. He was quick and intelligent and she enjoyed his company, but most of all his tranquility. He had brought her peace and joy.

Razvan held out his arms and Blaez and Rikki leapt onto his back easily, merging into his skin until he was decorated with detailed tattoos just as the rest of the pack joined with Ivory. They gathered the soil and the documentation of the experiments, and scanned meticulously before streaming out into the night and streaking fast across the sky toward the Carpathian settlement.

As they flew across the forests and meadows, they spotted evidence of vampires passing through the vicinity. Blackened shrubbery. Withered branches. Split tree trunks. In one area it was obvious a battle had taken place: the ground was blackened.

Ivory sucked in her breath. *They are out in force.*

He will come for me. Again his voice was absolutely calm. *No.*

Ivory dipped her wings and circled away from the ravaged wasteland below, taking them through a narrow pass and then over rolling hills dotted with small farms, but she felt his smile.

You will not be smiling long if you keep it up.

I was just saying.

You were provoking me.

I would not do that.

The female owl sent him a haughty look and began her descent, calling ahead to the prince to announce their presence. His house looked quiet. Deserted. She pulled up in alarm and settled into the tops of a tree to use the owl's acute sight to examine the area around the house.

They left in a hurry and they did not shift.

Raven is pregnant, fairly advanced in her pregnancy, Razvan reminded her. *Is it possible it is her time?*

The bad feeling inside of Ivory got worse. *Perhaps we should use our blood call to the healer,* she suggested uneasily.

Razvan didn't hesitate. He went inside himself to find the strain of healer blood running through his veins and sent a call: *We have need to speak with the prince but find his home empty. We both are uneasy. Is there trouble?*

There was a long silence, as if the healer might not answer, and then his voice came. Faint. Faraway. Stressed. Hesitant. *My lifemate cannot hold on to the babies. We are in the cave of healing, preparing a birth chamber. Lara and Nicolas have been injured.*

Razvan turned the owl's head and looked at Ivory before launching himself into the air, the female following this time. There were no words to say. If Nicolas had been injured, they had to have been attacked—and attacked deliberately. The master vampire—or Xavier— had determined who was saving the unborn children and had made a bid to remove that obstacle to his plans. *But how did they know to attack Lara?* Razvan questioned, remembering that brief hesitation from Gregori. *They think I am a spy in their camp and that I gave up Lara to Xavier.*

Immediately Ivory dropped toward the ground, shifting form at the last moment to pace through the snow with quick long strides of energy, radiating a fury that couldn't be mistaken. She had heard that small hesitation in the healer as well.

"We go, Razvan, and we could be walking into a trap. They might try to jump us, and, if they do, we will have no choice but to fight our way clear." She whirled around to face him, a slow hiss escaping. "Someone will die."

Razvan regarded her with dark, somber eyes, leaning against a tree trunk with casual ease, watching her move like quicksilver through the snow. He loved her ferocious protection, the fine fury that shone through her, radiating out like the brightest moon.

"I will go alone." He kept his tone quiet, very calm.

Her chin went up. "You will *not* be their sacrifice. They are upset. On edge. They need a scapegoat and they will make you one. We both know it."

"One of us has to speak with the prince. You are the better warrior. I do not mind them putting their hands on me or searching me. You would never tolerate such a thing, nor would I be able to allow them to touch you without respect. If you go, there *will* be a fight. If I go, there is a chance we can get to the prince with our evidence and help them."

"They do not deserve help." She snapped the words at him, enunciating each one.

He folded his arms across his chest as she took up pacing again, her hands in tight fists at her sides. He said nothing, merely watched her through half-closed eyes.

She stopped in front of him, her breath coming in ragged gasps, her heart there behind the tears swimming in her eyes. There was nothing more disarming than a warrior woman looking vulnerable and weeping. He lifted his hand to her face in wonder. "Don't cry for me, Ivory. I have always lived with my choices. I have to see that Lara is safe. And I cannot let babies die if we have a way to save them, and neither would you."

"If they harm one hair on your head—just *one*—there will be a war such as they have never seen."

His hands framed her face. He knew it only embarrassed her when he told her he loved her, because she had a difficult time answering him back. And it would probably be worse if he told her she moved him as no one and nothing else ever had or would. So he kissed her.

Razvan poured everything he felt for her into his kiss. Infinite love. Complete acceptance. Pride. Joy. Lust. Everything he was, he gave to her. She answered him, sinking into the heat of his mouth, giving herself up to that world of pure sensation mixed with love. She could live there, in his arms, their mouths fused together forever, her body sinking into his, her arms around his neck. Her home. Her shelter. Her everything.

When he reluctantly left the haven of her mouth, he rested his forehead against hers, drawing in a deep, shuddering breath. "If this goes wrong, *hän ku vigyáz sielamet*—keeper of my soul—know I will wait for you in the next life. Xavier must be destroyed. Before all else, he must be destroyed. Look at me and tell me you will come to me with your soul shining brightly."

"You ask too much."

"I do not, Ivory. I ask you to endure as you have endured for so many centuries, your eye fixed on the task given to you. We have had this time. A stolen moment of happiness. What they do—or do not do—matters little to us." He placed his hand over her heart, felt it beat into his palm. "We have a great purpose and we must see it through to the end."

The sob in her throat threatened to choke her as she swallowed it back down. "You terrify me with your calm acceptance, Razvan."

"I do not control others, Ivory, only myself. I do what I must, no matter the cost."

"I will hate them with all of my heart if they harm you."

"You are my light, Ivory. I need you to be that light. I count on that light."

"You ask more from me than you would from yourself. You would slay them all if they touched me."

"Yes." His thumb traced her fine bone structure. "You are the miracle, Ivory, not me."

His fingers curled around the nape of her neck and he

pulled her to him and simply held her in his arms until the stiffness and tension drained from her body and she lay against him, pliant and soft. Their hearts beat the same rhythm. In tune. His soul moved against hers. She felt the brush of his lips in her hair and then he put her away from him.

"Give me your documents and the soil samples. I will let you know if we are clear. If not, I will see you on the other side."

Reluctantly she handed them to him, ignoring that her hands were shaking. Razvan held out his arms and shrugged off the wolves, then knelt to bury his fingers in their fur, holding their heads and touching their faces as he rubbed their ears and necks before standing. When he turned away from her she caught his hand.

"Razvan."

He took a breath and turned back to her. "Beloved?"

"You are *my* miracle."

He smiled at her and walked away, carrying her words with him. It didn't take courage to walk into the lion's den. Whatever fate waited was nothing in comparison to what he had suffered at Xavier's hands. They would not torture him. Without Ivory they had nothing to hold over his head, no emotional pain they could give him. There was only death. He had accepted death as part of life a long time ago and he didn't fear it.

He walked with an easy pace, circling through the trees, making no attempt to hide his presence. He had left his weapons with Ivory, although he could summon them at will, and the Carpathians would know that.

He felt the first prickle of unease as he drew closer to the series of caves leading to the healing chambers. He knew they watched him. He heard the flutter of wings overhead as several owls settled onto the branches above his head. He kept walking.

Healer, I am coming in.

There was a small silence while Gregori relayed the information to others. Two owls floated down from the trees, shifting before they came to earth, resuming physical shapes. He recognized Falcon and Vikirnoff as they dropped in behind him to escort him. Above his head, the other owls took flight.

They have posted sentries, Ivory, and they are searching for you.

They will not find me.

He didn't allow his smile to show on his face as he entered the cave of healing. *I do not doubt you are right.* And he didn't. The Carpathian males continually underestimated Ivory. They should have known better, if they gave it any thought at all. Her bloodline. Her intelligence. Her determination to survive. Her hunting skills alone should have tipped them off that they were trying to chase a tiger.

Razvan continued into the tunnel connecting the series of caves. Grim-faced warriors were posted at each entrance. None of the faces was friendly. He felt the beat of their suspicions, the dark recrimination. He had been tried and convicted already. He didn't look at them as he walked past them, nor did he drop his head or quicken his pace. He felt, occasionally, the probe of a mind touch, but he had been with Xavier too long to ever allow anyone into his mind, no matter how strong the probe.

He knew that would only condemn him further in their eyes, but it mattered little to him. Gregori met him at the third entrance and fell into step.

"You know what they think."

"How is my daughter?"

"The attack came at dawn as they were out hunting, a time most vampires, particularly a master vampire, rarely rise. They had to have information not only that Lara was the one needed, but exactly where they had gone to hunt."

"How is my daughter?" Razvan repeated.

"She is healing, as is her lifemate. We had no choice but to complete the conversion and put them both in the ground. They went at her first. She was—mutilated." Gregori shook his head when Razvan stopped and looked at him. *Keep walking. This is a very difficult situation. Without Lara, we cannot break the cycle of the microbe attack. We sense their presence but they hide from us. We have no way to lure them to the surface. Being fully Carpathian, Lara will no longer be able to trick the microbe, but it was necessary to convert her. The women must rest in the ground, as do we, but then the microbes invade,* Gregori added telepathically.

"Tell me how she is." There was a bite to Razvan's voice. He felt Ivory stir in his mind, surrounding him with warmth. Deeply merged with him as she was, she heard every word and knew what his control cost him.

"It will take time, Razvan. The vampire wanted to make a statement. He went after her womb. I did the best I could, but I am not a miracle worker."

For a moment he couldn't move. Couldn't breathe. His daughter. Lara. She had suffered so much. He found himself on one knee, his head down, dragging air into his burning lungs. When he looked up at Gregori, his eyes burned with ruby-red flames and death stalked behind the fire.

I go no farther, healer, until you tell me her location.

You know I cannot. My daughters are at stake here as well. Savannah struggles to keep them within her. One is very weak.

We will lose her before this night is gone if I cannot find a way to defeat the microbe.

I bring you our best chance at it, but, unless you give me my daughter's location so Ivory can aid her, I will not go one step farther. And you are welcome to slay me, but I take your answers with me.

Gregori let out his breath in a long, slow hiss. "I know you are not guilty of the crime, Razvan. I have spoken out and defended you."

"I want my daughter to be whole. Ivory can see to it. We will call it my last request."

Gregori cursed in the ancient tongue, frustrated and angry to be put in such a position. *Mikhail. I believe he should have the chance to save Lara's ability to have children when I cannot. I know he is not guilty of these charges. You know what is inside of this man. He has a will of iron, and what he says, he means. He will go to his death, and for what? Tell me, for what?*

Give him the coordinates.

Gregori instantly passed Razvan the location.

Ivory sent another burst of warmth. *I will ask for Mother Earth's assistance. She has been good to us, Razvan, and I believe she favors you. She will give aid.*

He clung to the promise in her voice. Lara deserved a full life. He wanted her to have it all, even if he didn't live to see her happiness. He swallowed the rage and fear and forced a calming breath before he stood and resumed walking, again looking neither left nor right.

Tell me when it is done, Ivory.

Gregori guided him through a small series of caves and tunnels leading lower beneath the ground. Heat rose and swamped them, forcing them to regulate their temperature continually. Large crystalline formations burst from the walls and through the high ceilings, as well as rose from the floor. Instinctively he knew this was the warriors' council chambers, and this was where his fate would be decided.

The chamber held more male Carpathians than he'd known existed. As he entered, the giant columns hummed in welcome. Gregori glanced at him, and then his silver gaze slid around the room, marking each warrior's face. He remained at Razvan's side as the most despised Carpathian walked, head high, through the warriors and straight to the prince.

He inclined his head. "Mikhail. I understand there has been trouble."

"As if you did not know," a voice said.

Mikhail lifted his head, his gaze sweeping the crowd. "One more word and this room will be cleared. As you have seen, Razvan has entered of his own free will and the chamber welcomed him. I apologize for that unfortunate outburst," he added and stepped forward, clasping Razvan's forearms in the traditional greeting between warriors. "*Sívad olen wäkeva, hän ku piwtä*—may your heart stay strong, hunter."

"*Pesäsz jeläbam ainaak*—long may you stay in the light," Razvan replied.

"A master vampire attacked Lara and Nicolas as they went out to hunt in the early twilight hours. He knew where they would be. Nicolas fought them with valor. Had he not been the skilled warrior that he is, they would not have escaped. He killed three of the lesser vampires and nearly destroyed a fourth. Nicolas recognized the master vampire as Sergey Malinov. As he slashed up Lara, he told her that his sister sent her regards."

Razvan didn't flinch. He heard the soft murmur

swelling to outrage behind him, but he kept his gaze locked with that of the prince. "And you believe Ivory would order such a thing done to my daughter?"

"No, but the attack was clearly orchestrated, with the victims specifically chosen and information given about them."

"So there is a traitor among you."

The prince inclined his head. "I fear so."

"And it is easier for them to believe that I am the one who has betrayed your people," Razvan said. "As I already have been branded a traitor."

"I fear that is correct." Mikhail sighed.

"I bring you hope," Razvan said. "Before you carry this farce any further, let me deliver to you what we have found. Ivory worked for weeks to find something to combat the microbes. She has tested this life-form and believes it will destroy any mutated microbe in the earth. She, of course, wishes for more time for further tests, but wants you to see what she has found and make your decision."

He took the precious pouches of soil from his belt and handed them to Gregori, along with the small book documenting each experiment and her findings. "At least you will have a place to start."

Gregori bowed to him. "Thank you."

Razvan. Ivory's voice was tight, putting him on alert. *I have found the resting place, but it was being disturbed. Someone with a very large knife has been trying to unearth them.*

Fury pounded through his veins and thundered in his ears. *Who dares to try to kill my daughter and her lifemate? I will bring him to you.*

Do not come to this place. I think they are about to put me through some kind of trial to determine if I am their traitor.

Ivory hissed in his mind, and a very feminine, unwarriorlike image of retaliation on the lot of them made his groin throb, not with anticipation but in sympathetic pain.

"Razvan, the counsel wishes you to submit for testing from a chosen panel," Mikhail said. "Ancient warriors that lived under my father's rule. They do not know me well." He lifted his voice. "Though they are sworn to defend me, they do not trust my judgment and will have the choice when we are done here to leave this council and go their own way without heed, but also without allegiance to our people."

In essence, Mikhail was giving the ancients this one time of doubt and then he would not tolerate it again.

Razvan shrugged. "So be it."

Sun scorch them all. O jelä peje terád. Ivory bit out each word so that not only Razvan could hear, but Gregori, Vikirnoff, Natalya and the prince—everyone who had given them blood. Her contempt was palpable, blatant, reducing them all to maggots beneath her feet.

Razvan had to stop his grin from showing. He glanced at Gregori. *That is my lifemate.*

A rare one, Gregori agreed.

He sighed, obviously steeling himself for his task. He beckoned the chosen ancients near. Vikirnoff. Mataias. Tariq and Andre. Each one had to pronounce Razvan clean of Xavier and find no hidden agenda. One wrong thing and they would slay him. Gregori grit his teeth, hating that they had to appease the ancients. To him it was a slap in the face to question the wisdom of the prince.

Had they questioned their own prince, Razvan reminded him, *perhaps Ivory would have been spared her ordeal and Rhiannon would not be dead. The war between mage and Carpathian might never have taken place.*

Gregori marveled at the absolute calm and acceptance in Razvan. Gregori had no wish for others to invade his privacy to the point that Razvan would have them search his memories and know every humiliation suffered. It was cruel and wrong as far as the healer was concerned.

I love you, Ivory, Razvan sent gently. *More than life. Leave me now. Do not let them invade you as well.* Although these men would have knowledge of her as he did, the terrible things she had endured. *Wipe out the direction of our lair from my memory.* He knew she was capable. She was capable of far more than any of them knew.

Ivory complied and then she was gone, leaving him entirely alone once again.

Ivory had no patience for niceties. She marched onto the healing chambers, uncaring of the owls flitting through the trees and the grim-faced Carpathian males falling in behind her as she approached the series of caves. She felt the wrench of a safeguard and dragged the traitor through the mild barrier with her just to show those around her she didn't need to stop and unravel their pitiful safeguard for either her or the spy.

She entered the caves, looking down her nose at the guards, her expression haughty as she stalked through the tunnels, following her lifemate's scent unerringly. As she turned into the third cavern, making the descent, she was forced to protect her captive from the building heat.

Ivory moved through the tunnel, looking at none of the guards, her head up, her eyes unknowingly fierce, the boy, Travis, firmly in her grip. Her crossbow was slung across her shoulder, giving her wolves a clear view of front and sides as she made her way through the chamber.

Falcon made a movement toward her and she heard Sara gasp. She held up her free hand to halt them. "Take me to your prince, Falcon."

"Put down your weapons, Ivory."

"I am a weapon. I can bring down these caves and kill everyone inside, including your precious prince, and you know it. Do not argue with me. Take me to your prince *now*."

Falcon stepped in front of her, leading her through the long entry, through the tunnel lined with warriors. "Travis," he said gently, "you will be fine."

"No thanks to you," Ivory said with a sniff of disdain. "I hope you are a better warrior than parent, Falcon."

He flashed her one emotion-laden look over his shoulder, promising retribution, but she merely continued walking. The council chamber was packed with Carpathians, both male and female. Many turned their attention from the trial in front of them to her. She caught a glimpse of Natalya's face, blood-red tears tracking her cheeks, and she felt no sympathy for her at all. She would have liked to give her a reason to cry.

The lines of warriors opened for them, the men parting to reveal Mikhail, his face drawn and tired. Razvan stood to one side, and Ivory tried not to drink him in, tried not to show the relief sweeping though her.

She inclined her head regally at the prince. "I have brought you your traitor." She pushed the child into the circle.

Falcon caught the boy to him, wrapping one arm around him and holding him protectively. "What are you accusing him of? Being in league with our enemy?"

"Exactly. Were you planning on killing my lifemate in your need for revenge against Xavier? How inconvenient that I found the real culprit." She looked around at the faces of the counsel, her contempt obvious. "Whatever fate you chose for him, you now have an obligation to put on this boy."

Falcon pulled Travis closer to him. "She lies to save her lifemate."

Her eyes flashed at him. "I never lie. Healer, examine him. All of you, the entire mockery of accusers. The shadow of Xavier has found a home. The boy must have been hiding in the woods while we battled Xavier's abominations and we only destroyed one of the four shadow fragments. He carries one. He is your traitor, not my lifemate, who has fought to save a species not worthy of life."

Razvan said nothing as he looked upon his warrior woman. Fierce. Proud. Unbending. She looked far more regal than the prince. A queen among men, showing her utter contempt of their stupidity. She took his breath away with her beauty. With her absolute belief in him and her ferocious protection of him—in spite of his instructions. She didn't mind very well, but it was worth it to see her dress down the ancient warriors in the room.

"I examined Razvan as you asked," Gregori said, "although I was reluctant to put him through such an indignity when I already knew he was free of Xavier. I will examine the boy." He was grateful that he had gone first and no other Carpathian had relived Razvan's memories, although he felt it would shame them to know what the man had suffered, as it did him.

"You will not touch my son," Falcon said. "No one will touch him." He laid a hand on the hilt of his knife. His heart lurched. Startled, he looked at his belt. The scabbard was empty.

Travis snarled and flung himself forward, straight at

Mikhail, his small arm upraised, his face a mask of hatred as he attempted to plunge Falcon's knife into the prince. Gregori moved to intercept almost before anyone knew what was happening. He caught the boy's small wrist, marveling at the strength in the child as he fought to retain the weapon.

The knife fell to the floor at Mikhail's feet and Gregori held the child to him. "It's all right, Travis. Everything is going to be all right," he soothed, rocking the boy. "I've got to take him to the surface and remove Xavier's fragment."

"There are still two missing," Ivory said. "You will need to check everyone who was there that day. If Xavier managed to find other hosts, everyone is at risk." She turned cool eyes on Falcon. "Start with him. Perhaps the entire council should search him."

Ivory. Razvan said her name gently.

"Tell me of the progress, of your find," Mikhail said. "I want to take you to Raven and Savannah. Will you come with me now?"

Ivory looked to Razvan for the answer. *It is up to you.*
We came here to save the unborn children.

"I will return as quickly as possible," Gregori said. "Let me help this boy."

Mikhail nodded and then looked around the chamber. "We will need everyone to aid us in attempting to save our children. Those of you who do not care to keep your vow of allegiance, I free you from your blood-sworn vow. Go now and do not return." He waited but no one moved. "I will call when we need to draw energy for the healing chant." He gestured for Razvan and Ivory to follow him.

Ivory shot another look of contempt toward Natalya and her lifemate before walking beside Razvan, her head up as the prince led them through the crowded chamber.

She disliked any public display of affection, but she deliberately tangled her fingers with Razvan's to show solidarity. The entire lot of the Carpathian people could walk into the sun, for all she cared. She didn't have a high opinion of them and so far, other than Gregori and maybe the prince, nothing had happened to change her mind.

Ivory. Razvan said her name again. Gently. A reprimand.

It is merely my opinion, lifemate.

He hid his smile from the others, but she caught the brief flash of male amusement.

18

Savannah half sat in a bed of rich soil, her face swollen, her body bloated. Raven sat next to her daughter, holding her hand. She looked up and relief flooded her face when she saw Ivory. "Thank God you are here! Lara cannot come. Syndil, Skyler and Francesca have been doing their best without her, but Savannah's body is filled with toxins." She pushed down the little sob in her voice. "Can you help us? I told Mikhail to find you. I just have this strong feeling that you can help us."

Ivory forgot all about her anger at the Carpathian people and she crossed the chamber in a rush. Several of the women moved aside to make room for her.

"I am Francesca. We met when we were but girls. It was brief, you probably do not remember." Francesca smiled at her. "You were in the middle of ten strong warriors and you were difficult not to notice."

She drew Ivory away from the bed and the suffering woman, and lowered her voice. "I have done all I know how to do. Gregori, the greatest healer among us, will not be able to save this child. If you know anything I do not, please give us aid."

"If I can counter the effect of the microbes on Savannah's body, can you stop her labor?"

Francesca shook her head. "She is too far along. But we will have a chance to save the babies. The microbes are in the twins as well as Savannah, and they work to kill the babies. One is very weak and the microbes are working against us, shutting down her ability to live."

Ivory frowned. "I have never tested the reversal spell on Carpathians. Razvan was going to infect himself so I could try it, but we have not had time. I do not think it is a good idea on a woman already under duress. If I knew it worked . . ."

Razvan put a comforting hand on her shoulder, knowing Ivory was uneasy with the idea of trying an unproven experiment on a living person. "Do it now," Razvan said. "We know where to find the microbes. I will just let them attack me."

Ivory shook her head. "If Savannah is infected, doubtless they are well entrenched. I need someone who has had them for some time."

The woman she recognized as Syndil stepped forward. Tall and elegant, she had that same serenity that Ivory had noted before. "I am not pregnant. I know I am infected. Try your experiment on me."

"Syndil." Raven's voice was gentle. "You have given us too much already. You are so tired and worn. I am the prince's lifemate and Savannah is my child. I should be the one to do this for her."

Ivory's gaze dropped to Raven's swollen, very pregnant belly, and she shook her head. "No. Not you." She stepped back away from the prince's lifemate. "I will not risk a child."

"Please," Savannah choked out. "Whatever you're going to do, do it now. The contractions are increasing. I am fighting to give Gregori and Shea time to prepare the incubation cubicle, but I don't know how much longer I can keep the babies from coming."

Syndil flashed a calming smile, very reminiscent of Razvan. "Clearly it should be me."

Ivory closed her eyes. Her scientific need to experiment dozens of time, dozens of ways under dozens of conditions battled with the desperate maternal need to save Savannah's unborn children. To risk precious lives . . . *I cannot do this, Razvan. They cannot ask me to experiment on human life without other trials first.*

Perhaps the rich soil will buy us the time that we need. Razvan slid his hand from her shoulder down her arm to tangle his fingers with hers.

Gregori came striding into the healing cave, going straight to his lifemate. He took her hand, brought it to his heart and stood quietly looking into her eyes, obviously encouraging her.

"Gregori," Razvan said, "we brought you a gift of pure, untouched soil. We can bring it to the laboratory and have your people examine it to make certain it is fit for your lifemate. Perhaps the soil will buy you the time you need to prepare for the children."

Gregori inclined his head, his attention remaining on holding his daughters to their mother while they struggled and clung to life. "You must hurry."

The weariness in Gregori's voice shook Razvan. He knew how difficult it was to remove a fragment of evil, and Gregori was already stretched thin from trying to keep his children and lifemate alive.

"Can you hold off the birth three or four hours to give Ivory the chance to test whether or not she can neutralize the mutated microbes within Syndil?"

"She is advancing fast. I will try." Gregori sounded doubtful.

"What of the boy, Travis?" Razvan had great sympathy for the child. Travis obviously loved Falcon and tried to look and act like him. He followed the Carpathian everywhere. He would be ashamed at having attacked Mikhail, even though he wasn't to blame.

Just as you were not, Ivory pointed out, her fingers tightening around his.

"Travis will be fine," Gregori said. "I removed the fragment and destroyed it. There are two left. We checked everyone who was there. I know you are clean of the mage's taint, but are you certain one did not enter Ivory?"

"Ivory is clean of his evil as well."

"Then two more fragments are making their way back to Xavier. They will need hosts." Gregori sighed. "That was my mistake. I wasn't fast enough to incinerate them."

"I doubt you could have done much in the midst of an all-out battle," Razvan said. "I am glad the boy is all right."

"He loves Mikhail as well as Falcon." Gregori stopped abruptly and shook his head. They both knew the psychological damage the child would have from the incident.

Razvan took a breath and his gaze met Ivory's across the room, knowing she was thinking exactly what he was—Xavier had to be destroyed. He started to clap Gregori on the shoulder in sympathy, but let his hand fall to his side. He'd never had friends, and was unsure the protocol one used.

Ivory looked around the healing chamber. "I need a different place. Somewhere quiet. Healer, you must have a laboratory."

"Shea does," Syndil answered. "A very good one. I can take you there."

"Hurry," Gregori urged. "Francesca and I will do what we can."

Savannah let out a muffled sob and shook her head. "The little one, Gregori. She is so weak. I am losing her."

Ivory had taken a step away to follow Syndil but she turned back toward the birthing bed to see Gregori crouch down beside his lifemate. The frightening Carpathian who always looked invincible and all-powerful seemed so weary and more vulnerable than she thought possible. She hesitated and then went back to him. "Do you talk to her?"

"Yes, but she is not listening." There was a wealth of sorrow in Gregori's voice.

Ivory looked around her at the quietly sobbing women. Even Raven could not hold back her tears. Ivory bit down on her lip and closed her eyes. At once the anguish emanating from the women assailed her.

Gregori, feel the energy in this room. If she is highly sensitive, she will feel what I do—what you do. They believe—you believe—all of you believe she is already lost. Let me talk to her through you, through our connection. I have some experience with the will to live. Meanwhile, change the atmosphere in here. Anyone who cannot remain positive must remove their presence from this chamber.

Gregori looked at her and then to Francesca. He was too close to the sorrow, and Savannah's anguish consumed him. Francesca nodded her head.

Thank you, Gregori said. *Please do speak to her.*

The singing changed to the Carpathian lullaby, a soft musical melody, voices raised in song to soothe the babies as labor continued.

Little one. Your trial is great. You must rise above it and cling to life. Endure. I have fought to stay upon this earth and, though it is difficult, I know it is worth it. You are destined for greatness. Let me tell you a story of a great man, a healer among his people, a warrior unsurpassed and his princess. A beautiful woman with long, flowing hair and violet eyes. They love one another very much, but there is a terrible mage, a great wizard, who wishes to keep them apart.

The infants stopped slipping from the safety of Savannah's womb; instead, they pulled back to listen to the rise and fall of her voice, mesmerized by the story she began. *Your father will continue the story and tell you of the two little girls, mere babies, but strong beyond belief, who rose up to defeat the evil mage.*

She couldn't bring herself to put her hand on Gregori's shoulder to comfort him, so she gave him a quick, encouraging smile. "I told myself many such stories to hold despair at bay. Make them the heroines of the tale, and make the story long and involved and exciting so they listen and concentrate on that. I will work as quickly as I can."

Ivory waited for Gregori to pick up the story where she had left off. The voices around him fell into a soft accompaniment, lending excitement to the tale the healer wove for his daughters. Savannah added her own voice when she could to bring the tale to life.

Ivory and Razvan followed Syndil out of the caves and together they hurried to the building chiseled into the cliffs. Inside the large main room, Shea, a Carpathian woman with bright-red hair, and the human, Gary, who Ivory had already met, worked together with a seamless efficiency that suggested they had worked side by side for a long time and were used to a certain rhythm.

Another woman, who Syndil introduced as Gabrielle, was in a smaller room peering into a microscope. Ivory immediately recognized the silken pouches containing the soil samples she'd brought along with the open book of her records.

Shea whirled around. "I can't believe you have done this," she greeted. "How did you discover this? These life-forms are foreign to me. I've never seen them before. What are they? Where did they come from?"

Gabrielle looked up. "They seem to be abnormally high in iron." She stood up and crossed the room, a graceful woman. "I have studied all kinds of organisms and this is new to me as well."

"Which is why I was concerned with just dumping them in the soil," Ivory explained. "They will spread, and I believe they will eventually destroy all the mutated microbes, but I have not had enough time to determine what else could happen. I do not know the effect on humans or any other species. Plants. Insects. I have no idea."

"They don't touch the normal microbes," Shea said. "You're right, we have to be cautious, but I think you may have found our answer. We need you to work with us."

Ivory forced herself not to back away from the group. She was unused to being the center of attention and certainly was never in such close proximity to people crowding her.

Razvan. She reached to him for reassurance. The moment she did, she was annoyed with herself. She had become dependent on him.

His soft laughter eased the knots in her stomach. He was there instantly, flooding her mind with warmth. *As you should be dependent on me. There is still a part of you that would like to run from me.*

That is not true. Well, it might be true, but she wasn't admitting it to herself. She was braver than that.

His voice softened. Went tender. *I am always with you, Ivory. In your heart and mind. We share the same soul. Always, o jelä sielamak—light of my soul.*

Ivory forced a smile as she looked at the research team gathered around her. "I will help as soon as I have tried these reversing spells. Before I try this on Syndil, I want to try it on mutated microbes in the soil. If I can come up with a spell to reverse what Xavier has wrought, then I can teach it to all of you. Any Carpathian should be able to use it. It will be a temporary solution until the new organisms do their job and cleanse the soil. And until we can go to the source of the microbes and destroy it for all time.

"The spell will not reverse the mutation," Ivory warned. "It is only designed to reverse Xavier's dark command. We cannot really tell if it will work until we use it on someone the microbe is already attacking. I need to make certain this will not harm the living, especially a child. I am a little reluctant to try it on Syndil even now."

A sudden hush fell over the room. Ivory's skin prickled. The hair on the back of her neck and on her arms stood up. Her breath caught as an unfathomable anguish gripped her by the throat. Around the room, she saw the others freeze in their tracks, their eyes widened in horror. Syndil gasped and began to weep. Shea's face lost all color. The test tubes in Gary's hands began to shake while the glass slide in Gabrielle's numb hand fell and shattered on the floor.

For a moment time seemed suspended. Except, Ivory knew it couldn't be true, because she could feel the rapid thud of her heart, pounding inside her chest like a drum. If time had stopped, so, too, would her heart—wouldn't it? Dazed, uncomprehending, yet fighting an inexplicable urge to weep, Ivory reached blindly out to Razvan and felt the solid connection as his fingers closed around hers.

A broken, anguished cry shattered the stillness. *Help me! All healers to the cavern! We are losing them.*

Gregori, the impervious. Gregori, the all-powerful. Ivory trembled to hear him so desperate, so frantic, and it was clear the others were equally as shaken. Gabrielle and Shea dropped their materials and bolted for the door.

Syndil started to follow, but Ivory grabbed her arm. "What is it? What's happening?" She knew. She didn't want to know. The outpouring of grief gripped her heart, shredding it, and she knew she was feeling Gregori's emotions.

Tears had filled Syndil's eyes and begun to spill down her cheeks. "We're losing the babies. They cannot stop the birth."

"God help them." Ivory covered her mouth with one hand. Her knees were weak and rubbery and she leaned back into Razvan, gripping his arm to keep steady. They had come too late. Far too late. No matter what they learned now, they had not saved the fragile babies.

Vapor shimmered in the room and then Mikhail was there, his powerful presence filling the small space. "We have great need of you now, Ivory. They are slipping away. You are the last hope for my granddaughters."

"But I have never even tried it on soil, let alone a child," she protested, her stomach knotting. *Razvan.* She breathed his name as her talisman.

You will do this.

She shook her head. "Not on an infant. An untried spell. I will have to summon the dark magic in order to reverse what Xavier has wrought. Anything could go wrong."

Mikhail's face hardened. "It has already gone wrong. You must."

She forced down the lump threatening to block her

387

throat, grateful for Razvan's supporting arm. "Mikhail . . ." She broke off, swallowing hard. "There's no guarantee this will work—or even that I will not harm them more. Xavier is a powerful adversary. So much could go wrong."

"You *must* do this if we have even a small chance of saving them." Mikhail was implacable. "Everyone believes you are our best hope. Gregori asks this of you."

Gregori. The man who had fearlessly gone after the four shadow fragments Xavier had placed in Razvan to allow his possession. Gregori hadn't flinched. But infants . . . Ivory shook her head, swallowed hard and sighed.

You will do this, Razvan repeated with complete confidence.

"So be it," she whispered, hoping Razvan's calm would rub off on her.

"Make whatever preparations you must, but hurry," Mikhail urged. Then he was gone.

"Razvan," Ivory said, her voice hoarse with grief and worry. "You know how evil Xavier's spells are. I cannot go into a sacred birthing chamber and call forth the darkness. Anything can happen." Even as she protested, she used magic for cleansing, rather than her ritual bath, as time was of the essence.

"Nothing you have ever accomplished has been easy, *fél ku kuuluaak sívam belső*—beloved—but you have done it. This is too important not to try."

She leaned into him for the briefest of moments and then, gripping his hand, rushed to the birthing cave. The swell of voices held heavy grief, swamping her senses. The crowd parted to allow her through, and her heart pounded. Ivory felt as if she couldn't breathe with so many Carpathians gathered around Gregori and his lifemate, pressing close, as if by their nearness they could in some way keep the babies from slipping away to the next life.

"*Gregori!*" Savannah screamed her lifemate's name as her body expelled the first tiny life into his hands. She panted heavily as she watched him breathing for their child. "Is she alive? I can't feel her, Gregori. Please tell me she lives." She buried her fist in the soil as another wave of pain ripped through her.

"I've got her," Gregori said, but his voice was distant. Filled with grief.

Razvan, I cannot bear to see them lose these children.

Francesca stepped close as Savannah's body shuddered again, her face rippling with pain. Francesca's hands guided the second baby into the world. At once her face went distant, as she, too, breathed for the infant.

You can do this, Ivory, Razvan whispered in her mind, his voice gentle as she stood before Gregori and Savannah and the tiny babies laboring for life. *You were born for this moment.*

I was born to slay vampires and destroy Xavier. Not for this. Never this.

Like everyone else, she was spellbound, watching Gregori, blood-red tears tracking down his face, holding his tiny daughter in his arms while Shea poured the small stores of soil that Ivory had brought with her into the incubator, on top of existing layers of soil Syndil had already cleansed in preparation for the birth of the twins.

The child in Gregori's hands was too small to live, much too fragile. Even from where she stood, Ivory could see Gregori breathed for her. His hands shook, that strong man, the knowledge that he, the greatest healer of their people, was helpless to save his own child.

Ivory swallowed hard, took a deep breath and cleared her mind to block out all the sorrow and anguish, all the negative energy. She'd had Razvan go through each gesture and movement that Xavier had made as he cast his reprehensible spell. She knew he had poured his hatred and need of revenge into his spell as he commanded the microbes. She could do nothing about the mutation, but she could reverse the command. Every detail had to be exact. If Razvan had misremembered one tiny aspect—if she forgot so much as a single motion or word . . .

I did not, fél ku kuuluaak sívam belső—beloved. Nor shall you. You can do this, Ivory. I have faith in you.

She felt the brush of his lips in her hair, the warmth of his breath on the nape of her neck. She took a breath, started forward, and halted. "Gregori." When he looked up, his silver eyes were so lost she nearly wept. "You have to be certain, Gregori."

"I am certain," he replied grimly. "We have no other choice."

"Razvan, you will have to do the setup fast, but every detail must be precise." She lifted her face and looked around the crowd. "I am re-creating a very evil scene. Anyone who does not want to be here should leave, otherwise form a large circle of protection in case I make a mistake."

No one left. Even the Carpathians who had looked upon her and Razvan with distrust and perhaps even loathing now set aside their prejudices and submitted themselves to his direction. They formed a huge circle several layers deep. Those in the room, including Gary, who was human but seemed to know all Carpathian rituals, began a cleansing chant. Syndil, Shea and Gabrielle burned sage and moved through the room, sweeping high and low, paying particular attention to every entrance.

"Gregori, I need you and the babies in the center here."

Ivory pointed to the very center of the ring.

Without hesitation, Gregori and Francesca moved the incubators into the open area Ivory was preparing. Savannah gripped her mother's hand and whispered to Ivory, "Please, please."

That overwhelming grief shook her. Razvan's voice was closer as he surrounded her with warmth. *You can do this. There is only you and our mortal enemy. You were born to defeat him, Ivory. You can do this.*

"I need four women. Syndil. You choose those closest to the earth." She pulled her sword from her sheath. "They cannot flinch once we start. This thing, this great evil that Xavier wrought, will not go quickly or quietly. It will fight back. It will try to break us. So whoever you choose must have the courage to face whatever this evil might throw at them."

Syndil didn't hesitate. "Natalya. Shea." As the two women hurried forward, Syndil turned to a young girl. "Skyler. I know you're very young and perhaps I should not ask, but there are few as closely connected to the earth as you and few who have faced evil as bravely as you. Can you do this? *Will* you do this?"

The girl's face was pale, but she set her jaw and nodded before joining the others.

Once they were in place, Ivory lifted her chin and began to cast the circle of protection around Gregori and the infants, walking clockwise three times. She held her sword in her right hand, pointing it down, chanting as she walked.

Three times around this circle round
Bind all evil, sink into the ground.
That which is fire but born of ice,

I command thee now to clear this space.
Take that which is tainted and burn it pure
So that healing may be done in a place that is
    secure.

Ivory brought out four candles, one to be set in each of the four corners of the circle, representing the four directions and their elements. She set a white candle in the east for air and purity. A red candle went to the south for fire and the burning of evil. To the west she set a blue candle for water, representing cleansing. To the north she set a green candle, representing earth and rebirth.

Around the incubators she lit sticks of incense that filled the chamber with the rich scent of clove to keep out all hostility. To that she added sweetgrass and sage for purity and tuberose to ward off evil. Then as the incense and the candles burned, she took a deep breath, gathered her strength and her powers and lifted her hands in entreaty.

Power of night, mistress of light,
I am Ivory, daughter to Mother Earth who healed
    me.

A rush of memories assailed her. The scent of the earth as it closed around her torn body, welcoming her into the deeper recesses where nothing could reach her. She drew on the healing power that had surrounded her for centuries.

I summon thee to this place to that which is
    impure and tainted.
I ask this for all that is good
I know you will do this for me.

She brought her hands down to her sides, palms facing inward against her thighs and kept her head down, looking at the floor as she began to follow the unclean pattern Razvan had shown her. Three steps in, evil began to stir. Its presence whispered across the back of her neck, a faint disturbing prickle, like spiders crawling across her skin. She flinched and fought the urge to brush them off. Xavier's foul taint would do everything it could to lead her astray, to force her into making a mistake. She could not allow it. Her hands swept resolutely upward toward the ceiling. As her face lifted, she crossed her palms, and chanted.

Born of darkness
Ancient, old
I call thee forth
Unfurl, unfold
Taint the pairings—

She heard a slow hiss; a hideous voice whispered. Scorpions, stingers held high, crawled from beneath rocks and rushed toward the circle. Skyler wavered, started to lift her foot away from the oncoming insects.

"Stand firm," Razvan called, his voice carrying complete calm. "Do not break the circle."

Ivory continued to utter the foul words.

I command you to spread
Attaching yourself to womb and seed.
Seek out new life
I command you to this deed.
Taint the milk
Wither the seed on the vine

Destroy the ilk
Unborn and born, with blood thee I bind.

The flickering flames dimmed, nearly went out, so that shadows deepened, creeping along the walls and floors of the cave with grasping fingers. Overhead spiders oozed through cracks and foul voices murmured. Heart's blood bubbled up from the center of the room, a red so dark it appeared black. An unclean stench filled the chamber, polluting the air, contaminating it until they were all nearly choking on the fetid odor. The babies began to cry in protest.

Syndil gasped aloud. Shea and Natalya moaned softly, but they held their ground even though the microbes deep inside them ripped and tore at them. The crowd gasped and looked to one another while women pressed hands to their wombs as they felt the drawing of the microbes as they answered the call of darkness.

Ivory raised her hands in response to the darkness quickly spreading through the cavern. In her right hand she held high a boline, a harvesting knife, the handle of which was set with white bone. The boline was curved, bearing the mark of the crescent moon, made of precious metal from her sacred cave, the sickle edge serrated, ready for harvest.

With great caution, Ivory recited Xavier's foul spell backward, mimicking in reverse the movements that Razvan had so patiently taught her as she placed her feet carefully, weaving the pattern backward with her hands.

Ivory. I see you. I name you. Xavier's voice, harsh and cruel, whispered through her mind. Sickened her. Weakened her. *I see you.*

"No, he does not," Razvan said, his voice calm. He

flooded her with peace. "He feels your power and trembles. Do not let him break you."

Using the sacred boline in place of Xavier's blood-stained ceremonial knife, she cut the palm of her hand and allowed her blood to drip over the two babies, just as Xavier had shed his blood over the incubator of microbes. Three drops precisely over each child. The infants shrieked as if burning embers had been dropped on their innocent newborn flesh. Savannah cried out and staggered to her feet.

"Stop her," Razvan ordered. "She must not break the circle."

Savannah would have lunged toward her children if her own parents, Raven and Mikhail, hadn't wrapped their arms around her to hold her back.

"What is happening?" Gregori snarled.

"Evil fights back." Razvan eyed the Carpathian legendary healer bleakly. "It will get worse, Gregori. Much worse. You and your lifemate must both be strong. Talk to your daughters. Sing to them. Be strong for them. Tell them they fight the evil mage in your story for them. Now is their time."

While Razvan tried to calm an agitated Gregori, Ivory tried her best to silence the babies' screams from her mind. Xavier's evil was hurting them. She was hurting them.

No, fél ku kuuluàak sívam belső—beloved—you are saving them. You cannot stop no matter what happens.

She forced herself to continue moving, to continue weaving the patterns of the spell. When she had completed Xavier's entire ritual in reverse, she raised her knife to the cavern's chimney and pointed it toward the small sliver of moon that shone overhead.

I call on the lady of the dark moon,
She who stands at the crossroads,
Who counsels us that we must leave the old before
     we take up the new.
I seek the spiral.
Bring me forth to the center of stillness in absolute
     darkness
That I may dispel this evil with light.

Light flashed across the blade of the boline, as if the moon herself had entered the birthing cave. Overhead, the stalactites rocked and vibrated. Crystals sparkled like tiny, faraway stars scattered over the ceiling and along the walls of the cave. Veins of gold and silver intertwined and brightened, throwing light across Ivory's pale face. She placed the sacred boline carefully between the twin girls, the curved blade in the exact mirrored position of the outside crescent moon.

The infants writhed. One convulsed. Their skin grew hotter. Savannah fought her parents, tears pouring down her face.

"Please, Gregori," she entreated. "Stop this abomination. She's hurting them."

Gregori wavered, his face a mask of pain. The Carpathians began to murmur protests.

"Let them die in peace," Savannah pleaded, clasping her hands together, sagging against her father's restraining arms. "Give them to me. Let me hold them as they go into the next life."

"No, Gregori," Razvan protested. "Evil fights hard. Stay to the purpose."

"They wish to live, Savannah," Gregori said hoarsely.

Once again Ivory lifted her hands. Now there were tiny droplets of bloodsweat beading her body and her hands shook with the effort to bear the weight of evil. Razvan's reassuring presence, his warmth and belief in her, steadied her as she chanted.

> I call to the blight upon this earth, I see into your
> heart.
> You who were thrown into this soil, transformed
> and then torn apart.

"I will never forgive you, Gregori," Savannah screamed, tearing at her own flesh, digging great gouges in her arms so that blood spilled onto the floor. "Never. Do you understand? She's torturing our daughters and you're just letting her."

Gregori shook his head, the blood-red tears tracking down his face, but he remained stoic, his hands over each writhing infant.

Several women tried to break the circle to rush to the aid of the babies.

"Stop them," Razvan ordered. "Stay calm. Did you think he would go easily? Hold them. Mikhail, you must stop them."

"He is right," Mikhail said calmly. An uneasy stillness descended. Only Savannah and the babies could be heard weeping.

Ivory kept her mind firmly on the ritual, proceeding, trying not to allow the women to distract her.

> I call to that which was unmade, and then created
> to do harm to all.
> Come to me now as I call your name, so that I may
> take one and all.
> Twixt and twine, I seek to unbind, that which was
> woven tight.

Ivory took her cleansed crystals from a silken pouch hanging at her hip. The crystals had been left in the sunlight for one week, gathering the energies and cleansing properties she needed. She looked over the stones carefully before making her choice. She wasn't surprised when her fingers settled around a large chunk of pumice.

Pumice came from volcanic rock, and, though to some it wasn't beautiful, she found the light stone with its beige-white color unique. The airy stone was often used for banishing spells, yet also could be given to a woman to hold in her hand to aid in childbirth. Both rough and smooth, it was symbolic to her of life. She placed the stone in the eastern corner.

I look to the east, the morning light,
That which was born in darkness, now bring to
    light.

She bowed to the east, and made the sign of the cross. Her hands then formed the oval for the sacred heart where Xavier had poured heart's blood over the microbes, her sacred symbol replacing his act of evil.

She lit the piñon pine needle bundle and waved it over the entire area to purify and cleanse, mixing with the cleansing sage. The fragrance added to her power to help exorcise the demonic spell Xavier had cast over the microbes. She handed the incense to young Skyler, who remained in the eastern corner.

The moment Skyler's hands closed around the incense, shadows moved in the darkness outside the circle. Male laughter, ugly and taunting, slid slyly into the cave, echoing around Skyler. Whispers of obscene acts. She felt hands touching her. Sliding inside her clothes—

grasping at her soft skin, exposing her. A sob broke from her.

Dimitri cursed and stepped forward. It was well known that he was Skyler's lifemate, although she was still too young for him to claim.

"Illusion," Razvan said. "She's caught in an illusion."

Gregori waved a hand toward Skyler just as her trembling hand pulled back to fling the incense from her. She shuddered and held fast, her chin rising, but tears poured down her face. She looked once at Dimitri and then stood stoically under the assault of unseen evil.

There was a beat of silence. *Ivory. You must continue*, Razvan urged.

Ivory closed her eyes for a moment, took a breath and then selected garnet next. The fiery stone was used to enhance powers in rituals. To defeat Xavier, to overturn his horrific spell, she needed as much aid as possible. She also wanted the extra protection against the darkness in Xavier. Again it was a stone often used in childbirth. Her stone was multifaceted and a brilliant deep red, to combat the dark red of heart's blood. It was said that the great ark had been guided by a garnet, and she hoped the light would give her guidance in her time of great need. She placed the stone in the southern corner.

I call to the south, phoenix rise high
Casting your fire as you take to the sky.

Ivory bowed to the south, and then repeated the sign of the cross. Xavier had plunged a needle through the heart of a dove and then burned the body. She opened her hands and released a white dove, bearing an olive branch. The bird flew around the circle three times, reversed and repeated the action, and then winged her way out into the night sky.

The fragrance of Dragon's blood resin, collected and processed from the palm tree, filled the room, chasing away the evil of Xavier's ritual, adding to their protection and exorcising the high mage's abominations, consecrating and strengthening the potency of her ritual. She handed the incense to Natalya, who remained in the southern corner.

Natalya braced herself, but there was no preparing for her brother's face when she looked at him and saw—*vampire*. She gasped as the scales fell from her eyes and she saw inside him, past the illusion to his true nature. Deceiver. Flesh eater. Laughing as they tortured the infants. She needed to stop him. Drinker of his own children's blood. What had possessed her to believe in him again? She cried out in fear and anger at yet another heartbreaking deception at the hands of her twin.

Vikirnoff hissed with fear for her, his hand going to his sword. It was his brother, Nicolae, who restrained him with a hand over his sword.

"Whatever you are seeing, I do not," he said.

"Natalya," Razvan said gently. "See me."

His words, spoken in a calm command, dispelled the ugly illusion. Vikirnoff let out his breath and inclined his head in thanks to Nicolae.

For a moment, Ivory's trembling hand hovered between two stones: moonstone, one of her favorites, and her bright-red piece of precious coral, straight from the sea. The coral was an umbrella piece with fine jagged crevices, without a single chip or break. The piece symbolized life and blood force, and sheltered those from evil with its protection. Not really stone, the coral was made up of many skeletons of creatures from the sea itself, but it could be used for good since the piece was found on a long-ago beach, the life already morphed into a healing, protective element. She placed the coral in the western corner.

I call to the west, bring forth your breath,
Let the rains fall, clear and clean.

She bowed to the west and again made the sign of the cross before she sketched the fleur-de-lis into the sky, the symbol of purity, representing the three who were one, removing the abomination that Xavier had sketched before, a symbol of hatred and depravity.

The incense she chose was a mixture of lily and lilac mixed for protection and purity. She handed the stick to Shea, who braced herself in her position in the western corner.

She looked down at the hand holding the incense and saw her mother's hand withering, fading, the flesh shrinking, thinner and thinner, the voices around her stilling until there was silence—the silence of her child-hood. Long, endless days of hiding in a tomblike house, the sun burning her skin, the small child huddled in the corner trying to find enough food to feed her shrunken stomach.

"My love," Jacques whispered aloud. "I am with you."

Keep going, Ivory. I know you are doubting yourself, but the tide is turning. You are not harming these women or these infants. This evil must be stopped, Razvan encouraged.

Ivory's gaze shifted to him, to his beloved face. Her strength. His belief in her allowed her to continue. She straightened her shoulders and looked in her silken pouch for the last stone.

For her fourth and final stone, Ivory chose a stone

whose powerful magic was often used to aid childbirth and fertility as well as for protection. Golden amber, believed to bind earth, fire, air and water, but also highly symbolic of Mother Earth.

Amber, really a fossilized resin, was deep antique gold in color and seemed almost alive with its light. Her stone contained a completely formed honeybee in the exact center. The wings were outspread and the bee was a thousand years old. This particular chunk was her favorite. With great respect she placed the amber in the northern corner.

I call to the north, upon the earth, who can be
   reborn.
I seek to undo this thing.

She bowed to the north, and drew the sign of the cross into the floor, in the exact position where Xavier had poured his concoction of heart's blood, evil and hatred in his black circle. She lit another stick of incense, this time using a precious frankincense and myrrh, a powerful combination for purification and protection. Syndil took the potent incense and remained in the north corner.

Syndil knew what was coming and closed her eyes as her lost brother-kin's face floated in front of her, filling her mind. Savon reached for her, tearing with greedy fingers at her clothes, slamming his body into hers, hammering into her, hurting and tearing while his vampire teeth tore at her neck as he gulped great swallows of blood.

Barack filled her mind. The essences and warmth of who he was. Mate. Protecter. Lover. Everything. He joined with her, holding her close, sharing those memories of that long ago, but never forgotten, attack.

"I will not break," Syndil said. "Continue."

Ivory stood in the center of the circle and raised her arms, her tone one of entreaty mixed with respect.

> I call to thee, Mother, who once held me tight,
> Healing me whole so that I might continue the
> fight.
> Bring to me the power of all
> To undo that which was cast in spell.

The room shimmered with life in reaction. Flames leapt high from the candles, casting grasping shadows on the walls. A harsh wind howled through the cavern. The floor rippled with life and overhead the stalactites rocked and vibrated, threatening to shake loose. More dark-red dots of perspiration beaded across Ivory's flesh.

Evil burned through her veins, eating at her so that she was rotting from the inside out. The filth tainted her, stained her soul. She could feel the very flesh peeling from her bones. Xavier's face swam in front of her vision, his sly laugh echoing through her mind as he pointed a bony finger, the sharp, bloodstained nail directing her.

Slowly, reluctantly, Ivory dared to turn her head. The twin girls, tiny infants, lay lifeless—corpses, their bodies blackened like her soul. She opened her mouth to give a soundless scream of utter horror.

No! Razvan merged with her, poured his strength into her. *Keep going. You must finish this. He cannot win.*

Ivory took a deep, shuddering breath, her legs trembling, rubbery, barely able to support her. She needed Razvan's arms around her, his presence close. His mind moved in hers and she summoned her last strength, praying it would be enough.

Give to me the power to right this wrong,
Clearing all from this earth that we may continue
   on.
Clear the body, cleanse the soul,
Heal the mind and make us whole.
Give us once again the gift to raise our young so
   that we may continue to live.

She shouted the words in defiance. Power surged and
swelled, filling the room. Electricity crackled. Their hair raised
and waved in the bands of energy. A whip of lightning snapped
above their heads and then jumped to enfold Ivory. She glowed
with white-hot energy, sparks now flying from her fingertips.
Her tone changed, booming through the room with absolute
command.

The babies convulsed again, their tiny bodies slamming
hard into their father's hands, their breath coming in
ragged, torn gasps. Both glowed a bright, hot red as temperatures soared beyond what they could endure.

"Hurry, Ivory. For God's sake, hurry," Gregori implored.

Reverse this spell, I send it back.
I call for justice, let this fall upon Xavier's back.
I command thee to take him,
Bind him, seal him,
Let nothing be left or remain.
Bring forth your light encompassing this prize
As your radiance burns this darkness to light.

The room flashed with light. The flames on the candles
leapt higher. Wind rushed through the room, whirling
around in a twister motion, spinning through the soil,
touching each corner of the protective circle and then

subsided as if it had never been, leaving the candles flickering and the room smelling sweet and pure.

Ivory slumped in the center of the circle, and collasped to one knee, exhausted. Bloody sweat coated her body and made her tendrils of silken hair curl around her face. Skyler blew out her white candle. Natalya blew out the red one. Shea followed suit with the blue one. Syndil was last, blowing out the final one, allowing the smoke from the green candle to rise into the air, joining the smoke of the others to mix with the incense and purify the room.

The chamber went silent. Only the sound of breathing filled the room. Savannah struggled away from her father, her desperate gaze on her lifemate and their daughters.

Gregori closed his eyes and then opened them to look down at the tiny infants lying beneath the palms of his hands. Slowly, with great care, he lifted his hands away. His twin daughters stared back up at him with enormous, solemn eyes—eyes that had seen far too much already. Their skin was a healthy pink. Their fragile limbs kicked and pumped the air. Both breathed on their own. His breath burst from his lungs and his body sagged in relief. His silver gaze met Savannah's violet one. She cried out, her joy bursting through the room.

Gregori sank to his knees beside Ivory, reaching for her, not bothering to wipe the crimson tears from his face. "Her spirit is lighter. We can help her fight for life now. There are no words to give thanks. None."

She rolled over and looked up at the ceiling. "Razvan?" She was nearly translucent. She needed him desperately. *Razvan.* She couldn't face this crowd alone, not feeling so weepy and vulnerable.

He was there in an instant, reaching to draw Ivory into

his embrace. *Take my blood, fél ku kuuluaak sívam belső—beloved*. As she wearily accepted and buried her face against the warmth of his neck, Razvan looked over her head to the prince.

"The night is nearly over; Ivory must go to ground. The ritual has drained her of strength."

"You are welcome here," Mikhail said.

"Thank you, but no. I will take her home where she can rest. We will return when she is stronger. In the meantime, Gregori must teach the ritual to some of your most gifted people so they can protect themselves until the life-form in the uncontaminated soil has a chance to spread and we can destroy Xavier and his unholy factory."

"But—" Mikhail began a protest.

Razvan swept his arms around Ivory and simply took her away, flying them from the chamber.

19

Razvan woke with the pack curled around him and
Ivory cuddled into his body as if she sought shelter there. He opened the soil so he could look up
at the stars on the ceiling, a sense of peace stealing over
him. This was the moment he loved. Waking in the early
evening when the prisms of the gems embedded in the
opening allowed the moonlight to spill into the chamber
and across Ivory's face.

He ached every time he looked at her. One small smile
from Ivory was enough to make his soul soar. One touch
wiped out every memory of the torture and depravity of his
past. He had no idea how she did it, or why, when he was
with her, the world was such a different place, filled with
laughter and beauty and things he'd never dreamt of.

Raja stirred and lifted his head, rubbing his chin over
Razvan's arm in greeting. Razvan sank his fingers into the
deep fur, a miracle in itself. Already his heart had accepted
each of these creatures with their separate personalities.
Who had ever dreamed of burying a face in soft fur and
having a wolf guard and try to heal wounds?

Take the pack into the next room. I wish to be with my mate.

Raja's answer was a smile, his tongue swiping along
Razvan's arm, a rare gesture for Raja. Razvan greeted each

wolf as they woke and watched them lope into the next room, leaving him alone with Ivory. He turned toward her, his arm sliding around her waist, his body close as he studied her face again. The shadows and hollows, the exquisite bone structure. Her hair spilled out of the thick braid and his fingers itched to pull out the weave and spread that silken mass everywhere. He loved her mouth. She rarely smiled, but she had a mouth made for smiling—and loving.

There was no way he could tell her of the pride sweeping through him, the lump in his throat, the way his heart sang, and the terrible fear in his heart at her terrifying courage as he watched her battle Xavier's evil. He knew better than any other just how difficult the task had been. He had seen other mages battle and lose with Xavier's spells, and the mutated microbes were the culmination of his evil plot against his most hated enemy. She had chosen her equipment well; each article she used had been cleansed and prepared ahead of time, everything planned meticulously, just as she planned her battles. In the end, though, as things usually did, everything had gone wrong and, instead of trying a practice run, she had fought for the lives of infants—yet she had triumphed. Her finest moment.

He knew she would never see herself as he saw her—or maybe as any other had. She had been magnificent. Pride swelled. Tall, with a woman's soft, curvy body and slender arms, honed with muscle and sinew, her face lifted toward that small sliver of moon shining through the cavern's chimney.

Sometimes, when he looked at her, like he did now, he felt overwhelmed, his every sense so acute, on overload, with his blood thundering in his veins, filling his groin to bursting so lust was a vicious punch in his belly. His skin crawled for her. A spike hammered through his skull and without her touch there was a hole so deep, so wide, it cut straight through his soul. He waved his hand to slide a silken sheet beneath both of them.

Razvan bent his head and breathed into her mouth. *Awaken, fél ku kuuluaak sívam belső—beloved. Come to me.* Because he needed her. Needed to see her eyes grow hungry for him, the way he knew his were for her.

He gave her that first sweet breath of air, then took one from her to draw deep into his lungs. Her lashes fluttered and lifted and his shaft jerked in response to the sudden leap of his heart. She opened her eyes and all the emotion he could ever want was right there. Her amber eyes were enormous, filled from their very depths with love just for him. An endless well. There it was. *Everything.*

He smiled at her, a hungry, predatory smile, while she lay stretched out like a banquet before him. Tonight might be their last night together, and he was going to make it special for her. He dissolved right in front of her arms, turning his body to warm liquid, a blanket of heat and sparkling liquid, running over her like a million tongues, fizzing against her delicate skin, nudging her legs apart to wrap around them, run through them and nuzzle the junction between her legs lovingly.

She writhed beneath his administrations, her breath hissing out in a long slow *what* of shock. The bubbles teased her breasts and the taut nipples that tempted him to return to his physical form. He resisted, wanting her to match the fever of his need. The warm liquid coated her body, suspending her in a pool of bubbling water, seeking every hollow, every crevice, and filling the hot spaces with even hotter liquid.

She cried out when the water began to lap at her, gently at first, teasing her clit, bubbling inside of her, front and back until she was panting, crying out at the probing fingers of water pushing in and out of her. More fingers tugged her nipples and bubbles burst over and in every conceivable opening, bringing her to a fever pitch. He manipulated the liquid again, suckling now, fizzing and probing until it seemed a thousand mouths tormented her.

Razvan. She whispered his name as her body went into a series of orgasms, each one stronger than the last, and she found herself reaching for him, trying to find her anchor while the world erupted into a red haze around her.

He laughed softly, shifting easily, letting her fingers sink into his skin and hold there.

Her arms slid around his neck and she smiled. "I love waking up to you."

He pressed his forehead against hers. "That is good, warrior woman, because, if you woke up with someone else, the world as we know it would end."

She made a face at him and leaned forward to nibble her way across his chin to the corner of his mouth. "I doubt that. You are the calmest, most accepting man I have ever met."

Her breasts slid against his chest, soft and full, and tantalizing. Tiny flames flickered over his heavy muscles everywhere their bodies connected. Just touching her soft skin shook him. He kissed each eye and skimmed his mouth to the corner of hers.

"I am Dragonseeker, *fél ku kuuluaak sívam belső*—beloved. We breathe fire under certain circumstances. Finding you with another male would be one of those circumstances."

His teeth nipped her full lower lip. Once. Twice. He

captured that soft bow and tugged gently, wanting to devour her, to have her for dinner. He felt edgy with need, and just the gentle friction of her body rubbing along his increased his desire more than he thought possible.

"I doubt you have anything to worry about. You are very . . . *inventive.*"

Her hand drifted to the inside of his thigh, slid higher, between his legs, to cup his heavy erection. He reacted almost helplessly, pushing his hips into her hand, throbbing and hot, swelling against her palm until her fist was a tight glove surrounding as much of him as possible. Her thumb stroked caresses over the broad, sensitive mushroom head, smearing the tempting pearl drop over the soft, hot tip. She watched the shudder move through him with hot eyes— eyes that sent his temperature soaring even higher.

Her fingers on his skin felt like heaven, the stroking caresses wiping out every ugly memory from his past, so that there was only Ivory and his world with her. Tactile. Erotic. Sensory. His world instantly became one of feeling. His mouth moved over hers. Drank in the taste of her. Nectar. Sweet with just a bite of spice.

"I might like to see you breathe fire," she whispered into his mouth.

Her tongue tangled with his and his shaft jerked and swelled more against the tight fist of her hand. He deepened the kiss, the hunger blossoming with such urgent demand he felt edgy and a little desperate for her. It might have had something to do with the way her hand moved over his heavy erection and her mouth suckled at his tongue as if it was his shaft.

"No, you would not, *fél ku kuuluaak sívam belső*— beloved. You like me the way I am."

She laughed softly, the sound low and wicked, and then

she was kissing her way down his throat and chest, pushing him back, rising above him to nip at his belly with sharp little teeth. His breath hitched in his throat. That long, thick, silken braid dragged over his body, adding to the sensual sensations, robbing him of breath and reason. He reached up and tugged loose the tie so he could let it cascade over his body.

She was so sexy, her hair a little wild and disheveled, all soft skin and lush curves with that wonderful steel running beneath it. The combination always aroused him past sanity. His body ached and his heavy erection thickened and hardened somewhere in that subspace between pain and ultimate pleasure whenever she moved over him, her touch rubbing over his hot skin like velvet.

Her tongue licked along his skin, a cat lapping at cream, while her fingers stroked and caressed, drawing the essence from him. Her breath was warm on the head of his shaft and he felt every muscle tighten, but he didn't let himself move. He resisted the urge to catch her head and pull it down over his fiercely burning erection. The anticipation of her mouth, soft and hot and made for heaven, added to the tightening of his body and the need growing like an addiction in his blood.

He loved seeing her eyes, the glazed, dazed look that said she was falling into that same well of need and hunger, yet was still a little shocked and surprised that she could be so helplessly in love. Her hands trembled just that little bit, and as her breasts moved, soft and delicious and so tempting, fingers of arousal teased his thighs and danced over his shaft.

He waited. Holding his breath. Her hair pooled on his hips and thighs. He closed his eyes as he felt the warmth of her breath bathing his pulsing erection, the satisfying jerk of reaction, swelling more. Indulgent and lazy. He loved her generosity. The complete way she loved him, not in words, but with this, bringing him pleasure, just the giving of herself to him. That alone was the biggest turn-on to him, that ultimate gift that she gave completely and generously—she *wanted* his pleasure as much as or more than she wanted her own.

Her tongue flicked out and he groaned, lifting his hips helplessly, following her hot mouth, but she pulled away. Her palm cupped his aching balls, rolled and teased, her tongue sending streaks of fire shuddering through his body when she lavished attention, licking her way back up to his shaft.

His breath stopped. His heart missed a beat, and then began to pound. The roar in his head increased and he swore a jackhammer pounded there. His groin felt like a steel spike. He groaned, a soft, husky sound that seemed to compel her to action. She caught his hip in one hand, her fingers digging deep while the fingers of her other hand wrapped around him like a vise. He heard her heart match his own pounding beat. Heard the rush of her blood through her veins like the swell of a tidal wave. He swore in the ancient language, his voice not his own, but hoarse and desperate, and hungry with demand.

She licked him. Licked the broad mushroom head, swirling her tongue over that firm, velvet-soft tip and savoring the pearly drops he leaked in anticipation. His entire body tightened, shuddered, and this time he growled, the sound low, filled with lust while his vision went hazy. "*O köd belső*—darkness take it. Ivory, you might kill me."

He had to be in her mouth, in that tight, moist, secret haven. He caught fistfuls of her hair and pushed her head down on him, needing her desperately, unable to wait a moment longer.

Ivory kept her eyes on his, watching the changes in him, drinking them in, glorying in her ability to shake his usual calm. She loved it when he went all demonic on her, growling and bunching her hair in his hands, dragging her closer, thrusting his hips helplessly. She reveled in the way his eyes went from midnight blue to intense black. The way the stripes in his hair deepened. There was something very exhilarating and intensely sexy about the growls rumbling in his chest, the bunch of the muscles in his jaw, that little tic that made her know he was completely gone into another realm.

They were going out this night to hunt the most dangerous enemy the Carpathian people—the world—had ever known, and either might never return. Determination to show him how she felt, what he meant to her, what he brought to her, was in every mesmerizing stroke of her tongue and caress of her fingers. She engulfed his shaft completely, drawing him deep, hollowing her cheeks to tighten the suction around his hard flesh.

He moaned when her teeth scraped gently and her tongue swirled up his shaft to tease at the ultrasensitive spot beneath the flared head. She pulled her head back until her lips were barely skimming over him, watching him, watching his eyes go wide in pleasure, watching his breath come in ragged, harsh gasps.

"*Ivory.*" There was demand in his voice.

Gone was her slow, smooth lover, the one who took his time taking her over and over the edge, always in complete control, always the one to give so generously and drive her beyond anything she'd ever known. Joy burst through her and she swallowed him, taking him deep, feeling his entire body react, feeling him shudder again as intense pleasure vibrated through him.

The muscles in his thighs jumped with arousal, his stomach bunched in reaction, the heavy muscles of his chest rippled while his arms flexed. But it was his shaft, jerking and pulsing in her mouth, growing thicker even than he'd ever been, that thrilled her. She loved the way he stretched her lips, reveled in the way the hot length of him felt on her tongue, even the way he thrust in short, staccato bursts deeper down her throat where her muscles squeezed and massaged and milked him.

She had planned this moment, this giving to him, this taking, wanting the raw pleasure for him, the helpless, mindless ecstasy where he didn't have to worry about her or what she was feeling, but only taking what she gave him, what she offered to him. Heat flared through her when his teeth came together like that of a hungry wolf.

He shifted, floating them to the floor, his hands holding her head still while he thrust down her mouth, his eyes narrowed now, watching her throat work, watching the beauty of the woman now at his feet, kneeling in supplication, her eyes locked with his.

Do not look away from me, he commanded.

She had no intention of looking away, or of pulling from his mind. She wanted that exquisite feeling to go on forever. Her own thighs were wet, the junction between her legs pulsing with need for him to fill her, but she wasn't going to stop for anything. She wanted to take him down her throat, to be everything for him, to be used by him, to give him this one perfect gift so he would feel her love encompassing him.

Her tongue stroked and rubbed along his most sensitive spot and she heard a strangled cry escape his throat. His eyes went so deep blue they appeared black with no pupils. She felt his reaction. Burning alive. Going up in flames from his toes to the top of his head. Flames licked over his skin. His blood ran like hot lava, thick, almost too thick to make it through his veins.

Harder. The whisper was in her mind. *Oh, Kućak!—star. Ivory, harder.* His voice was ragged. Hoarse. Thrilling. *Andasz éntölem irgalomet!—have mercy, do not stop.*

Nothing could have stopped her. She was burning for him. Empty inside without him. Desperate for him, for this wild, sexy thrill. She increased her suction as he took control, as his body went out of control. He used her hair, holding her head still while he took her mouth, driving her head onto him until she felt the violent jerk. The swell. Heard his ragged cry of joy and ecstasy as he exploded, the hot jet rocketing down her throat in spurts.

She didn't let go, feeling his shudders as she continued to suck on him, gently now, her eyes locked with his. She rocked back on her heels as she finally allowed him to slide from her mouth. Her tongue did a slow, sensual sweep of her full, swollen lips.

Ivory watched his eyes change, go from that dark midnight blue to a yawning chasm of a deep ocean abyss. So hungry. So focused. All for her. Her heart leapt. Sometimes his hunger could unnerve her, like now, when his body was aggressive and she could feel the steel running through his muscles. It both drew and repelled her, thrilled and frightened her. Razvan was always so in control that when he lost it—as she loved him to—his intensity was terrifying . . . and rewarding.

His fist suddenly caught in her hair again to drag her up. He pulled her head back, exposing her neck. Her heart leapt. Every bone melted. She felt the burn in her lungs for air. His teeth sank deep, and sheer ecstasy rushed through her body like a tidal wave, swamping her. Her eyes drifted closed. How could she keep her senses intact when that delicious pleasure spread through her like a wave of heat? He drank from her as if he was starving, drawing the essence of life into his body, as if he might never get enough.

She loved it when he was just on the edge of his control, his mouth moving over her in a frenzied passion, and the ecstasy she felt was nothing compared to what her body and taste brought him. She loved touching his mind and feeding the chaotic male heat, the need and lust rising so sharp and terrible he could barely keep from devouring her. His teeth were small bites of pain that only added another dimension to the layers of desire and heat spreading and consuming her.

Every rising it was like this, the need to merge, to feel absolutely one, the heat and fire of their joining. She shuddered with pleasure as he took one last indulgent drink and swept his tongue across the pinpricks to close the small wound. His mouth suckled there for a moment, marking her, a further indulgence he'd never taken before. She felt . . . part of him. Part of his heart. Part of his soul.

His tongue licked at the ruby-red droplets of blood trailing down her throat to her breast. His tongue flicked her nipple and she sucked in her breath, but her hands caught his head to restrain him. Yet there was no restraining Razvan in his present mood. He growled something and took her breast into his mouth, biting down on her nipple and tugging until she cried out with pleasure.

He suckled strongly, ravaging her body, making it his. He took his pleasure from her, yet gave her back tenfold, as if he, too, knew this could be their last time together.

Neither voiced it, neither acknowledged it, but when he took her to the floor of the chamber, she was every bit as frantic as he was.

Her hands moved over his back, her nails digging deep as he laved her breast, sending those delicious flashes of lightning streaking through her. His tongue flicked at her hard peak with hot, slow licks that sent her mind reeling. His mouth took on a rhythmic motion that matched the push of his hips against hers. She could feel the hard length of him lying like a brand along her thigh. Each drag of his body along hers just made him grow hotter and thicker.

Electricity seemed to arc over their skin, sparks of arousal as she gasped for breath. He was switching back and forth, a man possessed, teeth and tongue and hot mouth driving her senseless. There was nothing in her world but Razvan, his hard body, his male scent of sin and sex filling the air around her, burning in her lungs in place of air.

He lifted his head, small flames burning through the piercing blue of his eyes. "Take my blood, Ivory. *Now.* Right now."

He lifted her with hard hands, fitting her on his lap, facing him, straddling him, so that she felt the hard length of him, aggressive and hot, against her wet, slick opening. His harsh gasps just drew her further under his spell. She felt mesmerized when he was like this, so desperate for the taste and touch of her. His hands never stopped moving over her skin, claiming every inch of her for his own. She loved the thrill of being his.

She lifted her head to lick over his chest and up to his throat. His stomach rippled. Bunched. His shaft, that terrible, wonderful steel spike, throbbed and pulsed against her thigh, waiting for an opportunity. She licked her lips.

Tasted him. His essence. Let him feel what that did to her, deep in her mind—in her body.

Her tongue swirled over his pulse as she nuzzled his warm throat. She loved the masculine feel of him, the heat of him. Her teeth nipped and she moved her body restlessly along his, a tempting enticement, so deep, so primal, she shook with her need. She lifted her face for his kiss, wanting—no—needing his mouth. That glorious mouth that could send her body skittering on the brink of a great precipice, too close to the edge, to that yawning abyss, or send her over, plunging her into a maelstrom of pleasure beyond anything she'd ever dreamt.

Her mouth melted into his. Fused. Welded. So hot. A scorching heat that filled her entire body, turning her fine, white porcelain skin to faint color. She looked up at his face, carved with hard edges, a man's face, his eyes heavy-lidded, possessive. She kissed him again, drinking him in, letting the rush hit her hard before kissing her way to the corners of his mouth. Licking. Tasting him. Biting with small nips to his chin and back to his lip. Tugging. Teasing. Wanting.

"You might kill us both," he warned.

She moved her body in a sensuous slide over the hot brand of his very hard erection, rubbing back and forth, trying to draw him inside of her.

His body jerked and he groaned. His fingers tightened in her hair, pulling her head back so he could stare into her eyes. "Take my blood now, Ivory." His voice had gone deep. Harsh. Hungrier. More sensual.

Her heart jumped. Nearly exploded. Her throat constricted. Her tongue already could taste him, that sweet, seductive, erotic taste of him. She felt her saliva form. Her teeth lengthened. She kissed his stubborn jaw, trailed more kisses to the side of his neck where his pulse was warm, alive and inviting. Her teeth grazed his skin.

Razvan sucked in his breath. "*Kućak*—stars, Ivory." Sweat gleamed on his body. "I do not know if I will make it through this."

He turned his head and guided her head to his shoulder, to exactly the vein from which he wanted her to take his blood. His eyes drifted closed as he lifted her hips, positioned himself and dropped her over him so she sheathed him completely.

Her craving grew until she couldn't think of anything but the scent and taste of him. His heartbeat matched hers. Adrenaline rushed through her like a fireball. Her teeth sank deep and he groaned and slammed his body home into hers. He didn't move, simply filled her, pushing his way through tight, scorching folds to seat himself completely within her.

She drew the first sweet drops of hot blood into her mouth, let it explode over her tongue, her body absorbing the essence of him. His hands caught her head, held her against his shoulder, and he bent his head to her soft, warm neck. His tongue licked along her vein.

Her body exploded around his. Pulsed. Rippled with life. Her heart jumped. Every muscle in her body tightened, squeezing down on him like a velvet vise. He gasped. Licked again. Allowed his teeth to graze her neck. Her response was another orgasm, this one harder than the first.

She gasped, tried to lift her head, but he held the back of it in his palm, all that glorious blue-black hair, and forced her to drink. His teeth pierced her neck, sank deep. She groaned, the sound vibrating through his body and surrounding his erection, stroking him, milking him, bathing him in rich, hot cream.

He drank from her while he drove her to another orgasm. And another. Each time his erection grew thicker. Hotter. Longer. He took his fill while she took hers, her climaxes rocking both of them. When they were both sated, they closed the pinpricks and looked at one another.

Razvan moved first, leaning down to capture her mouth with his, his blood pounding in his veins and his groin so full and hard and aching, he knew one more movement, one slight spasm of her body around his, and he would forget who he was. The moment his lips touched hers, it happened. She clenched the muscles of that exquisite feminine sheath and he groaned, broke the kiss and caught her hips in his hands.

He began moving, driving into her like a piston, his body slamming deep into hers, pulling her down onto his lap as he drove upward. Her breasts bounced against him, the friction sending darting arrows shooting to his groin. Her long hair, brushing his thighs, aroused him even more, so that he used the enormous strength in his legs to drive into her.

Her mouth opened. Her eyes widened. He felt the first ripple, strong—like a quake—ripping through her from breasts to sheath so she clamped down on him, dragging his seed from him. Jet after jet of hot seed poured out until he was drained and empty, her delicious screams echoing around him.

It was Ivory who floated them back to the relative safety of the rejuvenating soil. They lay locked together, arms, legs, his body deep in hers, staring into each other's eyes. Her smile was slow. Satisfied. A little shocked.

"You never cease to surprise me, Razvan."

He licked a small droplet of crimson blood from where it had run down unnoticed from neck to breast in their passion. She shuddered in reaction, producing another fresh wave of liquid cream, hot and unbearably sensual as she clamped down again, draining the last remaining drops his body could possibly produce.

"As long as I please you, *fél ku kuuluaak sívam belső*—beloved."

Reluctantly he loosened his hold on her and allowed her legs to drop from where she had them wrapped around his hips. The movement sent another shuddering pulse through both of them. She rolled over off him and lay with her arms spread out, her body still gasping for air.

"I think you might have killed me. At least my lungs are gone. And I am still having tiny, little, very amazing orgasms. How do you do that?"

He turned his head to give her a cocky grin. "It happens to be my job to keep you satisfied, and I take that task very seriously."

Her fingers found his. She closed her eyes and just savored him. Being with him. "I want you to know something, Razvan. It is very hard for me to say the things in my heart. It makes me feel silly to say them aloud but you have to know this."

She opened her eyes, locked her gaze with his and put one hand over her heart. "If things go wrong, and we both know there is every chance they will, this has been the best time of my life. I do not regret one moment with you. You made me feel alive again. You reminded me why I hold my brothers' memories in my soul. And you gave me such a gift of your heart. I want you to know that gift is treasured. I love you without measure."

The admission meant all the more because he knew it was truly difficult for her to express intense emotions.

"I love you, too." That didn't quite make it, as far as he

was concerned. He sent the emotion to her. Intense. All-consuming. Swamped her with it. Drowned her in it. Let her see into his heart and mind and very soul.

"You move me like no other could," she said and swallowed hard, blinking back tears. She sighed. "We have to feed well. Ourselves and the pack. This is our best chance to destroy the high mage. He will be weakened by what we did last eve."

"You are certain you want to take on this task."

She smiled and this time her smile was serene, matching his. "I have not changed my mind, nor would I let you go without me, as you are thinking. You need me if we are going to succeed, just as I need you. We have a better chance together than apart."

"We cannot lose this night, then, *fél ku kuuluaak sívam belsö*—beloved," Razvan said. "Let us choose our weapons and call the pack. If he escapes us it will be a long while before we—or anyone else—has this opportunity again."

"He will not escape us," Ivory said, and there was steel in her voice.

20

Flakes of snow drifted down as they streamed across the sky away from their home and toward the mountains where Razvan knew Xavier had taken up residence. They had found a small group of human hunters tracking deer through the forest miles from the village nearest to the Carpathian territory and fed well. With the pack sated and everyone at full strength, they immediately began the journey to the glacier mountain where Xavier had gone when his labyrinth of caves had been destroyed months earlier, allowing Razvan to escape.

They traveled through the sky, careful to leave no tracks, but stayed low so they could examine the ground carefully. Once out of the trees near an icy stream, a splash of color caught Ivory's eyes. The wolves reacted with unease. Ivory and Razvan hovered just above the ground, resuming their physical forms in order to study the tracks.

"There is a blood trail here," Ivory pointed out unnecessarily. "You can see where the carcass of a deer has been dragged from the shelter of the trees through the snow and toward the mountains. It is not wolves who killed the deer, nor human hunters." She pointed to the spike marks in the snow. "Bats."

She stood for a long time just studying it. Razvan said

nothing, enjoying watching the huntress in her puzzle out the trail. It was highly unusual for Xavier's mutated bats to feed any distance from the caves, but this had definitely been a bat attack. The evidence of the creatures walking on their wings was clear in the snow.

"They ambushed the deer here," she said. She pointed overhead. "Some dropped from above, some came from below, and they obviously surrounded it. The poor thing had no chance."

He didn't point out that she hunted with various wolf packs, aiding them in getting through the winter.

Ivory glanced up sharply, her gaze narrowing. "It is not the same thing. They take the blood to their master for evil purposes."

"That is true," he agreed. "Why do you read my mind when it just annoys you?"

"It only annoys me when you get that secret little smirk on your face. The male one." Because he melted her insides with it, and that just wasn't acceptable. Like he thought she was cute or something. *Cute*. What an irritating word. She shot him a look, a mixture of annoyance and embarrassment. There it was again, that little male smirk that made her want to jump his body right there in the snow and ice, with danger surrounding them. "You are distracting me."

His white teeth flashed. "I am simply paying close attention to the expert so that I might learn."

"You are deliberately distracting me and I—" She broke off, her eyes widening.

The smile faded from Razvan's face as he followed her gaze to an overhead tree limb. It looked fine to an untrained eye. The snow clung to the needles and weighed down the branches. He caught the flash of alarm in her mind.

"What is it?"

"Up there. High in the very top branches." Her voice was very low, barely a thread of sound. "The snow is disturbed."

It took a moment to see what she was talking about. In four small places, as if a bird had landed lightly on the thin branch, the snow had flaked off, revealing a smudge of bark.

"The bats?"

"No, they scratch lines in the snow but the bark does not show through. Hunters followed the bats." A note of fear crept into her voice. "They do not know who dwells in this place and what they face. We weakened Xavier with our ritual. We turned his hatred back on himself. If he manages to find a hunter . . ." She trailed off.

His stomach lurched at the idea of Xavier getting his hands on Carpathian hunters. Not only would the hunter suffer, but Xavier would be extremely powerful with a Carpathian's blood.

"Are you certain?"

In answer, Ivory shifted, streamed as vapor up to the treetop. She hovered in the air while she examined the branch and dropped back to earth beside him, careful not to disturb the snow. "Definitely Carpathian. There is no scent. Nothing else, just those two small telltale marks."

Razvan rubbed his hand over his jaw. "We have to follow them all the way in, Ivory, if they followed the bats. You know we will have no choice. We will not be able to leave them to Xavier. If we are very lucky, they will be very strong, experienced hunters."

"Xavier will not be alone," Ivory added.

"No, he will not. And he has many abominations to guard him, not the least of which is the undead," Razvan said.

She reached out to him, her fingers connecting with his. "We go then."

"All the way," Razvan agreed.

Ivory and Razvan moved with stealth, careful of disturbing even a single snowflake as they approached the outer rolling hills leading to the mountain where Xavier had begun to build his latest fortress. He needed the deep ice caves and network of caverns beneath the earth where he could conduct his evil experiments and wreak havoc on the Carpathian people. He had chosen an optimal location near the edge of the glacier, so he could use nature to carry his mutated extremophiles into the waterways leading throughout the mountainous range where the Carpathians dwelled.

If the hunters came this way, at least they left no other sign, Ivory said, using their telepathic connection, unwilling to risk sound carrying in the night.

A terrible feeling of dread had been growing in Razvan. As they approached the mountain, it grew stronger. He knew they were closing in on Xavier, but worse, he knew who the hunter—or huntress—was.

Natalya and her lifemate are ahead of us.

Ivory gasped. *Are you certain?*

Absolutely.

Razvan looked at Ivory and his midnight-blue eyes had gone so dark the pupils had nearly disappeared. Small flames flickered deep in the depths and Ivory shivered a little in reaction, a chill sliding through her.

He cannot have my sister. He bit out each word.

She leaned into him for just one brief moment, surrounding him with warmth. *No, he cannot.* She was fully committed to hunting Xavier down and ridding the world of his evil.

The wind began to pick up as they moved through the valley leading to the base of the outlying hills, just below the bursting peaks of bluish ice. No trees grew on the slopes of ice. Few ever tried to climb there, the sharp-rising ridges were too sheer and jagged. The winds increased as though in protest, and great spears of ice often came hurtling down upon hapless victims. It was a treacherous mountain and most shunned it.

As they neared the first of the hills, they felt the first impact of the safeguard. A low humming began, growing louder as they continued on their course. The pressure inside their heads grew, a painful burst that shook both of them. Ivory stopped and pressed her fingers to her throbbing temples, trying not to cry out.

Even an animal would feel that. No wonder there is no life close by, she said.

Which explains the tracks we have seen, the drag marks and bloodstains in the snow. Razvan placed his hand to her temple and flooded her with a healing warmth. At once the pressure lessened in her head. She glanced at him sharply. His face tightened only for a moment, and, when she touched his mind, it took a moment before he allowed her in.

The bats have to go farther than they did in the other caves to find prey, Razvan said before she could protest.

Ivory shuddered. She really detested fighting the bats. They had nasty little teeth and a liking for flesh. The blood trail led to a spot near the base of a small hill that rolled just in front of the sharper climbing flow of ice cliffs. She knew from experience that the ground near the spot where the bats had gone under would be a trap for some unsuspecting creature. If they ventured too near, the ground would give way.

Xavier has not had time to work out a better system, which means he is not in the best of shape, he continued. *I escaped when they moved here. He kept me weak, as he did my aunts, because he feared my resistance, but that also weakened him. He had me drained and could not use me to feed. He made do with mage and animal blood.*

Ivory didn't want to think too much about Razvan in Xavier's hands. She sent up a prayer that his sister was not in the high mage's fortress. Keeping her safe had been the only thing he had clung to, the reason he had survived. As long as Xavier lived, he was not going to allow Natalya into his hands. And now . . .

She clamped down hard on the thought. *I do not want to drop through the bat lair if we can help it.*

She had a sick feeling in the pit of her stomach as she hovered above the bloodstained snow. The carcass of the deer had obviously been dragged inside, but something else had gone in after it. Flakes of snow partially covered the stains, which meant something had disturbed the snow after the bats had returned to their lair with their prize.

It is an entrance. Razvan was pragmatic. *We have dealt with them before.*

The ground beneath them rolled. The mountain shivered and a great chunk of ice calved off the sheer cliff towering above them, driving the snow and ice straight down on top of them with little warning. Without hesitation, both reached for the ringed canisters in their war belts and dissolved into vapor as they leapt into the ominous hole covered by a thin layer of bloodstained snow.

The foul stench assailed them first, even before the sounds of highly agitated bats registered. The smell of fetid, rotting flesh burned their noses and offended their stomachs so that they had to fight to keep their present form and not react. The high-pitched angry shrieks swelled in volume as they descended through the narrow tube, scraping like sharp fingernails on the walls of their minds, shredding their nerves to the screaming point.

Scorch marks blackened the stains on the walls, although bats continued to pour out of the dark, sulfur-smelling holes in the tube, dropping down to join the fierce battle taking place on the floor of the cavern. Bits of rotting meat and splashes of blood and fur clung to the outer edges of each hole where the carnivorous bats dwelled.

Xavier has been warned that his fortress is compromised, Ivory said, irritation creeping into her voice. *Even weak, he is a formidable opponent. I had hoped to come on him unaware. I do not want him to escape us.*

He will not give up his fortress easily, Razvan predicted. *He has fewer and fewer places to go. He has not had time to fully make this one secure. This is our best chance whether he knows we are coming or not.*

Ivory refrained from saying Xavier was expecting two hapless hunters who had inadvertently stumbled upon the bats and probably was joyfully preparing for feasting on Carpathian blood.

Hurry, Ivory, they attack Natalya.

Xavier will order his guardians not to slay them—at least not to slay her. He will want her blood for himself, which gives them a slight advantage, she reassured.

They were close to the bottom of the long tube and could see the bats now. Hundreds of them, with black furry bodies and razor-sharp teeth, claws tipping the toes of their feet and their wings spiked at the tips. Swords swept violently through the mass of bats, slicing heads and bodies, but the sheer numbers were overwhelming. Vikirnoff and Natalya stood back-to-back, faces grim, blood streaking every exposed bit of skin. Both Razvan and Ivory had felt the tear of teeth shredding flesh from their bones and, at the sight of the Carpathians, the haunting memories rose up to taunt them.

Coming in, Ivory warned, using the more ancient common telepathic path that Vikirnoff would recognize. *What we are going to do is change the composition of air using our homemade grenades. The fire will burn hot, very intense, and you cannot draw this chemical into your lungs. You will want to panic and go toward the surface, but the fire will race upward*, she warned, giving them nearly the same instructions as she had given Razvan when she'd first used her chemical grenades with him.

Razvan reached for his sister, feeling her startle when he used their much older connection, one they had made as children. *Fight your way out of the center but stay away from the walls. When we materialize we will use the chemical, and then change back to vapor; do the same instantly, but remember, you will still feel the intense heat.*

I understand, Natalya sent back.

Razvan tried not to see the mass of bats attacking her. She looked fierce, her grim face a mask of concentration, her hair striped with the colors of a tigress.

Razvan positioned his body face-to-face with Ivory's. As soon as they materialized, he knew from previous experience, the bats would attack, ripping and tearing at their flesh. *Ready, kont o sívanak—heart of a warrior?*

Let us get it done, Ivory responded, as calm as always in battle. She could handle nearly any circumstance when it came to fighting without panic; yet when it came to emotion, she wasn't so good at hiding her nerves and vulnerability.

One more thing, fél ku kuuluaak sívam belső—beloved, I love you more than life itself. Now, Razvan added.

She wanted to hold him. Wanted to say it back to him. But he was already materializing and she had to match his rhythm. She burst onto the chamber floor, noting that Razvan's body, while protecting the front of hers, was angled to shield his sister.

The moment they donned their flesh-and-blood bodies, the bats went into a feeding frenzy, the scent of prey driving them insane. They ripped and tore, hurling their bodies at the Carpathians. The wolves roared, heads emerging, paws digging, ready to leap.

Stay! Stay! Ivory ordered frantically.

Raja and Blaez subsided, calling orders to the rest of the pack, although they snapped at the bats, grabbing heads and shaking, snapping necks even as the bats' claws shredded skin. Razvan and Ivory pulled the pins simultaneously. They had only five seconds to get rid of the canisters.

Ivory lobbed her grenade directly into the center of the chamber amid the sea of fighting bats. Some pounced on the canister, trying to bite through it with sharp teeth.

Razvan pulled back his arm to throw, and at least a dozen bats, drawn by the scent of Dragonseeker blood, leapt on him, the weight of their bodies pulling his arm down as he went to throw the oval-shaped canister.

Vikirnoff leapt forward, swinging his sword, sweeping it across the lot of them, missing Razvan by a paper-thin margin. Razvan sucked in his breath as the bodies toppled from his arm, leaving behind torn flesh. More rushed to feed on the open wounds, but he had already let the canister go.

Now! Now! Razvan warned his sister.

All four Carpathians dissolved into vapor. The chamber rocked with the explosion, the air raining bodies of bats and chunks of rock, ice and rotted carcasses, both human and animal. The flash of light was so bright it pierced their eyes despite them being in a different form. The intense heat ate through their natural shields as the composition of air changed to gas. Fire raged up through the chimney, burning through the holes and cracks in the rock, voracious for the air outside.

The ice melted, turning to boiling, hissing steam as the fire raged with orange-red rolling flames, flashing through the bats' burrows and roaring out and through every crack. The external pressure was so extreme, the molecules of their bodies threatened to collapse inward, imploding like the bodies of the bats. All around them, the mutated creatures erupted into hot flames, exploding as if a bomb had touched them, or simply coming apart.

The noise rushed over them, the thundering violence of a volcano erupting as the fire created its own wind so that it howled through the chamber, looking for hapless victims. The inferno was a fiery hell from which there seemed no escape. Vikirnoff and Natalya stayed only because Razvan and Ivory did, resisting the urge to try to rise to the surface and outrun the conflagration. The rock walls of the chimney blazed an ominous red, but the flames died out, leaving a hideous, blackened flood behind.

Burned carcasses and debris floated in the water pouring down from the melted ice and snow. Ivory led the way out through the chimney and away from the foul stench, taking care to avoid the glowing walls. They turned a corner and the tunnel widened into a large chamber. Ivory held up her hand, halting. The others crowded around her.

"What in the world made you decide to go down the bats' hole?" she asked. She didn't need to look after Razvan's sister, especially if the woman and her lifemate were foolish enough to go chasing Xavier's guardians into their burrows.

Razvan put a restraining hand on Ivory's shoulder, recognizing the cool contempt in her voice. She was standing up for him against the two people who she felt should have believed in him. *Some of their wounds were not made by the carnivores.*

Ivory took a breath and instantly regretted it as she drew the stench of burned flesh into her lungs. Now that she took a good look at the two, she recognized the wounds on Vikirnoff. "The undead." She answered her own question. "You followed a vampire."

Vikirnoff nodded. "A master vampire. He dropped into the hole. We knew what we faced, but believed we had a good chance to get through the bats, given they had a fresh kill. They rarely get too far from it without feeding first."

She was grateful he knew that much about the bats. "Xavier has taken up residence here. It is not a place you want to be."

"Did you come here looking for us?" Natalya asked, gripping her sword tighter and looking around the ice cave. "I should have known the moment I came in that Xavier would be drawn to this place."

"You were occupied elsewhere," Razvan pointed out. "You can get out through the tube. That entrance should be clear now."

Vikirnoff and Natalya exchanged a long look. Vikirnoff cleared his throat. He refused to look away from Razvan. "I will be the first to admit I was wrong about you, Razvan. Natalya suffered greatly when she believed you had turned vampire and had allied yourself with Xavier. We both realize Xavier possessed your body and wanted the world to brand you traitor."

"I do not blame you for protecting Natalya," Razvan said and shot Ivory a quelling look when she stirred.

It was the first time he had ever indicated that he might be displeased with her, and it was shocking to Ivory how much it hurt. She moved away from them only to have Razvan catch her arm, circling her wrist with his fingers like a bracelet.

"It is best to leave this place quickly," he continued. "The bats are his guardians and he will know intruders have arrived. If the vampire has come to aid him, this is no place to be."

"Yet you are here," Vikirnoff said smoothly. "You weakened Xavier, didn't you? Last eve, when you turned his spell back on him. That is why you're here today. You're hunting Xavier."

"And we have no time to waste," Razvan said.

"I agree," Vikirnoff returned. "Lead the way."

Ivory wasn't about to stand around arguing. She knew Razvan wanted Natalya as far from Xavier as possible, but they had this one opportunity and she was going to take it. Vikirnoff and Natalya could do as they wished. For that matter, so could Razvan. He could stay and protect his sister, too.

She took a step away from them, but Razvan didn't let go of her wrist. In fact, his fingers tightened. Ivory glanced down at his hand and then up to his face. His eyes glittered at her, black obsidian with just a hint of blue, but it was his hair that gave her pause. His hair seemed alive, electric almost, bands of black and white sliding through the color. His face was as tranquil as ever and, when she touched his mind, he appeared utterly calm, but his hair, eyes and that tight grasp on her wrist told her something else.

Do you honestly think I care more for a woman who I only held in my memories than I do you? Because I prefer she is not here? I prefer that you be far from Xavier as well, but I respect your fighting skills and your vow of purpose. This is a path we agreed on, and I will hold to my word, but as your lifemate, as the man who loves you above all else, this is the last place I would want you to be. This is not easy for me, Ivory.

Ivory stood there, heart beating fast, and realized that sick feeling inside of her had nothing to do with standing in an ice cave fortress riddled with traps belonging to the high mage, her mortal enemy, and everything to do with having their first fight.

"We go with you," Vikirnoff said. There was steel in his voice.

Razvan glanced at him, then at his sister. "So be it." He brought Ivory's hand to the warmth of his mouth and held her fingertips there against his lips. *You matter, Ivory. You are my heart and soul and everything good in this life. Let us destroy this evil and go home where I can show you just who really matters to me.*

Had she been jealous? She hadn't even recognized such a petty thing in herself. Why would she be jealous of Razvan's love for his sister? She wanted him to love and be loved by his twin, by his daughters and his aunts. So what was wrong with her . . .

Razvan abruptly dropped Ivory's hand and reached for the hilt of his sword, looking around the cavern, his gaze clearing enough to see the faint mist drifting like poison, curling around Ivory and Natalya.

"He knows we are here," he warned. "He's attacking, amplifying our fears and emotions."

Ivory's lips firmed, annoyed she'd been caught in one of

Xavier's more basic traps. She began moving cautiously deeper into the series of caves. One chamber opened into the next as they went deeper beneath the mountain. The ice walls were thick and rumbled ominously, the pressure from the tremendous weight causing continual buckling so that they had to watch for huge blocks of ice shooting out of the walls, a natural phenomenon Xavier used against intruders.

"He favors traps in the ground," Razvan cautioned. "Be careful. We will be walking through a minefield. Once we find the first one, I may be able to guide us through. He favors certain patterns."

The sound of dripping water was loud, adding to the noise of the ice creaking and rumbling. After a time, the noise drowned out everything else so that Ivory had to remember to keep the volume down and tune in to other things. She had long ago learned to hunt with all senses, but here, in Xavier's domain, the rules had changed and she couldn't count on her instincts.

They rounded another corner and Ivory nearly stepped down onto a floor of rock and ice. At the last second she pulled her foot back, studying the floor. Razvan came up beside her and Vikirnoff and Natalya peered around her shoulders.

"This is classic Xavier," Razvan said. "He always has a back door to escape and it usually is a trapdoor of some kind. This is not a man who will fight to the death. He runs away to fight another day. The squares indicate his pattern. In recent years, he has had trouble remembering, so he uses the same one all the time." He looked over the floor. "Seven squares from the opening and to the left is most likely where his escape route is. This room will be well protected. The floor is a trap. He will have a nasty little pet. And do not step into water or touch it as it seeps from the walls."

Clapping startled them. Above, on the far wall, Xavier appeared, applauding. He looked smaller than Ivory remembered from her youth, and his face was lined and aged, but he was in surprising shape when he should have died centuries earlier. He wore long robes and his beard was a flowing white, perpetuating his reputation as a tremendously powerful wizard. Beside him was his staff, innocent-looking enough, but the crystal ball on the end glowed milky white, and she could make out the dark-red spot in the center. Heart's blood, in the shape of an eye, stared back at her, sending a chill down her spine.

"Good then, boy. You have come home and you've brought guests with you," Xavier greeted. The mage's voice boomed out, and the walls rippled.

Razvan stepped forward, his body partially blocking Ivory's, keeping clear of her arms, but still putting him in a position to stop the force of the staff. He'd seen it too many times not to recognize the real threat to them all.

The floor pitched, threatening to throw them into the room, but Ivory, Razvan and Vikirnoff steadied themselves. Natalya was on a slight incline and the sudden roll sent her staggering. She flung out her hand and her palm brushed the wall.

Instantly the ice cracked and the weight of her body falling forward sent her hand and arm deep into the crack. The ice closed around her limb hard, slamming together, crushing bone, holding her tight. She tried to turn to mist, but her arm was held fast. She struggled as Vikirnoff whirled around to try to help her, frantically trying to dig her free while Natalya tried to heat the ice surrounding her arm to make it melt.

Ivory's gaze never left Xavier, watching for his next move. She was pleased that Razvan continued to watch as well. The mage deliberately had used Natalya to try to distract them. Already ice spiders poured from the cracks in the ice, rushing toward Natalya with their poisonous fangs.

Lara was friends with the ice spiders, Razvan said. *Turn them back on Xavier.*

Ivory, her gaze never leaving Xavier, immediately lifted her hands, tracing a pattern in the air.

Spiders, spiders of crystal ice,
We are not the enemies you seek.
We seek no malice,
Look to our hearts, see that which is pure
Remembering Lara, a friend who was dear.

At once the spiders halted, then turned abruptly, quickly crawling away from Natalya and back into their cracks.

Tiny spiders of crystalline ice
I call you now to weave and splice.
Send forth your minions as to war
To seek out evil, to banish it ever more.

Spiders dropped silken nets from the ceiling, enfolding Xavier even as thousands poured from the ice in a rush to get him. The nets came up empty. Xavier appeared on the closest ledge, laughing. A second and a third Xavier appeared—all laughing—all three identical and all with staffs. The three wizards raised their arms and a wind rose, rushing through the chamber. The spiders immediately retreated, seeking the cracks in the ice and safety.

Ivory refused to flinch or look away as the howling wind tore through the ice cave and straight at them, carrying ice missiles, large and small spears with deadly points. *Watch for the vampire*, she warned Razvan, never once taking her eyes from the wizard. Her hand swept up in a dismissive motion.

That which is ice, I now command
Bring forth a shield to protect and stand.
Stand as guard, protect us all,
Deflect these spears that evil calls.

The ice missiles shattered and fell harmlessly to the ground at Ivory's feet. She didn't so much as flinch or glance behind her to see if Vikirnoff was making progress freeing Natalya.

"I see you paid attention in my classes," the three wizards said with a mocking bow.

Behind them the wolves suddenly roared, their heads coming out of the skin. Vikirnoff heeded the warning, whirling to face Sergey as he flew at them from above. His face was a twisted mask of hatred. Dressed in war gear, he wore a vest of armor, thin yet tightly woven of a fabric Vikirnoff had never seen before.

Natalya stopped struggling to free her imprisoned arm, pushed down the excruciating pain and caught the sword that Vikirnoff tossed to her with her free hand.

"Vikirnoff," she cried. "Be careful. The walls are creeping forward." Every few moments she had to take a small step as the ice spread into her, the wall nearly bumping her foot in an effort to trap all of her. "I see two small shadows, splinters really. Look out for them, everything in their path withers."

The fragments Gregori drove from me, Razvan sent on the ancient pathway. *They have to be making their way back to Xavier. We have to destroy them, too.*

Leave Vikirnoff and Natalya to it, Ivory cautioned Razvan. *We have to trust them to keep Sergey off our backs. He is reaching for the staff. The one on the right is really Xavier. Watch where that staff aims. That will be the real target.*

How do you know?

The wind. It flowed past him without touching his beard. He has some kind of barrier erected around him to protect him. Watch the pattern of the wind flow.

Razvan didn't question her judgment. She had studied Xavier's ways with great care, and that was just the sort of thing the mage would do.

The mage snatched up his staff and aimed it, not at them, but at the far wall. The other two mages aimed their staffs at Ivory and Razvan. Neither moved, standing their ground as the wall close to them exploded with a thunderous blast. Chunks of ice and rock rained down, the falling debris triggering numerous traps as they hit the floor of the cave. The battle behind them was loud, Natalya fiercely trying to enter the fray, Vikirnoff blocking the vampire from getting close to her. The wolves raged, wanting to leap free, but Ivory restrained them, commanding them to wait—as she waited.

A single sound swept through the cavern. A roar of rage. Behind them, the hunter and vampire faltered. A chill went down Ivory's spine. Her skin itched as the wolves' hair stood on end, prickling her with a thousand sharp needles.

I cannot take my eyes from Xavier, Razvan. This is for you to deal with.

Consider it done.

It was his calm that settled her stomach. They were being attacked from all sides. Sergey battled with Vikirnoff ferociously. The ice walls continued to close inch by slow inch. Xavier had his staff in his hand and now something big was moving out of that rubble into the main part of the floor.

The head emerged first. The skull quite large, the large, curved teeth prominent as the large cat leapt into the room. It landed on a chunk of ice, keeping his claws from the floor, suggesting Xavier directed his movements away from the traps buried beneath the surface. Shorter than a lion by a foot or so, the cat was at least twice as heavy, all muscle and lethal-looking teeth.

Razvan. Get me out of this ice. I know what to do, Natalya said unexpectedly. *Hurry.*

Razvan whirled around, his gaze moving over the solid wall holding Natalya prisoner. Xavier had used such things to imprison the aunts. He wasn't the best at spells, but Natalya was. He threw his enormous strength behind hers. Without hesitation, Natalya lifted her one hand, palm toward the ice and chanted.

I call to Mother air, earth, fire and water,
Come to me now, fill my desire.
Set free now that which is caught in ice.
I name thee fire, bring forth your breath.

Water poured from the wall around her arm and she tugged until she was free. Thrusting her sword into her brother's hands, she leapt into the air, her hair striping as she shifted, making the change—a beautiful, glorious tiger, a little more modern but all female, her alluring female scent filling the room. She landed hard, her front paw obviously injured as she favored it, holding it up off the ice block. The male roared and she answered.

Sergey leapt toward Vikirnoff as he half-turned to look at his lifemate. He slammed the sword aside and punched through Vikirnoff's chest, reaching for his heart, standing toe to toe, grinning evilly. Blaez and Rikki dug paws into Razvan's back and pushed off, hitting Sergey hard, from the side, driving him back away from Vikirnoff, who staggered, blood spraying across the ice. Raja and the rest of the pack leapt free to circle Vikirnoff protectively as he healed the great gaping hole in his chest.

The vampire had little time to lick his fist to get a taste of Carpathian blood and power. Razvan threw a vial of holy water over him. Sergey screamed as the water burned through his skin all the way to the bone, leaving behind great holes in his flesh. Smoke rose, the stench fetid. Razvan followed the water with a series of arrowheads, snapping them hard so they buried deep, going up the vampire's chest.

The vest stirred as though alive, the fabric parting as if torn and then smoothly going back into place. Razvan rushed him, following the arrows. Sergey tried to shapeshift, but the coating on the arrows prevented him from doing so. Razvan punched through the vest. The moment his flesh touched the fabric, the threads came alive, winding around his fist, racing up his arm toward his shoulder and face. Tiny parasitic worms with sharp teeth, ripping and digging into his flesh. He stepped back, trying to sweep the creatures from his body. Sergey flung himself at Razvan but the wolves interceded, slamming into the vampire with full force, driving him over backward and going for his throat.

Ivory never moved. Never looked back. She had one

purpose, and he was in front of her. The tigers snarling at one another, the battle raging behind them—none of it mattered, only Xavier, only the man lifting his staff with hatred on his face and his gaze fixed on Razvan. She knew he would go for her, not Razvan. He wanted her lifemate to suffer for his perceived betrayal, for the Dragonseeker blood that had held out for centuries against him. For his escape and his newfound strength and power. Razvan was the symbol of everything he hated. And she was Razvan's lifemate.

As if in slow motion, she saw him bring the staff across and down his body. Time slowed down, her world narrowing. The end of the staff began to glow bright as he pointed it at Razvan. Ivory noted the red eye in the center of the crystal fixed on her, not on her lifemate. She felt power move inside of her. Everything she was. Everything she had ever been. Was it enough?

Razvan poured everything he was into her, leaving the pack to deal with Sergey while they merged, trusting Vikirnoff to guard their backs along with the wolves. Trusting Natalya to lead the tiger away from them.

The staff glowed bright orange-red. Ivory lifted her hands, palms facing the wizard. A flash of bright light hurt her eyes as the crystal shot out a bolt of energy directly at her. Razvan stepped up beside her, lifting his hands to the exact same height as hers.

I call to Hell's Gate, Ivory chanted.

Let lightning strike, Razvan invoked.

I call to the power that which is light, Ivory chanted.

Take form from this darkness, Razvan invoked.

Let angels walk forth, Ivory pleaded.

Opening their arms, draining evil's force, Razvan chanted.

Take that which is heart's blood. Power filled Ivory's voice.

Straining it pure. Razvan merged completely with Ivory. They chanted together: *Let it only abide in one that is pure.*

Already weak without Carpathian blood to sustain him and from her previous spell, the combination of Razvan and Ivory together was too much for Xavier. The dark blood in the center of the crystal exploded outward and Xavier clutched his heart. Blood burst from his chest. Snarling, cornered, terrified he was losing his final chance at immortality, the mage used his last, most secret weapon. He dropped his staff, clutched his chest in an effort to stem that black, bubbling blood and unleashed his wrath on the Carpathians.

The sun burst overhead. Bright. White-hot. A turbulent, seething, volcanic mass. Winds roared, tearing through the ice caves as the heat blasted them from all sides, melting the ice faster than anything possible. Water poured down on them, searing, boiling water. Steam rose, but, as the orange-red ball spun, it flung threads of fire. Dazzling light radiated through the chamber.

Skin smoked. Blistered. Melted. Sergey screamed and tried to dissolve again, and this time the arrowheads fell from his chest as his acid blood ate through the coating. The two fragments seeped into his pores just as he shifted.

To my back! Ivory ordered the pack, holding out her arms.

The wolves leapt for safety as the water rose fast, rushing through the chamber, boiling everything in its path, including the saber-toothed tiger. The Carpathians shifted to vapor, their only hope of escaping, just as Sergey had done, but, even in that form, the sun burned the molecules that made up their forms.

Ivory flowed toward Xavier as he crawled along the edge,

leaving a trail of black blood behind. The blood bubbled and burned into the fast-melting rock. He opened a crack that was spewing water wide enough for his body to pass through, but she was on him, her hands coming out of the vapor. The burns went to the bone, her skin dissolving first into a mass of blisters and then melting. Still, even with her bones, she held him, preventing his escape.

Razvan's fist came out of the vapor, suffering the same fate as Ivory, the skin burning off as he slammed it deep into Xavier's chest and extracted the burst heart. He threw it into the raging fires and then followed it with the body.

The four Carpathians streaked out of the rapidly collapsing cavern using Xavier's escape route. The spinning mass of heat and light stayed behind them as they shot down a tube and into the cool darkness of the caves. The mountain rumbled ominously as they made their way through the tunnels to the outside hills.

All of them rolled in the snow, trying to ease the burning, vicious pain.

"We need to go to ground right now," Vikirnoff said, his teeth chattering, his body in shock. *Gregori, we have need of you. Healers! Come to us!*

"Not here. Not anywhere near his evil," Ivory advised. "Find a clean spot and let Mother Earth have you."

"Gregori and Francesca are on the way. They will meet us," Vikirnoff said.

Shivering with the terrible pain, Ivory and Razvan took to the air together, leaving Vikirnoff and Natalya to do the same.

21

Razvan gripped Ivory's hand as they approached the ceremonial cave. Gregori's summons had reached them just before dawn, with his invitation to the naming ceremony, and both had been nervous before they had succumbed to their rejuvenating sleep. They had spent so long in the ground recovering from wounds, both had thought the naming would have already taken place, but Gregori had honored them by waiting, which meant they had little choice but to attend.

"They are not going to search you this time," Ivory teased. "I think."

"They try that this time and the dragon in me may just come flaming out." He gripped her hand tighter.

Ivory looked up at his face. Instead of his usual calm, he looked strained. She knew it had nothing to do with the distrust of the Carpathian ancients and everything to do with his daughters and sister.

She halted and tugged him around to her, lifting her palm to frame his beloved face. "You are *hän ku pesä*—protector. You are *hän ku meke pirämet*—defender." Her voice softened. Her eyes swam with love. "Most of all, you are *hän ku kuulua sívamet*—keeper of my heart."

He caught her face in his hands and lowered his mouth

to hers. He couldn't have spoken. Not with love shaking him and setting his hands trembling, or with the lump in his throat so big he might choke. He could only pour everything he felt for her into his kiss. When he lifted his head, her eyes had gone antique gold. "Thank you. I needed to hear you say you loved me."

She parted her lips to protest. She hadn't actually gone that far, but he kissed her senseless again, scattering her wits until she could barely remember her own name, let alone what she'd said to him.

"Razvan!" Natalya rushed them. "You came."

They had barely time to break apart before she threw herself into her brother's arms, rocking them both so hard Ivory had to catch his arm to steady them.

"Of course we came. Gregori said it was a naming ceremony. I have never been to one." Razvan gently set his sister back on her feet, looking her over for injuries. The time spent rejuvenating in the ground had done her good. She bore little evidence of the encounter with Xavier and Sergey.

"You have to come to see Lara. Gregori let her up for the ceremony. She's fragile and weak, but he said, whatever Ivory did, she can still bear children." Natalya's eyes were bright.

"Mother Earth saved her, not me," Ivory protested.

Natalya ignored the protest as well as all personal barriers, catching Ivory's arm and tugging her toward the ceremonial cave. "Hurry. Everyone is waiting inside for you."

"Give them a chance to catch their breath, Natalya," Vikirnoff advised with a small smile. He tucked her beneath his shoulder. He still had a couple of burn marks on him from having shielded Natalya.

"I do not wish to upset Lara, especially in her fragile state," Razvan objected, halting abruptly.

Ivory swung around to him, her hand actually curling around the hilt of her knife. *We do not have to do this.* She wasn't going to have *anyone*—sister, daughter, ancients, *anyone*—make him feel unwelcome or less than what she believed him to be: a great hero.

Shockingly, Razvan laughed and the sound was carefree. He swept his arm around her. "You are a treasure, *fél ku kuuluaak sívam belső*—beloved. *My* greatest treasure. I believe you would stand between me and . . ."

"*Anything.* Anyone." Her eyes deepened from her light amber to that antique gold that always sent his heart stumbling.

He brushed a kiss on top of her head. "Let us go to the naming ceremony for Gregori's sake. He has done much for us and, if this pleases him, it is a small thing to us."

Natalya frowned. "Lara wants to see you, Razvan. And Nicolas is *dying* to see his wonderful little sister Ivory. He can scarcely believe what you did—what the two of you did. What a relief it is to know Xavier is gone from this world."

"Not entirely," Ivory cautioned. "No one must ever forget those two fragments found a host in a master vampire. He was terribly wounded, but he will rise again, and with the shadow of Xavier dwelling within him, he will be more evil than ever."

"We have warned the people," Vikirnoff assured. "A hunting party went out, but no trace of Sergey was found." His eyes met hers. "I am truly sorry about your brother. He was a great warrior once."

Ivory forced a smile, and was grateful for Razvan's understanding. He didn't touch her, which might have been her undoing, but he surrounded her with warmth. "My brother has been long dead. What is in his place is truly evil and bears no resemblance to the man I love, but I thank you for the thought."

Young Travis ran up to them. His eyes were bright again, his hair long and tied with a thin leather cord. "Gregori says to get a move on."

Laughing, they followed him to the entrance of the cave, but got no farther. A young teenaged girl Ivory recognized as Skyler stood waiting just inside. Her shoulders were square, her gaze hesitant. Francesca, the female healer and her adoptive mother, stood with her, shoulder to shoulder, her hand on Skyler's back.

Ivory's heart jumped. There was no denying this girl was Razvan's child. She was beautiful, but in her eyes, eyes very much like Razvan's, there was far too much knowledge. The girl had been through hell and back again. This was going to break Razvan's heart. Ivory wanted to wrap her arms around him and get out of there, take him far away where no one else could hurt him.

"This is my daughter, Skyler," Francesca said. She wore a smile, but her expression was strained. "You might remember that she aided in fighting Xavier's evil."

"Yes, of course," Ivory said. "You were amazing. Everyone thinks so highly of you, Skyler, obviously for a good reason. I am Ivory and this is my lifemate, Razvan."

She felt the impact when Razvan raised his head. The punch to his gut, hard and deep. He hadn't really paid attention to anything but protecting Ivory from Xavier's evil and trying to keep everyone calm. Now, there was no mistaking this child. Or the trauma she'd suffered. He swallowed hard, but his expression didn't change. Only Ivory felt the terrible blow.

"I am Dragonseeker then," Skyler said, her chin up. "That is why I can sense the earth in the way Syndil does, although she is not Dragonseeker, but has the gift of bonding with earth as the Dragonseekers do. I am part Carpathian, although for some reason, unlike others who are half, I have not needed blood."

Razvan took a breath, let it out. Ivory reached for his hand, clung. She didn't know which of them needed the support more.

"You are my daughter." He made it a statement, although he had no recollection of her mother. He must have been buried deep, suppressed by Xavier when the mage had impregnated the woman. Skyler had been spared being kidnapped and taken because her blood had not called to Xavier, the Dragonseeker in her hiding deep, probably sensing a mortal enemy. It was her eyes that gave her away. Had Xavier looked closer, had he not been so greedy for the "right" blood, he would not have allowed Skyler and her mother to escape so easily.

What happened to her? Razvan asked his sister. When he sensed her hesitation, he snapped an impatient order. *Tell me.*

Ivory put her hand on his shoulder. It was the first time she'd seen him really shaken. She felt him tense beneath her hand, but he didn't pull away.

Natalya bit her lip and then capitulated. *Her mother ran when she was a mere infant. For years Skyler believed the man her mother married was her birth father. He was a very bad man and sold her to other men. Francesca rescued her.*

Razvan closed his eyes briefly. Only Ivory's touch steadied him. His children seemed destined to live with pain and suffering even when Xavier didn't get his hands on them. He opened his eyes to look directly at Francesca. "I am grateful to you."

He had no idea what to say to this young girl. His

daughter. A girl he knew nothing about, who had lived in hell and had far too much knowledge of monsters in the world. "I do not know what words I can give you, Skyler, other than to say I am sorry I have not been in your life to protect you from all the horrors of this world. Had I been able, I would have protected you."

She shrugged her shoulders, far too mature for her age. "That was a little impossible, as you didn't even know I existed."

"I do know now," Razvan said, "and I hope you are willing to get to know me. I will never take the place of your parents, but I certainly want to be a part of your life, if you will have me. You are someone any parent can be proud of. You stood your ground against evil, and I hear you work with Syndil to heal the earth. That alone is a miracle."

The tension seemed to leave her. "I'm glad we met." She held on to Francesca's hand, seemingly unaware she did so even as she reached out to touch the scars webbing his arm. "You destroyed Xavier. Gregori told us what happened."

"Without the others, Skyler, I would not have been able to do so. We worked together."

"They are waiting for you inside," Francesca said. "I wanted to look at you and Ivory again. I had hoped you would stay and allow us to heal you after the initial session."

Razvan and Ivory exchanged a long look. There had been so much pain. The Carpathian people had gathered to help speed their healing, but neither could stay in such close proximity. They needed their own sacred ground and they had gone together to the cave where Mother Earth surrounded them with her richest soil. Both still bore the scars, but, like Vikirnoff and Natalya, the scars were fading.

"Thank you, Francesca," Razvan said, with a slight,

formal bow. "We both appreciate your aid. You probably saved our lives."

"I doubt that." Francesca led the way through the cavern to the ceremonial chamber where everyone waited.

A hush fell over the crowd as they entered. Ivory moved closer to Razvan. She could smell sage and lavender. Candles adorned every conceivable crevice and ledge, the flickering lights casting soft shadows over the walls. Above their heads, crystals adorned the ceiling, and the dancing lights sent the gems sparkling on and off like a blanket of stars. Ivory slid her arm along Razvan's, shocked that such a crowd of people ringed the room—staring at them.

Mikhail glided from the center of the room, closing the distance between them. He clasped Razvan's arm in the formal manner of greeting between two experienced and respected hunters. "*Pesász jeläbam ainaak*—long may you stay in the light. Thank you for your great service to our people."

Razvan didn't move. Didn't speak. He stared over Mikhail's shoulder even after Mikhail turned to Ivory and clasped her arms in the same formal manner.

"*Sívad olen wäkeva, hän ku piwtä*—may your heart stay strong, hunter," Mikhail greeted. "Your people thank you for your great service." He stepped back and bowed, a long, low sweeping bow indicating great respect.

To Ivory's shock, the entire room bowed with him. Emotion choked her, constricting her throat, and she glanced to Razvan. He hadn't moved. Hadn't changed expression, as if he were frozen there, his face carved in stone. He hadn't seen the tremendous tribute. He hadn't taken his eyes from across the room. She turned her head to follow his gaze.

There was no mistaking who the woman was seated

beside Nicolas De La Cruz—*Lara*. Ivory couldn't drink in her beloved Nicolas, not when Razvan's heart shattered into a million pieces. He just crumbled inside. Outside, he appeared aloof and apart from everything. Inside, he simply dissolved. His inner peace was gone—destroyed. He couldn't breathe; his heart accelerated to the point she feared it might explode.

Every memory, every horrendous detail of this child's life, crowded into his head. The scent of her blood. The feel of his teeth tearing into her flesh, unable to stop, unable to do anything other than warn her, try to get her to run. Yet there was nowhere for her to run. No place for her to go, and he was helpless to save her. The hopeless despair and weight of terrible guilt drove him to his knees. Tiny red beads tracked down his face. His hands were unsteady as he tried to push himself up.

Razvan just knelt there beside her, and, for the first time, Ivory felt panic. He wasn't ready for this. She should never have allowed him to come to this place. She dropped to her knees beside him, her arms around him in spite of the fact that he didn't want her comfort. He didn't feel he deserved it. He had been unable to protect his child not only from Xavier, but from himself, from the monster Xavier had forced him to be. To Razvan, possession was no excuse. This child, his beloved Lara, had been born of him, but, like Skyler, she had been in the midst of monsters.

He knew her. He loved her. Even when he couldn't feel the emotion, it had been there, far off, remembered. His sense of family, the Dragonseeker blood, calling to him, to her.

"Father?" The voice was a child's voice.

Razvan looked up and there she stood, right in front of

him, tears sliding down her face. Lara wrapped her arms around him and held him to her with Ivory.

"It's all right. Really. I'm all right. Nicolas has taken great care of me, and now that you're here with us, and I know you really were trying to get me out of there, everything is all right."

"I do not deserve you."

Lara smiled. "Neither does Nicolas, but I love him all the same." The smile faded and she looked serious. "I am proud to be your daughter."

Nicolas helped Razvan to his feet. "And I, your son." He grinned a little mischievously, something that shocked Ivory as he leaned over to brush a kiss on her cheek. "Hello, Mother."

Ivory gave him a mock scowl, but the ease in Razvan was worth the unfamiliar teasing.

Razvan found a smile forming in his heart. "Take my daughter and sit where she can rest," he instructed, "so they may get started."

Ivory touched his mind again. The terrible pain had eased, but she knew he still felt it. She wrapped her arm around him tightly and clung there while the prince walked to the middle of the room and the hush fell again.

Gregori and Savannah carried their babies into the center of the room. The crowd erupted with joy, the walls expanding as though they couldn't contain so much happiness. Razvan wrapped his arm around Ivory's waist and held her close.

"Everyone will pledge to love and support those children," Ivory said, remembering the ceremony from her childhood. "All of us are expected to educate, love and become family to them so that, should anything happen to their parents, they will not feel alone in the world." She brushed a kiss along the side of his face. "More children for you."

He flicked her a promise of retaliation at the laughter in her voice. "We will have to have at least ten more."

Ivory sucked in her breath and scowled at him. She didn't know the first thing about babies—give her a sword every time.

Razvan made a little snorting sound and even the wolves stirred as if they were laughing.

Gregori handed his daughter to the prince. The baby seemed impossibly tiny to Ivory, but she had all her fingers and toes and a head of thick, dark hair—and she was alive. Her head turned and her eyes met Ivory's. There was awareness there. Ivory's throat tightened more.

"Who names this child?" Mikhail asked.

"Her father," Gregori answered.

"Her mother," Savannah proclaimed.

"Her people," the entire crowd chanted back.

"I name you Anastasia Daratrazanoff," Mikhail said. "Born in battle, crowned with love. Who will accept the offer of the Carpathian people to love and raise our daughter?"

"Her parents, with gratitude," Savannah and Gregori answered formally.

The second infant was handed to Mikhail with great care. She was visibly smaller and a little more fragile, with the same head of dark hair. She, too, looked at Ivory as Mikhail held her high in the air for the Carpathian people to see. Elation swept through the room at the sight of the small baby, an almost electric excitement that had tears swimming in Ivory's eyes. She smiled at the baby and was shocked when the infant smiled back.

"Who names this child?" Mikhail asked.

"Her father," Gregori answered. His voice sounded

choked, as if he could barely get the words past the lump in his throat.

"His mother," Savannah replied, cuddling little Anastasia protectively against her body.

"Her people," every man, woman and child in the room proclaimed in unison.

"I name you Anya Daratrazanoff," Mikhail announced. "Born in battle, crowned with love. Who will accept the offer of the Carpathian people to love and raise our daughter?"

"Her parents, with gratitude." Gregori and Savannah accepted the tremendous honor and duty together.

The crowd erupted into singing and chanting, joy filling the ceremonial chamber. Laughter broke out. Ivory caught sight of Travis hugging Falcon. He looked happy and carefree. She found herself smiling right along with the rest of them.

"I suppose we should swear allegiance to the prince," she whispered.

"I suppose," Razvan agreed, "but not now. Now, I want to take you home and start on those ten children we are going to have."

Ivory laughed and placed her hand in his. She doubted the ten children thing was ever going to happen, but she certainly had no objections to the trying.

Appendix 1

Carpathian Healing Chants

To rightly understand Carpathian healing chants, background is required in several areas:

1. The Carpathian view on healing
2. The Lesser Healing Chant of the Carpathians
3. The Great Healing Chant of the Carpathians
4. Carpathian musical aesthetics
5. Lullaby
6. Song to Heal the Earth
7. Carpathian chanting technique

1. THE CARPATHIAN VIEW ON HEALING

The Carpathians are a nomadic people whose geographic origins can be traced back to at least as far as the Southern Ural Mountains (near the steppes of modern-day Kazakhstan), on the border between Europe and Asia. (For this reason, modern-day linguists call their language "proto-Uralic," without knowing that this is the language of the Carpathians.) Unlike most nomadic peoples, the wandering of the Carpathians was not due to the need to find new grazing lands as the seasons and climate shifted, or the search for better trade. Instead, the Carpathians' movements were driven by a great purpose: to find a land that would have the right earth, a soil with the kind of richness that would greatly enhance their rejuvenative powers.

Over the centuries, they migrated westward (some six thousand years ago), until they at last found their perfect homeland—their *susu*—in the Carpathian Mountains, whose long arc cradled the lush plains of the kingdom of Hungary. (The kingdom of Hungary flourished for over a millennium—making Hungarian the dominant language of the Carpathian Basin—until the kingdom's lands were split among several countries after World War I: Austria, Czechoslovakia, Romania, Yugoslavia and modern Hungary.)

Other peoples from the Southern Urals (who shared the Carpathian language, but were not Carpathians) migrated in different directions. Some ended up in Finland, which accounts for why the modern Hungarian and Finnish languages are among the contemporary descendants of the ancient Carpathian language. Even though they are tied forever to their chosen Carpathian homeland, the wandering of the Carpathians continues, as they search the world for the answers that will enable them to bear and raise their offspring without difficulty.

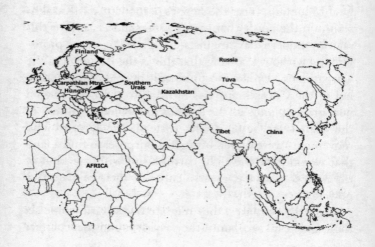

Because of their geographic origins, the Carpathian views on healing share much with the larger Eurasian shamanistic tradition. Probably the closest modern representative of that tradition is based in Tuva (and is referred to as "Tuvinian Shamanism")—see the map on the previous page.

The Eurasian shamanistic tradition—from the Carpathians to the Siberian shamans—held that illness originated in the human soul, and only later manifested as various physical conditions. Therefore, shamanistic healing, while not neglecting the body, focused on the soul and its healing. The most profound illnesses were understood to be caused by "soul departure," where all or some part of the sick person's soul has wandered away from the body (into the nether realms), or has been captured or possessed by an evil spirit, or both.

The Carpathians belong to this greater Eurasian shamanistic tradition and share its viewpoints. While the Carpathians themselves did not succumb to illness, Carpathian healers understood that the most profound wounds were also accompanied by a similar "soul departure."

Upon reaching the diagnosis of "soul departure," the healer-shaman is then required to make a spiritual journey into the nether worlds to recover the soul. The shaman may have to overcome tremendous challenges along the way, particularly: fighting the demon or vampire who has possessed his friend's soul.

"Soul departure" doesn't require a person to be unconscious (although that certainly can be the case as well). It was understood that a person could still appear to be conscious, even talk and interact with others, and yet be missing a part of their soul. The experienced healer or shaman would instantly see the problem nonetheless, in subtle signs that others might miss: the person's attention wandering every now and then, a lessening in their enthusiasm about life, chronic depression, a diminishment in the brightness of their "aura," and the like.

2. THE LESSER HEALING CHANT OF THE CARPATHIANS

Kepä Sarna Pus (**The Lesser Healing Chant**) is used for wounds that are merely physical in nature. The Carpathian healer leaves his body and enters the wounded Carpathian's body to heal great mortal wounds from the inside out using pure energy. He proclaims, "I offer freely my life for your life," as he gives his blood to the injured Carpathian. Because the Carpathians are of the earth and bound to the soil, they are healed by the soil of their homeland. Their saliva is also often used for its rejuvenative powers.

It is also very common for the Carpathian chants (both the Lesser and the Great) to be accompanied by the use of healing herbs, aromas from Carpathian candles, and crystals. The crystals (when combined with the Carpathians' empathic, psychic connection to the entire universe) are used to gather positive energy from their surroundings, which then is used to accelerate the healing. Caves are sometimes used as the setting for the healing.

The Lesser Healing Chant was used by Vikirnoff Von Shrieder and Colby Jansen to heal Rafael De La Cruz, whose heart had been ripped out by a vampire as described in *Dark Secret*.

Kepä Sarna Pus (The Lesser Healing Chant)

The same chant is used for all physical wounds. "Sívadaba" ["into your heart"] would be changed to refer to whatever part of the body is wounded.

Kuňasz, nélkül sivdobbanás, nélkül fesztelen löyly.
You lie as if asleep, without beat of heart, without airy breath.

Ot élidamet andam szabadon élidadért.
I offer freely my life for your life.

O jelä sielam jŏrem ot ainamet és soŋe ot élidadet.
My spirit of light forgets my body and enters your body.

O jelä sielam pukta kinn minden szelemeket belső.
My spirit of light sends all the dark spirits within fleeing without.

Pajňak o susu hanyet és o nyelv nyálamet sívadaba.
I press the earth of our homeland and the spit of my tongue into your heart.

Vii, o verim soŋe o verid andam.
At last, I give you my blood for your blood.

To hear this chant, visit: http://www.christinefeehan.com/members/.

3. THE GREAT HEALING CHANT OF THE CARPATHIANS

The most well known—and most dramatic—of the Carpathian healing chants was *En Sarna Pus* (**The**

Great Healing Chant). This chant was reserved for recovering the wounded or unconscious Carpathian's soul.

Typically a group of men would form a circle around the sick Carpathian (to "encircle him with our care and compassion") and begin the chant. The shaman or healer or leader is the prime actor in this healing ceremony. It is he who will actually make the spiritual journey into the netherworld, aided by his clanspeople. Their purpose is to ecstatically dance, sing, drum and chant, all the while visualizing (through the words of the chant) the journey itself—every step of it, over and over again—to the point where the shaman, in trance, leaves his body, and makes that very journey. (Indeed, the word "ecstasy" is from the Latin *ex statis*, which literally means "out of the body.")

One advantage that the Carpathian healer has over many other shamans is his telepathic link to his lost brother. Most shamans must wander in the dark of the nether realms in search of their lost brother. But the Carpathian healer directly "hears" in his mind the voice of his lost brother calling to him, and can thus "zero in" on his soul like a homing beacon. For this reason, Carpathian healing tends to have a higher success rate than most other traditions of this sort.

Something of the geography of the "other world" is useful for us to examine, in order to fully understand the words of the Great Carpathian Healing Chant. A reference is made to the "Great Tree" (in Carpathian: *En Puwe*). Many ancient traditions, including the Carpathian tradition, understood the worlds—the heaven worlds, our world, and the nether realms—to be "hung" upon a great pole, or axis, or tree. Here on earth, we are positioned halfway up this tree, on one of its branches. Hence many ancient texts often referred to the material world as "middle earth": midway between heaven and hell. Climbing the tree would lead one to the heaven worlds. Descending the tree to its roots would lead to the nether realms. The shaman was necessarily a master of movement up and down the Great Tree, sometimes moving unaided, and sometimes assisted by (or even mounted upon the back of) an animal spirit guide. In various traditions, this Great Tree was known variously as the *axis mundi* (the "axis of the worlds"), Ygddrasil (in Norse mythology), Mount Meru (the sacred world mountain of Tibetan tradition), etc. The Christian cosmos, with its heaven, purgatory/earth and hell, is also worth comparing. It is even given a similar topography in Dante's *Divine Comedy*: Dante is led on a journey first to hell, at the center of the earth; then upward to Mount Purgatory, which sits on the earth's surface directly opposite Jerusalem; then farther upward first to Eden, the earthly paradise, at the summit of Mount Purgatory; and then upward at last to heaven.

In the shamanistic tradition, it was understood that the small always reflects the large; the personal always reflects the cosmic. A movement in the greater dimensions of the cosmos also coincides with an internal movement. For example, the *axis mundi* of the cosmos also corresponds to the spinal column of the individual. Journeys up and down the *axis mundi* often coincided with the movement of natural and spiritual energies (sometimes called *kundalini* or *shakti*) in the spinal column of the shaman or mystic.

En Sarna Pus (The Great Healing Chant)
In this chant, ekä ("brother") would be replaced by "sister,"
"father," "mother," depending on the person to be healed.

Ot ekäm ainajanak hany, jama.
My brother's body is a lump of earth, close to death.

Me, ot ekäm kuntajanak, pirädak ekäm, gond és irgalom
türe.
We, the clan of my brother, encircle him with our care and
compassion.

O pus wäkenkek, ot oma śarnank, és ot pus fünk,
álnak ekäm ainajanak, pitänak ekäm ainajanak
elävä.
Our healing energies, ancient words of magic, and healing
herbs bless my brother's body, keep it alive.

Ot ekäm sielanak pälä. Ot omboće päläja juta alatt o jüti,
kinta, és szelemek lamtijaknak.
But my brother's soul is only half. His other half wanders
in the netherworld.

Ot en mekem ŋamaŋ: kulkedak otti ot ekäm omboće
päläjanak.
My great deed is this: I travel to find my brother's other
half.

Rekatüre, saradak, tappadak, odam, kaŋa o numa waram,
és avaa owe o lewl mahoz.
We dance, we chant, we dream ecstatically, to call my spirit
bird, and to open the door to the other world.

Ntak o numa waram, és mozdulak, jomadak.
I mount my spirit bird and we begin to move, we are under way.

Piwtädak ot En Puwe tyvinak, ećidak alatt o jüti, kinta, és szelemek lamtijaknak.
Following the trunk of the Great Tree, we fall into the netherworld.

Fázak, fázak nó o śaro.
It is cold, very cold.

Juttadak ot ekäm o akarataban, o sívaban és o sielaban.
My brother and I are linked in mind, heart and soul.

Ot ekäm sielanak kaŋa engem.
My brother's soul calls to me.

Kuledak és piwtädak ot ekäm.
I hear and follow his track.

Saɣedak és tuledak ot ekäm kulyanak.
Encounter I the demon who is devouring my brother's soul.

Nenäm ćoro; o kuly torodak.
In anger, I fight the demon.

O kuly pél engem.
He is afraid of me.

Lejkkadak o kaŋka salamaval.
I strike his throat with a lightning bolt.

Molodak ot ainaja komakamal.
I break his body with my bare hands.

Toja és molanâ.
He is bent over, and falls apart.

Hän ćaδa.
He runs away.

Manedak ot ekäm sielanak.
I rescue my brother's soul.

Alədam ot ekam sielanak o komamban.
I lift my brother's soul in the hollow of my hand.

Alədam ot ekam numa waramra.
I lift him onto my spirit bird.

Piwtädak ot En Puwe tyvijanak és saγedak jälleen ot elävä ainak majaknak.
Following up the Great Tree, we return to the land of the living.

Ot ekäm weńćä jälleen.
My brother lives again.

Ot ekäm weńća jälleen.
He is complete again.

To hear this chant, visit: http://www.christinefeehan.com/members/.

4. CARPATHIAN MUSICAL AESTHETICS

In the sung Carpathian pieces (such as the "Lullaby" and the "Song to Heal the Earth"), you'll hear elements that are shared by many of the musical traditions in the Uralic geographical region, some of which still exist—from Eastern European (Bulgarian, Romanian, Hungarian, Croatian, etc.) to Romany ("gypsy"). Some of these elements include:

- the rapid alternation between major and minor modalities, including a sudden switch (called a "Picardy third") from minor to major to end a piece or section (as at the end of the "Lullaby")
- the use of close (tight) harmonies
- the use of *ritardi* (slowing down the piece) and *crescendi* (swelling in volume) for brief periods
- the use of *glissandi* (slides) in the singing tradition
- the use of trills in the singing tradition (as in the final invocation of the "Song to Heal the Earth")— similar to Celtic, a singing tradition more familiar to many of us
- the use of parallel fifths (as in the final invocation of the "Song to Heal the Earth")
- controlled use of dissonance
- "call and response" chanting (typical of many of the world's chanting traditions)
- extending the length of a musical line (by adding a couple of bars) to heighten dramatic effect
- and many more

"Lullaby" and "Song to Heal the Earth" illustrate two rather different forms of Carpathian music (a quiet, intimate piece and an energetic ensemble piece)—but, whatever the form, Carpathian music is full of feeling.

5. LULLABY

This song is sung by women while the child is still in the womb or when the threat of a miscarriage is apparent. The baby can hear the song while inside of the mother, and the mother can connect with the child telepathically as well. The lullaby is meant to reassure the child, to encourage the baby to hold on, to stay—to reassure the child that he or she will be protected by love even from inside until birth. The last line literally means that the mother's love will protect her child until the child is born ("rise").

Musically, the Carpathian "Lullaby" is in three-quarter time ("waltz time"), as are a significant portion of the world's various traditional lullabies (perhaps the most famous of which is "Brahms' Lullaby"). The arrangement for solo voice is the original context: a mother singing to her child, unaccompanied. The arrangement for chorus and violin ensemble illustrates how musical even the simplest Carpathian pieces often are, and how easily they lend themselves to contemporary instrumental or orchestral arrangements. (A wide range of contemporary composers, including Dvořák and Smetana, have taken advantage of a similar discovery, working other traditional Eastern European music into their symphonic poems.)

Odam-Sarna Kondak (Lullaby)
Tumtesz o wäke ku pitasz belső.
Feel the strength you hold inside.

Hiszasz sívadet. Én olenam gæidnod.
Trust your heart. I'll be your guide.
Sas csecsemőm, kuńasz.
Hush my baby, close your eyes.

Rauho joŋe ted.
Peace will come to you.

Tumtesz o sívdobbanás ku olen lamtad belső.
Feel the rhythm deep inside.

Gond-kumpadek ku kim te.
Waves of love that cover you.

Pesänak te, asti o jüti, kidüsz.
Protect, until the night you rise.

To hear this song, visit: http://www.christinefeehan.com/members/.

6. SONG TO HEAL THE EARTH

This is the earth-healing song that is used by the
Carpathian women to heal soil filled with various toxins.
The women take a position on four sides and call to the
universe to draw on the healing energy with love and
respect. The soil of the earth is their resting place, the place
where they rejuvenate, and they must make it safe not
only for themselves but for their unborn children as well
as their men and living children. This is a beautiful ritual
performed by the women together, raising their voices
in harmony and calling on the earth's minerals and healing
properties to come forth and help them save their children.

They literally dance and sing to heal the earth in a ceremony as old as their species. The dance and notes of the song are adjusted according to the toxins felt through the healer's bare feet. The feet are placed in a certain pattern and the hands gracefully weave a healing spell while the dance is performed. They must be especially careful when the soil is prepared for babies. This is a ceremony of love and healing.

Musically, the ritual is divided into several sections:

- **First verse**: A "call and response" section, where the chant leader sings the "call" solo, and then some or all of the women sing the "response" in the close harmony style typical of the Carpathian musical tradition. The repeated response—*Ai Emä Maγe*—is an invocation of the source of power for the healing ritual: "Oh Mother Nature."
- **First chorus**: This section is filled with clapping, dancing, ancient horns and other means used to invoke and heighten the energies upon which the ritual is drawing.
- **Second verse**
- **Second chorus**
- **Closing invocation**: In this closing part, two song leaders, in close harmony, take all the energy gathered by the earlier portions of the song/ritual and focus it entirely on the healing purpose.

What you will be listening to are brief tastes of what would typically be a significantly longer ritual, in which the verse and chorus parts are developed and repeated many times, to be closed by a single rendition of the final invocation.

Sarna Pusm O Maɣet (Song to Heal the Earth)

First verse
Ai Emä Maɣe,
Oh, Mother Nature,

Me sívadbin lańaak.
We are your beloved daughters.

Me tappadak, me pusmak o maɣet.
We dance to heal the earth.

Me sarnadak, me pusmak o hanyet.
We sing to heal the earth.

Sielanket jutta tedet it,
We join with you now,

Sívank és akaratank és sielank juttanak.
Our hearts and minds and spirits become one.

Second verse
Ai Emä Maɣe,
Oh, Mother Nature,

Me sívadbin lańaak.
We are your beloved daughters.

Me andak arwadet emänked és me kaŋank o
We pay homage to our mother and call upon the

Pōhi és Lōuna, Ida és Lääs.
North and South, East and West.

Pide és aldyn és myös belső.
Above and below and within as well.

Gondank o maɣenak pusm hän ku olen jama.
Our love of the land heals that which is in need.

Juttanak teval it,
We join with you now,

Maɣe maɣeval.
Earth to earth.

O pirä elidak weńća.
The circle of life is complete.

To hear this chant, visit: http://www.christinefeehan.com/members/.

7. CARPATHIAN CHANTING TECHNIQUE

As with their healing techniques, the actual "chanting technique" of the Carpathians has much in common with the other shamanistic traditions of the Central Asian steppes. The primary mode of chanting was throat chanting using overtones. Modern examples of this manner of singing can still be found in the Mongolian, Tuvan and Tibetan traditions. You can find an audio example of the Gyuto Tibetan Buddhist monks engaged in throat chanting at: http://www.christinefeehan.com/carpathian_chanting/.

As with Tuva, note on the map the geographical proximity of Tibet to Kazakhstan and the Southern Urals.

The beginning part of the Tibetan chant emphasizes synchronizing all the voices around a single tone, aimed at healing a particular "chakra" of the body. This is fairly typical of the Gyuto throat-chanting tradition, but it is not a significant part of the Carpathian tradition. Nonetheless, it serves as an interesting contrast.

The part of the Gyuto chanting example that is most similar to the Carpathian style of chanting is the midsection, where the men are chanting the words together with great force. The purpose here is not to generate a "healing tone" that will affect a particular "chakra," but rather to generate as much power as possible for initiating the "out of body" travel, and for fighting the demonic forces that the healer/traveler must face and overcome.

The songs of the Carpathian women (illustrated by their "Lullaby" and their "Song to Heal the Earth") are part of the same ancient musical and healing tradition as the Lesser and Great Healing Chants of the warrior males. You can hear some of the same instruments in both the male warriors' healing chants and the women's "Song to Heal the Earth." Also, they share the common purpose of generating and directing power. However, the women's songs are distinctively feminine in character. One immediately noticeable difference is that, while the men speak their words in the manner of a chant, the women sing songs with melodies and harmonies, softening the overall performance. A feminine, nurturing quality is especially evident in the "Lullaby."

APPENDIX 2

The Carpathian Language

Like all human languages, the language of the Carpathians contains the richness and nuance that can only come from a long history of use. At best we can only touch on some of the main features of the language in this brief appendix:

1. The history of the Carpathian language
2. Carpathian grammar and other characteristics of the language
3. Examples of the Carpathian language (including the Ritual Words and the Warrior's Chant)
4. A much-abridged Carpathian dictionary

1. THE HISTORY OF THE CARPATHIAN LANGUAGE

The Carpathian language of today is essentially identical to the Carpathian language of thousands of years ago. A "dead" language like the Latin of two thousand years ago has evolved into a significantly different modern language (Italian) because of countless generations of speakers and great historical fluctuations. In contrast, many of the speakers of Carpathian from thousands of years ago are still alive. Their presence—coupled with the deliberate isolation of the Carpathians from the other major forces of change in the world—has acted (and continues to act) as a stabilizing force that has preserved the integrity of the language over the centuries. Carpathian culture has also acted as a stabilizing force. For instance, the Ritual Words, the various healing chants (see Appendix 1), and other cultural artifacts have been passed down through the centuries with great fidelity.

481

One small exception should be noted: the splintering of the Carpathians into separate geographic regions has led to some minor dialectization. However the telepathic link among all Carpathians (as well as each Carpathian's regular return to his or her homeland) has ensured that the differences among dialects are relatively superficial (e.g., small numbers of new words, minor differences in pronunciation, etc.), since the deeper, internal language of mind-forms has remained the same because of continuous use across space and time.

The Carpathian language was (and still is) the proto-language for the Uralic (or Finno-Ugrian) family of languages. Today, the Uralic languages are spoken in northern, eastern and central Europe and in Siberia. More than twenty-three million people in the world speak languages that can trace their ancestry to Carpathian. Magyar or Hungarian (about fourteen million speakers), Finnish (about five million speakers), and Estonian (about one million speakers) are the three major contemporary descendants of this proto-language. The only factor that unites the more than twenty languages in the Uralic family is that their ancestry can be traced back to a common proto-language—Carpathian—which split (starting some six thousand years ago) into the various languages in the Uralic family. In the same way, European languages such as English and French belong to the better-known Indo-European family and also evolved from a common proto-language ancestor (a different one from Carpathian).

The following table provides a sense for some of the similarities in the language family.

Note: The Finnic/Carpathian "k" shows up often as Hungarian "h." Similarly, the Finnic/Carpathian "p" often corresponds to the Hungarian "f."

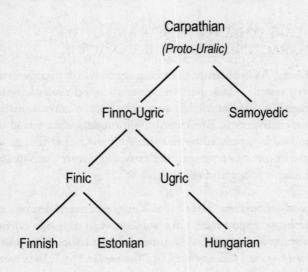

Carpathian
(Proto-Uralic)

Finno-Ugric   Samoyedic

Finic   Ugric

Finnish   Estonian   Hungarian

Carpathian	Finnish	Hungarian
(proto-Uralic)	(Suomi)	(Magyar)
elä—live	*elä*—live	*él*—live
elid—life	*elinikä*—life	*élet*—life
pesä—nest	*pesä*—nest	*fészek*—nest
kola—die	*kuole*—die	*hal*—die
pälä—half, -side	*pieltä*—tilt, tip to the side	*fél, fele*—fellow human, friend (half; one side of two)
		feleség—wife
and—give	*anta, antaa*—give	*ad*—give
koje—husband, man	*koira*—dog, the male (of animals)	*here*—drone, testicle
wäke—power	*väki*—folks, people, men; force	*val/-vel*—with (instrumental suffix)
	väkevä—powerful, strong	*vele*—with him/her/it
wete—water	*vesi*—water	*viz*—water

2. CARPATHIAN GRAMMAR AND OTHER CHARACTERISTICS OF THE LANGUAGE

Idioms. As both an ancient language and a language of an earth people, Carpathian is more inclined toward use of idioms constructed from concrete, "earthy" terms, rather than abstractions. For instance, our modern abstraction "to cherish" is expressed more concretely in Carpathian as "to hold in one's heart"; the "netherworld" is, in Carpathian, "the land of night, fog and ghosts", etc.

Word order. The order of words in a sentence is determined not by syntactic roles (like subject, verb and object) but rather by pragmatic, discourse-driven factors. Examples: *"Tied vagyok."* ("Yours am I."); *"Sivamet andam."* ("My heart I give you.")

Agglutination. The Carpathian language is agglutinative; that is, longer words are constructed from smaller components. An agglutinating language uses suffixes or prefixes whose meaning is generally unique, and which are concatenated one after another without overlap. In Carpathian, words typically consist of a stem that is followed by one or more suffixes. For example, *"sívambam"* derives from the stem *"sív"* ("heart") followed by *"am"* ("my," making it "my heart"), followed by *"bam"* ("in," making it "in my heart"). As you might imagine, agglutination in Carpathian can sometimes produce very long words, or words that are very difficult to pronounce. Vowels often get inserted between suffixes, to prevent too many consonants from appearing in a row (which can make the word unpronounceable).

Noun cases. Like all languages, Carpathian has many noun cases; the same noun will be "spelled" differently depending on its role in the sentence. Some of the noun cases include: nominative (when the noun is the subject of the sentence), accusative (when the noun is a direct object of the verb), dative (indirect object), genitive (or possessive), instrumental, final, supressive, inessive, elative, terminative and delative.

We will use the possessive (or genitive) case as an example, to illustrate how all noun cases in Carpathian involve adding standard suffixes to the noun stems. Thus expressing possession in Carpathian—"my lifemate," "your lifemate," "his lifemate," "her lifemate," etc.—involves adding a particular suffix (such as "*-am*") to the noun stem (*"päläfertiil"*), to produce the possessive (*päläfertiilam"*—"my lifemate"). Which suffix to use depends upon which person ("my," "your," "his," etc.) and whether the noun ends in a consonant or a vowel. The table below shows the suffixes for singular nouns only (not plural), and also shows the similarity to the suffixes used in contemporary Hungarian. (Hungarian is actually a little more complex, in that it also requires "vowel rhyming": which suffix to use also depends on the last vowel in the noun; hence the multiple choices in the cells below, where Carpathian only has a single choice.)

Note: As mentioned earlier, vowels often get inserted between the word and its suffix so as to prevent too many consonants from appearing in a row (which would produce unpronounceable words). For example, in the table on the following page, all nouns that end in a consonant are followed by suffixes beginning with "a."

person	Carpathian (proto-Uralic)		contemporary Hungarian	
	noun ends in vowel	noun ends in consonant	noun ends in vowel	noun ends in consonant
1st singular (my)	-m	-am	-m	-om, -em, -öm
2nd singular (your)	-d	-ad	-d	-od, -ed, -öd
3rd singular (his, her, its)	-ja	-a	-ja/-je	-a, -e
1st plural (our)	-nk	-ank	-nk	-unk, -ünk
2nd plural (your)	-tak	-atak	-tok, -tek, -tök	-otok, -etek, -ötök
3rd plural (their)	-jak	-ak	-juk, -jük	-uk, -ük

Verb conjugation. Like its modern descendants (such as Finnish and Hungarian), Carpathian has many verb tenses, far too many to describe here. We will just focus on the conjugation of the present tense. Again, we will place contemporary Hungarian side by side with the Carpathian, because of the marked similarity of the two.

As with the possessive case for nouns, the conjugation of verbs is done by adding a suffix onto the verb stem:

Person	Carpathian (proto-Uralic)	contemporary Hungarian
1st (I give)	-am (andam), -ak	-ok, -ek, -ök
2nd singular (you give)	-sz (andsz)	-sz
3rd singular (he/she/it gives)	— (and)	—
1st plural (we give)	-ak (andak)	-unk, -ünk
2nd plural (you give)	-tak (andtak)	-tok, -tek, -tök
3rd plural (they give)	-nak (andnak)	-nak, -nek

As with all languages, there are many "irregular verbs" in Carpathian that don't exactly fit this pattern. But the above table is still a useful guideline for most verbs.

3. EXAMPLES OF THE CARPATHIAN LANGUAGE

Here are some brief examples of conversational Carpathian, used in the Dark books. We include the literal translation in square brackets. It is interestingly different from the most appropriate English translation.

Susu.
I am home.
["home/birthplace." "I am" is understood, as is often the case in Carpathian.]

Möért?
What for?

csitri
little one
["little slip of a thing," "little slip of a girl"]

ainaak enyém
forever mine

ainaak sívamet jutta
forever mine (another form)
["forever to-my-heart connected/fixed"]

sívamet
my love
["of-my-heart," "to-my-heart"]

487

Tet vigyázam.
I love you.
["you-love-I"]

Sarna Rituaali (**The Ritual Words**) is a longer example, and an example of chanted rather than conversational Carpathian. Note the recurring use of *"andam"* ("I give"), to give the chant musicality and force through repetition.

Sarna Rituaali (The Ritual Words)

Te avio päläfertiilam.
You are my lifemate.

Éntölam kuulua, avio päläfertiilam.
I claim you as my lifemate.

Ted kuuluak, kacad, kojed.
I belong to you.

Élidamet andam.
I offer my life for you.

Pesämet andam.
I give you my protection.

Uskolfertiilamet andam.
I give you my allegiance.

Sívamet andam.
I give you my heart.

Sielamet andam.
I give you my soul.

Ainamet andam.
I give you my body.

Sívamet kuuluak kaik että a ted.
I take into my keeping the same that is yours.

Ainaak olenszal sívambin.
Your life will be cherished by me for all my time.

Te élidet ainaak pide minan.
Your life will be placed above my own for all time.

Te avio päläfertiilam.
You are my lifemate.

Ainaak sívamet jutta oleny.
You are bound to me for all eternity.

Ainaak terád vigyázak.
You are always in my care.

To hear these words pronounced (and for more about Carpathian pronunciation altogether), please visit: http://www.christinefeehan.com/members/.

Sarna Kontakawk (The Warriors' Chant) is another longer example of the Carpathian language. The warriors' council takes place deep beneath the earth in a chamber of crystals with magma far below that, so the steam is natural and the wisdom of their ancestors is clear and focused.

This is a sacred place where they bloodswear to their prince and people and affirm their code of honor as warriors and brothers. It is also where battle strategies are born and all dissension is discussed as well as any concerns the warriors have that they wish to bring to the Council and open for discussion.

Sarna Kontakawk (The Warriors' Chant)

Veri isäakank—veri ekäakank.
Blood of our fathers—blood of our brothers.

Veri olen elid.
Blood is life.

Andak veri-elidet Karpatiiakank, és wäke-sarna ku meke arwa-arvo, irgalom, hän ku agba, és wäke kutni, ku manaak verival.
We offer that life to our people with a bloodsworn vow of honor, mercy, integrity and endurance.

Verink sokta; verink kaŋa terád.
Our blood mingles and calls to you.

Akasz énak ku kaŋa és juttasz kuntatak it.
Heed our summons and join with us now.

To hear these words pronounced (and for more about Carpathian pronunciation altogether), please visit: http://www.christinefeehan.com/members/.

See **Appendix 1** for Carpathian healing chants, including the *Kepä Sarna Pus* (The Lesser Healing Chant), the *En*

Sarna Pus (The Great Healing Chant), the *Odam-Sarna Kondak* (Lullaby) and the *Sarna Pusm O Maɣet* (Song to Heal the Earth).

4. A MUCH-ABRIDGED CARPATHIAN DICTIONARY

This very much abridged Carpathian dictionary contains most of the Carpathian words used in these Dark books. Of course, a full Carpathian dictionary would be as large as the usual dictionary for an entire language (typically more than a hundred thousand words).

Note: The Carpathian nouns and verbs below are word stems. They generally do not appear in their isolated, "stem" form, as below. Instead, they usually appear with suffixes (e.g., *"andam"*—"I give," rather than just the root, *"and"*).

agba—to be seemly or proper.
ai—oh.
aina—body.
ainaak—forever.
ak—suffix added after a noun ending in a consonant to make it plural.
aka—to give heed; to hearken; to listen.
akarat—mind; will.
ál—to bless; to attach to.
alatt—through.
aldyn—under; underneath.
alǝ—to lift; to raise.
alte—to bless; to curse.
and—to give.
andasz éntölem irgalomet!—have mercy!

arvo—value (*noun*).

arwa—praise (*noun*).

arwa-arvo—honor (*noun*).

arwa-arvo olen gæidnod, ekäm—honor guide you, my brother (*greeting*).

arwa-arvo olen isäntä, ekäm—honor keep you, my brother (*greeting*).

arwa-arvo pile sívadet—may honor light your heart (*greeting*).

arwa-arvod mäne me ködak—may your honor hold back the dark (*greeting*).

asti—until.

avaa—to open.

avio—wedded.

avio päläfertiil—lifemate.

belső—within; inside.

bur—good; well.

bur tule ekämet kuntamak—well met brother-kin (*greeting*).

ćaδa—to flee; to run; to escape.

ćoro—to flow; to run like rain.

csecsemō—baby (*noun*).

csitri—little one (*female*).

diutal—triumph; victory.

emi—to fall.

eći—to fall.

ek—suffix added after a noun ending in a consonant to make it plural.

ekä—brother.

elä—to live.

eläsz arwa-arvoval—may you live with honor, live nobly (*greeting*).

eläsz jeläbam ainaak—long may you live in the light (*greeting*).

elävä—alive.

elävä ainak majaknak—land of the living.

elid—life.

emä—mother (*noun*).

Emä Maɣe—Mother Nature.

én—I.

en—great, many, big.

én jutta félet és ekämet—I greet a friend and brother (*greeting*).

En Puwe—The Great Tree. Related to the legends of Ygddrasil, the *axis mundi*, Mount Meru, heaven and hell, etc.

engem—me.

és—and.

että—that.

fáz—to feel cold or chilly.

fél—fellow, friend.

fél ku kuuluaak sívam belső—beloved.

fél ku vigyázak—dear one.

feldolgaz—prepare.

fertiil—fertile one.

fesztelen—airy.

fü—herbs; grass.

gæidno—road, way.

gond—care; worry; love (*noun*).

hän—he; she; it.

hän agba—it is so.

hän ku—prefix: one who; that which.

hän ku agba—truth.

hän ku kaśwa o numamet—sky-owner.

hän ku kuulua sívamet—keeper of my heart.

hän ku meke pirämet—defender.

hän ku pesä—protector.

hän ku saa kućaket—star-reacher.

hän ku tappa—deadly.

hän ku tuulmahl elidet—vampire (*literally: life-stealer*).

hän ku vie elidet—vampire (*literally: thief of life*).

hän ku vigyáz sielamet—keeper of my soul.

hän ku vigyáz sívamet és sielamet—keeper of my heart and soul.

hany—clod; lump of earth.

hisz—to believe; to trust.

ida—east.

igazág—justice.

irgalom—compassion; pity; mercy.

isä—father (*noun*).

isäntä—master of the house.

it—now.

jälleen—again.

jama—to be sick, wounded or dying; to be near death.

jelä—sunlight; day, sun; light.

jelä keje terád—light sear you (*Carpathian swear words*).

o jelä peje terád—sun scorch you (*Carpathian swear words*).

o jelä sielamak—light of my soul.

joma—to be under way; to go.

joŋe—to come; to return.

joŋesz arwa-arvoval—return with honor (*greeting*).

jŏrem—to forget; to lose one's way; to make a mistake.

juo—to drink.

juosz és eläsz—drink and live (*greeting*).

juosz és olen ainaak sielamet jutta—drink and become one with me (*greeting*).

juta—to go; to wander.

jüti—night; evening.

jutta—connected; fixed (*adj.*). To connect; to fix; to bind (*verb*).

k—suffix added after a noun ending in a vowel to make it plural.

kaca—male lover.

kaik—all.

kalma—corpse; death; grave.

kaŋa—to call; to invite; to request; to beg.

kaŋk—windpipe; Adam's apple; throat.

kaða—to abandon; to leave; to remain.

kaða wäkeva óv o köd—stand fast against the dark (*greeting*).

Karpatii—Carpathian.

Karpatii ku köd—liar.

käsi—hand (*noun*).

kaśwa—to own.

keje—to cook; to burn; to sear.

kepä—lesser, small, easy, few.

kidü—to wake up; to arise (*intransitive verb*).

kim—to cover an entire object with some sort of covering.

kinn—out; outdoors; outside; without.

kinta—fog; mist; smoke.

köd—fog; mist; darkness.

köd alte hän—darkness curse it (*Carpathian swear words*).

o köd belső—darkness take it (*Carpathian swear words*).

köd jutasz belső—shadow take you (*Carpathian swear words*).

koje—man; husband; drone.

kola—to die.

kolasz arwa-arvoval—may you die with honor (*greeting*).

koma—empty hand; bare hand; palm of the hand; hollow of the hand.

kond—all of a family's or clan's children.

kont—warrior.

kont o sívanak—strong heart (*literally: heart of the warrior*).

ku—who; which; that.

kuć—star.

kućak!—stars! (exclamation)

kule—to hear.

kulke—to go or to travel (on land or water).

kulkesz arwa-arvoval, ekäm—walk with honor, my brother (*greeting*).

kulkesz arwaval, joŋesz arwa arvoval—go with glory, return with honor (*greeting*).

kuly—intestinal worm; tapeworm; demon who possesses and devours souls.

kumpa—wave (*noun*).

kuŋe—moon.

kuńa—to lie as if asleep; to close or cover the eyes in a game of hide-and-seek; to die.

kunta—band, clan, tribe, family.

kuras—sword; large knife.

kure—bind; tie.

kutni—to be able to bear, carry, endure, stand or take.

kutnisz ainaak—long may you endure (*greeting*).

kuulua—to belong; to hold.

lääs—west.

lamti (or lamt)—lowland; meadow; deep; depth.

lamti ból jüti, kinta, ja szelem—the netherworld (*literally: the meadow of night, mists and ghosts*).

lańa—daughter.

lejkka—crack, fissure, split (*noun*). To cut; to hit; to strike forcefully (*verb*).

lewl—spirit (*noun*).

lewl ma—the other world (*literally: spirit land*). *Lewl ma* includes *lamti ból jüti, kinta, ja szelem:* the netherworld, but also includes the worlds higher up *En Puwe*, the Great Tree.

liha—flesh.

lõuna—south.

löyly—breath; steam (*related to* lewl: *spirit*).

ma—land; forest.

magköszun—thank.

mana—to abuse; to curse; to ruin.

mäne—to rescue; to save.

maɣe—land; earth; territory; place; nature.

me—we.

meke—deed; work (*noun*). To do; to make; to work (*verb*).

minan—mine.

minden—every, all (*adj.*).

möért?—what for? (*exclamation*).

molanâ—to crumble; to fall apart.

molo—to crush; to break into bits.

mozdul—to begin to move, to enter into movement.

muonì—appoint; order; prescribe; command.

musta—memory.

myös—also.

nä—for.

ŋamaŋ—this; this one here.

nélkül—without.

nenä—anger.

nó—like; in the same way as; as.

numa—god; sky; top; upper part; highest (*related to the English word: numinous*).

numatorkuld—thunder (*literally: sky struggle*).

nyál—saliva; spit (*related to nyelv: tongue*).

nyelv—tongue.

o—the (*used before a noun beginning with a consonant*).

odam—to dream; to sleep.

odam-sarna kondak—lullaby (*literally: sleep-song of children*).

olen—to be.

oma—old; ancient.

omas—stand

omboće—other; second (*adj.*).

ot—the (*used before a noun beginning with a vowel*).

otti—to look; to see; to find.

óv—to protect against.

owe—door.

päämoro—aim; target.

pajna—to press.

pälä—half; side.

päläfertiil—mate or wife.

peje—to burn.

peje terád—get burned (*Carpathian swear words*).

pél—to be afraid; to be scared of.

pesä—nest (*literal*); protection (*figurative*).

pesäsz jeläbam ainaak—long may you stay in the light (*greeting*).

pide—above.

pile—to ignite; to light up.

pirä—circle; ring (*noun*). To surround; to enclose (*verb*).

piros—red.

pitä—to keep; to hold.

pitäam mustaakad sielpesäambam—I hold your memories safe in my soul.

pitäsz baszú, piwtäsz igazáget—no vengeance, only justice.

piwtä—to follow; to follow the track of game.

poår—bit; piece.

pōhi—north.

pukta—to drive away; to persecute; to put to flight.

pus—healthy; healing.

pusm—to be restored to health.

puwe—tree; wood.

rauho—peace.

reka—ecstasy; trance.

rituaali—ritual.

sa—sinew; tendon; cord.

sa4—to call; to name.

saa—arrive, come; become; get, receive.

saasz hän ku andam szabadon—take what I freely offer.

salama—lightning; lightning bolt.

sarna—words; speech; magic incantation (*noun*). To chant; to sing; to celebrate (*verb*).

sarna kontakawk—warriors' chant.

śaro—frozen snow.

sas—shoosh (*to a child or baby*).

saɣe—to arrive; to come; to reach.

siel—soul.

sisar—sister.

sív—heart.

sív pide köd—love transcends evil.

sívad olen wäkeva, hän ku piwtä—may your heart stay strong, hunter (*greeting*).

sivamés sielam—my heart and soul.

sívamet—my love of my heart to my heart.

sívdobbanás—heartbeat (*literal*); rhythm (*figurative*).

sokta—to mix; to stir around.

soŋe—to enter; to penetrate; to compensate; to replace.

susu—home; birthplace (*noun*). At home (*adv.*).

szabadon—freely.

szelem—ghost.

tappa—to dance; to stamp with the feet; to kill.

te—you.

ted—yours.

terád keje—get scorched (*Carpathian swear words*).

tõdhän—knowledge.

tõdhän lõ kuraset agbapäämoroam—knowledge flies the sword true to its aim.

toja—to bend; to bow; to break.

toro—to fight; to quarrel.

torosz wäkeval—fight fiercely (*greeting*).

totello—obey.

tuhanos—thousand.

tuhanos löylyak türelamak saγe diutalet—a thousand patient
　　breaths bring victory.

tule—to meet; to come.

tumte—to feel; to touch; to touch upon.

türe—full; satiated; accomplished.

türelam—patience.

türelam agba kontsalamaval—patience is the warrior's true
　　weapon.

tyvi—stem; base; trunk.

uskol—faithful.

uskolfertiil—allegiance; loyalty.

veri—blood.

veri ekäakank—blood of our brothers.

veri-elidet—blood-life.

veri isäakank—blood of our fathers.

veri olen piros, ekäm—blood be red, my brother (*literal*); find
　　your lifemate (*figurative: greeting*).

veriak ot en Karpatiiak—by the blood of the prince (*literally:
　　by the blood of the great Carpathian; Carpathian swear
　　words*).

veridet peje—may your blood burn (*Carpathian swear words*).

vigyáz—to love; to care for; to take care of.

vii—last; at last; finally.

wäke—power; strength.

wäke kaδa—steadfastness.

wäke kutni—endurance.

wäke-sarna—vow; curse; blessing (*literally: power words*).

wäkeva—powerful.

wara—bird; crow.

weńća—complete; whole.

wete—water (*noun*).

Turn the page for a glimpse at some previously unpublished deleted scenes . . .

Deleted Scene 1

"They are whispering again, Gregori," Savannah said with a small smile on her face. "In their own language and I fear they are up to no good."

"They are in incubators, Savannah," Gregori pointed out, glancing toward the twin cubicles his girls were in. "It isn't like they can get into trouble."

Savannah's eyebrows shot up.

Gregori frowned. "What? What could they possibly do?"

"If someone doesn't stay in the room with them every single second, Anastasia finds her way into Anya's incubator."

He whirled around to glare at the infants. "No way is that possible. They fit into my palm. She would have to remove the oxygen leads and float into the incubator and refit the leads. She was born too early and is only a week old. That is impossible."

"And yet we keep finding her in Anya's incubator," Savannah said.

Gregori took a step toward the small cubicles, halted and pushed a hand through his dark hair before placing both hands on his hips. "Tell her to stop it."

"I did."

"Forbid her."

"Exactly what do you plan on doing to her if she disobeys?"

"Well she . . ." He broke off. "Savannah. You cannot let her get away with that. It could be harmful to her. Just reason with her."

"I tried reasoning with her. Perhaps she needs to hear it from you."

Gregori straightened his shoulders and put on his sternest face.

"Honey," Savannah said. "You can't frighten her. You look like a thunder cloud. Perhaps you should be sweet."

"Were you sweet with her?"

"Of course."

"I don't see that it did much good." He stomped across the room, his chest out, his silver eyes glittering dangerously. "Anastasia. You are not allowed under any circumstances to float over to your sister's incubator. Do you understand me, young lady? I absolutely forbid it and you'll be answering to me if you defy me." His voice was low, but roared like thunder.

His daughter stared up at him with her huge violet-blue eyes, very reminiscent of her mother. Her face crumpled. Her little heart-shaped bow of a mouth trembled. The lower lip quivered, and then her lips parted. Her face scrunched more. A loud, thin wail came out of her mouth and then she began to weep in earnest.

His heart nearly stopped right there in his chest. "Savannah! Get back in here!"

The wail grew louder, sounding even more distressed. Now his heart pounded and his mouth went dry. "*Savannah! Veriak ot en Karpatiiak* – by the blood of the prince! Get in here *now*."

Anya added her wail to her sisters.

Savannah glared at her lifemate. "What is going on? Did you just swear?"

"Do something. She's crying. Get over here. I made her cry. Why is she crying? I just told her to stop doing that. Why would she cry?" He sounded panic-stricken even to his own ears. Soon he was going to start sweating blood. Nothing sounded worse to him than his own babies crying.

"It isn't the end of the world," Savannah soothed.

He glared at her. In spite of her voice she was obviously amused, definitely not grasping the gravity of the situation. "No, you don't understand, those are real tears."

"I wasn't the one to make her cry, Gregori," Savannah pointed out righteously.

Gregori reached into the incubator and lifted out his tiny daughter. "Don't, baby, nothing is so bad we can't fix it. I didn't mean to sound loud and stern, it's just that if you lose your concentration when you're levitating you could fall and hurt yourself. And you need oxygen."

Anastasia continued the most pitiful sound, but snuggled against his hand as if the contact soothed her in some way.

"She doesn't like being alone," Gregori said, giving Savannah another panicked look. "She needs to be in with Anya." Very gently he put his daughter beside her sister and leaned down to give both of them a kiss.

Instantly both babies quit crying and looked up at their father with smiles. His heart melted and he smiled back.

Deleted Scene 2

"Gregori," Razvan asked, "how much rich soil will you need for the incubator? I can get you a bed of pure untouched soil. It is a distance away."

"How long will you need?"

Razvan was shaken at the sound of that weary voice. He knew it was difficult to remove a fragment of evil, as he had with Travis, and Gregori was already overtaxed in trying to keep his children and lifemate alive.

"Can you hold off the birth another three or four hours if Ivory manages to reverse the mutation on the microbes within her womb?" The sacred cave was a good distance away and he would have to get there and back before the birth.

"Savannah is advancing fast, but we both will try." Gregori sounded doubtful.

"What of the boy?" Razvan had great sympathy for the child.

Travis obviously loved Falcon and tried to look and act just like him. He followed the Carpathian everywhere, even when he wasn't supposed to. He also looked up to Mikhail, and attacking him had to have been traumatic. The boy would feel shame for attacking the prince, even though he wasn't to blame.

As you were not, Ivory pointed out, always quick to defend him.

"We appreciate your offer of the soil," Mikhail said. "If it is anything like the samples you brought us, it should aid the twins."

"If we can keep them alive through the birth," Gregori said, his voice low.

"Go now, Razvan," Ivory said. "I will be fine on my own. If I do not have the reversing spell correct I will contact you to replay the scene and images in your head in case I missed one small detail."

"Travis will be fine," Gregori added. "I removed the fragment and destroyed it. There are two still unaccounted for. We've checked everyone who was there in the vicinity at the time. Are you certain one did not enter you, Ivory? I have been in you, Razvan, and know there is no part of Xavier dwelling within you."

Razvan's head came up sharply. His eyes held death in them, a dark, piercing warning. "Ivory is clean of his evil as well. No one will subject my lifemate to the inquisition which I allowed. *No one*." He looked from Mikhail to Gregori, ignoring all others in the cavern.

"I give you my word," Mikhail said.

"And mine," Gregori added.

Razvan visibly relaxed. "Then two more fragments are making their way back to Xavier. They will need hosts."

Gregori sighed. "That was my mistake. I wasn't fast enough to incinerate them."

"I doubt you could have done much in the midst of an all-out battle," Razvan said aloud. "I am glad the boy is all right."

"He loves Mikhail—" Gregori stopped abruptly and shook his head. They both knew the psychological damage the child would have from the incident.

Razvan took a breath and his gaze met Ivory's across the room, knowing she was thinking exactly what he was—Xavier had to be destroyed.

Gregori bent toward Savannah, took her hand, brought it to his heart and stood quietly looking into her eyes, obviously encouraging her. His expression was soft, filled with love, with concern. He put his hand on her rippling stomach and then bent to whisper to his twins. His voice shook with tenderness.

"Stay with your mother just a little longer. Be brave, we are with you, holding you to us, and we will not fail you." He looked up at Razvan and Ivory. "We are counting on you both."

Razvan lifted a hand to clap Gregori on the shoulder in sympathy, but let it fall to his side. He wasn't a man with friends, and was unsure of the protocol one used.

"I'll bring back the soil as fast as possible."

Razvan started out of the chamber but stopped and turned to face them all. "Last time Ivory and I had a little fun. We were not in a hurry so we took no offense at being followed. This time should anyone try to follow me to this sacred place, I will treat them as an enemy and I will defend us."

"Understood." It was Mikhail who answered. "Anyone trying to follow you will be considered an enemy by my people as well." His voice was very low but the sound carried into the outer chambers where most of the warriors had already gathered and begun to chant to aid the women and healers in saving Gregori's unborn children.

"Take the pack," Ivory said. "You may need them. And travel fast, Razvan. Hurry."

Deleted Scene 3

Razvan smiled at Ivory, his teeth flashing white, his grin boyish. Her heart did that little double flip she had come to associate with him. There was something so endearing, so charming about him when he was being a mischievous boy. And she had to admit to herself, she was actually having fun with him—even though ancient Carpathian hunters were tracking them. Razvan didn't seem at all ruffled by their persistence; in fact, he laughed and appeared younger than ever, so much so that Ivory found herself laughing with him and actually feeling a little carefree.

"What are you doing?"

"Creating your fantasy."

Her eyebrow shot up. "I had no idea I had a fantasy."

"Well you do now." He waved his hand and she found herself wearing a long white gown, shimmering with beads that glittered in the lights of dozens of paper lanterns strewn through the trees. He grinned at her. "Of course, a little bit of my fantasy may be mixed in as well." The dress showed the swell of her breasts and clung to her tucked-in waist and the curve of her hips. Her silver wolf coat appeared quite stylish and warm, swinging down the length of the dress to reach the ground. "They may as well have fun too."

She knew the wolves were really on sentry duty, watching their backs, but she wasn't going to ruin the spirit of his fun by pointing out the obvious. He waved his hand again and he was in a white suit with tails, looking very elegant. She knew he'd chosen white for safety, to blend in with the snow, but she didn't let that ruin the illusion of his magical realm. Danger surrounded them, but suddenly it didn't matter. That was simply their life, and maybe that was what Razvan had wanted to show her all along. They couldn't control anyone else, but they could always control themselves. They could choose to have fun.

He lifted his hand and she put hers into his. Music began, violins and then more, an entire orchestra. If she looked close, she could see them, the images translucent at first, and then shimmering into life. His arm slid around her back and she put a hand on his shoulder. They swayed together to the soft strains of a waltz.

How had he known that was one of her secret desires? She had seen dancing from a distance, staring into homes and watching festivals, careful to keep from being seen, but the thought of floating across a floor, graceful and free in the arms of a man she loved, had been a hidden longing since she'd been a girl. Of course, back then, the dances had been much different, but she'd practiced in her lair, moving around the small confines of each room, with careful steps, trying to capture the elusive feeling—of *this*.

Euphoria. Pure happiness. Ivory felt beautiful and young, gliding around the small outdoor ballroom to their own private orchestra. She smiled up at Razvan. He looked handsome. Younger. His body was warm and strong, his hand at her back guiding her perfectly, so perfectly, she knew he had taken the time to look at the step-by-step instructions in her dance books at their lair. He must have also pulled her self-taught lessons right out of her memories.

Their gazes locked and for a moment she actually seemed to be dancing in the clouds. Wings fluttered overhead, and she looked to see several snowy owls circling. Slowly they descended, shifting as they did, until other couples joined them on the floor.

The frozen stream mirrored a rainbow of colors from the paper lanterns hanging in the icy branches as the dancers whirled and glided. Snow leopards padded down from the higher elevations to join in the fun. They too shifted, emerging as more Carpathian couples. She recognized Natalya dancing with a strange man and suddenly she began to laugh, realizing just what Razvan was doing. The winter wonderland would continue long after they were gone, another confusing illusion that would delay the ancients following them.

Razvan bent his head to hers and took her mouth, a slow sensual assault that sent butterflies winging through her stomach. Her womb clenched. She wanted to go home with him. To be there now, to be in his arms. Floating as she was, dressed so regally, feeling so in love, overwhelmed her with happiness.

"You have a very wicked sense of humor," she accused.

"I am wicked in a lot of ways," he admitted and danced her out away from the crowd. "I have every intention of showing you all of them. If you would not mind, perhaps you would do me the honor of a simple, yet very effective, confusion spell."

She curtsied. "I would be more than happy to help."

Ivory reached upwards, toward the silver moon bathing them in shining light.

Mother shining full and bright.

I seek your cover while confusing sight.

She held her arms wide to encompass the snow swirling around them as they danced.

Little flakes of crystalline form.
Dance and swirl,
Hold tight to form.
Let your beauty be seen by all.
Slowing passage by those enthralled.

The Carpathians dancers continued circling the small clearing, dresses catching glints of silver from the moon, the men handsome in their suits and ties, the women breath-taking in their long gowns.

Razvan framed Ivory's face with his hands and bent to capture her mouth. His lips were soft and firm. His mouth hot. His tongue sliding over hers with so much finesse she wanted to crawl inside of him and shelter there in his strength. All the while the dancers whirled and dipped to the strains of the waltz throughout the night.

Vikirnoff held up his hand, as they neared a clearing, crouching low, elation on his face. He cast one swift look at Gregori, before indicating the clearing. "They're there, in the clearing, dancing." His tone was a mixture of smug satisfaction and annoyance that the couple they were chasing had so little regard for them that they would take the time to dance.

Peering through the veil of drifting mist they could make out Razvan and Ivory circling the clearing, her in a white gown that clung to her curves, a silver wolf coat falling to her ankles and moving almost as if it was alive around her. Razvan wore a white suit and tie, his dark hair streaked with white as they glided gracefully, swaying and turning, looking as if he knew what he was doing as he guided his partner.

"They aren't alone," Nicolae pointed out.

Vikirnoff squinted, trying to make out the dancing couples as they moved in a circle. He swore every third or fourth couple was cloned to look like Razvan and Ivory. "They think they can fool us with such a simple cloning spell? We have only to wait. They cannot keep up this nonsense all night," he added in a sneering tone.

Nicolae nudged him. "Is that Natalya? In that dress? She looks beautiful."

Vikirnoff nearly rose, leaning forward to look at his lifemate. She was more than beautiful as she whirled around the dance floor. She looked spectacular. Her red-gold hair shone beneath the moon. The dress clung to every abundant curve. The neck plunged nearly to the waist and one side of the clingy dress was slit up her thigh. Her partner held her close—too close—moving her around the dance floor with authority and grace, staring down admiringly into her eyes.

"*Veriak ot en Karpatiiak*—by the blood of the great Carpathian," Vikirnoff swore. "What is going on?"